The CHASE

Continue the ICON Trilogy with
THE GAME,
coming soon from
Vanessa Fewings
and HQN Books.

The
CHASE

VANESSA
FEWINGS

HQN™

HQN™

Recycling programs
for this product may
not exist in your area.

ISBN-13: 978-0-373-80411-5

The Chase   JUL 1 1 2017

Copyright © 2017 by Vanessa Fewings

www.HQNBooks.com

Printed in U.S.A.

For Mum

Acknowledgments

Embarking on this new series with Zara and Tobias has been a thrilling journey, one that would not have been possible without the support of many people. I have the deepest gratitude and respect for my editor, Ann Leslie Tuttle; her kindness and enthusiasm is inspirational, and I'm so honored to work with one of the romance industry's most renowned senior editors. Thank you to Gina Macedo for your time and precision. Thank you to the entire HarperCollins and Harlequin team for all they've done for the ICON Trilogy.

This series exists thanks to agent Kimberly Whalen, and I'm constantly wowed and grateful for her expertise and passion. Thank you for sharing in my vision for this series and encouraging me to write it!

Thank you to Tara Carberry. Her enthusiasm for Wilder right at the start spurred me on to create an inspiring book boyfriend for us all.

Thank you to Peter Katz and Guy Birthwhistle for their support and generosity.

My gratitude for all the bloggers and reviewers who have supported me from the very beginning. Many of you have actually become friends, too, which leads me to thanking Hazel Godwin, Lauren Luman, Heather Pollock and Louise Sandford for their continued support.

Thank you to those reviewers who are new to me for taking a chance on my novel and recommending this series to your readers. They are the living force behind each author, and we couldn't do this without them!

Endless gratitude to SueBee at Goodreads for her librarian skills and determination to take care of our beloved readers.

Nina Grinstead and Jenn Watson at Social Butterfly PR, thank you so very much for lending your powerhouse talent to the promotion of this series along with your entire team. A big thank you to Lisa Wray, publicist extraordinaire at Harlequin, for directing such a great promotion.

A shout-out to my incredible Facebook friends who are always cheering me on; thank you for telling your friends about my books! I hope you enjoy spending time with Wilder!

For Brad, my wonderful husband, who has supported me from the very beginning and has been there for every moment of my journey—thank you for making me see the funny side when I get too serious and reminding me there is a world outside the window when I become too obsessed with writing.

A big hug for Liz and Mand, my beloved sisters, who cheer me on.

To my beloved readers, thank you so very much for spending time with Tobias and Zara and joining me on this wild ride of their adventures together!

I hope this book inspires many of you to return to your favorite museums and to perhaps discover new galleries.

"Art is not what you see, but what you make others see."
—Edgar Degas

Prologue

The Courtauld Institute of Art

The stillness of the Witt Library embraced me as I sat at a corner table, my breaths slow and steady, my thoughts wandering, slipping almost into a trance. I tried to see the events that had transpired through his perspective as though I'd been there with *him*.

This faceless man who'd seized my every waking thought.

Closing my eyes, my fingers traced the file. I'd combed through every detail of this three-week-old report, a precise translation from French to English by the Police Nationale. As an employee of Huntly Pierre, London's most prestigious investigative art firm, I'd been permitted exclusive access.

It wasn't only that I'd been tasked with hunting him down, or his obvious passion for art that seemingly equaled mine, drew me to him. Rather there was an unfathomable connection to this stranger that now consumed my days and nights. Perhaps this was only the inevitable shakiness of a newbie forensic art specialist finding her way through the precarious underworld of corruption.

Though that didn't explain why he'd visited my dreams as though we shared a deeper connection.

Forcing these nonsensical thoughts away, I tried to focus on the details in the file. I could see this theft had presented our suspect with a technical hitch like no other. There were so many irregularities to plan for when breaking into a private estate at three o'clock on a crisp Sunday morning. I imagined the kind of preparation it would have taken. More than requiring a disciplined mind to navigate through complex innovations in home defense, the job would also have demanded brute force. He'd abseiled into a privately owned, billion-dollar rotunda displaying some of the most priceless masterpieces in existence around its curved wall. The kind most people would never see. The estate was owned by the Burells, who had made their money through the family business. Their private contractor company used the guise of combat support to deploy well-trained mercenaries into war. Their impressive art collection was proof that business was booming.

Resting my hand upon the small samples of evidence collected, I envisioned him wearing black khakis with a tight T-shirt pulled over a sculptured torso. After all, given that the climbing harness he wore would suspend him fifty feet in the air, he'd have to be fit. Peering through his night-vision goggles, without which he'd be in pitch blackness, that sheer drop beneath him was an exhilarating rush that was all part of the allure.

The kind of bravery I coveted.

That's all this was, surely? A curiosity for the kind of recklessness I'd never dare experience. The kind that brought freedom. A life fully realized without societal constraints.

Until we locked him away, irrevocably.

The evidence proved he'd been on track with claiming his

prize, namely a glorious 1566 self-portrait by Tiziano Vecelli, more commonly known as Titian.

A print of the painting had been placed in the file, and I now marveled at Titian's remarkable technique. He'd immortalized himself on that oil on canvas, masterfully capturing the charisma of an elegant seventy-eight-year-old and highlighting his sharp features in those rich deep shades. Should one look closer, there was a dash of melancholy too. Titian's black-robed attire was an understated reflection of his modesty, despite his great wealth. That final touch of his right hand holding a paintbrush reflected his brilliance. Hailed by his contemporaries as "The sun amidst small stars."

I shared the thief's exhilaration of being so close to such a treasure.

I imagined what he'd felt as he surveyed the room and zeroed in on his target. Adrenaline fueling his descent until he'd paused to run through his options.

Failure was out of the question. He'd come too far.

The hole he'd drilled into the glass ceiling was altering the fine temperature control that protected the other paintings, and had there been any other way in he'd no doubt have used it. That breach had exposed the room to the humid French climate. Though luckily the weather forecast for Amboise had promised no rain.

He wasn't a complete bastard; because one downpour would have left nothing but ruin.

A jolt of envy hit me that it had been him and not me experiencing all that inaccessible beauty.

Our man was clearly arrogant, well educated based on his grasp of this advanced technology, and already wealthy from previous heists. I sensed he'd been touched by the kind of charm that forged a blunt sense of entitlement. A self-serving desire to own whatever he set his sights on.

He'd not gone for the *Saint Veronica* by Robert Campin, a strange-looking baptism by Giovanni di Paolo or an overvalued Paul Cezanne. Trying to wrap my head around this fact there was also the consideration of his infamous MO.

He only ever took one.

Our man had researched this space until he knew it intimately and had even been prepared for that emergency generator kicking in after he'd cut the power. Because he'd hacked into their security firm's database, he knew all about the pressure-sensitive marble floor tiles, finicky laser detectors and the temperature monitor set to go off after five minutes.

He'd burned through a few minutes when he must have looked up at the sky and spotted an enormous squawking raven perched on the end of the glass hole that he'd taken precious time to saw through.

Had he experienced a jolt of fear before returning to the Zen-like calm he must have possessed to do a job like this? Somewhere, I'd read a bird's eyesight was sensitive to ultraviolet light. Something about visual pigments in their retinal cones. I'd stored this in the "interesting stuff of no current value" corner of my brain.

But for this case it couldn't have been more vital.

Because there were two things I knew for sure. First, the ultraviolet flashlight strapped to his utility belt, standard equipment for any self-respecting thief, had been on and had caught that raven's attention. Second, that very bird had dived straight toward the invisible layers of those state-of-the-art motion detectors.

Opening my eyes, my fingers traced the sample of black feathers found at the scene, proving he'd tried to prevent the bird from landing.

The only consolation was the raven had been found alive

and happily perched atop a whimsical 1889 still life: *Vase with Fourteen Sunflowers* by Vincent van Gogh, worth millions.

Though minutes before, there had been the inescapable mayhem of a swinging climbing rope, flying feathers and scrambling hands to rein in the chaos.

Basically, he was fucked.

And he'd still gotten away with a Titian.

Closing the file, my heartbeat quickened with a fierce resolve to see this case closed and have this heist go down in history as the one that got him caught.

1

One week earlier

She'll be safe here.

Since I'd first made the decision to leave her at The Otillie, I'd been reciting this mantra to reassure myself. I can even remember what I was wearing that early winter morning when I'd first set eyes on my beloved *Madame Rose.*

To me, my *Madame Rose* was so much more than a painting. She represented my childhood, my innocence, my strongest connection to my father. Rose had been a woman of her day—my father had told me this as he'd raised his bidding paddle and with one sweep of his wrist he'd secured *Madame Rose Récamier* as ours, outbidding every other art collector at Sotheby's. Adding another masterpiece to his already vast personal gallery back when I'd called Kensington home.

Zara, within the texture lies the truth, he'd told me as he nudged me closer to the canvas. *Can you see?*

As I'd taken in—or at least tried with the perception of a ten-year-old—the brilliance of that French artist on that century-aged painting, I'd sensed life would never be the same. I'd known in the depths of my soul art would always be my one true love.

Tonight, I'd been so fazed about coming here that I'd forgotten to wear a coat that would have offset the chill of a London autumn and the cold temperature the gallery was kept at to preserve its treasures within.

Art galleries were quiet places with hushed whispers as respectful visitors paid homage to the genius of artists who'd left their indelible mark. Many of these painters had languished in poverty even after giving so much. As a child I'd always wanted to travel back in time to watch them work and tell them their talent had been worth all they'd sacrificed.

My stilettos clicked along the marble uncomfortably loudly as I neared *Madame Rose Récamier.* She'd hung in my bedroom and watched over me for years.

Stepping closer, my gaze roamed over her, marveling at those pristine strokes giving Rose a stunning realism.

I gave the softest sigh.

The year was 1803 when Jacques Momar had captured a moment in time with this Parisian socialite and, as I trailed my fingers through my auburn locks, I recalled how I'd wanted to be her. Chestnut irises, we had that in common, but her fiery gaze reflected a life of daring—one she'd chosen to live on her terms. *Madame Rose Récamier* had been known for her love of neoclassical fashion and her controversial interest in politics. She'd stunned Paris with her tenacity. Her reputation to enamor with her smart wit and intelligence had been expressed so beautifully as she reclined on that satin chaise lounge, her head thrown back and her gaze held firmly on the artist Monsieur Momar. In her expression there was love. As time went on I'd realized that look proved an affair had transpired between them. The kind of passion I'd only ever read about.

I saw something I'd never noticed before—uncertainty—the emotion starkly vivid and painfully real.

In his will my father had left *Madame Récamier* to me. And now I was leaving her here.

"She's haunting," Clara whispered, shaking me from my daydream. It was just like her to know I needed a few moments alone with Rose to say goodbye.

It felt comforting having my best friend here.

No matter how many months went by without seeing Clara, it felt like mere minutes had passed between us. She'd always come through for me, and I for her.

Her diamante-crystal, halter-neck dress made her look gorgeous, as always. She had a couple of inches on me and her thick blond curls were a contrast to my long auburn hair. Her high cheekbones were a reflection of the confidence that had helped her succeed as an advertising photographer. Her voluptuousness was a contrast to my smaller curvy figure. "Rubinesque," she'd called herself, which matched her vibrant personality, and her bright eyes and warm smile were always welcome in my world that always seemed more complicated than hers.

As if sensing I needed it, she came over now to give me a hug. "She's beautiful." Clara squeezed me into her side.

"First time I saw her I was wearing my favorite floral dress." I rested my head on Clara's shoulder for a moment. "Red shoes. I loved those shoes."

"Oh, Zara, this was a good decision."

"Yes. She's meant to be here."

She paused for a moment and studied me as though being careful with her words. "What about the others?"

The three other paintings we'd saved that night...

Flames rising from our house and licking the air with those monstrous oranges and reds; a hellish glow...

The stench of toxic smoke in my clothes. My hair. My skin. My doll lost to the flames.

Stubbornly, I shook my head, not wanting to remember anything more about that night. "There was always this sense we were protecting *Madame Rose* by hiding her away."

Now it was time to step away.

Let it all go. And move on.

"You okay?" came Clara's reassurance.

I nodded to let her know I was.

It was behind me now, all that grief of dealing with the complex issues of my father's estate and those endless meetings with softly spoken solicitors where coffee was my only friend. And those journalists who'd begged for a scoop on what plans I had to take the Leighton family legacy into the twenty-first century.

I had no real plans for anything, not really.

Other than settling into my new career. Moving on felt cathartic.

Clara tutted. "Dreadful thing."

Shaken back into the room, I asked, "What is?"

"No one's reckless enough to steal from a gallery. Not with all this." She peered up at one of the discreet cameras.

She was referring to that theft in Chelsea: a portrait by Henry Raeburn had been stolen from a private estate.

"You're right," I agreed.

She patted my arm. "You'll sleep better knowing she's here."

"You don't think it's connected to what happened in France, do you?"

Rumors had reached the community that some of the wealthiest families in Paris had suffered at the hands of an art thief and that news had set the city's private dealers and their customers on edge.

"Let's get some bubbly." Clara led me back down the hallway. "You have some hobnobbing to do with these art-loving crazies."

"Thank you for being here."

"Wouldn't miss it."

I forced myself not to look back.

Making our way down the hallway, we continued to admire the collection, pausing here and there until I sensed Clara's restlessness.

"That's a nice blouse," she said. "Gold brings out your eyes."

I tugged on my pencil skirt. "Marks and Spencer."

"I thought you were going to say some posh designer. You're getting close to that birthday."

Which was Clara's tactful way of saying my inheritance would kick in on the eve of my twenty-third birthday. Pride had turned my thoughts away from it but these rising costs of living in London had me rethinking that. The idea of having to decide what to do with fifteen million pounds made me nervous. That decision wouldn't come until next year and I still had time to nudge that thought far away.

A wave of guilt settled in my gut that my inheritance came from my father's will. I spun round to face Clara. "I got the job!"

"What? Why didn't you call me?"

"I wanted to tell you in person."

"Oh, darling, that's wonderful!"

"I'm officially a forensic art specialist at Huntly Pierre."

I'd landed my dream job at a high-end firm in the middle of The Strand, and I couldn't wait to start.

"Zara, that's wonderful." She leaped forward and hugged me. "I'm so excited."

Years of studying art and I was finally being let loose.

"They know about your dad's penchant for collecting priceless art, then?"

"No, I got this on my own merit." I lowered my brow, hoping my family name of Leighton wouldn't follow me around forever. "Have a knack for detecting forgeries apparently."

Within the texture lies the truth.

Everything Dad knew he'd taught me; an education like no other. It wasn't only studying at the Courtauld that had given me the talent for knowing the difference between an Uccello and a Masaccio, but my education had begun when my father had instilled in me his rare insight into art before I could even walk, hoping I'd follow in his footsteps.

"It's in my blood."

She winked. "The commission you'll make when you confirm a piece is real should be quite something. These things are worth a fortune."

"You can't place a value on pieces like this," I said wistfully, admiring Constant Troyon's oil on canvas *A Clump of Trees*, with its soothing layers of greens and yellows. "For the first time I feel like I'm putting my knowledge to good use."

"You know what else needs to be in your blood? Booze. More specifically, champagne." We laughed too loudly as we neared the lift.

Standing back a little, I watched Clara hit the down button and the silver doors slid open. Peering inside that gaping chasm of metal, I felt my haunting phobia of lifts returning, the light inside flickered to taunt me, and my feet refused to move forward as that familiar fear swept over me.

Terror spiked my veins. "Let's take the stairs."

She raised her left foot to show off her heels. "I'll break my neck."

"You sure?"

"Zara." She sounded baffled.

"Meet you down there."

"This is why you have great legs," her voice echoed after me. "You're always taking the stairs."

Her laughter followed me down the stairwell.

I peeled off each shoe and in stockinged feet burst through the fire escape door. I descended fast, round and round, counting the floors as I went.

Breathing in the chilled air, I rekindled the feeling that what I'd done tonight was one of my better decisions. Clara was right. The security was great and the responsibility of protecting all of Dad's other pieces would soon be lifted as they made their way here.

It made me happy to think of other people getting to enjoy them too, and my feet flew down with a bounce in my step.

With a shove on the security rail I pushed open the heavy fire door and went on through into the dimly lit hallway.

Realizing I'd gone too far I turned to go back. The door was locked from this side.

Ouch.

As if right on cue my garter belt snapped off my thigh-high stocking and I hurried onward to find somewhere private to fix it.

My feet carried me away from the lift and along the hallway. At the end was a door stamped with a sign: Staff Only.

I went on in and saw the long mirror right in front of me. I neared it and gave myself a reassuring smile. I looked pretty tonight and was actually a little less geeky than usual, having switched out my cardigan and flat heels for my favorite gold silk blouse and black skirt, and even my hair was miraculously behaving. After putting my shoes down, I eased up my hem and attempted to reattach my stocking top.

Fiddly thing.

My fingers slipped so I hiked my skirt higher to better work

the intricate reclipping. With that accomplished, I straightened my eggshell-blue high rise panties.

And then I spotted a movement across the room—

I yanked my skirt down, my mouth forming words of
apology but failing to say them. I bent over to scoop up my
shoes and rushed toward the door, my hand reaching round
to neaten my skirt.

Oh no, my hem still exposed my bum.

Cheeks reddening further, I grappled with the unreasonable
material and sucked up my embarrassment so I could throw
a wave of apology to the stranger.

My gaze fixed on the living, breathing sculpture.

Making it to the door, I tried to force my stare away from
the strikingly beautiful specimen of a man who was looking
at me with a mixture of surprise and delight.

Finally exhaling, I was riveted by his sun-kissed torso with
its finely chiseled abs, his black trousers low and revealing
a hint of a V. An intricate tattoo on his left upper arm that
vaguely reminded me of a Polynesian design, with its swirls
in black ink and an image in the center.

My heartbeat quickened as I searched my memory for where
I knew him from. I was awestruck by this breathtaking Adonis,
who was reaching for a white shirt hanging on the back of
a chair. He was tall and devastatingly handsome in a rugged
kind of way. Thirty, maybe? Those short, dark golden locks
framing a gorgeous face, his three-day stubble marking him
with a tenacious edge and that thin wry smile exuding a fierce
confidence. His green irises were a startling contrast to his
lightly tanned complexion; his intense, steady glare stayed on
mine as he calmly pulled his arm through a sleeve and covered that tattoo before I could make out more.

A gasp caught in my throat as it came to me that we'd
never actually met, probably because this was Tobias Wil-

liam Wilder, a billionaire. He moved in the kind of refined circles one would expect from a business magnate and inventor who owned TechRule, one of the largest software companies in the world.

And I'd given this playboy mogul his very own peep show.

He'd popped up on my radar a year ago when I'd read an article on him in *Cosmo*, featuring his Los Angeles–based art gallery, The Wilder. It was an acclaimed museum that was one of the most prestigious in the world and it was also right up there on my wish list to visit.

Wilder was even more dazzling in person.

I'd imagined one day I might bump into him with the art world being relatively small, but never had I imagined a scenario as racy as this.

Why the hell hadn't I worn my sexy panties?

"I'm looking for the stairs," I managed.

"That way." His refined American accent felt like another blow to my reason.

That alpha-maleness made him look like he'd just returned from a dangerous adventure in the Himalayas or even the jungles of Peru—

Where he'd spent his days hunting in the wilderness, or naked while fishing in a fast-running stream, and then making a campfire at night with those elegant hands, and then saving his friends from beasties that attacked our campsite.

His smile reached his eyes. A blush burned my cheeks.

He arched an eyebrow, amused.

Was he mocking me?

"I was looking for a signal." I broke my gaze to hide my lie. "For my phone. You know, Wi-Fi."

"Try the foyer. It's a security issue."

"I know that." Which made no damn sense.

It was impossible to think straight because someone had

made the executive decision to suck out all the oxygen from the room, or so it felt.

With a tug of his shirt he hid that other tattoo to the right of his lower abdomen, a Latin inscription leading to his groin immortalized in italic black ink.

"Excuse the—" He gestured to his state of undress. "I'm running late."

This kind of manly perfection obviously knew just how beautiful he was, the way he blinked at me casually: the way he firmly weaved that bow tie around his collar without using a mirror and making quick work of forming that silk into a neat knot, and all the while his eyes not leaving mine.

Until I dragged my gaze from his to look around the room. On a table close by to him rested a black motorcycle helmet with its tinted visor down. Leather gloves beside it.

He moved with a sophisticated elegance that had me doubting I'd caught his body inked so seductively. A waft of expensive musky cologne reached me with its sensuous allure and did something crazy to my body. Trembling slightly, I shifted my gait and leaned farther back against the door, spellbound.

Nature might have bestowed this man with the ability to leave a trail of heartbreak in his sexy-arse wake but it had also provided me with the ability to detect danger.

"You might want to put some clothes on," I said firmly.

"Well, now I'm dressed."

Yes, he was, and this was a changing room, apparently, and I'd not exactly represented a pillar of virtue.

"Well, that's good." I swallowed my pride. "Please keep it that way."

His gaze lowered to my feet.

And I remembered my strappy stilettos were flirtatiously dangling from my left hand, those spiked heels hinting at a sexy side I wished I had.

Intrigue marred his face, and then his expression softened again as his jade gaze returned to hold mine and he broke into a heart-stopping smile.

The seductive dazzling kind that threatened to melt my panties. I left in a rush—

Shaken with just how this man had affected me merely with a smile, my heart racing, I reconsidered risking the lift to take me as far away from him as possible. Embarrassment scorched my cheeks and made me glad I'd not worn a coat.

Taking a second, I leaned against the wall and stared back.

That alluring inked-up vision had taken my mind off the reason I was here. I felt an inexplicable need to run back in and continue to bathe in the aura of the most enigmatic man I'd ever met.

2

"You all right?" Clara rested her palm on my forehead.

"The stairs took it out of me," I fibbed and gestured to get the attention of a waitress.

She came over, and with a nod of thanks I lifted a flute of champagne off her silver tray and took several sips to quench my thirst.

My thoughts drifted to the basement and my run-in with Tobias Wilder. These were the kind of moments I cherished— me dipping my toe in the dangerous side of life—but I knew the moment I saw reason, I'd pull it right out.

The only romance I would ever indulge in again was the fantasy where everyone lived happily ever after.

Oh no, I'd really embarrassed myself down there.

Clara narrowed her gaze and it made me smile. It was the kind of smile you give when you doubt yourself beyond all reason.

"Happiness is the best revenge," she offered brightly. "I'm happy you're here."

It was still difficult to accept Zach wasn't coming back. He should have been here tonight and it hurt so bad that I'd had to tear up my invitation because it had his name on it.

I tried not to think of the way his copper locks flopped over his deep blue eyes, or how his refined nose made him look so cultivated and that endearing way he emanated his free-thinking spirit.

A month or so after my father's funeral, Zach Montgomery, the man I had been destined to marry, complained my grief was causing him too much stress. With our finals looming he couldn't be "distracted." He needed a break from *us*, just for a little while. I'd lovingly given it to him.

I'd seen my understanding nature pay off when he'd graduated with an MA in art curating.

Afterward, when the intensity of our studies was over and I could see the strain lifted from his handsome face, I'd met him for dinner at our favorite pub, The Old Ship, and reassured him I'd pull back on all this unnecessary drama of grief. I'd truly believed he'd realize his mistake after our exams were over. Even with Clara's disapproval I couldn't have refused him had he changed his mind and asked to come back to me.

Until the dreadful truth came out.

That stark memory returning along with that knot in my stomach, and I felt like I was there again—

Tucked away in my favorite corner of the Witt Library, with my head buried in a book. I'd been reading about Vermeer and how he'd painstakingly chose his expensive pigments. Colors I'd once run my fingertip over, acutely aware of the privilege of such intimacy that came with ownership. One of the few from my secret stash that not even Zach knew of.

Snug in my oversize jumper to ward off the chill of the Witt, I'd been happily reading away until those familiar voices of my classmates had caught my attention. I'd placed my fingertip on the page to keep my place…

Their hushed gossiping the catalyst that sent my life into a tailspin: Zachary Montgomery was now living it up all the way across the world in a little town called Tivoli, where he'd taken a job in an art gallery.

The news came as a blow, not least because I'd had no idea he'd even left London.

The whispers went on to reveal a few of the other students had received their invitations to the wedding of Italian beauty and fellow student Natalia Donate to Zachary Montgomery.

Those late evenings Natalia had spent hours with us studying at my flat had provided her with access to more than just my art acumen. She'd made a play for my boyfriend and come out the resounding winner.

If paintings taught me anything with their endless portrayals of human suffering, it was that heartbreak is inevitable and we are fools to be surprised by it. Trust is an ill-fated pursuit.

Although Clara believed in true love and had no doubt found it, I questioned whether I was ever going to experience it again.

Clara tutted. "He doesn't deserve one more second of you."

I leaned in and hugged her. I'd tell Clara about my risqué adventure once I'd gotten control over this flush that threatened to rise each time I thought of him. I imagined over the course of the evening one of the many artists here or even sculptors would spot the infamous Mr. Wilder and try to persuade him to pose for them.

Naked. Preferably.

I treated myself to that thought.

"So what do you think?"

My attention snapped to Clara.

"They've gone all out, haven't they?" she added as she looked around.

"This is more than I expected." Using a pillar for a shield, I looked for Tobias in the crowd. "Can't get over it."

"They're wooing you for the other paintings." She turned to look at me.

"It does look like it, doesn't it?"

"You never talk about them?" she said.

"They're all I have left of Dad."

She rubbed my back, knowing well enough not to push me. "He'd be so proud of you."

The black marble tile almost clashed with the pink marbled pillars lining the room either side. Along those pristine cream-colored walls hung the finest eighteenth-century Italian paintings, which were apparently on loan from the Vatican.

Suppressing my melancholy, I vowed to enjoy tonight.

The Otillie was one of my favorite places to visit and easily one of the most prestigious galleries in the world, with a unique collection of both modern and ancient art.

Despite such grandeur, it was also famed for showcasing new and up-and-coming artists before anyone else had discovered them. Like the young painter Liza Blake, who stood alone in a corner looking a little forlorn. She'd been easy to spot with her blue hair, and her boho chic dress looked cute on her, those round rimmed glasses perched on the end of her nose. Artists were always so interesting, their perspectives so profound, and I admired their tenacity for following their hearts and sharing their emotional power. Perhaps it was the only way to find ours, through their vision of just what we were capable of.

"Let's go say hello to Liza." Excitement flushed my cheeks that I was here again.

I took in the other guests, a handful of well-known socialites, some I recognized from past events, the avid art collectors circling The Otillie's rising new talent and ready to invest in their promising careers.

"Look who's here," whispered Clara. "Your favorite person."

I almost coughed up my drink.

A well-worn face and yet strangely handsome in a highly bred kind of way. The Right Honorable Lord Nigel Turner stood out in the crowd with his high cheekbones and overly refined nose. His tweed jacket with that perfect bow tie made him seem extra quirky and yet moneyed. His chin rose with an air of superiority as he perused the other guests. Nigel was apparently related to "the Turner," or so he told us. He worked at *The London Times* as their senior art critic and wielded the kind of power that could make or break an artist's career.

I'd crushed on him back when Lady Zara Leighton had a nice ring to it. Right before I'd actually met him.

We made our way over to Liza, and she smiled with relief when she saw us. I got her talking about her favorite subject, modern art, and she soon relaxed as she chatted away about the latest piece she was working on.

Together we mingled with the other guests, sipping champagne and popping back way too many caviar hors d'oeuvres.

Clara arched an amused brow when I reached for another flute from a passing waiter's tray. I'd never tolerated booze well, very often getting tipsy on merely one glass. Still, this night was the first real evening I was letting myself go in what felt like ages, and I soon found myself having fun. With Clara's mischievous insights into the other guests, she had me and Liza struggling to keep our laughter down.

Nigel nudged up against Clara. "You're looking lovely tonight."

"Thank you." She offered him a polite smile.

"You didn't bring your camera?" he asked.

"Taking the night off. The staff get nervous when they see a photographer taking photos of their priceless paintings. Something about copyright."

His overly critical gaze found me. "I was sorry to hear about your father."

"Thank you," I said. "I appreciate that."

Those difficult few months were behind me now and for the first time tonight I'd felt that wedge of pain in my heart lifting. I swallowed my grief with a sip of champagne and broke Turner's gaze, hoping he'd talk to Liza.

"I hear a rumor you're hiding away more paintings?" he said.

I shook my head, not wanting to go there.

"One step at a time," Clara whispered.

Nigel narrowed his gaze. "Your skills could be put to good use."

"Excuse me?"

"That fire at your father's home?" he said.

"I don't remember much." Other than the bitter taste of ash.

"She was ten," snapped Clara. "For goodness' sake."

"Interesting that Walter William Ouless's *St. Joan of Arc* has turned up in Venice?" he went on. "Have you heard?"

My throat tightened. "That's impossible."

"And yet." He smirked.

A wave of panic circled my stomach.

Part of me wanted it to be true. Needed to believe our beloved *Joan of Arc* had survived that fire. But with that revelation would come a truth so vivid I wasn't sure I'd survive it. All I'd known would be proven a lie.

I'd missed her terribly; Ouless had masterfully painted one of France's most beloved heroines. Her legacy included visions of Christ that inspired her heroic reclaiming of France from the British. Of all my father's collection she'd both inspired and scared me the most, perhaps because some part of me knew I'd never be capable of that kind of bravery.

Clara piped up, "Maybe Ouless painted more than one?"

Nigel tutted. "How likely is that?"

"Sounds very likely," she said. "Probably loads of them out there."

I cringed too soon, revealing I knew all too well this remarkable British painter was known for his one-of-a-kind masterpieces. Ouless was considered one of the nineteenth century's best known portraitists and his *Joan of Arc* had been sought after by too many collectors to count. My father had rejected every offer.

Nigel lit up with triumph. "There's a chance it wasn't destroyed as alleged."

"I'm afraid it was," I said through clenched teeth.

Clara sounded distant. "Really, Nigel? This is Zara's evening to celebrate her dad's legacy."

"What's left of it," he muttered.

I reached out to the marble pillar to steady my legs.

"Any plans to visit the painting?" he added. "If that piece is real—"

"Of course it's not," I said.

"It's coming to London for final authentication apparently," he said.

My legs wobbled with the unsteadiness of my feet.

"Are you sure?" asked Clara.

"That's the rumor." Nigel frowned his disapproval.

Dread shot up my spine. "Who is this mystery dealer?"

Who was the outrageous person willing to put his or her reputation on the line?

"Have no idea," said Nigel. "I'm sure you'll want more answers?"

"Yes." *No.*

I want to forget.

The resurfacing of that old lie proved jealousy for my father's collection still went deep. I wasn't ready to give up the others, not yet.

Black spots flashed across my vision—

Tobias Wilder strolled out of the crowd toward us carrying two glasses of champagne, and I sucked in a sharp breath of surprise. He offered one of them to me; bubbles rising to the surface, the chilled glass making my fingers tingle as I accepted it from him.

Soothed by his beautiful striking face and that rugged stubble clashing with his styled locks he'd since run a comb through.

"Thank you," I said, amazed my underwear fiasco hadn't scared him off.

"My pleasure." Tobias gave a self-possessed nod and then gestured to the waiter beside him. The young man handed out more champagne flutes to the others in our group. Two more waiters hurried forward and held out their trays laden with china plates full of hors d'oeuvres.

Nigel, Liza and Clara all helped themselves to the assorted small bites of food with obvious glee, seemingly recognizing him too. With a wave of my hand and a kind smile, I declined an appetizer.

"That's awfully nice of you," Nigel said.

"Mind if I join you?" Tobias showed off that dazzling smile. "What a fantastic venue. Love this place."

The staff hurried away.

Dragging my teeth over my bottom lip, I tried to think of something to say, perhaps draw his attention to the Raphael directly behind him. In that painting the Italian artist had captured the beguiling image of a young lady with a unicorn on her lap.

"You like that one?" Tobias asked me with his back still to the painting.

"Yes." I loved it and adored the crisp gold and burgundy of the subject's dress, her delicate beauty, her eyes exuding innocence and the way she held that small animal on her lap so very carefully.

"Is that a unicorn?" asked Clara.

"A conventional symbol of chastity," I told her.

"The allure of High Renaissance." Tobias turned to take in the portrait and then spun round and fixed his gaze on mine—

Liquefying my insides and making my chest tighten.

Oh, bloody hell.

He was still staring at me.

At least when I'd met him briefly in the basement there had been some distance between us, but now, with that intense green stare locked on mine and that delicate waft of heady cologne reaching me he'd made my thoughts freeze.

"Mr. Wilder?" Nigel proffered his hand. "It's such a pleasure to finally meet you." Tobias turned toward Nigel and reached out to shake.

"I was in LA when The Wilder hosted the Samurai collection," Nigel told him. "Japanese art is my specialty."

"That was five years ago." Tobias turned to us. "The Taka Ishii Gallery generously loaned us a few of their most treasured pieces. First time in the US."

"I'd have loved to have seen that," said Clara. "Will it come to London?"

"Afraid not," said Tobias. "The collection is at home in Tokyo now and won't tour again in our lifetime. Though we are hosting a collection by Sandro Botticelli." His face lit up with happiness. "It's quite something."

Sighs of admiration rose from everyone circling him.

"You're all invited of course—" his gaze fell on me "—if you're ever in the neighborhood."

My heart fluttered at the thought of seeing those early Renaissance pieces by an artist who'd captured the deepest emotions in his subjects' eyes.

Who was I kidding? My heart was fluttering over this hottie.

Tobias smiled wistfully. "Seeing *La Primavera* up close is a privilege."

I wanted to tell him how much I'd always wanted to visit The Wilder Museum, but held back, not sure if that would come over as a little forward.

Tobias slipped into a smile. "Nigel, may I call you Nigel?"

"Absolutely."

"I enjoyed that piece you wrote about the Tate."

"The one on Anna Lea Merritt?"

"That's the one," he said. "Very insightful. Love her work."

"She married her tutor," I muttered.

Tobias looked my way, his eyes narrowing in interest, and he made me blush.

Clara's eyebrows popped up, and I hoped she was the only one who'd caught my visceral response to this man. For some reason my mouth had stopped working and this was unusual for me. I loved taking part in this kind of conversation and Clara knew it.

"So what brings you to London?" asked Nigel.

"Business," he replied.

With Tobias conveniently distracted, I took a breath and admired him discreetly. He moved with such refinement, and yet his earthiness made him less threatening. I kicked myself that I'd had him all to myself down in the basement and not taken the time to talk with him and get to know this enigma better.

Tobias tucked his left hand into his trouser pocket casually and took a sip of bubbly.

That lick across his bottom lip, that tilt of his head, that intensity in his expression as he listened to Nigel.

God, he was gorgeous.

A rush of excitement flooded my chest as I realized he was still hanging out with us.

I let out a wistful sigh.

And earned a flicker of amusement in Tobias's expression; his eyes crinkled into a subtle smile.

Oh no, he'd sensed me staring.

Reason kicked in as I recalled my first instinct had been to run when I'd met him. He'd no doubt have a slew of women chasing after him and all of them from his world of beautiful socialites. The European supermodel types who took perfection all too seriously.

And based on the passing glances from the other guests surrounding us, many of them seemed just as enamored and more than proved my glum musing that men like this could only be enjoyed from afar.

There was an evening of Googling Tobias Wilder ahead of me when I got back to my Notting Hill flat. See what he was up to now and perhaps find a clue to why he was in London. I'd dig up some dirt on him, no doubt, some article to confirm my gut feeling about him. Tobias Wilder was out of my league for all the right reasons.

He stepped forward to shake Liza's hand and then Clara's, his smile reaching his eyes. Their faces lit up in delight at meeting this charismatic man.

"Pleasure's all mine." He turned to me and took my hand firmly in his. "Tobias."

"Zara."

His smile faded and he blinked at me.

"Zara Leighton," I said brightly.

His hand slid from mine and he looked away as though distracted.

"Tonight's a celebration for Zara," explained Nigel. "She's given her painting to the gallery. It's quite a find. Have you seen it?"

"She's beautiful," said Tobias. "The painting. Well, I should go. Thank you for the great company. It's been…insightful."

"But you only just got here?" said Clara.

"I have an appointment across town."

"Where are you staying?" asked Nigel.

But Tobias was already weaving his way through the crowd and heading fast for the door.

That masterful stride carrying him away from us.

We all swapped wary glances with each other at his quick exit, and I felt Clara's arm wrap around my waist to comfort me.

Tobias's attention had been short lived and someone or something had drawn him away all too briskly. Taking another sip of champagne, I feigned there had never been any hope it might have been me.

3

With my morning latte in hand, I wound my way up the fourteen-story staircase of The Tiriani Building toward the top floor. My fear of being late clashed with my claustrophobia. Taking the elevator was impossible, though, but as every building had stairs it was never an issue and on the positive side it was great for my bum.

During my interview three weeks ago I'd been wowed by the sprawling view that stretched as far as Canary Wharf, and the interior's decor of steel and silver solidifying its cutting-edge reputation.

Pausing between floors to catch my breath and take delicate sips, careful not to spill my drink on my new blue silk blouse or Ralph Lauren skirt, I was close to being late for that 9:30 a.m. staff meeting. My first introduction to Huntly Pierre's elite crack team of investigators had kept me up all night with a mixture of excitement and nerves.

I patted myself on the back with how well I'd already coped with disaster this morning. My curling iron broke seconds after switching it on so I'd had to shove my wayward locks into a neat chignon.

Huntly Pierre took up the top six floors and was a modern masterpiece of architecture smack-dab in the middle of The Strand, and the kind of real estate that proved the company was thriving. I'd been brought on for my special brand of expertise garnered from that art history degree I'd earned at Courtauld. This was truly my dream job. I would soon be hanging out at galleries all day, chatting with other art lovers, and my nosy personality would get its daily fix.

My face flushed as I recalled last night's highlight at The Otillie, meeting the enigmatic Mr. Wilder. I'd fallen asleep with my laptop open on his pretty boy face.

One thing was for sure, he was the outdoorsy type and had a thing for motorbikes and sports cars, or any kind of speed, for that matter.

Soon after I'd gotten home from the gallery I'd sat riveted to my screen as I'd watched what was hailed as a rare insight into his life filmed last year and aired on national television. He'd taken the interviewer on a private tour of his Los Angeles gallery. As they'd strolled through The Wilder, perusing his fine collection of paintings, Tobias had sincerely expressed his passion for seeing art education continued in schools.

I'd let out a sigh as I'd watched him express his belief that students benefited greatly from learning to see beyond the ordinary—

"They must be taught to look closer," he'd fervidly expressed. "They must be shown how to peer through the enlightened lens of art and develop the skills that will lead them to experience creative lives."

That short journalistic piece had highlighted his serious nature, which I'd glimpsed last night. Though when Tobias had finally relaxed a little, enough to smile into the camera, he might as well have been looking through the screen at me.

My face burned brighter at the seeming chink in that bad boy charm that threatened to disarm my defenses.

Though there was tragedy in his past too. I found an article on him from five years ago, written in the *Telegraph Online*. His parents had died in a plane crash when he was a boy. Perhaps this was why he was so driven; he was running away from the pain. He'd refused to comment on that aspect of his life, preferring instead to keep it private.

There had been photo after photo of the press catching him making supersonic exits at every opportunity, his hair messed up and his sunglasses shielding those stunning green eyes. The press had christened him "Mr. Elusive" and it suited him.

Now that I knew it wasn't unusual for him to perform a disappearing act I didn't feel like it had been me who'd scared him away with any number of my usual social blunders.

I wished I'd savored that sun-kissed body a little more but I'd been so shocked to see a living, breathing masterpiece subtly flexing his muscles in The Otillie's basement.

I felt a wave of melancholy that I'd never know the meaning of that Latin inscription on his well-toned torso. I wondered if he had any more of those mysterious inked inscriptions on any other part of his body.

I flinched and almost bit through my lip.

And burst through the top-floor exit with a little too much gusto.

That caffeine had evidently kicked in, and I startled Elena, the receptionist, forcing her to spring to her feet to greet me.

"Morning exercise," I managed breathlessly.

"Good morning, Zara." She sang the words in that heavy Glasgow accent.

I'd fallen for Elena's easy breezy charm the day of my interview when she made me laugh with her cheeky humor. She'd worked here for years and seemed to know the inside scoop on everyone. I loved her fashion sense, that daring miniskirt just above her knees and those fine leather boots, which seemed a statement of her unwavering confidence—I'd overheard her on the phone handling difficult clients—her purple sweater added a dash of color.

A rush of movement came at me.

Danny Kenner swept past me with the biggest grin. "Hi there."

His accent reminded me of Tobias's, but Danny had a Californian lilt whereas Tobias's had an indistinguishable husky edge.

His ripped jeans and Lacoste jumper, along with his Nike sneakers, revealed Huntly Pierre's more casual approach to their dress code.

I smiled after him.

Danny had made me feel welcome during my first visit here, and we'd hit it off straight away with our shared love of "anything" by Rembrandt and Starbucks.

Elena beamed at him. "They got a fingerprint on the Jaeger case."

My gaze snapped after Danny, wanting to run after him and hear more.

Last night, the same evening I'd dropped *Madame Rose* off at The Otillie, there'd been a theft from a private house in Holland Park.

This morning, I'd been riveted to the TV as the BBC newscaster had reported that nothing else had been taken. The Jaeger family had lost their greatest heirloom, an 1896 Edvard Munch, and were predictably devastated.

This second theft in under a month in London was sending the art community into a spin. The police were scrambling for clues and had brought in the team at Huntly Pierre.

Part of this job was also comforting the victims and I prided myself that with my tragic history I'd flourish with that aspect of my profession. I knew what it felt like to lose what had essentially become a friend; for some, art had a way of drawing you in and holding you spellbound for a lifetime.

I felt a rush of excitement that I was finally here.

"Your meeting with the staff got pushed," she said. "The boss has a last-minute change in schedule."

"I imagine everyone's crazy busy," I said. "How are you handling the press?"

"Everything goes through Mr. Huntly."

"Of course."

"He'll come get you when he's ready."

"Great."

"Let's show you around."

She introduced me to the rest of the staff, and I was greeted with warm smiles. Everyone seemed friendly and acted happy here, which was a great sign. The large windows allowed sunlight to flood in and the warm tone of those cream-colored walls gave the central cubicles a spacious feel.

When we made it to the room that would become my office I saw the small brown paper bag on the desk.

"It's a muffin," said Elena. "My treat to make you feel at home."

"Thank you, Elena. That was so kind of you." I peeked into the bag. "Now this is a perfect way to start the day." It made my mouth water just thinking of it.

"Here's what you'll need to get started." She handed me a file. "You'll find everything on our private website. Just hit Staff Access. Change your codes and shred this."

"Got it."

She left me to get settled, and I sat in the leather swivel chair and fired up the desktop computer in front of me.

There was an empty bookcase flush against the right wall,

a filing cabinet in the corner and a stack of empty files on top of it. The blank wall in front was just waiting for a painting. That view was something else: the River Thames looked beautiful with the morning sunlight reflecting off it.

I dragged my gaze away and tapped my code into Huntly Pierre's database and began navigating the software. Taking a bite of that delicious blueberry muffin, undoing all the good of those stairs.

"Good morning, Ms. Leighton." Adley Huntly leaned a shoulder casually on the door frame. His friendly face beamed a warm welcome.

Brushing crumbs off my hands, I pushed myself to my feet.

His white hair gave my boss an arty flair. He was strikingly tall and slim and his tailored suit rounded out his aristocratic air. Adley was well respected in the community as one of the most successful consultants in the industry. Working for him was going to be life changing.

I made my way over to him. "Sir, it's a pleasure to see you again."

"Likewise, Zara." His handshake was firm and his smile reassuring. "Do you have everything you need?"

"Yes, thank you. Elena's been wonderful."

"Glad to hear it. Ready to get to work?" He gestured. "We're in the conference room."

He led me back through the foyer and down a long sprawling hallway. I'd not seen the east wing yet and tried not to gape at the whitewashed walls upon which hung a line of forgeries of the Old Masters.

"I want to thank you again for this incredible opportunity," I said.

"We're delighted to have you onboard." He checked his phone as we walked.

I paused before the stunning replica of Vincent van Gogh's *The Starry Night*.

"Good, aren't they?" he said.

"They are." I let out a sigh of wonder as we strolled passed a Salvador Dali. "Will I be part of the Jaeger team?"

"Perhaps. The painting's gone. Lost without a trace, apparently."

"Sorry to hear that."

"Actually, we have a new assignment for you. A client needs an authentication on a piece he's considering purchasing." His face crinkled into a smile. "Thought we'd break you in slowly."

"Of course," I said, "Whatever you think is best." Adley went on ahead into the conference room.

I glanced behind to take in one of my favorite paintings by John Singer Sergeant, affectionately known as *Portrait of Madame X*. A lifelike image of an elegant young woman wearing a long black evening dress, her hand casually resting on a small table as she stared off wistfully.

Virginie Gautreau had been an American beauty who'd garnered a notorious reputation for her rumored infidelities. The painting had caused a scandal during its 1884 debut in Paris.

My focus was captured by its guilty secret. This portrait was a brilliant forgery that could have slipped past the experts. It was that good.

"Ms. Leighton?" Adley called out.

Virginie Gautreau masked her true feelings so well. Like I was doing now.

My feet melting into the floor as my breath caught.

Adley had taken his place at the head of the table and beside him sat a stunning thirtysomething, her hair a striking platinum blond up in a neat chignon.

And sitting beside her—Tobias Wilder.

Now cleanly shaven, he'd outdone his last suit with this three-piece pinstripe number that highlighted his finely formed physique, his short dark blond hair perfectly combed and those striking eyes…were locked on mine.

What was he doing here?

There was no sign of that dashing warm smile. His mouth was fixed in a tense hard line of scrutiny and those irises were now a startling jade.

I dragged my gaze away from his and looked over at Adley.

He was studying my reaction. "Those forgeries have a knack of getting to you, don't they?"

Catching my breath, I gestured to the paintings. "How do you ever get any work done?"

Tobias pushed himself to his feet and came over. "Miss Leighton."

"You know each other?" asked Adley.

Tobias reached out to shake my hand. "Had the pleasure of meeting last night at The Otillie."

Right after I'd caught him half-naked, I secretly mused, holding on to his hand for a second too long, the sensation of his touch temptingly addictive.

Cringing inwardly, I tried not to think about me unwittingly flashing him yesterday.

Casually, he tucked his hands into his pockets. "The gallery's a favorite to visit when I'm this side of the pond. I'm good friends with Miles Tenant—"

"The Otillie's curator," said Adley. "Great chap. Knows his art."

I went to ask him if it had been Miles who'd invited him to the party but thought better of it. Maybe later, when the formality of the meeting was over.

"Already broken the ice, then?" Alder's gaze fell on me. "Good to hear."

"One of my dad's paintings," I told him. "I've donated it to the gallery. They were kind enough to hold a reception in his name."

"Of course, *Madame Rose Récamier*?" he said. "How was the reception?"

"Great," said Tobias. "The usual crowd."

"Got anything else hidden away?" said Adley cheekily.

I wore my best vague expression.

They didn't need to know about my little secret stash of art gems. Amongst the collection was a tour de force from a painter who'd influenced the landscape of Western art. I'd already drawn too much attention, and what was left of our paintings threatened to disrupt the kind of peace I'd come to crave.

"Would anyone like a doughnut?" I gestured to the plate in front of us.

"No, thank you." Tobias's jaw muscles tightened and flexed, and he swapped a wary glance with the woman.

That spark of recognition on his face last night when he'd first met me had probably come from a Huntly Pierre memo he'd read with my name on it. Realizing this made me feel a little better.

Damn, this place was fantastic. I already loved working here. The kind of clients this place attracted was astonishing.

"Ms. Arquette." Tobias gestured toward her. "My attorney."

"So happy to meet you," I said brightly. "Can we get you anything?"

"I'm fine," she said with a softly spoken Swedish accent. "Any more coffee and I'll never sleep again. Please, call me Logan."

"Logan," I said, "welcome to London."

She started to say something but Tobias answered for her. "She lives here."

"Oh, that's lovely," I said.

"I'm bicoastal, Ms. Leighton." She flashed a grin at Tobias. "Sometimes LA. Sometimes here. I go where needed."

Her neat chignon was showing mine up—whereas hers didn't have a hair out of place, mine looked like I'd gone for the other end of the spectrum with wisps of hair fighting for freedom.

Tobias took a step toward me, closing the gap between us, and he raised his hand toward my mouth, his intense stare fixed on mine. I leaned back slightly, but his thumb was already brushing over my lower lip in a sensual sweep and it pouted naturally beneath his touch.

My breath stilted as a rush of tingles circled my chest and my cheeks felt flushed. Time slowing...

His irises were speckled with amber. That revelation, along with his mind-altering cologne wafting my way, caused a wave of giddiness.

The shadow of his touch on my lip...

"Crumb," he said huskily and lowered his hand to his side.

"Muffin," I managed and went for a seat near Adley, avoiding Logan's ice-cold glare. Tobias gripped the back of my chair and nudged me forward into the desk.

"Thank you." I wished I'd brought a pen and notepad now so I could pretend to write. "It was a gift from Elena. The muffin, I mean." I offered a polite smile to Logan. "Our receptionist. It's blueberry. With blueberry bits in there."

Logan smirked as though amused.

He didn't seem to notice, merely rounded the table and took his seat again right next to her.

"Careful," said Logan, "don't up-sell Elena too much or I might headhunt her."

Tobias swiveled casually in his chair. "Let's leave their staff alone."

He'd brought his left leg up and crossed it over his right, showing off those fine highly polished leather shoes, and he looked so damn confident, so relaxed, so ridiculously dashing.

"Elena's been with us for years," offered Adley. "We'd be lost without her. Shall we go over the details?" Adley opened the beige folder in front of him.

I settled back in my chair, pretending that Tobias hadn't fixed his stare on me. This seemed like cruel karma after I'd ogled him for a little too long last night.

I avoided his scrutiny by showing interest in the paintings surrounding me. More fakes hung from the walls. The large Jackson Pollock to our left was breathtakingly real. The original was safe in the National Gallery, a tube ride from here. A home away from home during my student days.

Pollock, one of America's most famous abstract artists, had left a legacy of canvases splashed with brilliant roiling lines and blotches that even today stirred a visceral response. This one, if it had been real, would have fetched at least thirty million pounds if sold today. Luckily, it was in here and off the market so some poor unsuspecting collector with too much money didn't throw it away on a counterfeit.

I'd once watched my father throw a mug of tea at a forgery. He'd told me afterward the artist had plagiarized the heart and soul of the painter. There was only one explanation for hanging these cruel betrayals up in the east wing. They were used for training.

Dragging my gaze away from the Pollock, I returned my focus to Adley.

He peered over his rounded spectacles at Tobias. "The plan is to authenticate before you buy?"

"It's a time issue," said Tobias. "It's the kind of investment I'm willing to make but only if we can confirm its authenticity."

"Which painting?" I asked.

"Mr. Wilder is hoping to move fast," said Logan.

"You're not going with an American firm?" said Adley.

"Discretion is essential," replied Logan.

"It's in the UK?" I wondered why he was not going with the firm he usually used. After all, his vast collection had been authenticated.

"It's a well-sought-out piece," said Tobias. "I need discretion."

"We're ahead of the curve with this one," said Logan. "We want to move fast."

"Huntly Pierre guarantees a strict privacy policy," said Adley. "Our service is confidential."

Logan's glare locked on me. "How long have you worked for the firm?"

"Well, I've been with Huntly Pierre—" I looked over at Adley.

He gave a reassuring smile. "I can assure you Ms. Leighton's art pedigree is exceptional."

"If you don't mind," said Logan. "We're merely crossing our t's."

"Of course." Adley gestured for her to continue.

Tobias picked up a pen embossed with the company insignia and tapped it on the desk. "Tell us more about you, Ms. Leighton."

"I studied art here in London." I smiled, hoping that would allay their concerns. "I've loved art all my life."

Logan opened the beige folder in front of her and read. "Courtauld Institute of Art?"

There was a flipping folder on me?

A wave of nervousness circled my stomach. "Yes, I graduated—"

"With honors." Tobias's stare locked on mine. "Impressive."

"The Courtauld's just down the road," I told them brightly. "I can arrange a visit if you like."

Logan's frown narrowed. "We're more interested in your current experience."

"Oh, well, I've not been with the firm that long. But I've been immersed in the art world all my life. My father was an honorary member of the Royal Academy of Arts."

"Are you a member?" asked Logan.

"No," I said, "you have to be voted in. Members are usually practicing artists."

Tobias reached out for that folder and slid it toward him along the desk. Turning the pages slowly, he seemed to be reading every single line of whatever was in there. If silence could have been considered a weapon he'd mastered the art of using it.

That Jackson Pollock was jarring my nerves, those swirls of white on black, those yellow blotches had hit the canvas with precision. To an untrained eye they would have appeared like a madman's call for help.

Adley leaned forward. "Zara has a natural flair for—"

"Is this your first day?" Logan sounded incredulous. Tobias's stare slowly lifted to hold mine.

Making me feel like I'd been caught in a lie. The unfairness of being thrown into the deep end hit me. The fine hairs on my forearms prickled.

"Ms. Leighton?" she said sternly.

"Zara?" Tobias sounded tense.

He'd gone from friendly American to scary interrogator with that steely gaze fixed on mine.

I straightened my back defensively. "As it so happens, yes."

Logan's skeptical glare shot toward Adley. "This is your best man?"

"My team is currently invested in a high-profile case," said Adley.

"You're essentially saying your staff is too busy for us?" Logan looked annoyed.

Adley seemed unfazed. "Well, as you probably know there have been a couple of art thefts, right here in London. We've been brought in by the Met to do what we can to help. See if they're connected."

He went on to explain the details. As my world crumbled around me.

This day was meant to be bloody awesome. Now I was about to prove to my new boss I had no right to be here.

Why had I even bothered? Why had I even believed I could make a place for myself in a world that had turned away from my family? I was destined to be discovered as a fraud myself. Might as well just hang me up on the wall.

I was starting to regret ever meeting Tobias Wilder. Even if my thighs were squeezed tight and that tingling between them was disagreeing with my current conclusion: he was beginning to look like a class-A rogue who always got his way. Yet my thoughts kept carrying me back to his secret tattoo, the first Latin word meeting the tip of his V and conveniently leading off toward his forbidden zone.

That video of him I'd watched last night had probably been a ruse to soften those hard edges of his public image.

He seemed willing to do just about anything to own that mystery painting. I'd seen that same determination in my father. These were the kind of men who let nothing stand in their way when it came to possessing that certain coveted masterpiece.

Adley and Logan continued to debate the wisdom of hiring such an obvious newbie with no fieldwork experience.

Tobias's expression remained unreadable. The way he played

with that pen made me want to snatch it out of his hands and ram it into the middle of that Jackson Pollock—

Those maddening swirls mirrored my racing heartbeat and those yellow blotches significantly matched the artist's adoration for placing bright colors just so, a brilliant rebellion against order and a show of pride against expectations and yet setting them where our subconscious reassured us they were meant to be. That hint of a blue canvas beneath all that profound color was hard to fake, if not impossible, and I didn't need to stick my nose up against it to know there was only one man who could pull off a Pollock as good as this one—

"Zara?" said Tobias.

I blinked his way as though stirring from a dream.

The way he'd spoken my name made me feel as though he'd touched me all over again.

My fingertips traced my lips.

We don't like him, remember?

"Want to add anything, Ms. Leighton?" asked Logan.

Great, I'd suddenly developed ADD too, apparently.

Not wanting to embarrass myself or Adley one more second, I rose to my feet. "If you'll excuse me…" *I need fresh air.* "I'll get us some more water."

"Well, this has been a colossal waste of time," muttered Logan.

I folded my arms. "Excuse me?"

She gave a thin smile. "I was merely advising my client we're running late."

My arm shot up and I pointed toward the Pollock. "Look."

Logan followed my gaze.

I took a sharp inhale of breath. "It's a Pollock."

Adley arched a brow as though inviting me to elaborate.

I rose and strolled over to it. "This is a sixty-million-dollar painting and the coffeepot is boiling just ten feet away from the canvas. Mr. Adley, whoever appraised your artwork needs retraining."

"That would be me," he said calmly.

My apology stuck in my throat and I swallowed to budge it, my brain replaying the last ten seconds to check if I'd sworn out loud.

I was too thrown to even cringe.

"And it just happens to be hanging in your coffee room?" said Tobias, smiling over at Adley. "A remarkable discovery."

No, he wasn't going to fill me with doubt.

Logan stared over at it. "Shouldn't you x-ray it before jumping to a conclusion?"

"The evidence is backed by the frame, Ms. Arquette," I said. "See? The frame is modest." My gaze swept over the canvas, my heart sympathizing with this masterpiece and feeling just as misunderstood.

Adley gestured with open palms toward Tobias and it looked like resignation, or worse, an apology on my behalf.

Tobias's fingers were resting on my file. "Thank you, Adley. I believe we're done here." He closed it and pushed to his feet.

Words were exchanged between him and Adley. A shake of hands. A promise to be in touch.

Tobias lowered his head, tucked his hands into his pockets and left the room without looking at me. Logan threw me a thin smile and followed him out.

I stood frozen, regretting the sudden delivery of my outburst as I watched them leave, realizing it was too late to salvage the meeting.

I spun to face Adley. "Sir, I'm so sorry. I don't know what came over me."

"You're going to have to learn to keep a lid on your emotions, Zara."

"Yes, of course." I plopped back down in my seat.

Had I just blown my career on my first day? Yes, I bloody well had.

Adley's attention went from the door to where Logan and Tobias had just exited and moved swiftly over to the Pollock, his attention lingering there. "Well done."

I blinked my confusion.

Adley gestured to the painting. "Most people assume they're all fakes. They don't see beyond the other scoundrels hanging around them. They assume if one is fake, then they all are."

Startled, I sat back.

"Our client requested a demonstration of your skills. I made a call."

I wondered how much this had cost the firm. The security detail alone would amount to thousands. It had to be the kind of investment that would pay off when it nabbed a high-paying client. Adley stared in admiration at the painting and I stared at him, marveling at his faith in me to pull off this feat.

"They left in an awful hurry," I muttered.

He shrugged. "Looks like we're officially lending you to Wilder."

My breath caught and my fingernails dug into the armrests.

"He's requested an exclusive consultation," he added.

"He asked for me personally?"

But Adley was already on the phone and chatting with a curator about having that Pollock they'd borrowed just this morning returned to the National Gallery.

4

My Range Rover handled the off-road terrain well.

Tobias Wilder's Oxfordshire estate was tucked away in the middle of nowhere, though thanks to my navigational skills I was right on time. This place was not on the map, nor were the dusty tree-lined lanes that led me here.

And at 7:00 p.m. I'd not had the advantage of daylight.

There came a thrill of intrigue at seeing Tobias again, and I knew that the secret painting he wanted me to authenticate would also reveal more about him. As would seeing the inside of his home.

It'd taken me over two hours to drive from the city, and it felt good to stretch my legs and ease the stiffness from my limbs as I'd made my way up the driveway toward his door. The only way I'd known I was in the right place was that I saw a helicopter perched on the roof.

You'll see it from the driveway, Logan's instructions via email had said. Though she'd not mentioned the driveway went on for three miles.

And as most Brits didn't have sleek-looking helicopters on their roofs or a line of silver Jaguars parked outside their multimillion-dollar houses, I knew this was it. Something told me Tobias liked toys. The expensive kind.

My modest flat was a shoe box compared to this place. My bedroom looked like a hurricane had swept through the place. I'd changed my outfit so many times and even now doubted this was the right choice. Black slacks, a white chiffon blouse, Ralph Lauren heels. I'd treated myself to a trip to my local salon for a professional blow-dry and now my unruly locks were shiny curls tumbling down my shoulders, and I might have spent a little longer than usual on my makeup.

I'd left my parka in the car.

The last time I'd seen Mr. Wilder was at the meeting yesterday morning. He apparently needed me in the field immediately. I was curious why time was such a factor. The art world moved at a snail's pace right up until a painting went to auction. Then all hell broke loose with bidders scrambling to release funds so they could possess that certain piece they'd been waiting to come onto the market. Sometimes for years.

I knocked several times on the front door. With no answer I took the liberty of heading on in. There was sure to be security to signal my arrival.

Tobias's foyer had a minimalist's opulence.

Modern, if not futuristic, with chrome-lined trimmings and stark white marble tiles and yet vaguely homey in a high-tech kind of way.

"Hello!" I called out again.

My voice echoed, my fingers tense from holding my phone too tightly. I went to call out again—

A blur of movement shimmered in the far corner.

The petite geisha was dressed in the traditional kimono and moved swiftly toward me, her head bowed, her lips marked with a red kiss of lipstick, her movement serene as she made her way into the center. Her black hair was rolled into several elaborate buns and her striking features were highlighted by her pure white foundation.

Why was I not surprised that Tobias had a pretty woman working for him? She came closer, her hands held together in greeting and her fingers eerily pale.

"I'm Zara. I'm expected by Mr. Wilder?" I gave a quick "I hope so or that would be awkward" smile.

She raised her line of sight and stared at me. *"Yōkoso."* Unease rose in my chest; a sense something was wrong. She vanished.

I staggered back, my handbag slipping from my grip and my iPhone joining it on the marble with a loud crack as it bounced at my feet.

My throat constricted with fear.

Blinking around the foyer, all air gone from my lungs, heart racing, my brain telling me to run and yet my legs too weak to respond.

The geisha girl was back before me. Right there. Her head respectfully bowed, her gaze rose to meet mine, her line of sight exact. And yet—

"Yōkoso." She bowed low.

These impossible seconds unfolded like a cruel nightmare. Her fading image flickered back into focus.

"What the fuck…" I hissed through clenched teeth.

"She's a bit glitchy." A male voice. My stare shot toward it.

Tobias Wilder stood at the top of the stairs with his hands tucked casually inside his trouser pockets, his thoughtful frown deepening. He was more striking than I'd remembered him, that dark blond hair crowning his handsome face and his green eyes were mesmerizing as they held mine. His well-defined physique was now dressed sharply in a classically styled tuxedo, his white shirt open at the collar with no bow tie.

I chastised myself for staring too long. The geisha was gone.

Blinking furiously, my brain tried to process what I'd seen. Tobias made his way down the stairs. "The uncanny valley."

"I'm sorry?"

"A hypothesis." He paused on the last step. "From the field of aesthetics." He raised his gaze to the ceiling. "The brain triggers unease. It clearly senses what it's seeing isn't real. What was your initial emotion?"

My thoughts swirled, my jaw easing its tension.

If try not to pee yourself was an emotion, that would be it.

He gave an assured nod. "Revulsion? Even if she is pretty."

"A hologram?" I wanted to tell him that was wrong in so many ways.

He arched his eyebrows playfully. "I started off with a rat. That did not go down well."

This man was bloody insane.

And I was in the middle of the country and quite possibly alone with him.

Trying to pull back on my startled expression, I said, "You have a beautiful home, Mr. Wilder?" It came out as a question. "Long driveway."

"Please, call me Tobias."

My gaze darted around to see if anyone else was here.

"Would you like a drink?" He gestured to the left.

I knelt to retrieve my handbag and cringed when I saw the shattered glass on my iPhone's screen.

He stood above me in that devilishly handsome pose, his face calm as though he'd not just scared the crap out of me and smashed my phone. I peered up to see his intense stare locked on mine, and a rush of ill-timed excitement flooded my veins.

He'd frozen me there with his stare.

"I'll get you a new one," he said firmly. "You're three models behind, Zara. This will not do."

My gaze swept over my phone.

He held out his hand, and I felt his firm grip as he assisted me up. I stared at him. "That won't be necessary."

"I think you'll find contradicting me is unwise." He winked.

God, I'd forgotten how gorgeous he was. How his striking green eyes crinkled so seductively when he smiled.

"I insist." He waved it off.

My cheeks scorched with embarrassment as I followed him out of the foyer. This was my first day out in the field, and I intended on getting my act together and impressing both Tobias and my boss when he reported back to him.

For now, I'd have to tuck my cheeky retorts away.

His cologne wafted around me and I subtly sniffed him in. The scent of a fresh forest in the morning, and something spicy, something forbidden. A poorly timed vision of his naked, toned torso flashed through my thoughts.

I wondered if Tobias's messy-yet-artful, post-fucked hairstyle was on purpose. His flawless bespoke tux showed off his tall frame and broad shoulders and his onyx-and-silver cuff links shone as they caught the light. He had the kind of walk that proved his unwavering confidence as he went about intimidating those who dared to enter his stratosphere.

He'd either come from a posh dinner or was heading out to one. Probably with some übersexy vixen who made me look like the girl next door. Might as well have worn that parka, it wasn't like he was going to be admiring my curves anytime soon.

"This shouldn't take long," I reassured him.

He turned and flashed a heart-stopping smile. "I've already had the pleasure of a demonstration of your skills, Zara."

"The Jackson Pollock?"

"Quite a gift." He gave a ghost of a smile and his American

aura oozed approachable and yet those stunning good looks were unnerving.

We made our way into a large sitting room, sparse like the foyer, a leather couch facing the long sweeping window from floor to ceiling. Beyond the view lay miles of lush green grass that eventually met with a forest that stretched out for miles.

All that lovely nature extended in here too with those tall thriving plants that gave the place an earthy feel. To the left there was a clear wall of glass with falling water echoing like rain along the full length of the room.

The beauty of it took my breath away.

"The house is run by solar," he said when he caught me staring at it.

"Why the hologram?" I asked. "Is it part of your security system?"

"I tinker."

"With holograms?"

"Inventions."

Of course, I'd read that about him but hadn't expected to see one so soon, and certainly not such a brilliant demonstration of what he was capable of.

Tobias made his way over to a chrome bar. From behind there he opened a fridge door and brought out an impressive bottle of Krug champagne and a carafe of orange juice and set about making us drinks. "You made a fine test subject."

"You observed my reaction?"

"Software failed. The experiment was compromised."

"What else do you invent?"

He arched a brow. "The nature of an invention is to create that which does not exist."

"Obviously."

Tobias paused as though I'd offended him.

"I'm sure it's all top secret." I softened the moment.

"Failure is common."

"Didn't Edison say something about being so close and not giving up? That you're usually right there when you give up."

"And how would one test such a theory?"

My teeth scraped over my lower lip as I ran through that logic.

He turned around and reached up to the glass cabinet behind him and brought down two champagne flutes.

"I'm driving," I said. "Water would be nice."

"Not tonight."

"I meant when I leave later."

He spilled a trickle of orange juice onto his hand and licked the tip of his finger; a curl of his sensual mouth, a flash of tongue.

He threw me a mischievous grin. And I almost melted on the spot.

Being in the same space with him addled my thoughts, and I had to force myself to pull back on my imagination, which was teasing how wonderful his gorgeous body would feel against mine. A fantasy that felt impossible.

"Thank you for driving all the way out here," he said.

"It's my pleasure. I'm glad to be of help. Do you rent the property when you're in town?"

"I own it."

Of course he did, and it felt like such a silly question now.

He peered out the long window. "I'm not too popular amongst the neighbors. Whoever submitted the schematics for the height of the fences got their metric system muddled with the foot units and measured it all wrong."

I had noted how tall the gates were as I'd driven through his property.

"Turns out," Tobias continued, "fox hunters can't jump the gates during a hunt." He uncorked the bottle of champagne.

"And their hounds are too big to fit through. So those foxes use my land as a sort of sanctuary. Naughty foxes."

I caught his cheeky grin.

"Well, that's quite wonderful," I said.

"In the winter I like to stand right where you are now and look out and watch them play in the snow."

With a tilt of champagne and a dash of orange juice he'd prepared two mimosas. My gaze roamed over him in awe.

He caught me staring and straightened his back. "Perhaps now is a good time for us to go over my expectations."

I stepped forward, eager to hear. "Of course."

"Now that you work for me—"

"Technically I work for Huntly Pierre."

"Who have officially loaned you to me." He caught me with his glare. "Let's toast to a successful evening." He raised a glass and offered it to me.

I took it. "Cheers."

"We were discussing the ground rules."

"I'd be happy to hear your expectations."

He took a sip. "I expect confidentiality—"

"That goes without saying."

"Unquestioning loyalty—"

"Of course."

"I expect you not to interrupt when I'm speaking—"

"I was merely—"

He arched a brow.

His overly confident manner sent my equilibrium reeling and I had to stare out of that long glass window to regain my composure.

"Let's discuss tonight," he said.

He wasn't just into controlling holographic geishas apparently. I looked around. "Sir, perhaps I could see the painting?"

"Tobias."

I gave a thin smile. "Tobias, I'd love to see it. The painting, I mean."

He raised his glass and took several sips, his stare holding mine.

Mirroring him, I took a sip, enjoying the delicious tang of orange and expensive champagne, and ran over what I knew about him. He was a self-made billionaire but so far he'd not acted spoiled. Though from what I'd seen he could be considered bossy.

He was the kind of challenge I usually rose to but I was here to please him. *The client*, my addled brain corrected my erotic musing.

Wilder might as well have had *heartbreak central* stamped on his forehead. And I'd had more than my fair share of that. Those internal alarms were there for a reason.

"Are you going out? Am I making you late?"

"Follow me."

"May I get my equipment from the car?"

"No need."

Behind his back, I took a gulp of bubbly.

I set the glass on the bar and followed a few steps behind him, relieved to be getting to the reason why I'd driven all this way. Strolling down the well-lit hallway and vigilant for any more geisha-like surprises.

"Perhaps I could see more of your inventions?" I said softly. He threw me a doubtful smile.

"Perhaps a warning next time? Before you show it to me." I wondered what other stuff he was working on. "What kind of application does the hologram have?"

"Security, mainly. I'm currently working on a touchable hologram. One that reacts to movement."

"That sounds incredible." I secretly ogled his bum.

Tobias had the kind of height and confident stride most

women would swoon at. We'd not gotten to the place where I could pry about his personal life. I wondered if we ever would. My lips pressed together when my brain nudged me to ask the meaning of his Latin tattoo.

"No 3-D glasses, Zara, did you catch that?" He smiled my way. "Don't tell anyone what you saw."

"Of course." I breathed out in a rush of giddy excitement, realizing I'd witnessed something special.

The fact Tobias had trusted me made me beam with happiness. Being here was fricking amazing. "So the seller lent you the painting so you could have it appraised?"

He pushed open a door.

Inside the modest room there was merely a central island. A couple of boxes resting on top of it.

One wall was a mirror from carpet to ceiling. There, in the corner, hanging on an ornate tall cupboard, was an elegant black satin gown, the kind you see worn on the runways of Paris. Tobias strolled over to the island and lifted the box sitting in the center. He opened the lid to reveal the strappy silver shoes inside.

I caught my breath. "Those are pretty."

He was showing me his girlfriend's things, and I feigned this wasn't awkward at all. I looked around for the painting. There wasn't one.

"You'll need this." He gestured to the box beside the shoes.

My frown deepened as I stepped forward, lifted the lid and rifled through the soft tissue paper, looking for the handheld X-ray scanner.

I pulled out a strip of black silk material and realized I was looking at Coco de Mer lingerie.

My breath left me in a rush as the bra slipped from my fingers back into the box. He came closer, his expression intense, his green irises fierce under the light.

"Tobias?" My gaze dragged from his and fell back onto the tag on that thin strip of material that was meant to serve as a bra and it was my cup size. My cheeks blazed like fire. "What's this for?"

He glanced at the dress. "Please, put on the Alexander McQueen."

"Why?"

"You can't go dressed like that."

"Go where?"

"To see the painting." He brushed a strand of hair out of my eyes and tucked it behind my ear.

It felt as though I'd been struck by lightning and the echo of his touch lingered where his fingers had brushed my cheek; my eyelids fluttered. "We're not staying here?"

"No, Zara."

"We're going out?"

He gave the kindest smile. "Yes."

My stare returned to the sexy underwear and then moved from the strappy shoes and hovered over the dress. "That's for me?"

He gave an assured nod. "Meet me in the foyer."

Tobias left and his heady cologne lingered behind him, its effect just as powerful.

I leaned on the central island and clutched the edge, knuckles white, fighting this wave of light-headedness.

As though rising from a dream, the situation became glaringly clear. I'd stepped inside the world of the truly wealthy and just proven I was out of my depth. Yes, I'd come from money, but it had all been tied up in property and paintings and never had I experienced moments of decadence that took my breath away—

Until now.

5

Reason caught up with my arousal and nudged it out of the way, helping me see clearly without the distraction of that sex god clouding my view.

You don't invite a professional woman over to your home, which is in the middle of nowhere, show her some erotic lingerie and tell her to put it on, and then force her to wear a gown from one of the world's top designers. No matter how much it must have cost or how gorgeous those strappy straps looked with that risqué off-the-shoulder design and elegant ruching, and the way it fell to flatter a woman's curves just so.

Even if you do go around flaunting you're the sexiest man alive and a hero to wildlife, with the ease of someone who pretends he has no effect on those around him.

"No, you bloody well don't." I stomped down the hallway, through the foyer and out into the cold night air.

And headed for my Range Rover.

From what I'd seen, everyone back at Huntly Pierre seemed reasonable. I'd merely relay my concerns about our client's eccentricities and be off the hook—

A burst of noise above.

A blinding fluorescent white lit up the house.

I forced my lips shut against the tornado of dust and leaves swirling around me and brought my hands up to protect my face from the scattering debris, crouching against the metal monster looming above, the force of wind shoving me back and blasting my clothes.

Whirling blades came into view—

The sleek helicopter turned a 180 and landed smoothly before me. Heart pounded, blood roared in my ears, my legs weakened.

The chopping lessened as the blades stilled. The air now quiet.

I blinked against the bright blur of headlights directed at me. Out climbed Tobias.

He walked toward me with that casual swagger of confidence, wearing a bow tie now to round out his intimidation, looking even more formal than before, even more handsome, with that familiar earthiness and a splash of bad-boy billionaire.

He stopped short of where I stood and locked his gaze on me.

Brushing off a few leaves that were stuck to my trousers and dragging my fingers through my hair to remove a few more to make my point, I raised myself to my full height, trying to regain some decorum.

That's right, buddy, I'm not wearing it.

I stared him down.

Tobias stepped toward me, closing the gap between us.

And closer still until he towered over me, his expression calm.

Slowly, my chin rose as though daring him to kiss me and earn himself a slap. I knew better than to let this man in despite my thoughts scattering like those wayward leaves still finding their way around my feet.

I hardly knew anything about Tobias and yet he was seducing me with the ease of a man who always got what he wanted.

That was twice he'd scared the hell out of me. I was damned if I was going to give him the chance to do it again. He still hadn't touched me, his hands tucked inside his trouser pockets in that seductive pose.

I flashed a glare. "It appears we have a misunderstanding, Mr. Wilder."

"Yet I see the situation clearly."

"Really?"

"Zara." His breath felt warm on my mouth.

"Yes."

He tilted his head slightly and his left cheek hovered near mine, his mouth close to my ear as he whispered, "It's just a painting."

I tried to remember the last time I'd been this daring and nothing came close to being whisked away by a gorgeous man in a helicopter to view a secret masterpiece. My universe was all about respectful whispers around century-old paintings housed in well-lit galleries in carefully controlled settings.

Was I going to let this adventure slip through my fingers?

"I promise to keep you safe." He looked sincere. "Aren't you even a little intrigued?"

"A little."

"I want you to want to come," he said without a hint of sarcasm.

My gaze moved over to that flashy helicopter.

"Say yes," he whispered.

Whoever that girl was who'd stormed out of his house was nowhere to be seen now.

Instead, with my hand firmly in his grip I followed him

back in and we walked through the foyer and down the hallway and back into the room with the dress.

He guided me into the center.

"I'll put it on." My gaze swept over the dress.

"I appreciate that, Zara."

He was gone again, and I was left staring at my own stunned reflection.

It didn't take me long to undress, peeling out of my underwear and then putting on his Coco de Mer. Staring at the mirror, I marveled how the lingerie flattered my figure, the bra with its delicate design that barely skimmed over my breasts and the Venetian lace panel on the back of the panties showing off my pert bottom. All self-consciousness left me, all embarrassment, as though it was quite natural to stand here wearing Tobias Wilder's gift that barely covered anything.

My nipples beaded and nudged my bra.

A rush of blood to my head that he might have cameras installed in here and from another part of the house might be ogling me. The thought of me arousing him sent tingles between my thighs, his strong arms pulling me into him and holding me tight against his firm body and delivering a kiss so fierce it took my breath away; his full lips, his tongue teasing mine and delivering that unspoken promise he'd fuck me harder than I'd ever experienced.

The kind of passion that had women screaming for more.

I'd never reached those kinds of erotic heights with Zach. Not even close.

There'd been too many intimate moments where I'd feigned release with him because I just couldn't get there, that elusive orgasm well out of reach, and until now I'd believed there was something wrong with me.

My breathing stuttered as my reflection came back into view and I realized I'd never thought of myself as sexy until now. Auburn curls tumbled over my shoulders and brushed my breasts.

I'd never been turned on by my own reflection. *Until now.*

Keeping my focus on why I was actually here was essential if I wasn't going to lose my way, or lose my heart again and screw this up.

Within minutes I'd pulled myself together and put on the Alexander McQueen. I took a few more minutes to admire how well the dress fit over my curves and how incredibly gorgeous it looked on me. The intricate crystals woven into the material proved this was worth at least three months' salary for me.

I used the counter for balance to slide into the high heels that were surprisingly comfortable. I opened my handbag and found my lipstick and dabbed my lips with a soft pink.

I went in search of Tobias, hoping he'd be pleased at least with the way I looked. I found him texting on his phone in the foyer.

When his gaze rose to mine he viewed me like something he'd created; his back stiffened as he stood taller.

A flash of excitement burned in his eyes.

Despite the fact that he was a virtual stranger, I somehow trusted him. This alluring enigma that was Tobias William Wilder was seductively hypnotic.

I loved being around him, and never had I met anyone as exciting as him.

I wanted, *no*, needed his approval. "Will I do, Mr. Wilder?" Searching his face for any sign of attraction to me, I forced a confident smile.

He merely held a fixed, stern expression and blinked my way.

I broke his gaze. "I'm afraid my handbag doesn't match."

"Do you have your magnifier?"

"Yes." Rummaging through my bag, I felt for my miniature magnifier.

He stepped forward and took it from me. "Thank you." Tobias tucked it into his jacket pocket. "You don't need your bag."

"But my phone—"

"Please—" He gestured for me to set it down on the table near the stairs. "You won't need it."

With each step toward it I questioned the sanity of leaving my phone behind and my credit cards, but his glare edged me on.

"Good." Tobias gave a reassuring smile.

Staring through the glass window, I caught sight of the helicopter. "We're really going in that?"

He gestured for me to follow. "Of course."

Following him out into the crisp night air, I said, "I feel like Cinderella." I giggled at my cuteness.

"I'm not sure what that makes me." He smirked as he opened the passenger-side door of the helicopter and beckoned for me to get in. "Cinderella, we have to get you out of there before midnight."

"Out of where?"

"Blandford Palace."

My heart fluttered with joy.

We were heading to one of England's most beautiful estates and seeing inside it had been merely a pipe dream. The manor was closed off to the public, and its rumored impressive collection of artwork was inaccessible, until now.

I vaguely remembered reading that large country estate was owned by one of the wealthiest siblings in England—the Blandford twins, their empire merging old money with the new from a thriving news corporation.

Tobias shrugged off his jacket and turned to face me, placing it over my shoulders. The warmth was welcoming. Until now adrenaline had made me forget the chill. I pulled his jacket around me and snuggled into it.

Focus, Zara, be professional.

The dashboard was all black leather and shiny controls.

When he wrapped his fingers around the central phallic control I had to look away to hide my blush.

Tobias handled his surroundings like his toys, with a focused intensity. That, and the way he broke into a relaxed smile had an addictive quality.

I counted myself lucky to be merely a professional colleague. God knew what kind of damage this man could do if you let him get under your skin.

A few equipment checks later and a brief chat into his headphones with air traffic control, we lifted off smoothly. Gravity forced us into our seats as we made a fast ascent.

With my heart in my throat and my knuckles white from gripping the seat belt too tightly, we banked left, and Tobias's home shone brightly like a beacon below.

Within minutes we were flying over countryside, homes, farmland, and the city lights shrunk beneath us.

As I scanned the flickering lights below, it was easy to forget we were suspended merely in a machine, and now and again I braved a glance over at Tobias, who seemed lost in his own thoughts too.

We landed in the middle of a field and, after the blades stilled, we made our way over to an Aston Martin parked beside a deserted barn. This trip had been well thought out apparently.

We sped off into the night.

Large oak trees lined the driveway, arching above as a wooded tunnel and grandly welcoming visitors with its dramatic forest. Onward through the surrounding acres, their landscape shielded by darkness. When we drove over a bridge there came the view of two great lakes.

"They won't let us land close?" I was forced back into my seat—Tobias accelerated around a corner.

"No-fly zone over the house," he explained.

The drive up to the mansion was no different to the flight here, with Tobias quiet and our conversation lacking. With him focused on his speed I was happy to let him concentrate.

I could only assume my meandering back at his house had lost us time and he was trying to make up for it.

My breath caught at the sight of the monumental seventeenth-century Baroque palace that dominated the horizon. It was truly the most striking home I'd ever seen. Vast stone pillars towered at the entryway, and before it spread out a splendorous courtyard.

"Wow," I said in a rush.

"You're starting to sound like an American," he said playfully. "We can't have that now, can we?"

I was too exhilarated to stop my giggle and slapped my hand to my mouth before I embarrassed myself any further.

We parked left of the house, his Aston Martin fitting in perfectly with the other high-end Bentleys, Ferraris and Mercedes-Benzes.

He leaned right and his arm brushed mine. He opened the glove box and reached in and removed two masks. One black and simple, masculine, and the other, which he handed me, was beaded with shiny studs and delicate feathers rising from the top.

"Put this on." He gestured for me to turn my head so he could help me secure the ribbon behind, his fingertips moving against my hair and making my scalp tingle.

I couldn't wait to share my adventures back at the office.

Elena was going to freak out when I told her about what kind of mission Adley had unwittingly sent me on.

After repositioning my mask to fit perfectly, I pulled down the rearview mirror. My reflection was that of a mysterious sultry siren.

Tobias of course looked gorgeous in his and when he caught me staring at him flashed a grin. "Ready?"

"Yes, I'm excited."

"You look beautiful."

I was grateful he'd already gotten out of the car and hadn't caught my reaction to his compliment. Tobias Wilder had a kind side. And as we were about to spend the evening together at a party, discovering this about him would make tonight easier.

I wondered if it was a Rembrandt we were going to see, and my toes curled with the thrill of seeing the kind of priceless masterpiece reserved for stately homes like this.

Thanking Tobias for holding my door open, I appreciated his strong hand taking mine to help me out of the car.

We strolled up to the front door, which loomed grandly above. Taking those stone steps beneath the elaborate archway highlighting the Roman-themed grandeur.

I straightened my dress. "Why do we have to be out by midnight?"

"Not we, you." His lips curled into a smile. "I need to protect your innocence."

I flashed a smile back. "Oh, it's that old-fashioned tradition where the men retreat to the smoking room in some kind of archaic sexist ritual."

He wrapped his fingers around my left upper arm. "No, Zara, it's because that's when the fucking starts."

6

The front door opened—

And I'd given up breathing.

Tobias ignored my death glare and gave a nod of greeting to the butler, and said, "Vis-v-vis."

He removed a cream envelope from his jacket pocket and handed it to him.

The door opened wider.

Tobias's ironclad grip led me in and past the stocky young butler who probably doubled as a bouncer.

A young waitress stepped forward too. She extended a silver tray with crystal flutes of champagne. I tried to keep my gaze on the bubbly and not stare at her nakedness. She wore a black thong, and that was it, unless you counted the nipple clamps. She was petite, and her pretty eyes narrowed with intrigue from behind her mask.

Tobias thanked her for the drinks and lifted them off the tray. He handed one to me. I resisted gulping it down and turned to face him.

"Ms. Ruby Ryan?" The butler looked up from the invite he'd peeled open and held my gaze.

Tobias gave a nod. "Which way?"

"Welcome." The butler nodded left.

Tobias's grip tightened on my arm and he led us off in that direction.

"Black tie, sir," shouted the butler after us.

Tobias threw me a look of apology and removed his jacket from my shoulders. He shrugged back into it, rounding out his dashing, moneyed appearance.

My thoughts raced with confusion for what Tobias was getting us into, and I almost tripped when we hurried by Pierre-Auguste Renoir's painting of *Les Grandes Baigneuses*, depicting nude women bathing. The impressionist painter had a gift for capturing the dreaminess of his subjects.

His work stirring controversy even today for his promiscuity with color—oh the scandal—or the way he ignored lines and composition.

This was a taste of what Renoir must have felt with his decadent, impetuous behavior in Paris.

No, I reasoned, I've stepped inside a Picasso.

This was more like Pablo Picasso's 1903 *La Douceur*, the erotic oil on canvas with its delicate watercolors of a woman going down on a man as he leisurely lay back and enjoyed the moment, watching himself in the mirror.

And I was smack-dab in the middle of this explicit fantasy.

My heels clipped on stone, the cold a welcome relief to reduce the burn of embarrassment that scorched my face.

When we reached a door, he knocked once.

With no answer, Tobias headed on in and pulled me with him.

A quick glance around at the wood-paneled room made me realize what this was. Not a coatroom, no, but a room for the dresses that the female guests had worn to this event and then removed and safely placed on chrome free-standing racks.

From the number of dresses, hundreds of women had already arrived and stripped down to their underwear.

My Coco de Mer lingerie now made sense. Evidently, Marks and Spencer's panties didn't make the grade. Addled, I silently thanked Tobias for his forethought.

Careful not to spill my drink on my dress or the plush burgundy carpet, I set it down on a coaster on a corner table.

Tobias took a sip from his glass. And then another. "This is a Krug Clos d'Ambonnay. Very nice." He placed his glass next to mine.

What the fuck.

I went for the door.

Tobias wrapped his hands around my waist and spun me around and nudged me gently until my back pressed against the wall.

His mask made him look edgier and sexy as hell. I went to take mine off—

He stopped me. "Before you say anything." He gestured for me to be quiet. "I need you to listen."

"What is this place?"

"We have a mission. To view a painting. Authenticate it. And get out. Whatever else you see has nothing to do with us."

"Is this a secret society?"

He pressed his body against mine. "Keep your voice down. Let's not stand out any more than we did when we arrived."

"Who is Ruby Ryan? And why did he think that's me?"

"She's a friend who pulled some serious strings to get us in here." He turned his head toward the door as though listening. "Think of the invite as the equivalent of a golden ticket."

It was hard to suppress my sarcasm. "Like *Charlie and the Chocolate Factory*? Only instead of chocolate…"

He looked amused. "Yes, if you like."

"So you're not a member?" I studied his face for the truth.

"No, otherwise it'd be my name on the invite."

I tried to think straight but it was difficult being this close to him. "The painting still belongs to the owners?" I grabbed his biceps, and his firm muscles flexed beneath my touch, rousing a sense of safety.

"It's due to go up for auction in a few weeks," he said. "Sotheby's doesn't allow for anyone else to authenticate a piece other than their own staff. I don't want to outbid the room only to end up with a forgery."

"You should trust them, they're the best—"

"I've been burned once before. Never again."

"Isn't what we're doing illegal?"

"We're merely guests at a party. We just happen to come across a painting and admire it. No one needs to know. Trust me, everyone, including the hosts, will be otherwise distracted."

"Is this an orgy?"

"No, Zara, it's a tea party." He looked amused.

"I hope you don't think—"

"Please." He rolled his eyes. "I need you focused. You nearly gave us away back there."

"How?"

"Your response to the waitress."

"She's buck naked."

"I noticed a thong."

I glared at him. "A warning would have been nice."

"This opportunity can't be lost."

And right now I was hard pushed to recommend any staff at Huntly Pierre who'd raise their hand when invited to an orgy. I hadn't worked there long enough to know who'd be up for a mass banging.

"Do I have your commitment to complete our objective?"

He didn't budge, merely leaned his weight, further pinning me to the wall.

"Yes." My lips trembled with a thrill of excitement when his erection dug into my stomach. This searing heat of arousal between my thighs.

A wave of exhilaration.

His lips brushed close to mine. "It's just in and out, Zara."

The pressure of his cock now placed perfectly at my groin sent sparks of pleasure between my thighs.

We both froze as though equally stunned by the intensity of this position. Swirls of pleasure. A yearning for him to be inside me.

A soft sigh escaped my lips.

I shoved at his firm chest, trying to push him off before I weakened any further and begged for it. This man was pure muscle, pure alpha, and he'd captured me with the intensity of his stare.

My nipples nudged through my dress and there was no doubt he'd feel them through his shirt.

"Zara, I need you focused. Professional. I need you at your best." He stepped back. The loss of his body left me bereft and I tried not to show it.

"I don't have to do anything rude?" The question was my way of denying he'd affected me.

"No."

"I need my X-ray machine."

"It'll stand out." He waved his hand. "Just do what you did with the Pollock."

"What do you mean?"

"I'll get you in the room. Just tell me if it's an original."

"It doesn't work like that."

"I saw you do it."

"No, I know the Pollock intimately. I sat at the National

and stared at it for hours." I broke his gaze. "I was trying to understand what Pollock was telling us."

"What about your reputation? Your knack for fakes?"

"Art intuition? I suppose it runs in my family."

Tobias blinked at me. "Do your best. That's all I'm asking."

I gave a reluctant nod. "Can I keep my dress on?"

"You'll stand out."

"You're sure about that?"

"Yes."

"I just have to look at the painting and then we can leave?"

"I promise."

"You'll be with me the entire time?"

His eyes crinkled with kindness. "Won't let you out of my sight."

My breath stilted when I realized he was waiting for me to take off my dress.

He turned around.

How far was I willing to go for a painting? The question was glaring.

It's like being at the beach, my nervous thoughts reassured me. *This is no different to wearing your bikini.*

I shimmied out of the gown and found a hanger to place it on. I left it at the end of the rung so it'd be easy to grab later.

Dressed merely in my underwear, or rather strips of silk barely covering me, my palms cupping my cheeks, I waited for him.

"Zara? Can I turn around?"

"Yes." I assumed a confident pose, even though I didn't feel it, and straightened my back and raised my chin.

Tobias blinked as he took me in. A flexing of his jaw muscles.

"Do I look okay?" I wanted to hear him say I looked beautiful to him.

The way his taut posture betrayed his secret desire for me spiked this dizzying rush of exhilaration.

My delight rose that he found this moment just as thrilling, never had I felt so desirable, so capable of this stark sensuality that had a man like Tobias Wilder looking so confounded.

"Don't cover yourself." He snapped back to unreadable and swept his hand through the air. "The women here are comfortable with their bodies." His gaze swept over me and he gave a nod of approval. "Own your sexuality and you'll do fine."

Which I assumed was "Tobias" for act confident.

My left hand twitched to reach out and grab his hand to soothe this vulnerability.

This grand house kept too many secrets. I didn't want to be in and out, I wanted to stroll along the hallways and drink in the art, saturate my soul with the work of the Old Masters.

This was not how I'd seen the evening going. Not even close.

"If anyone asks you a question, defer to me."

"Did we just go back a hundred years?"

"We're trying to maintain a low profile."

I wanted to be ready for him, for them, but fear threatened to incapacitate me.

He took my hands. "You look beautiful. Do this and I'll reward you well."

"Like, with a bonus?"

He smirked. "Don't push it. I'm already getting you a new phone, remember?"

I frowned, wondering how else he'd reward me, then.

He neared me and tipped my chin up. "I'll make it up to you in more ways than you can ever imagine."

My body trembled with this growing need of arousal and

I bit my lip hoping I didn't dampen my panties, my breaths short and sharp.

The pad of his thumb rested on my lower lip and he freed it from my bite. "Just do as I say."

"I'll try."

As though lost in thought, his eyelids closed for a beat. "Mr. Wilder?"

He stepped away and walked over to his glass, and took a sip. "Let's get this over with so we can get you home."

His hand rested at the arch of my back as he led me out. Swooning at his touch and trying not to show it, I reminded myself I could leave at any time.

And, after all, I was wearing a mask.

Back within the vast foyer, the chill hit me again. Whoever had decided that women shouldn't wear clothes needed a punch. It was bloody cold, and with a quick glance down I was horrified to see my areolae were not quite covered. Instinctively, I reached up to hide my breasts.

"Zara," Tobias warned.

My arms flew to my sides as though I'd already stepped into the role of lover. "Next time I'm picking my own bra and panties."

His lips quirked in a smile. "I've had the unusual pleasure of glimpsing a sample of your personal knicker collection back at The Otillie. Quite the experience. My new favorite color just so happens to be eggshell blue."

I gave him a "you're a cheeky bastard" glare. "Not that there'll be a next time," I clarified.

"Okay, then."

We strolled down the dimly lit hallway.

Music carried along with laughter, clinking glasses, the revelry of a party.

Tobias spoke with two intimidating-looking bouncers

guarding a large double door. He sounded fluent in the Italian words he shared with them, and I sensed it was a password.

They both reached for their respective doorknobs.

So many questions. How did he know about this place? Who was Ruby Ryan and what was his relationship with her?

A woman who was obviously into this—

Inside a fluorescent red room, topless burlesque dancers were performing, with one twirling on a pole, another blowing fire out toward the awestruck crowd, the others swirling sensually on chairs. Garish theatrical music flooded the room.

A few hundred tuxedo-wearing men watched the performance, all of them with skimpily clad women by their sides, who mirrored what I was wearing. Their luxury lingerie hid nothing. A few dared to go topless. This could have been a Victoria's Secret photo shoot. The variety of stunning lingerie was breathtaking.

A rich man's playpen.

Booze flowed from silver trays carried by thong-wearing waitresses, who offered fresh flutes of champagne or golden spirits that were no doubt the very expensive kind.

The music changed to sultry French lyrics, setting the scene for arousal. The atmosphere crackled. I'd lost track of time and wondered how close to midnight we were.

Tobias led me to the far corner of the room, right up to the large mantel where a hearth burned brightly, orange logs sparking and exuding the kind of heat these old houses desperately needed. Rising out of those flames burst the scent of pinecones and rosemary.

I turned to face the marble mantel and warmed my hands against the dancing flames.

Glancing left and then right, this was also a perfect vantage point to view the other guests, and despite their masks it was obvious the men came from wealth and the women with their tall, slender figures were merely trophies, perhaps some of them coming from money themselves.

"Turn around," Tobias whispered.

I did so with a huff of rebellion and nudged up against him. His palm rested against the arch of my lower spine, sending shivers up it.

"I'd love to visit your gallery," I said. "The one in LA."

He dipped his head to my ear. "We're wearing masks for a reason. Let's not give any clues to who we really are."

"Sorry."

"You're forgiven."

I raised my chin. "You're not. Forgiven, that is."

His hand slid lower and he gripped the back of my thong— and tugged.

I gasped when my thong rubbed my clit and it ignited in a shock of bliss. My sex thrummed with pleasure.

He smirked. "Something wrong?"

"You're not allowed to do that," I said in a rush.

"Clearly I am."

"No, we're merely pretending to be lovers."

"Lovers?"

"Well, whatever the kind of relationship these people have—" I swept my hand into the crowd.

"They seem happy to me."

"I'll take a rain check."

He grabbed my arm. "Not without me."

"Why?"

He gave a polite smile to a couple standing close. "They'll stop you. And then give you back to me."

"Lucky me." I waggled my eyebrows playfully.

He looked amused. "So, how does it feel to step outside your comfort zone?"

"You like living dangerously?"

"There's no danger here. Just decadence, power and privilege. Nothing we can't handle."

Despite standing beside her tux-wearing partner, the pretty masked blonde nearby was clearly flirting with Tobias. Her boyfriend, with his striking red hair and cold gray eyes, caught her leering our way and instead of there being any kind of fallout to Blondie's teasing, he merely nodded respectfully toward us.

Tobias gave a subtle shake of his head.

That closed that offer down, then, and my mind ran off with the kind of scenario Blondie might have suggested. An unfamiliar wave of jealousy jolted me into realizing I was falling for him.

Tobias was staring right at me and was annoyingly giving me the kindest, most reassuring smile.

"I'm not your girlfriend," I muttered defensively.

"We've managed by some miracle to make it to the level of friends. I've felt comfortable enough to show you one of my inventions and you've dared to show me your assets." He arched a brow.

"Are you like this with your girlfriend?" I looked up at him.

"Are you fishing for clues on me, Zara?"

"Merely making polite conversation."

His eyes glittered in the firelight. "I fuck, yes."

I pretended not to be thrown and fluffed a strand of hair to distract him from my shock.

"How about you?" he said.

"God, no, won't be trying that again. Dating, I mean."

No matter how amazing one night of wildness with Wilder sounded.

"Someone broke your heart?" he asked softly.

"Doesn't that come as standard?"

He turned and stared at me for the longest time.

I forced a smile. "Art's my only love. And it always will be."

His intense green eyes seared into me as though trying to scorch my soul, causing a thrill to surge up my spine. My flesh thrummed with aliveness from being this close to him as though unwittingly craving even more...heartache.

I stepped toward the blonde. "Which way is the loo, please?"

She leaned toward me. "Shall I show you?"

"No, thank you, though." Now that we had a reason to wander off, I smiled back at Tobias.

Her boyfriend's lust-fueled glare ate me up and sent an uneasy shiver down my spine.

Tobias narrowed his gaze at the man, proving his disapproval, and the redheaded stud turned away, his smirk looking like a permanent fixture.

The blonde pointed left of the stage.

"Come on," said Tobias, and we headed in that direction.

"That was easy," I muttered.

Tobias's grip tightened. "Not now."

We weaved our way through the crowd, who were totally absorbed by the dancers. Two of the showgirls on stage were getting it on and taking this lusty extravaganza to the next level.

My jaw gaped when one of them kneeled before her lover and buried her face between the other girl's legs, the woman responded eagerly thrusting her sex forward, her eyelids flicking and her moans rising.

"Oh my God," I whispered.

"Then don't look," snapped Tobias.

He navigated us around a couple who were stripping. We were closing in on midnight apparently.

We slipped out a side door.

Music and cheers lessening behind us as we sped down the

hallway, me in four-inch heels and trying to keep up with Tobias.

We paused at the fork in the corridor. Three choices lay ahead of us. "You Americans are a bunch of perverts," I bit out.

He snapped his glare my way. "Excuse me?"

"That's a den of iniquity."

He pointed at my shoes. "What's that beneath your feet?"

I leaned forward to better look down.

"That's England, Zara. These are your people."

I fisted my hands and rested them on my hips. "Where is it, then? I want to see it."

"I hope you're referring to the painting?" He grinned. "Sure you don't want to go back and take another peek? Dabble a bit?"

"Quite sure."

He stepped closer. "I'm leading this mission. Just so we're clear."

"I thought it was a brilliant ruse."

"Except the restrooms for the guests are in the opposite direction of where we need to be." He shrugged out of his jacket.

"Have you been here before?"

"No." He rested his jacket around my shoulders.

I breathed in his soft cologne and soaked up the warmth, grateful to cover myself as I tugged it around me.

Tobias pulled out his phone and slid his fingertip along the screen and then stared down, engrossed.

I frowned his way.

"I'm checking the score. Dolphins are winning." He looked up at me.

"American football? Seriously?"

He looked incredulous. "No, Zara, I'm looking at a map." He pointed west. "This way."

"Have you ever taken part in one of those?" My breath stilted as I waited for his answer.

Tobias wrapped his arm around my waist. "I don't share. Ever."

"Even your toys?"

"You were referring to my women. So was I," he said as he started running.

"Are you going to give me a clue?" I asked as I followed him down a series of endless corridors.

"No," he said brightly. "I want to see your reaction." The intrigue spurred me to run faster.

We rounded another corridor and right past a masked couple who'd also strayed from the party. When they faded from sight we paused at the door at the end.

Tobias opened it.

He stepped in partially and then quickly backed out, closing it again.

"Wrong room?" I said.

"No, there's a couple. Well, a ménage. To be accurate."

"In there?"

He looked thoughtful. "Full-on."

"Oh, well that's inconvenient."

"Certainly is."

"We'll wait here, then?"

"They're almost done. From the sounds of…"

A woman's wails of pleasure flooded out into the hallway.

"We can wait," I agreed.

"Sure."

"We have the time, right?"

"Are you warm enough?"

"Yes, thank you. I can't wait to see the painting."

He glanced upward at the ceiling, hinting we were probably being watched.

"Isn't this place incredible?" I whispered.

Tobias forced a smile and gave a nod, proving he was in no mood for small talk.

It made my heart sink a little as I realized we had nothing to talk about, proving we had nothing in common. Standing here now with him staring at the ground and me leaning against the wall, I imagined what kind of woman Tobias usually went for.

Hearing those rising moans wasn't helping.

I avoided his gaze and admired the arching stained glass windows, and beyond them sprawled a large courtyard and in the center sat a fountain and around it elegantly arranged benches positioned just so to catch the morning sun. The old me would have loved to have visited during the day and brought a picnic and a good book and sat on one of those benches and savored being there.

I'd stepped behind the veil of the elite, beyond the safety of my world, having never explored this sensual side of me before, never allowed myself to imagine ever taking part in such a daring escapade, like searching out masterpieces in ancient castles, with an orgy as a backdrop.

And with a man like Tobias as my guide, who made me feel as though wildfire was burning me from the inside out.

Falling for his enigmatic charm would be so, so easy.

"What was his name?" Tobias looked at me.

"Who?"

"The man who broke your heart?"

"Zach."

"Zach's an idiot. Don't take him back."

The door flew open and a scantily dressed masked woman burst out, her cheeks flushed, her laughter loud, her hair a mass of post-fucked curls, and following behind hurried two men, their clothes as disheveled as their hair.

Tobias gave them a respectful wave as he watched them head off down the hallway. He reached for my hand and pulled me in—

A state room, perhaps where visiting dignitaries would be welcomed and no doubt impressed with the finery. Plush red carpet, white-and-gold wallpaper, candelabras, a few statues here and there on podiums, and the most striking collection of wall-to-wall paintings by Francisco Goya.

"The last of the great masters." My breath caught as the words fell away.

Turning around and around to look at the others, I smiled brightly, exhilarated to be given the chance to experience these rare wonders, a private collection that rivaled those shown in the finest galleries.

I wanted to leap onto Tobias and wrap myself around him in a hug to thank him for bringing me.

He moved fast and gestured me to follow quickly.

Above the large unlit fireplace hung *La Maja Vestida*, an exquisite oil painting by Goya, finished somewhere around 1805.

The beautiful subject held a timeless smile, her long chaste white dress showing off her curves, over which she wore a short yellow jacket. A pink sash snug around her waist. Her hands were held above her head as she reclined in a sensual pose on a couch.

"This is her?"

Tobias's gaze held the painting.

I admired her natural beauty, flushed cheeks from wine or making love, her eyes twinkling as though humoring Goya with her patience to sit still as he painted.

Tobias neared me and reached inside his jacket pocket, his strong hand brushing my thigh as he searched for it. "One second."

He removed my small magnifier and handed it to me.

Easing off my mask, I let it hang from my neck by the ribbon.

He walked across the room and pulled a chair over to the fireplace and gestured for me to climb up. I kicked off my heels and used his hand to support my balance as I stood on the chair. I sprang into action, peering through my magnifier and studying the elegant strokes of Goya's signature.

I lowered the magnifier and handed it back to him. "We have a problem."

He tucked my magnifier away. "Metric frame?"

"Yes."

"Two hundred years ago they hadn't gone metric."

"Exactly."

"Keep going."

"Do you think they've started?" I asked.

"What?"

"The orgy?"

"Zara, the painting, please." He suppressed a smile.

"I need to see the back." I glanced at the door. "Can we take it down?"

"Sure."

Together we lifted the portrait off its hanger and carried it over to an antique table, laying it down with the reverence both deserved.

"The framing's modern." Ruefully, I shook my head. "There's our first clue. Though it could have been reframed. There's no hint of exposure to open fires or pipe smoke, or any other signs of aging to the canvas. Unless this was stored in an oxygen deprived facility...which..."

"They didn't have back then."

"Sorry, Tobias."

He reached for the back of the frame and inserted his fingers between the canvas and ripped hard, separating it from the other. "How about this one?"

My palm slammed to my mouth.

"Focus," he said, amused.

"What did you do?"

"Look."

"Behind it?"

"Yes." He gestured for me to come closer.

Stepping forward, I peered over the top of the frame and there she lay, *La Maja Desnuda*, the exact same painting we were just looking at but the subject now completely nude, her pose mirroring the first.

"Oh my God," I said in a rush. "She's gorgeous."

"Whenever you're ready." He handed me back my magnifier.

I peered through it with one eye. "She's painted in oil, so easy to replicate."

"Tell me something I don't know."

I threw him a glare and he threw one back, and then he grinned and it was one of those cute, heart melting smiles, reminding me this was an adventure like no other.

He came round to stand beside me and his expression turned to awe. "Look at the detail. The colors are exquisite."

"She really is beautiful."

"Zara, do you feel her presence? She stirs a visceral response."

"Yes."

"So much secrecy around her."

I gave a nod, mesmerized by the way the artist painted the light around her. "*La Maja* was never exhibited during Goya's lifetime."

Peering through my magnifier again, I leaned closer. "Colors are pure. No modern palettes. All the touches of Goya, his diagonal signature is the same sweep of an *a*." I raised my line of sight to look at Tobias. "Perhaps you can ask to see the paperwork? Track its provenance?"

He waved that off. "Later."

Admiring the colors, I went to run my fingertip along the lower corner. Tobias grabbed my hand.

"Of course," I said. "It's instinctive."

"No fingerprints."

A door slammed from somewhere out there and made me jump.

"Seen enough?" he said.

"I need more time."

His jaw clenched with tension and he gave a sharp nod.

Goya's bold technique, a dash of daring freestyle, his ability to read the truth in the eyes of his subject, reveal their very soul, proved his profound understanding of the human condition. Had Goya's illness, which had left him permanently deaf, been the catalyst for such unearthly insight?

This painting had gotten him into a lot of trouble. He'd been summoned before the Spanish Inquisition to explain *La Maja Desnuda*, a rare nude in a sea of religious paintings that had been commissioned that year. He'd lived out his days in exile in France after the political upheaval of 1824. He'd died in Madrid, which was where this painting should have been hanging. The fact it was hidden behind another was heartbreaking and raised so many questions.

"How did you know?" I said.

He looked at the door.

Footsteps…

Laughter…the sound fading.

I breathed a sigh of relief as I watched him tuck my magnifier into the pocket of his jacket that still hung from my shoulders.

With a white handkerchief, Tobias dusted off his finger-prints and then secured the back of the frame to hide the painting, reusing the tape and smoothing it over. Together we carried the painting back over to the mantel and with a hefty tug we managed to get it resecured on the wire hanger.

Taking a step back I let him straighten the frame and con-tinue dusting our prints off, which he did with ease.

I slipped back into my heels and kneeled to work on the straps around my ankles.

"Zara, put your mask back on, please."

I used the antique mirror to straighten it and stared at my dazed eyes.

"You okay?"

He broke me from my trance and I gave a nod. "I'm fine."

I was better than fine, I was in my element and wanted to spend the night here and move from painting to painting until each brushstroke of the subjects' faces became branded into memory.

Strolling over to take a better look at the other paintings, my gaze drank in the miniature of Alberto Giacometti, an oil on cardboard capturing red roses. "This is pretty."

Tobias's firm hands wrapped around my waist and he spun me to face him, and with an ironclad grip he cupped my face. His lips crushed mine, forcing my mouth wider as his tongue possessed it, circling, setting every nerve alight with his in-tensity, owning me with his passion.

Weakening in his arms, surrendering, I let go and let him in, gripping his strong forearms and digging my fingernails into taut muscle. His hands left my face and moved to grab my wrists, and he yanked them behind my back and held them together, tight, forceful, dominating me with an un-matched strength.

Pleasure swelled low in my belly.

He'd chosen the perfect setting for our first kiss and my joy from being here fused with this electric current surging through me, flaring from his intensity and, despite our daring, never had I felt safer.

"Oh yes." I moaned into his mouth, shocked at his stunning show of power, my core alight, my body trembling with his unbidden heat, nipples erect against his chest. This was how I'd always yearned to be kissed, as though loved, this initial burst of control easing into a leisurely snog.

Tobias pulled away and his fierce glare held mine, his mask making him look so damn sexy. My lips reached for his again, unable to resist his fiery eyes that stared into mine, that green ablaze with desire.

This lure of need rising below—

He turned his head slightly and smiled toward the doorway, his grip still firm, my body still crushed against his.

"Warming her up," he said darkly.

My gaze snapped to the door.

Two tall men wearing masks and tuxedos stood just inside.

One of the men raised his hand. "Sir, the party's this way."

"One second." He waved them out. "It's her first time."

With a nod of permission the men turned on their heels and left. Tobias beamed my way. "I think we fooled them, don't you?"

My jaw was gaping.

"Zara?"

"Yes, absolutely." I righted my footing as he pulled away, my scorching cheeks and racing heart needing more time to recover. "Totally convinced." Trying to swallow this lump of embarrassment in my throat.

I tugged his jacket around me.

"I need it back," he said kindly.

Reluctantly, I eased it off my shoulders and held his jacket out to him, watching Tobias nonchalantly pull his arms through as though we'd not just shared an incredible kiss.

He used the same mirror to straighten his shirt and tie and fix his mask.

In a blur I followed him, glancing back at *La Maja Desnuda* as though I'd been the one naked and exposed.

7

We headed down the hallway following the men back toward the foyer. The door to the party was up ahead.

Music carried from within the vast room. Some rhythmic rave number, an erotic backdrop to spur those within on and tease them into an unending wave of lovemaking.

If I saw inside that room, my life would never be the same.

The taller of the two bouncers rested his hand on the door handle.

I reached out and grabbed Tobias's arm, wanting to say his name and knowing that was forbidden.

From beneath those double doors the thump of a bass bled out and seeped all the way inside me, surging through my veins. A rush of jumbled thoughts as I judged which way to run.

They'll stop you. And then give you back to me, Tobias had threatened before. "Turn around," he said firmly.

My feet stuck to the ground.

Following Tobias's lead, I feigned we were here for the party, hoping not to alert them to the real reason we'd snuck into their state room.

That chill found me and soaked into the depths of my limbs, my body trembling.

"I need you to trust me," he whispered, pulling his necktie from around his collar.

I turned and waited, my breathing stilted, the ringing in my ears disorientating.

We'd gone too far with our ruse.

Fragile, more unsure than I'd ever felt, I was going to break apart if I didn't relinquish to Tobias these remnants of faith I'd once guarded so fiercely, having doubted I'd ever let anyone this close. And this was more of a risk than I'd ever known, the equivalent of walking on hot coals, or skiing down a sheer ice face, or exposing the most vulnerable part of myself, the most sacred facet of my sexuality.

My breathing stilted as I reached back for him.

His warm hand rested on my nape and my skin tingled beneath his touch; with a gentle caress he reassured me.

Holding my mask in place I felt the material of his necktie wrapping over it to cover my eyes. A tug as he tied it behind my head.

The hard lines of Tobias's body nudged up against me. "Do exactly as I say."

I gave a nod.

"Don't let go." His palm slipped against mine and our fingers interlocked. "I've got you."

The relentless thumping of the rave grew louder.

In a haze of dizziness, I gripped Tobias's hand as though my life depended on it. And in a way it did.

This visceral revelation felt like an awakening and tonight without question, there was proof *this* really existed. My innocence, though not essentially pure, was under threat from what we were about to experience—

Had that brief time in Tobias's home been when he'd studied me? Assessing if I would mold to his will and endure a night of debauchery at one of England's most exclusive palaces?

My hand was squeezed tight by his, his thumb caressing my wrist as we walked through. The room felt warmer. Scented with expensive perfumes merging with richly textured colognes. Vibrations beneath my stilettos, crackling electricity surrounding us as though the air itself was magnetized, moans rising and falling—

I could hear the sounds of men and woman fucking all around us.

Tobias guided me onward, gently coaxing our way around tables, or perhaps lovers in the throes of passion, or goodness knows what, my imagination swirling with what I sensed unfolded from behind this makeshift blindfold.

And if removed…

A sea of bodies interlocked.

Low voices and moans carried around us, offering their demands of need, their squeals of laughter, proving that whatever they were doing was consensual, these men and women wanting to be here and from the sounds of pleasure that echoed their gratification was real and for some blindingly brilliant.

The sound of spanking. Erotic wails resonated.

My own arousal betrayed me and dampened my panties as if a Romanesque orgy was socially acceptable and their reckless lovemaking was normal for a weeknight.

To our left a scream of an orgasm tore out. The dreaminess of not knowing, never seeing. We paused for a beat and I froze.

"Almost there," came Tobias's low voice.

Coldness enveloped me and I sensed we were out as fading groans trailed behind until the doors closed and muffled the music and everything else, those rolling waves of lust now silent.

My heels clicked on stone.

Another door, another room and, warm again, I sensed we'd made it. My suspicions were confirmed as Tobias guided me to raise my arms into the air, the soft material of the beautiful Alexander McQueen gown being tugged over my body as he redressed me.

The blindfold lifted from my eyes. "Are you okay?" He studied my face.

I managed a nod and turned to the mirror to fluff my hair.

"That wasn't part of the plan," he said. "Obviously."

Blinking, I watched him place his tie back around his collar. He wrapped it into a neat bow. "I screwed up."

It was impossible to show I wasn't affected, my breathing ragged from walking through that lust-filled ballroom.

He threw me a look of apology, and I turned away and fiddled with my shoulder strap as though it needed it.

My shoulders relaxed and I exhaled a deep breath as though I'd been holding it the entire time.

"Let's get outta here." He took my hand.

Through the foyer we walked out into the night, the crispness welcoming our freedom and highlighting what we'd left behind.

To our left rolled a silver Bentley pulling out of its parking space. It drove our way.

Nervously, I stared at Tobias to see if he'd caught it.

The car idled in front of us and the side door flew open, and a young man with spiked short ashen hair climbed out. His face was friendly, his demeanor respectful toward Tobias, and I caught sight of his worn jeans and smart black blazer as he rounded the car and opened the rear door for us.

He handed Tobias a thick woolen scarf and Tobias wrapped it around his neck.

"Can I take my mask off?" I said.

"In the car."

I hugged myself and sucked up the cold, secretly coveting his scarf.

Tobias's eyes reflected intrigue. "Sure you're okay?"

"Oh yes, used to belong to a book club. Every Friday night we'd end the evening in a full-on orgy. Books everywhere. You can't imagine the horror of a damp paperback."

He laughed and his eyes lit up with joy.

I let out a wistful sigh. "Just wished we'd had more time to enjoy the art."

"I know." Tobias gestured for me to get in. "Cooper will take you home."

"Where are you going?"

"Another appointment."

"We're not riding together?" I cringed at my awkwardness.

"No." He gave a nod to the driver.

Cooper ran around the front of the Bentley and got back behind the wheel.

"Did I do okay?" I whispered.

Tobias snapped his attention back to me. "You were great."

Peering over his shoulder, I yearned to return on a day when the activities were more conducive to enjoying its vast collection of art. "We did it."

"We did." He peeled out of his jacket and wrapped it around my shoulders. *Again.*

And I couldn't help but feel enraptured each time he did that, every show of kindness endeared him to me more, despite what he'd put me through.

I beamed, secretly knowing I'd have an excuse to get his jacket back to him.

"I'll have it collected," he said. "Cooper will come get it."

Disheartened, I broke his stare and peered at the ground. "Thank you for watching over me."

"Thank you for trusting me." He gave an assured nod.

"I'll pass on my thanks to Adley, and request an invoice first thing tomorrow." He glanced at his watch. "This morning, I should say."

"Sounds great." Though now I only had a few hours of sleep ahead of me before I'd have to get up for work. "I'll send Adley your regards."

"I appreciate that."

"What about my car?"

"I have the keys," he said. "We'll get it back to you tomorrow. You usually take the tube into work, right?"

I gave a nod, wondering how he knew that, and ducked my head low to get in—then thought better of it.

I eased out and stood facing Tobias again and stared directly into his eyes. "For the record, Mr. Wilder."

"Yes?"

"It's never *just* a painting."

He pulled off his scarf and placed it around my neck, and then used it to pull me closer to him. Tobias leaned in and kissed my forehead.

This man's allure was unending, and as I closed my eyes I allowed myself this one last moment of his affection, a ripple of excitement.

He broke away.

Trying not to swoon, I remained still as he wrapped that soft scarf snuggly around my neck, weaving it neatly around my throat.

"That was quite the adventure," I said.

"Yes, it was."

I climbed in, dragging my gaze from his, and settled in the backseat, the scent of leather filled the car, the welcome warmth of the heating having been on for a while. Relief washed over me when I saw my handbag on the backseat. My house keys were in there. Cooper had obviously stopped by

Tobias's house to grab it for me. Though my car keys were still back at his place.

I peeled off my mask and rested it near my bag.

Tobias shut the car door and headed away with his hands tucked inside his pockets. I watched him stroll over to his Aston Martin. He opened the door and climbed in.

I breathed a sigh of relief he wasn't going back into the palace. Our Bentley pulled away.

Tobias's Aston Martin sped past us and raced on ahead; leaves and debris spun out behind his car. This dreamy sense of having been caught up in his world had left me remarkably untainted.

"Thank you," I said. "I'm afraid I live in Notting Hill. It's a bit of a drive."

"I have your address, ma'am," soothed Cooper in his American accent and he smiled at me in the rearview. "Got you up on the GPS."

"You know my address?"

"Of course."

"How?"

"My boss, ma'am."

"Call me Zara."

"Thank you, ma'am."

I was too exhausted to correct him. "How does Mr. Wilder know where I live?"

"I believe he obtained it from your company." Cooper must have read my dazed expression because he added, "Mr. Wilder wanted to make sure you got home okay."

Peering into the night, I took in the rolling fields now covered in a blanket of sprawling mist, obscuring those large lakes from view.

I'd probably never see Tobias again. The mission accomplished.

The client seemingly happy.

And then I realized as I spun round in my seat to look back at that striking palace fast fading on the horizon—

Tobias had forgotten to ask me if the painting was real.

8

Sleepy eyed after dozing off in the Bentley, I slipped into my babydoll nightdress. I eyed that Coco de Mer lingerie that I'd stripped off and thrown onto the bed, hoping that wasn't going to have to go back when I returned Tobias's jacket and scarf.

The Alexander McQueen hung elegantly from a hanger on my bedroom door, and it was hard to pull my gaze away from the satin gown adorned with intricate crystals. That would have to go back, as well.

I picked up his black jacket and buried my face into the lining, sniffing Tobias's cologne, and imagined him looking at me the same way he'd adored *La Maja Desnuda*.

This infatuation was going to be short-lived.

I tried to tame my excitement from such a whirlwind evening, a decadent adventure I couldn't wait to tell Clara about.

It felt good to be home.

This southeast flat had once been owned by my mother before she'd married my dad. After her death, Dad had rented it out and then rarely visited it. There was comfort drawn from knowing Mom spent time here. I walked the same pathway she'd taken from the small kitchen to the bedroom or the living room to the bathroom. I wondered if she, like me, ever read in the tub or sipped her morning tea while watching the world awaken.

So many memories had been lost to time.

There were boxes upon boxes back in Dad's old place that I still had to go through, all of them secured in the basement, and I had the only key. A task I'd put off over countless weekends.

I'd renovated this place back to its original glory of Victorian splendor, with its whitewashed walls reaching high to meet the elaborate crown molding. I'd gone for a fresh vintage decor, with crisp, clean pastels that were charmingly cozy and merged exquisitely with the more modern pieces.

I loved padding around barefoot on the hardwood floors or burying my toes in the faux fur rugs. I'd bought that large blue sofa from another favorite store lost to the spiraling costs of living in this city. The large mahogany bookshelves I'd retrieved from home. The place now poised to go on the market as soon as I was ready to let it go. Though the house was restored, the worth of the land it stood on was remarkable.

My thoughts carried me back to Blandford Palace and a sinking feeling washed over me at my naivety. Still, I'd felt safe beside Wilder and had drawn strength from his tenacity and even now I felt the wake of his charisma.

Tobias no doubt sparked chemistry in every woman who met him. It was his assuredness, his confident swagger, his ability to command without question. That Ivy League education had forged an already brilliant mind and gave him an unfair edge. Money and brains was a heady combination and Tobias wore it well. That arrogant curve of his lips, his bossy bastard demeanor, the way he crushed his body next to mine...

Tobias Wilder was the perfect storm.

And I was glad my feet were back on dry land, home safe, where I belonged.

After folding his scarf into a neat square, I placed it next to his jacket on the back of the chair, near the door. I'd take it into work tomorrow. I should have just handed it over to Cooper tonight and braved the cold from the Bentley to my flat, but I'd been too sleepy to think straight.

Writing my report for Adley was going to take some finagling. The big reveal of Goya's painting turning up out of the blue was going to set the entire office alight with excitement. Tobias could now bid away with confidence when that portrait went on sale.

I wondered which house he favored more: Sotheby's or Christie's.

I'd peeked behind the curtain of aristocracy and still couldn't believe people dared to get naked in front of each other. Tobias hadn't blinked an eye at all at that debauchery, though it seemed nothing much fazed him.

Only in the art world could the most decadent of parties be topped by the revelation of a Goya concealed behind another painting.

First thing tomorrow, I was going to make some discreet inquiries into that Goya's paper trail. It might also explain why a multimillion-dollar piece was hidden away.

A knock at my front door startled me.

At 2:00 a.m. it could only be Cooper. He'd probably realized I'd strolled off with his boss's jacket and scarf and had come to collect it.

I made my way to the front door and decided with each step there was no way I was mentioning the underwear. The Coco de Mer would serve as my consolation prize.

That thought made me smile.

Peeking through the eyehole I almost bit through my lip. After sliding off the catch I opened the door ajar.

Tobias's grin widened. "Hope I didn't disturb you?"

"No, it's fine." I'd forgotten how disarming his smile was. "I'll get your jacket." I closed the door and headed back toward the chair and lifted off his coat and scarf.

I yelped—

Tobias stood inside my flat with his back pressed against the closed door. "Bad time?"

"I was going to bed." I blinked at him. "Have to be up early."

Oh dear God, I was wearing my skimpy nightdress and the hem was dangerously short. If I bent over he'd be treated to a peep show.

His gaze swept over me.

"Were you happy with everything?"

"Yes." He stepped forward.

"You left suddenly."

"Sorry I didn't drive you home myself. Coops is very reliable, though."

"Where did you go?"

"Prior engagement. A meeting I couldn't cancel." At my look of doubt, he added, "Canterbury."

Whoever he'd visited sounded important to him.

Tobias seemed to sense what I was thinking. "Sarah's in her seventies." He looked like he wanted to tell me more but shrugged instead.

"You're here for your jacket?"

"No, to see you." His expression softened. "To thank you for lending your expertise."

"Oh right. Of course, it was my pleasure. I was happy to help." I drew in a deep breath and hugged his jacket. "So, your painting has a pure signature, which lends itself to the expected precise downward sweep."

Tobias stepped forward and gave a nod of approval.

I continued confidently as though I wasn't wearing merely a babydoll. "The layers of paint appear consistent. Perhaps we can x-ray at the Courtauld. I studied there."

"I remember."

"We can borrow their equipment."

He leaned in and gently kissed my neck. "Good to know."

Where his lips brushed my skin he ignited heat, my heart thundering, my body trembling, each and every cell sparking from the thrill of being this close to him.

His lips pressed against my naked shoulder. The strap slid down my arm, loosening the cup of my nightdress, revealing a hint of nipple.

"There were no stray paint hairs," I added softly.

"Well, that's good." He nipped my earlobe.

My core flinched, my nipples perking with desire and giving away my secret crush. I stuttered through another breath. "The scent is pure antique. The painting, I mean."

He chuckled and reached up to free my lip from where I'd nervously caught it between my teeth. His thumb caressed my lip to ease the sting.

I blinked up at him. "Perhaps you can request its provenance?"

"You can stop talking now, Zara." He gave a heart-stopping smile as he took his jacket from me and threw it on the back of the chair.

He repeated the way he'd kissed me in that state room, cupping my face with his palms, his mouth forcing mine open, his tongue searching, evoking a soft moan of pleasure from me. His hold also mirrored the way he'd kissed me before, back when we were in the palace and faking our affection for those sinister onlookers.

His lips widening mine, drawing my breath out of me, a high voltage of passion as his firm chest pressed against me, shocking me into stillness as I gave myself over.

We weren't faking it now. This was more real than I'd ever known, more passionate than I'd ever experienced, his tongue demanding control over mine, his mouth rough and urgent and needful, his blinding touch so emboldened as if we weren't strangers but lovers who knew each other intimately.

Pressing my eyelids shut, I went with this rush...

His hardness dug into my lower abdomen, the hugeness startling, as he continued to ravage my mouth with his.

I rose onto my toes and my body naturally fit against his, my hips gliding left and right, his erection growing firmer.

He moaned as his mouth left mine, as though he struggled with breaking away. He slipped a finger beneath my shoulder strap and brought it back up. And then pulled me into a hug, my face crushed against his firm chest and his arms wrapped around my back to hold me there. He held me like that for a while and I let him, breathing in his sexy scent, feeling safe, and aroused, and saying damn it to that part of my brain warning me this was too soon.

He peered down at me. "I wanted to check on you."

"Because of the orgy?"

"The Goya."

I nuzzled in and closed my eyelids. "How did you know it was there?"

Tobias let me go. "Zara, that discussion we had before we left my home..."

"Yes."

"Will it be honored when you return to the office?"

"When I write my report?"

"With our previous agreement in mind, yes."

"Can I mention the painting?"

"I'd rather you didn't."

"The location?"

"No."

I stepped back. "That's going to make it difficult—"

"We agreed on your discretion."

"But not from Mr. Huntly?"

"From everyone. Even your closest friends."

I narrowed my gaze, saying with my eyes what I'd dared not speak, *Were you trying to manipulate me?*

A wave of vertigo. "Is this why you're here?"

"I needed to make sure you're okay. We'd already agreed you'd proceed with discretion. This is a moot point, to be honest." He gave a shrug. "I'm sure it was the Goya that really swept you off your feet."

I held his gaze, wondering if I came over that reserved, showing my feelings had become an issue for me, a way to protect myself.

Yet I felt so safe with him.

"Zara?"

"How am I going to explain to my boss—"

"Come here."

I blinked at him, still shaken.

He opened his arms to me. "Zara, come here, please."

I took a careful step toward him and peered up at his beautiful face.

He took my hands in his, and his thumb brushed back and forward over my hands, soothing me.

I glared defiantly and tried to drag my hands from his. "I need to think about it."

"There's nothing to think about." He cupped my face in his hands again. "Thank you for all you did."

That ill-timed rush of arousal flooded through me again, my core tightening with tension, and my face flushed when he brushed his groin against mine. His lips now close to mine again, my wriggling against his body was futile. I yearned for his kiss, yearned for more of him.

"If there's written evidence of what we did it will affect my reputation. You agreed to your discretion. I need you to keep that promise."

"What happens when Adley asks for details?"

"He'll respect my wishes. I just need you to."

My eyelids flickered in response to these rousing feelings.

He leaned closer and trailed kisses along my neck. "I'm glad we're talking about it. So there's no confusion."

I'd been starved for this kind of affection, this pure passion. I'd not allowed myself to get this close to a man after the pain Zach caused me, for fear of getting hurt, couldn't bear to go through that heart-wrenching agony ever again.

All I had to do was learn to trust...

His gentle kisses trailed along my shoulder, sending me hurtling into the center of arousal, my nipples beading, my gaze on his lips as my sigh gave away my weakness. "Tobias," I said the rest with my eyes—*please...take me.*

He stepped back and pivoted gracefully to stare down the hallway. "This is a nice place. Did you decorate it?"

"Yes."

"You have great taste."

"You can come in if you like. I mean in the sitting room."

"Great location."

"Are you going to stay?"

"I'm afraid I can't."

"Would you like some tea before you go?"

"No, thank you."

His irises were speckled with amber. I saw that now because

I was brave enough to hold his gaze for more than a few seconds. That soft white hue of light framed him from behind, providing an almost angelic aura.

"Will I see you again?" I said.

A familiar confusion marred his face.

Trailing my fingertips over my mouth, caressing that tingle from where he'd scorched my lips, the shadow of his kiss lingering.

He hesitated for a second and then said softly, "There's no room in my life for love, Zara. Don't look to me for that."

I swallowed past the dryness in my mouth.

"I'm not the one for you," he said.

Cringing inwardly, I feigned his rejection wasn't triggering my self-doubt, wasn't taking me back to that dreadful time when I'd given everything, every part of me.

That same clawing regret wrenched my stomach. Hadn't I learned my lesson? Seen how these games played out…

He offered a kind smile. "You misunderstand me."

"No, you're quite clear."

"I'm too brutal for someone as gentle as you."

"How do you mean?"

He gave a defiant nod. "You'd never withstand the hard fucking I'd deliver."

Oh God.

I reached out to the wall to steady my feet as that same wave of powerlessness washed over me.

"Get some sleep. Everything will feel different in the morning. Your head will clear and you'll see reason."

He blinked as he stared downward, his teeth clenched with tension. I followed his stare between my thighs. My night-dress had ridden up. His eyelids became heavy as though fighting his will.

Tobias reached low to tug the hem to cover me. "I want

a copy of your report." He retrieved his jacket and scarf and flung it over his forearm. "First thing, please."

I straightened my nightdress, trying to retrieve my dignity. "Of course, Mr. Wilder." I too could turn glacial. "Right away."

"Call me Tobias."

Raising my chin proudly. "I much prefer formality." Even if I was standing here half-naked I could still hold my own. "Keep things professional."

"As you wish." His fingers disappeared inside his jacket pocket and he pulled out my magnifier.

He set it down on the hall table.

"I'll get the dress."

"Please, keep it."

That threw me a little and I went to argue that it was too much but he gestured his insistence.

"Mr. Wilder, you never asked me if the Goya is authentic."

"Didn't need to."

I braved to take a step toward him, feigning he had no effect over me.

He gave a warm smile. "I saw the wonder in your eyes."

"Good night."

He looked hurt. "For the record, I kissed you because I wanted to."

I watched him leave.

When the door shut I ran forward and locked it, my hands trembling as I replayed our passionate kiss, allowing those same sensuous sensations to wash over me, fighting this urge to burst into the hallway and call after him.

Tell Tobias I wanted him to stay.

9

I let out a sigh of appreciation and stepped back.

Liza Blake's painting looked perfect on the front wall of my office. This striking portrait deserved to be the only piece in here. Its bright modern blues and reds, that splash of gold soothing my soul as only contemporary can, with no lines to distract the mind, no images to evoke questions.

I straightened the painting.

My office was starting to look cozy. Stacking the shelves with those few art books I'd brought in and lining up my design journals.

Keeping busy was my way of forgetting last night. Forgetting *him*.

His kiss…

His body crushing mine, his cock promising no end of pleasure, each word he spoke, each look, each touch, sending me reeling.

I spun around and gulped tea from my mug—

My mouth gaping at the burn of heat at drinking it too soon and yet it burned so much less than knowing that brief interlude with Tobias Wilder was over.

It was a challenge to push away the memory of him and those precious few hours spent inside Blandford Palace.

Laughter rose from outside. Staff were trickling in and readying for their day.

There was a delicate bonsai tree resting in a small blue pot on my corner coffee table. The envelope beside it had my name embossed in gold. All that was written inside the card were Japanese symbols. I'd ask Elena who it was from.

That delicate tree with its miniature green leaves was a tranquil promise on how I hoped my day would go.

Elena burst in breathlessly. "How did it go with the hottie?"

Suppressing a fateful smile, I asked her, "Are you okay?"

She sucked in another breath. "Came up the stairs. You inspired me!" She turned to show me her bum. "How does it look?"

"Extra pert."

"That's what I'm going for." She burst out laughing.

I grinned at her enthusiasm.

Her eyes widened when she saw the Blake. "Is that a print?"

"Original. She's a friend."

"Wow—" Her gaze snapped back to me. "How was it, then?"

"Last night?" My cheeks flushed at the thought of him.

"Yes, last night."

I rounded my desk. "Tobias's—"

"First name terms?" She sat in the chair opposite. "Didn't see anything online about him being married."

"He's not."

"God, Americans are so sexy. Don't you think?"

And on her reaction, I added, "It was all business, Elena. Very professional."

She waved it off. "How are you settling in?"

"Good. I mean great. I love it here."

"Adley told me he once met your dad."

"He didn't mention that."

"Your dad knew everything there was to know about art."
I smiled. "His knowledge was impressive."

"Apparently, he was well loved in the community." She
looked sheepish. "Your lineage. Is it true?"

"A dynasty lost to history now," I said.

"So your great-great-grandfather came from the Russian
royal family?"

I perked up a little. "Yes."

"Your ancestors owned one of the greatest art collections
in Europe."

"Yes, well, after the Vatican, of course," I murmured.

"So you're related to the house of Romanov?"

I gave a nod. "As you probably remember from your history,
it all ended terribly. Marxist leaders revolted and my great-
grandparents were exiled by the Bolsheviks. They moved here
to escape. I never once heard my father speaking Russian. I
don't think he could, to be honest."

"Does that make you a princess?"

I gave a shrug. "My mom was Welsh. I take after her apparently. All wayward hair and barefoot wildness."

"Talking of wildness—" She waggled her eyebrows. "Did
you get the gossip on Wilder?"

"He's very private."

"You can tell me. I saw the forms in my inbox on my way
in."

"Forms?"

"His office emailed them over. Your copy of the nondisclo-
sure agreement that you need to sign for our files. I'll send the
signed forms back to them in the post. I've forwarded the doc-
uments to you. Looks like you can't discuss his personal life.
Can't discuss where his private address is and stuff like that."

I leaned forward and rested my chin on my palms. "He doesn't want me to write an official report, either. Well, that's not strictly accurate. He's asked me to exclude where we went and what we saw. Which is basically my official report."

"Where did you go?" she whispered.

I broke her gaze as that grand palace flashed into memory, those elite men who'd taken living the high life to an entirely different level.

"Zara?"

"To be honest, Tobias is intense. I wouldn't want to cross him."

"Was he rude?"

"No, nothing like that. He's just very…" warmth flushed over me "…mysterious."

His kiss…his strength and the firmness of his body…

Squeezing my thighs together, I tried to push thoughts of him away. Hoping with all my heart he'd not complain about me to Adley. He'd not exactly left my flat on amicable terms.

"That's pretty." She was looking at the bonsai. "Who's it from?"

"There's no signature." I pushed myself to my feet and walked over to it and picked up the note card. I handed it to her.

"It's made from luxury paper." She held it up.

"Adley?"

"All his gifts go through me." She flipped it over to show me the Japanese symbols. "What does it say?"

"Have no idea."

"Good morning, ladies," said Logan, bursting through the door in a flurry of pink Chanel suit and a perfume to match, a soft floral scent contradicting her demeanor.

"Did we have an appointment?" Elena looked worried.

"Brief visit," said Logan. "Have a matter with Ms. Leighton to discuss."

"Did Mr. Wilder send that?" asked Elena.

Logan sneered at the plant. "I send these out all the time for Mr. Wilder. Cooper delivered it this morning."

"It's lovely," I said. "Please thank him."

"Sure."

"Can I get you a coffee, Logan?" I offered. "Tea?"

"No, thank you."

"What does this say?" asked Elena, holding up the card.

Logan shrugged it off and handed me the large manila envelope. "Thought we'd get this out of the way, Ms. Leighton."

From Elena's expression, Logan had decided to hand deliver the forms herself.

My gaze returned to the bonsai as a rush of excitement flooded over me that it had come from Tobias. Maybe last night hadn't gone as badly as I'd thought.

Logan peeled open the envelope, withdrew the papers and handed them to me. "Sign here."

"Perhaps I should get Mr. Adley to look over it first?" I suggested.

She slid a pen my way. "My advice, sign it. We don't want to unleash…"

"Unleash?" I held Logan's gaze.

"Hell," she said. "Mr. Wilder has little patience for noncompliance."

As I've discovered, I almost muttered. "Still, I'd like to get my boss to approve."

"Zara had fun last night." Elena widened her eyes playfully. "Not that she's told us anything."

"Mr. Wilder seemed happy with everything," I confirmed.

"We'd love to know the gossip on him," said Elena with a glint of mischief.

I threw her a wary glance.

Logan scowled at me. "All these years I've known him he's never once wasted his time on anything trivial. He's possessive of his time."

I arched a brow and let her follow my gaze over to the bonsai. "I better Google how to take care of it. Looks expensive."

"Hope you've got green thumbs, Zara. Bonsais are very sensitive. One wrong move and it withers."

"Oh, I'm always up for a challenge," I said.

Elena rose out of her chair. "We have a couple of clients arriving any minute. If you'll excuse me." She waved to me as she headed out.

Logan sat casually on the edge of my desk. "I'll wait while you sign it."

"As an attorney you know the wisdom of having a lawyer review any document before you sign it."

"Yes, but this is for *my* client."

"I'm aware of that."

"Don't make me show you what I'm capable of, Zara."

I stood stock-still, staring at her.

"I don't have time for this." She huffed out her frustration.

No, I didn't do bullies.

She headed for the door.

"Please tell your client we'll be in touch," I called after her.

I left my office and strolled toward the east corridor, needing to put distance between us. I'd reassured Tobias I was going to proceed with discretion and wanted him to believe me. And if I was forced to sign anything, I'd need Adley's approval first.

I found Elena in the conference room chatting with a middle-aged couple, and even from behind the glass I could see the conversation was tense.

Elena's expression softened when she saw me and she signaled for me to join them.

Inside, fresh brewed coffee filled the air, and at the end of the table sat a plate of uneaten doughnuts. Those fraudulent paintings hung on the walls to mock us. That Pollock now gone, returned to its rightful place at the National.

The couple rose to their feet and reached out to shake my hand. They both looked worn with worry, and their tattered coats gave away their modest lifestyle.

"This is Zara Leighton," said Elena. "One of our art specialists." She gestured to me. "Zara, this is Mr. and Mrs. Fairweather. They've come all the way from Lancashire."

"Please, call me Harriet." Mrs. Fairweather pointed to her husband. "Stewart."

"Zara," I said, joining them at the table.

Elena went on to explain they'd come down on the train to have a painting appraised. They'd inherited a house full of antiques from Harriet's mom who'd lived in Pendlebury, and had found this painting—the one on the table—and were eager to see if it was worth anything.

Only, what they hadn't accounted for was Huntly Pierre's ten-thousand-pound appraisal fee prior to the assessment.

"But I thought it came out of the profit if we sold it?" explained Harriet.

Stewart nodded in agreement. "If it's worthless, then we're down ten thousand pounds."

"I'm so sorry for any confusion," said Elena.

Harriet looked nervous. "It's just Stewart lost his job a few years ago and we could really do with the money. We can't afford it if it's worthless."

"I'm sorry to hear that." Elena swapped a wary glance with me.

"I'm sorry we wasted your time," said Harriet.

"Not at all," I said. "We love to see paintings."

She rose and leaned over the desk and began rewrapping the canvas.

I stepped forward, throwing a smile at Elena. "Don't you just hate rules?"

Harriet paused and curled her fingers into her chest, her expression now hopeful.

Rules be damned...

Especially when they come from sexy, controlling Americans.

I refocused on the canvas.

Elena's face flushed with mischief. "Shall I get the X-ray? The one you'd use if you were going to appraise it?" She winked at me.

"Good idea." I rolled a chair out of the way and moved closer.

Elena stepped out and quietly closed the door behind her.

"Laurence Stephen Lowry." I leaned in. "Matchstick men and women."

Upon the canvas was Lowry's distinctive style of painting stick people scattered within an urban industrial landscape. This piece was titled *Going to Work on a Sunday*, and as I peered closer I ran through my checklist.

"Ms. Leighton," said Harriet nervously. "I'm afraid we can't proceed. We can't afford it."

"Totally understand," I said. "Perhaps if you change your minds and agree to Huntly Pierre's terms, I'll share with you what I find."

She gazed at the canvas lovingly. "I found it hidden in between several other paintings."

"Well, that would explain the fact that the paint itself is so vibrant. Daylight ages the colors." I lifted it and turned it over. "Love the frame. Is it yours?"

Harriet looked to her husband. "The painting didn't have

one. We thought it best to place it in one. We really weren't trying to trick anyone."

"Lowry never varnished." I retrieved a magnifier from the side table and peered through it. "See this, the discoloration in his figures. The solitude. The clarity despite the thick texture. Looks simple to replicate but it's not. He trained for years and his technical skills are hard to copy."

"Looks easy to copy to me," said Stewart. "Can't see the appeal." He earned a nudge in his ribs from Harriet.

"Lowry's the most faked painter on the market," I told them. "He only used five pigments. He dabbled in a different white but that was in his earlier works. You should only see five here. Look, there's my favorite, Prussian blue." I hovered the magnifier close again.

"How much do you think it might be worth if it's real?" said Stewart.

"If real, possibly millions."

Stewart cleared his throat. "Pounds?"

I set the magnifier down. "Quite possibly."

"My mom looked after Elizabeth, his mom, when she became poorly," said Harriet. "She was very hard on her son. My mom told me Lowry would wait for his mom to fall asleep and then go paint."

"Your mom really knew Lowry?" I said.

"They lived in the same town. He wrote her a lovely note after his mom died and gifted her this." She gazed at the painting.

My back straightened. "Do you still have it? The letter?"

Harriet rifled through her handbag and withdrew the plastic sandwich bag and removed a folded letter.

It was impossible not to smile. "This counts as provenance."

"I'm not sure I know what that means?" said Harriet.

"Paperwork that tracks the painting's origins. It's as valu-

able as the painting sometimes. Now and again it's the decid-
ing factor on whether a painting is deemed authentic."

"Do you think it might be real?" she said.

I beamed their way.

Harriet's eyebrows shot up with excitement.

"That was extraordinarily kind of you, Ms. Leighton," said
Stewart.

"Oh, did I just let it slip you own an authentic painting by
Lowry?" My lips curled into a mischievous smile. The joy on
their faces was adorable.

Elena appeared in the doorway.

I headed over to her. She must have read their happiness
because she suppressed a grin.

"Send them to Sotheby's," I told her. "It's worth at least
two million."

"Shall I bill them?" she said. "You'll get the commission."

"Leave it to their discretion." I glanced back.

"Adley wants to talk with you." She gestured for me to
follow her out.

"Everything all right?" I said.

She lowered her voice to a whisper. "Not sure what Logan
told Adley, but he's pacing."

"What does that mean?"

She looked nervous. "It's never good when he paces."

10

Adley refused to let up.

And I refused to unfold my arms and agree I was wrong.

He was sitting behind his desk and I was standing in front of it. Apparently, the moment I'd left my office, Logan had stormed into Adley's to discuss my refusal to sign the NDA. And to think I'd believed it was best to have my boss review legal paperwork first.

"You and I have already discussed your attitude, Zara," he said. "You can't talk to Mr. Wilder's staff so disrespectfully."

"I merely advised Ms. Arquette I'd have you look over the form first."

He rose to his feet, rounded me and shut the door. "We have clients who require discretion. Even from me. A little unusual, I know. You'll get used to it."

"But from you?"

He looked sympathetic. "There's a gray area."

"Mr. Wilder gave me a bonsai tree." I pointed to my office. "And a thank-you note. I thought he was happy."

"Probably sent out as standard."

This felt like a catch-22. If I explained to Adley I'd been

dragged through a palace half-naked to see a stashed-away painting, I'd breech the client's trust, but not sharing this made me appear as the ungrateful employee who'd recklessly threatened a relationship with a respected businessman. I had gone above and beyond.

Way beyond.

Adley slid the form across the table.

I picked up a pen from his desk and leaned over, signing my name along the dotted line.

"Apologize to him," he said.

I raised my gaze to his.

"Win back Mr. Wilder's respect for Huntly Pierre."

"You make it sound like I'm meeting him."

"You're taking him to lunch at Sketch." He waved to the door. "Table's booked."

Mayfair? One of London's poshest areas?

"Today?"

"Elena will give you the company credit card. Put it on that. Express your sincere apology and let our client know they can expect a professional when or if they ever require a field specialist again."

Maybe, just maybe, I silently mused, *you should pay your staff danger money for when the client wants them to get half-naked and run through a—*

"We have an understanding?" said Adley.

"Yes, sir."

He brightened. "I'd appreciate your insight on the Jaeger heist. We're set to approve the case for their insurance claim. Another set of eyes and all that."

"Thank you," I said, feeling a rush of excitement. "I'd love that."

The Jaeger's high-profile case was going to be my first chance to shine.

"We have a meeting at two. That'll be all."

"Thank you." I left Adley's office with mixed feelings.

I'd never visited Sketch until now and realized why as I blinked away to take in the restaurant's lavish pink seating, pink flooring and, well, pink everything, including the walls, which also showcased drawings by satirical artist David Shrigley.

I saw Tobias and Logan tucked away at a corner table. By the time I reached them my heart was pounding too fast and my hands were trembling. No doubt Logan was going to eviscerate me publicly, and I'd have to endure it until I could get out of here.

I thanked the mâitre d' and braved a look at Tobias, waiting for his invitation to join them, my breath stilted as his frown deepened further.

Even though he'd dressed down in ripped jeans, a white shirt and black jacket, he still oozed sophistication; his gorgeous face framed by ruffled hair as though perfection just fell in line around him. Those sleek lines of his jaw flexed and his eyes sparked with curiosity as they roamed over me.

"Hello." I forced my friendliest smile.

With no response from him, I glanced over at Logan. "I have your form. I signed it."

His glare fell on Logan. "You arranged this?"

She looked triumphant as she held out her hand.

I reached out and gave her the envelope. "Thank you for inviting me." Though reading his confusion I added, "Or not? Don't want to intrude."

Tobias's eyes searched the table. Clearly he wasn't expecting me.

Feeling the burn of the attention of the other guests, I said, "May I join you?"

He rose to his feet and I was again reminded how tall he

was, how he moved with assuredness. With a slight nod he gestured for me to join them, and then he sat back down.

Classical piano played softly in the background and I vaguely mused over whether I recognized the piece.

"This is nice." I seriously considered mentioning the weather.

That uncomfortable glance swapped by Tobias and Logan made me wince. Reaching for the glass of water to my left, I took a sip and then another, my throat too dry, my nervousness rising.

Their stares stuck on me.

I'd just sipped from Tobias's glass. "Sorry."

He suppressed a smile. "Hungry?"

I wasn't but I gave a polite nod anyway.

Glancing from Logan and back to Tobias, I watched him order from the menu, surprised he didn't ask us what we wanted and went ahead and ordered a selection of sandwiches, scones and pastries for all three of us.

From Logan's calm expression she was used to this.

Our waiter opened a bottle of chilled white wine and began pouring chardonnay into the glasses.

When he went for mine I held my hand over the top. "Not for me, thank you."

"Go ahead and fill it, please," Tobias told him.

The waiter complied.

I pulled my hand away and watched him pour my glass.

"You had something you wanted to say to us?" Logan edged me on, her gleam of pleasure bright on her face.

She was already enjoying playing with me. I took a sip of chardonnay.

My wine was chilled to perfection but there was no way I could let my guard down and forget how heady alcohol made me.

I made a mental note not to have any more.

"I'm sorry if I offended you in any way, Mr. Wilder," I said softly. "It wasn't my intention."

"Offend me?"

"I waited too long to sign it." I gestured to the envelope.

He reached for it and pulled out the document. Tobias tucked it back in and handed it back to Logan. "Would you excuse us, please."

Logan's smile thinned. "In view of the circumstances I believe it's in your best interest if I stay."

"Circumstances?"

"Her refusal to sign."

"It's signed."

"Because of my insistence."

He gave her a comforting smile. "I can deal with Ms. Leighton from here."

"Toby?" Her expression looked pained, and I found myself feeling sorry for her. There was sadness in her eyes that told me they were more, or perhaps I'd merely picked up on her yearning to be more.

I'd seen what a riled-up Logan was capable of. "I can go if you like?"

"Please." His tone was intense. "I want you to stay."

I put his demeanor down to running a billion-dollar company. The kind of power that would place him in the center of his own universe.

Logan shot to her feet and threw me a defiant glare. Tobias took a sip of wine as he watched her navigate around the table.

"I'll call you," she said.

"Sure."

With her gone this was going to be a little easier, though that thought was switched out by the awkwardness of Tobias's silence.

All I could think of was the way he felt against me when

we kissed, that gentleness fused with his masculine hard edges. Us fitting together as though made for each other. My breasts swelled as his delicate cologne reached me.

I concentrated on straightening my napkin, hoping not to give myself away. "You weren't expecting me?"

He tore his gaze from mine. "No."

"Sorry."

"It's good to see you. Why don't you take off your coat?" He frowned. "The concierge didn't offer—"

"I wasn't sure I'd be staying." I pulled my arms out of my parka and laid it beside me. "I'm here to apologize."

"For?"

"Offending you."

"Logan told you that?"

"Adley. He called me into his office." I looked down. "I speak my mind."

"So I've discovered. It's a good trait to have." He smiled playfully. "I'm surprised you haven't filed a complaint."

"Against Logan?"

"Me."

"Why would I complain about you?"

He arched a brow. "I led you half-naked through an orgy."

"The blindfold helped." I flushed and broke his gaze.

"I'm glad."

I took several gulps of wine. "It was kind of exciting."

"What do you normally do for fun?"

"Stay home and read."

He studied me carefully. "What do you like to read?"

"Romance." I silently screamed at myself for telling him that. "Books on art."

"Romance? Happy-ever-after?"

"Yes."

"That's why it's called fiction." He smiled at his joke. "And yet if you risk nothing—" His gaze held mine. "Sorry, that was inappropriate. As you can see, I've lost my faith in humanity. You're still relatively unscathed by life. Try to keep it that way."

"I've seen a few things."

"Well, that's good."

"Last night—"

He reached for his napkin and placed it on his lap.

"When will Goya's *La Maja Desnuda* go on sale?" I asked.

"Not sure."

A silver-tiered platter of sandwiches was placed on the table, the lowest tier holding scones and a selection of rich pasties.

I paused until the waiter walked away and then whispered, "Why was the Goya hidden?"

Tobias held my stare. "Because that's what men do with beautiful things."

These undertones of sexual attraction made it hard to concentrate. I sensed he was fighting it too from the way his stare roamed over my body, that burn in his gaze morphing into confliction.

The way he broke into a heart-stopping smile. "It's good to see you." He reached for that jug of water and topped up my drink and then his own. "Let me know if you'd like anything else."

I took a sip to quench my thirst. "How did you know it was behind the other painting?"

"This is scandalous, isn't it?"

"What is?"

"We should be drinking tea." He raised his eyebrows. "As you know I'm a bad influence."

"Tea would be lovely."

He raised his hand for the waiter and when the man approached he asked for English breakfast tea.

The waiter scurried off.

"Where in America are you from?" I said.

"Massachusetts. Originally."

"It's pretty there?"

"Beautiful in the fall."

"You miss it?"

"I travel a lot for work but love to go back when I can. I have a home there as well as an apartment in New York, Washington and, as you know, in Oxford. I call LA home." He frowned as though regretting sharing that with me.

A pot of tea arrived and was placed between us. A teacup was set down to my left, and I poured a little milk in.

"Where is your family now?"

Having read about his parents, I wanted to stay far away from that kind of painful conversation. There'd been no mention of siblings when I'd read up on him.

"My only living relative lives in Paris."

"I'm sorry."

"Actually, he's my favorite uncle."

"So you're a bit of a science buff?"

"I've always loved science."

"Because science shows you how to control things?"

"Just the opposite. Science proves just how unstable the universe is."

"It is?"

"It was created by the big bang." He demonstrated an explosion. "Humanity is against the clock. Unless we change our ways."

"I recycle."

"There's hope for us yet."

I perked up. "It must be wonderful owning your own gallery."

Happiness swept over his face, making him look younger, and those traces of tension lifted. "Yes."

I smiled. "Who was your first?"

He set his glass down.

"My first was *Madame Rose Récamier*," I said softly.

He nodded, appreciating my cheekiness.

"She hung on my bedroom wall," I continued. "Felt like she was watching over me."

I knew every angle of her face, every shadow thrown on the canvas, every delicate brushstroke. There came a rush of guilt I'd not returned to The Otillie to visit her.

Tobias's gaze met mine. "Fuseli, *The Nightmare*." He watched my reaction. "Painted in—"

"1781." A chill washed over me.

Johann Henry Heinrich Füssli had stunned the art community with his painting of a woman sprawled out on a bed seemingly asleep, or even unconscious, with an incubus crouched on her chest and his sinister glare peering out at us. The only other witness was a horse, nostrils flaring, emerging from behind a veil to witness the monstrous act of control the beast had over the woman.

"Why that one?" Uneasiness rose in my chest.

Waiting for him to answer, I downed the rest of my wine.

He lowered his gaze. "It represents entering another's dreams."

"Yes, it does."

"It offers uncertainty. Drama. Possession."

My mouth was still dry, but I was too shaken to reach for my water. "How old were you?"

"Ten." He slipped into a warm smile. "When the realization hit me that art was capable of stirring a visceral response. Alighting the soul. Awakening a person consciously. That

Fuseli haunted my dreams and terrified my days. There came an awareness of the inherit power of art to terrorize."

"You didn't love the painting?"

He grinned. "If I did, what would that make me, Zara?"

"Fucked up." I let out a laugh.

"And some. I felt driven to save the damsel and kill the beast."

I breathed a sigh of relief, and my shoulders relaxed from where they'd been holding their tension.

"You asked me for my first," he clarified. "Not my first love."

"True."

He looked thoughtful. "Goya."

"Which one?"

"Ferdinand Guillemardet."

"Of course, *The French Ambassador*, any young man would be struck by his confidence."

"And later, I understood the profoundness of the portrait, the life radiating off the canvas, the ambassador's calculated pose to exude intelligence."

"You admired his power?"

"Actually, it's what's captured in Ferdinand's eyes. They reflect that he'd seen so much. Goya understood his pain and the wisdom that had come from that. Goya's bright palette was truly remarkable. I wish you could see it up close. He believed this was his finest painting. To be honest, there are too many of his great works to choose from."

"I'm sure Goya enjoyed the vibrant conversation while the ambassador posed for him," I said.

"Most definitely. A shame he later lost his hearing."

"Where did you see *The French Ambassador*?"

"The portrait hung in the living room of my uncle's villa

in Reims. I stayed with him for a while." Tobias brightened. "My uncle bequeathed the painting to the Louvre."

"No wonder you were willing to go to any means to see the Goya."

"To know she was real—" He placed his palm on his chest to say the rest.

"I'm happy I could help. Do you speak French?"

"*Oui.*" He continued to speak, his tone poetic as though reciting a sonnet.

Making my toes curl. "What did that mean?"

"I was thanking you for brightening my day."

He made me smile, his flair for language adding a sexy dimension to the already heady Tobias Wilder.

"I'm grateful for your talent, Zara. And your continued discretion."

"Adley was okay with it."

"Of course he was."

"I wanted to get lost in that palace. Spend the night running from room to room and savor every second."

"Art should be shared. It's a travesty to hide them away."

Looking down, I hid my shame. My father's legacy had been all about hoarding the paintings and keeping them just for him.

A legacy of secrecy that I too was guilty of now.

That elegant hand reaching out across that ancient canvas...

"There's a beautiful mystery to art." Tobias reached for his glass. "I see myself as a steward."

"I feel the same way, only I'm honoring its authenticity."

"You didn't need to come here and apologize," he said. "I'm the one who put you through a difficult ordeal."

"I liked seeing the painting."

"I meant stripping you naked and dressing you in next to nothing. To ensure we'd mingle."

My cheeks burned from the warmth of the wine.

Not the wine…

I let out a deep sigh. "It felt like an awakening…"

The silence was no longer a threat and as his stare reached all the way inside me, I was sure he too felt this electrical pulse between us, this thrill, a familiar shiver, and these stirring memories of when he'd kissed me passionately and forced my surrender in his arms.

"I'm leaving for LA tomorrow," he said softly.

I dug my fingernails into my palms. "Going home?"

"Yes."

"That's…" *Probably a good thing.* "It's been lovely meeting you."

"Likewise."

"Maybe next time you visit London we can have drinks?"

He looked away and then those green eyes locked on mine, and with that one look he'd shut down my embarrassing suggestion.

Though he was hard to read as his jaw tensed and relaxed.

The men in my life had more than proven I didn't make their impossible grade.

"Zara, seeing you again would actually be—"

"I'm dedicating myself to my career right now." I took a bite out of a muffin and munched away, remembering he'd already shut down there being an *us* back in my flat.

Tobias placed a sandwich on his plate and glanced inside the slices of bread. He nudged his plate away.

I felt like that sandwich, never destined to be good enough.

That subtle check of his wristwatch proved I was either boring or keeping him from something far more important.

"Do you have to return to work?" he said.

"Yes, I should go. I have a meeting. I'm being brought in on this very important case." I reached for my coat. "Thank you for the bonsai tree."

"I'm glad you liked it."

"Card was pretty. What do the Japanese symbols mean?"

"It was a thank-you for all you did. You almost executed every requirement flawlessly." He quirked a smile.

Almost?

I rose from my seat and pulled on my coat. "I'm glad we're leaving each other on good terms, Mr. Wilder."

"And breathtaking memories." He waggled his eyebrows playfully. "You stun in Coco de Mer. A gorgeous Russian princess."

My cheeks burned again.

"Your impressive ancestry was noted in the file Adley gave us."

As if any of that mattered now.

He ran his fingers through his perfect hair. "You were an erotic delight to the senses. Impossible to forget." His gaze locked on mine. "Zara, I—"

I scoffed. "I'd not be surprised if you had royal blood too."

"Why do you say that?"

"You looked quite at home at Blandford Palace."

He folded his arms across his chest. "More interesting still, so did you, Zara Elizabeth."

It was too late to hide he'd gotten to me.

My full name had probably been noted in the report Adley had given him during our meeting.

"Forgive me," he said.

"What for this time?"

"I lied about what was in that note that came with the bonsai."

"Oh." I fisted my hands and rested them on my hips and they slid off my parka.

"It actually states in kanji you'd make an incredible geisha."

I sucked in my breath at his cheek.

"Now you need to read up on Japanese culture if you think that's an insult." He narrowed his gaze. "Oh dear, did I just upset your Jane Austen sensibilities?"

I plopped down next to him and leaned into his ear. "It's a good thing you and I are saying goodbye."

He looked taken aback. "Why is that?"

I lowered my voice to a whisper. "Because, Tobias, you'd never withstand the hard fucking *I'd* deliver." I gave a look of defiance.

High five, chardonnay, my loyal wing-wine.

I pushed myself to my feet and walked away. A few tables down I realized—

And stopped in my tracks as my eyelids squeezed shut with the ridiculousness of having to go back.

Rallying my resolve I returned to our table. "I'm meant to pay."

He gave a wry smile. "I've got this one, Leighton."

11

It was strange to miss a man I hardly knew, I thought, wrapping my hands around my coffee mug as I tried later that day to stay warm in the overly chilled conference room.

I refocused on Danny Kenner, a relatively new hire to the firm like me but with a background in security.

"There are cameras in the Jaegers' Holland Park home," he said. "But each one was disabled prior to the theft of the Edvard Munch." Danny's eyes scanned over each of us.

Elena had given me the scoop on everyone here before I headed on in. I was grateful to be included so soon on such a high-profile case, especially as it had been Adley who'd invited me.

This was a tight-knit group with Abby Reynolds at the helm, a forty-year-old who was considered a highflier in the company after leaving the Met at the rank of inspector. Her African heritage had given her those sharp cheekbones and her intelligent eyes sparkled with insight and highlighted Abby's pretty complexion.

Her rugged counterpart was Shane Hannah, an ex-policeman too, though he'd spent his years in Special Branch, and a back injury had apparently forced his early retirement. That cane he walked with was testament he'd put his job first.

Beside him sat Brandon Forbes, Huntly Pierre's senior techie who hailed from Wales and was rumored to be able to hack into anything.

They talked over each other with the ease of friends.

Everyone seemed relaxed around Adley, proving this was their stomping ground. They avidly listened to Danny and at times threw in even more relevant details. Their notebooks were open in front of them as they each waited a turn to present their own findings.

Adley leaned back casually at the head of the table and scribbled away, taking his own notes. "The family was in the house?" he asked. "Asleep upstairs?"

"Yes," said Abby. "They had silverware out in the same room, but nothing else was taken."

"The thief didn't get greedy," said Shane.

"Insurance won't match the worth of the painting," said Danny, "so it doesn't look like insurance fraud—" He looked over at me. "Shall I bring you up to speed?"

I gave a nod of appreciation.

He continued for me, "The theft was a quick break-in. No alarm was set off and nothing else touched. However, there was a partial fingerprint, but whoever left it isn't in the National DNA Database. We're running the staff right now in case it came from them. None of them are suspects but their prints will be all over the house and we need to eliminate them. The Met's Arts and Antiques Squad are leading the investigation but, with their resources short, they're happy to share updates and join resources. I have a meeting with them right after this over at New Scotland Yard. We're going to compare the Chelsea theft of a Henry Raeburn with this latest case."

"That burglary involved Raeburn's 1815 *Portrait of a Lady*," Abby said as she continued to update me on this robbery.

Free-flowing information had proven beneficial in other cases, she told me.

"How the hell does a man get into a house, steal a painting and leave no evidence?" said Brandon. "I mean nothing. Not one lead."

"And we know it's most likely to be a man," Abby threw in.

"Statistically," said Shane, "women are more likely to be arrested for theft."

"Apparently," said Abby, "the entire power went out on the Jaeger house in Holland Park right before the theft."

"The thief didn't stop there," said Shane. "The Holland Park neighbors had wall-to-wall cameras, which were also affected by the outage. That cuts the chance of our guy being caught on film entering or leaving the premises."

"The thief knew the painting was there. It wasn't random," I realized. "He's done this before."

Adley slid a file over to me marked Jaeger/Confidential.

I rifled through it, taking note of the paperwork full of proof of ownership, the legalese, including a Christie's tracking number for the painting. From a quick glance the family had inherited an Edvard Munch. A trip to Christie's would be all it would take to verify the provenance and validate their story. The investigation might not turn up the painting, which was quite possibly stashed away in a private collection by now, but at least it would assist with their insurance claim.

The meeting ended with an agreement for all of us to reconvene at five. This team knew each other well, from the way they huddled in a group and chatted away, forming a circle of trust that excluded me.

I felt like an outsider.

Taking the hint, I carried the Jaeger file back to my office

and set about making an appointment with Christie's apprais-
als and evaluations department. They'd be able to authenticate the family's ownership of the Edvard Munch and confirm
the painting had indeed come through them. The paperwork
went back as far as 1902.

After a few clicks on Christie's website I'd secured a
7:00 p.m. with Andrew Chan, their senior documentation
curator.

A blur of movement in the doorway.

My eyes rose to meet the startling gaze of Tobias's—

I shot to my feet, wondering how long he'd been there.

I felt like I'd been struck by lightning, a storm soon to follow in its wake.

He walked in with the stature of a man who owned any
space he entered, turning briefly to close and then lock the
door before heading over to the window. His fingers curled
around the thin pole of the blinds, twisting them closed and
throwing shade on the room.

My heart rate took off and my breathing stuttered as I
watched him move across my office.

"I want to talk with you," he said huskily, "about our last
conversation."

I rounded my desk and leaned against it with my arms
folded and I tried to feign I was unaffected by his ardent stance.
"Me paying for lunch?"

He chuckled and came over to stand right in front of me.
"Before that."

Racking my brain, I ran through our last interaction, trying to guess which one of my snappy retorts might have riled
him up and caused his expression to become so imposing, his
posture straight and his presence commanding. His height
easily intimidated, his stance proving a fierce determination.

My cheeks blushed with the realization…

Tobias watched my reaction. "May I clarify your statement?"

"Yes," I said in a rush, my breath stuttering as he crushed his lips against mine. That first shock of his hold weakened my defenses, proving my inability to deny I'd wanted this more than life itself.

I reached up and grabbed a fistful of hair and held him to me.

God, yes.

His lips forced mine wider and then he began leisurely flicks with his tongue into my mouth, and my sigh morphed into a moan. His fingers trailed down my blouse, unbuttoning as he went, easing it off my shoulders, and I leaned back, raising my arms and shimmying slightly to help him remove it.

I'm going to burn up from this, I thought. *I'll be left a wreck.* And yet instead of pushing him away, I held him to me as my tongue dared to enter his mouth and tangle with his.

When his lips broke from mine, I let out the softest moan of a need unquenched.

His kisses trailed down my neck and farther still, until he suckled my left nipple through my bra. My fingers curled over the lace cup and I tugged it down, giving him full access to that pert nipple. A burst of pleasure shuddered through me as he circled and suckled with determination, moving to the left now and dragging his teeth over it and eliciting a shock of bliss.

My head fell back and locks of my hair spilled behind me. "It's too much."

He cupped my face with his hands. "I need to be inside you. Do you understand?"

Blinking, jaw gaping, I stuttered through another breath, realizing my final words to Tobias had set me up for this and it was here in my office, with people on the other side of that door carrying on regardless, with no idea what was going on in here.

I exulted in the rush of danger of having Tobias taking me like this.

He feels it too, I told myself, *he's just as drawn to me as I am to him, a magnetic pull that neither of us can fight anymore*. This mysterious, brilliant man, an astounding vision of masculinity, all hard muscle and powerful stride.

He shrugged out of his jacket and threw it across the room, making quick work of his shirt and yanking that off too.

Tobias stepped toward me and paused as though measuring my reaction.

A wave of dizziness struck me when I ran my hand over his firm torso, my fingertips running along that intricate Polynesian tattoo on his left shoulder. My gaze flittered to the Latin writing hidden by his trousers, and he caught me looking there.

"What does it say?" My fingertips traced the edge of his belt.

He tipped up my chin. *"Secretus."*

"You mean it's a secret?" I hardly knew any Latin but I knew that.

"I'm not here to discuss me."

Tobias oozed virility, masterfully comfortable with every move he made, with each easy action proving he was a fierce alpha claiming his prize.

He shoved me back along the desk and his hand cupped behind my head to protect it as it went, and then he gripped my hips and dragged me toward him, sliding up my skirt and hiking it up around my waist. Nimble fingers tugged at my panties and dragged them down my thighs and off my legs, and then he opened my thighs with his firm hands and leaned in between my parted legs, his face inches from my sex.

Staring at the ceiling, my face on fire, my breathing ragged—

Arching my back as his tongue circled my clit, steadily thrumming, his fingers peeling back my folds farther to allow him longer sweeps that sent me hurtling close to the edge.

"Please," I managed.

"Want me to stop?" His breath was warm on me.

"No, never stop." My back arched higher when he slid two fingers inside me and my muscles clenched against his gentle thrusts, milking him. I let out a gasp when he pressed my G-spot and at the same time his tongue came down on my swollen clit and he began a mind-blowing rhythm.

His right hand reached for my mouth. He muffled my groan as I came, wave after wave of pleasure that felt never ending, eyelids squeezed shut, shuddering through.

Tobias lifted his head. "I wanted to taste you like this the first moment I set eyes on you."

My face burned like fire as my brain flashed that image of our first meeting in The Otillie basement, the realization unhinging my equilibrium.

In a wave of dizziness, the back of my head struck the desk.

Swooning, lost to reason, I let him turn me over up onto all fours, my head low and my forehead meeting the desk, my arse up in the air as he dragged me back toward him.

"Ready?" he said huskily.

The sound of a packet ripping open.

I peeked to see him glide on that condom over his hefty erection, his cock curled upward and achingly stiff, immovable.

No.

"Leighton, are you ready?" he repeated.

"Yes," I managed, biting down on my hand, readying for his first thrust.

"Shush," he soothed, his hand reaching around to run along my cleft, finding and flicking that perfect place on the hood of my clit sending a pulse of pleasure...

Sending me into euphoria.

My throaty groan of need subdued as I pressed my mouth against the back of my hand.

At the same time the tip of his cock tapped my entrance, before easing in, pausing inch by inch as he waited for me to stretch and accommodate his hugeness.

"Both hands on the desk," he commanded.

Bracing myself, I readied for him, holding my breath, this sudden fear caught in my throat.

"Hold on tight." Easing all the way in, Tobias's languid glide felt surreal, as though he'd tuned into my body's needs, its limits, with each passing second altering his movements until I relaxed against him, arching my spine and tilting my butt up to greet him and ease his glide all the way in, my sex rippling around him, my overly sensitized clit throbbing each time his balls struck there.

It wasn't enough, I yearned for more...

As though reading my mind, his hand swept round to play with me again. "Oh yes." I pushed back.

My need for faster, harder strikes were sensed by him too, his pummeling teasing me, leading me on, keeping me at the height of ecstasy as though he alone could control when I came.

Curling his left hand through my hair and gripping it tightly, he tugged my head back, lighting this primal yearning to be taken, my wish fueled as he drove into me fiercely, the soft sound of him slapping against me, the feel of his balls striking my sex until I could no longer hold back and had to let go, becoming his, my body lax, my thighs trembling in response to his pummeling.

The climax captured me, mind, body and soul splintering like glass, this pleasure so intense, so blinding, that I barely caught my last thought that I'd never experienced anything like this.

I'd never felt so enraptured.

Never had an orgasm owned me beyond all reason.

"Leighton." He moaned. "You feel incredible. I knew you would." Swirling his hips in a circle.

Couldn't speak, couldn't think…too much pleasure was centered in my core to be able to string any thoughts together.

"So good." He drove onward. "I need to be deeper."

Tobias lifted me and brought up my legs until they wrapped around his waist, my arms flung naturally around his neck, my face nuzzling into his neck, and breathing him in, his heady musk mingled with his intoxicating scent.

He lifted me up and carried me with him still inside me—

My back struck the wall but the coldness behind me was muted by the distraction of the heat coming off him. Tobias was all sleek muscle and bold motion, a chiseled perfection. That jolted thrust, my tautness pulling him in as his full length filled me again with its vastness.

He whispered huskily near my ear. "I'm balls deep inside you. Do you feel that?"

"God, yes," I breathed in a rush.

Propelling his hips against mine, taking me so hard that another orgasm snatched my breath away, and I buried my face in the nook of his neck as I came, dissolving into the purest intimacy, as though we'd always known each other like this, our oneness so natural, his firm hold making me his willing prisoner.

Tobias stilled, spilling his heat inside me. "Leighton…"

Resuming, gliding in and out and proving he too wanted

this to go on forever. Suspended against the wall I remembered to breathe again.

He pulled back slightly, his cock still buried deep, his eyes searching my face. "I couldn't stay away any longer."

My body shuddered at those words.

He eased out of me and set me down, and my legs felt shaky as my feet touched the carpet. He disposed of his condom and then returned to my side.

I stood there stunned into stillness, allowing him to redress me, his expression unreadable as he clipped the clasp together on my bra strap, his fingers sensually easing my breasts back into their lace cups, my nipples tingling as the pad of his thumb brushed over delicate skin.

He strolled over to the tissue box and pulled out a few.

My jaw went lax with embarrassment as I watched him wipe my sex with gentle sweeps, the intimacy so mind-blowing I lost my voice. His touch almost sent me over again.

Tobias gave a slight smile and kissed the end of my nose and then threw the tissues in the bin beneath the desk.

With the ease of a worldly man he knelt at my feet and helped me slide back into my panties, before raising them up my legs and pulling the thin strap of my thong into place. He continued to dress me.

Left to work on my hair and get these wayward locks back into some level of neatness, I watched him zip up his trousers, and then slip on his shirt and jacket, his eyes on the carpet as though avoiding mine.

He refastened his cuff links.

"Tobias?" I whispered.

He neared me and rested his hand on my neck, and I tilted my head to rest it in his palm, our eyes met, our gazes locked as we drew out this moment of affection.

"Leighton," he said softly.

"Yes," I breathed.

"Your beauty is haunting."

All air left the room; my eyelids flittered at the delirious-ness of his words.

My mind searching for answers about a man I hardly knew, my focus returned to the desk where he'd just taken me. "What just happened?"

He broke away and ran his fingers through his hair to tone down the mayhem of his dark blond locks. "I'll pick you up at seven."

"What for?"

"Dinner."

I let out the softest sigh of happiness. A smile shimmered across his lips.

Then I remembered. "I have a meeting at seven at Chris-tie's. Can we push it an hour?"

He strolled over to me. "Cancel it."

"Not sure I can."

He flicked a stray hair out of my eyes. "Do I need to fuck some sense into you?" He arched an amused brow. "Again?"

"That won't be necessary."

He leaned in and kissed me leisurely, his scalding hot mouth owning mine with each sweep of his tongue. "Good."

My body liquefied when he broke away.

Tobias strolled over to the blinds and with a curl of his fin-gers sunlight burst back into the room.

He let out a deep sigh. "You're extraordinary."

Rousing from this luxurious reality, I felt like I'd reached the surface after swimming from the very depths of the ocean to awaken—

Letting him take me like this couldn't go on. I couldn't re-peat this level of intensity and continue as though I'd never met this man. He was leaving for the States, for goodness' sake.

Yet I knew denying myself him was near impossible. Oh my God, I'd just done *it* in my office.

With *him*.

A man I hardly knew, gorgeous, yes, but outrageously controlling.

I straightened my skirt. "This is Britain, Mr. Wilder, not the Wild West."

He paused by the door and gave a heart-stopping smile.

Damn him, for making me giddy with excitement, my knees weak, these butterflies in my stomach threatening to last forever.

Tobias unlocked the door and strolled out with the same swagger he'd walked in with.

I could still smell him on me.

Wilder had just branded me with his scent.

12

Huntly Pierre's team were gathered for their five o'clock meeting.

I put my game face on, conveying a purely business attitude, not wanting to give anything away about my late lunch meeting that had morphed into a sex romp around my office with one of our most distinguished clients.

Tobias William Wilder, *fricking hell*, even his name was fused with sensuality.

Having spent the last twenty minutes gathering myself in the restroom, working on my hair and reapplying makeup, I now tried to wipe this ridiculous grin off my face.

My insides were melting just thinking of him.

Tobias had just turned my world upside down and I kept reliving every delicious detail, savoring every kiss, every touch and every move he'd made to rock my world just now.

Pulling out a chair, I blew out a concentrated breath to get me back in the zone as I joined them at the conference table.

Lead investigator Abby Reynolds sat at the end of the table working away on a text. Her sharp eyes seemingly not missing anything when they rose to meet mine, and she frowned her response.

I threw her a professional smile and self-consciously ran my fingers through my hair, reassuring myself I'd tamed these post-fucked curls.

Shane Hannah sat beside her and offered me a welcoming smile. I imagined nothing shocked either of these two ex-police officers. Next to Shane sat Brandon Forbes, his laptop open in front of him, proving his tech skills were poised if needed.

Danny Kenner was busying himself for his presentation at the front of the room, setting up the audiovisual display system and deftly working the cables into the high-tech equipment. He'd just returned from Scotland Yard and was excited to share what he'd learned from the team directing the investigation.

The scent of freshly brewed coffee and sugary doughnuts permeated the air. Adley hurried on in and took the seat beside mine.

He leaned toward me. "Heard you authenticated a Lowry?"

I braced myself for his annoyance.

"You talked the couple through the process?" he clarified.

I turned to face him. "They really did seem financially challenged."

"They're going through Sotheby's?"

"I believe so." Warily, I held his gaze.

"Harriet Fairweather's requested an official report and paid her deposit. Good work, Leighton."

A wave of relief washed over me. "Thank you, sir."

"We'll get your 10 percent commission deposited into your account." His smile reached his eyes. "Let's have our clients' payment go through first, next time."

"Got a bit carried away."

"You're art obsessed." His grin widened. "Which makes

you perfect for us." He swiveled in his chair to face the others. "Okay, where are we on this?"

There was something comforting about hearing Danny's accent, his voice booming with the confidence Americans always seemed to have. Even his mannerisms reminded me of Wilder—the way Danny beamed a smile when asked a question, his patience when interrupted by Adley or Shane, or even when Abby asked him to clarify an issue.

"We've been invited to participate in an Interpol investigation." Danny's gaze stayed on Adley. "Sir, we'd benefit from the insurance commission so it's financially viable."

"I'm listening," said Adley.

"Interpol has tracked a series of thefts across Europe," Danny began. "The heists all have the same modus operandi, with there being a series of two to three robberies in each country. All from private homes. Then the spate ceases abruptly. Paris seemingly being the last city hit so far. Right before London. They believe it's connected to the other cases we've been tracking. Which means the ones in London are part of a bigger picture."

"Same power cuts?" asked Abby.

"Lights out building-wide on either side of the theft," confirmed Danny. "Power outages every time, sometimes entire streets out for hours. But more important, the CCTV cameras are dead during the theft."

"In case a street camera catches him going in," I realized.

"Not one scrap of forensic evidence left?" asked Shane.

"Have they matched the fingerprint?" I asked.

"Belonged to their housekeeper," Danny confirmed with a nod. "Our man is in and out and there's nothing to prove he was even there. Except one heist where he made a mess of their ceiling when he used it as his entry point—"

"So we know we're looking for a man," Adley confirmed.

"The strength alone needed for these thefts points to a man," said Danny. "Interpol believes he scaled a castle wall for one of them. Château de Falaise, in Normandy."

"The thrill of the chase?" Brandon mused.

"And back in France during a heist, our culprit once left with the painting still inside the frame," Danny said incredulously. "Interpol is putting it down to a man due to the size and weight of the frame."

"He couldn't get the canvas out?" I muttered.

"Must have really wanted it," agreed Abby.

Shane made a note in his book. "He didn't want to cut it and reduce its value?"

"Or perhaps he cares about the art?" I sat up. "The frame was important for the provenance. Do you think he considered that?"

"How do they know it's not a team?" asked Shane.

"The underworld gossips," said Danny. "Prisoners' gossip. Whoever is doing this is a professional, and they look like they're working alone."

"So if they think this is connected," said Abby, "we have one theft left and the guy's gone."

"Off to the next city," Adley agreed.

"So, this is the same MO as the Jaeger case?" I asked.

Danny gave a nod. "Three thefts per city. There's a total of seventeen so far."

"He's methodical," I mused.

"Order works for him," said Abby. "So far."

Shane threw his pen down. "Shit, we're against the clock."

Danny turned on the wall-sized projector screen. "There's the mother lode of a payout for our man. If we find him it'll land Huntly Pierre a ten-million Euro reward." He waved his hands with excitement. "We're all looking for the same man."

Abby spoke up. "As Danny says, with two homes already

hit he's plotting another theft, if he's following the same pattern. We need to confirm the London thefts are related to those in Europe."

"Study the patterns," said Adley. "Collate the specifics of the other thefts. Research every detail of every painting. Are the Met willing to share?"

"Yep," said Danny. "It's a team effort."

"Maybe the thief works for a private collector?" suggested Adley. "We could work backward."

"I can gather a list of all the paintings involved," I offered. "And confirm their provenance over at the Witt."

I was excited at the thought of returning to my old alma mater, The Courtauld Institute, more specifically its library. The Witt's vast database contained information on millions of paintings from over seventy thousand artists, and with my privileged access I could be a real asset to the investigation.

"Love the idea," said Abby. "You'll need help."

"I'll go," said Danny.

I threw him a smile. "That would be great."

Danny blushed a little and turned sharply away, flicking a switch to bring up a photo on the screen of a large rotunda, the lighting drenched in gold. The round walls covered in wall-to-wall paintings by the Old Masters. An abandoned wire hung from the center.

"What are we looking at?" asked Adley.

Danny pointed to the screen. "That's how he got into the Burells' family home in Amboise in France, three weeks ago. Their security is state-of-the-art. No way in unless you descend through the glass ceiling. He cut his way through using a power tool and left a big hole in their million-dollar stained glass window. He stole a Titian."

I wondered why he changed his MO, and then realized saying, "No other way in."

Danny picked up a clear plastic bag containing what looked like feathers. "Guess what happens when you make a hole in a ceiling?"

"Are those crow feathers?" asked Abby.

"Raven, a littler larger than a crow," he said. "Interpol gave me a few feathers for us to examine. During the heist the thief also had to tackle a bird that flew in."

"Did he kill it?" asked Abby.

Danny shook his head. "No, the police found it alive and perched on a painting inside the rotunda."

"Can I take a closer look at the file?" I asked.

"Sure." Danny slid the bird feathers over to me. "I'll copy the file for you."

"I appreciate that." I raised the bag and marveled that our man had the guts to see the job through. "Did the bird set off any of the alarms?"

"Didn't trigger motion detectors or the floor panels," said Danny.

"Most people would have panicked and abandoned the heist," I said. "I mean, he was against the clock."

Abby agreed with a nod. "Son of a bitch is unflappable."

"He's going to be a challenge to catch," said Shane. "This guy's professional."

"We need to think like him," I said. "Get into his head."

"He's achieved more art thefts than any one man in history." Danny tapped the screen.

Abby let out a sigh of frustration. "Who the hell is he?"

Danny's face lit up with a mixture of intrigue and awe. "Icon." A chill descended on the room.

Taking a moment to read our reactions, Danny's gaze lingered on each one of us as though giving us a moment to consider this. "That's what they're calling him."

13

Clutching my notepad and leather satchel to my chest, I waited just inside the door.

Two analysts were holding up a stereomicroscope to a Monet, focusing on keeping it still and at the same time protecting the masterpiece. I recognized Andrew Chan from the website, and I held back a little when I saw he was deep in conversation with a male colleague.

I'd never had the privilege of visiting Christie's lab until now. The cold, stark room was situated in the basement and here and there were paintings on countertops awaiting their turn for authentication. The owners of each piece having to endure the long wait to see if their family heirloom was worth anything. If so, Christie's would handle the auction right here in this celebrated house.

My father had brought me to Christie's auction room as soon as I'd learned to walk, and I couldn't remember a time when this place hadn't been part of my life.

The heritage of Christie's was exceptional and the founder himself, James Christie, had been painted by Thomas Gainsborough in 1778—an oil on canvas that now hung at the Getty Museum.

The fondest memories washed over me. I'd raised my first gavel here and won my father a Giovanni Francesco Barbieri. What six-year-old could have resisted an angel with wide sweeping wings? Luckily, Dad only had to pay out a few thousand pounds for my mistake.

That one had been taken in the fire too.

I refused to slip into melancholy, right when things were getting good.

Just this afternoon I'd had the most mind-blowing sex of my life with the most incredible man I'd ever met. Even if Tobias was mysterious and off-the-charts bossy, my calling was to get to the center of each mystery and shine a light on it.

On him.

It wasn't only that Latin tattoo that had me intrigued, I yearned to know more about his entire world of business and innovation. What else had he invented? And where did he spend his days tinkering? The thought of visiting his LA gallery filled me with the anticipation of discovering even more life-changing delights surrounding him.

Why was I continuing to give him free rein within my thoughts? He'd already admitted he was leaving for LA.

Before I'd met Tobias nothing had felt so right and after him…

I shouldn't give him a second thought and no way should I pursue a relationship. No matter how incredible he made me feel and no matter how deliciously forbidden it felt with the way he touched me.

My core tightened with the thought of how easily he'd flung me around and controlled me like he had a right to my body. There came a cruel comfort knowing my days would predictably return to normal and I'd be saved from being drawn into a man hotter than the sun.

That tattoo was so damn sexy I'd almost buried my teeth in it like a wanton hussy.

Bloody hell.

Get a grip, Zara.

Your mind is meant to be on Icon, I chastised myself.

Being part of the team involved in one of the world's greatest spate of robberies was exhilarating. My dad would have been so proud of me.

I pulled out my iPhone, cringing at the cracked glass, and shot off an email to Logan, asking her to advise Mr. Wilder I was running late. It didn't seem fair I had to go through her to contact him. Perhaps if I'd been thinking straight I'd have remembered to have asked him for his number.

I couldn't wait to see him again; my mood lifted with the thought.

Andrew threw me a wave.

He was tall and dashingly cute, those dimples setting off his Asian dark eyes that lit up with his smile. I put him at thirty, though his colleague was much older.

From their enthusiasm they both looked to be in their element, tucked away down here where no one bothered them.

"Hey." I headed on over. "Didn't want to break your concentration." Andrew placed the scanner down and gestured for me to come closer. "I'm Zara, from Huntly Pierre."

"Hey, Zara," he said. "We had a last-minute cancellation. Usually you're looking at a two-week wait."

"Lucky me, then," I said, unable to take my eyes off the Monet. "Gorgeous."

"This is Sam, our tech."

I shook Andrew's hand and then Sam's. "What's your conclusion?"

"Let me know what you think first," said Andrew with a glint of delight as he stepped back to give me room.

"I'd be honored." I neared the painting.

Claude Monet, one of France's most talented impressionists, was famed for painting the same scene again and again, though each time offering a different perspective on light and seasons. I'd always found his work soothing.

"Signature's reassuring," I said.

"Isn't it," agreed Andrew.

"Monet was good friends with Renoir," I said. "They often painted the same landscapes at the same time. Even swapped them at the end of the day sometimes."

"The birth of impressionism." Andrew smiled at me. "You know your history. Royal College?"

"Courtauld. Studied under Professor Liana Belmont."

"Impressive," said Sam.

"May I?" I picked up the magnifier and used it to view the colors. "Water lilies, so dreamlike." Then I saw that one single cracked lily. "'The truth will out.'"

"Shakespeare," said Andrew, recognizing my quote.

"How can you see that without this?" Sam pointed to the stereomicroscope.

"It's the intricacy of the white." I set the magnifier down. "Monet had a gentle touch." I turned the painting over. "The forger used antique nails to secure the canvas. Clever. He also aged the backing. There's an official gallery sticker but it's stained with tea to make it appear aged. I'm going with Typhoo tea."

"Okay, wow," said Andrew.

I let out a laugh. "If only I was *that* good." They both swapped amused smiles.

I gave a shrug. "Still, it's more likely to be tea than coffee from the lighter stain."

"You're hired," said Andrew.

"I applied to work here," I admitted. "Not enough experience, apparently."

"That's because the higher-ups don't know talent," he said. "Don't quote me."

"The art world is competitive," I said. "A clique of experts that's difficult to break into."

"How did you know?" Andrew stared at the Monet.

"Couple of things, the forger used a hair dryer to mimic the minute spiderweb effect of an aging canvas, but he was too heavy-handed with the heat." I beamed at them. "To be honest you both looked excited right up until you read the results on the scanner. Let me take a guess, the machine picked up titanium white?"

"Didn't exist back in Monet's day," agreed Sam.

"Do the criminals really think you won't check?" I said.

"They're duping the buyer," said Sam. "Newbies to art have no idea that the pallets today weren't around in Monet's day."

"It's like any con, isn't it?" Andrew scrunched up his nose and mimicked with a sly tone, "We have to move fast. I have another buyer interested. This is a once-in-a-lifetime opportunity to own a painting that will change your life."

"Cruel." I ran my fingers over the Monet. "Making people part with their savings for a fake."

"So what do you have for me?" Andrew gestured to my satchel.

"The Jaeger case."

"Great, let's take a look."

Andrew and I headed to his corner office, and I removed the paperwork the Jaeger family had provided to prove they'd owned the Edvard Munch for generations. Together, we examined each piece of evidence, which included a sales receipt and a letter of authentication stamped with Christie's name and address. Mr. Jaeger had even provided a black-and-white photo taken in 1920 of his grandfather sitting at a kitchen table with the painting hanging behind him.

Time dissolved as I took detailed notes and cross-referenced what I had.

Half an hour later, Andrew led me through the auction house and we settled at a large oak table in the center on the library. Shelf after shelf of ancient-looking books surrounded us, filling the air with a musky scent.

Andrew ran his fingers over the line of Christie's sale ledgers, until he found the one for our year.

There, clearly in black ink was written proof that the painting had been purchased by the Jaeger family. Copies were made and the rest of the paperwork compiled. After an hour I had what I needed to proceed.

With a glance at my phone I was disappointed to see no reply from Logan. At least I could show this as evidence to Tobias that I'd tried to contact him.

I respected Tobias's time and he needed to respect mine. No matter how sexy that dominating tone of his was, I wasn't dropping my plans on a whim to please him. I'd already compromised my usual high standards for him at the palace and proven I was flexible—

I pushed aside these reckless thoughts of him.

And signed Christie's visitor's ledger, scribbling a side note referencing the reason for my visit. I slid the book back to Andrew and smiled at the charm of still using a ledger.

"Old traditions die hard," he said knowingly. "I'll enter this into the database." His frown deepened. "You're not Bertram Leighton's daughter, are you?" He sounded incredulous.

"Yes, did you know him?"

"No."

"He passed away."

"I read his obituary in *The Times*. Online. Not the newspaper." He cringed. "Not sure why I said that."

"It's okay."

"I'm sorry for your loss."

"Me too. He was a good man."

"His collection?"

"Most of it gone."

"A house fire?"

"You read about that too?" I lowered my voice. "It's heartbreaking to be honest."

"Zara, I'm so sorry. It must be hard trying to earn your reputation back."

I swallowed hard. "Are you referring to those dreadful rumors?" He looked apologetic. "You know my dad was vindicated, right? Those lies were disproven?"

"No one told you?"

My back stiffened. "About what?"

"Walter William Ouless's *St. Joan of Arc*."

"That went, too, I'm afraid."

"Your dad reported it destroyed?"

"Yes. He was devastated." Then I remembered that awful conversation with Nigel at The Otillie and a shudder ran up my spine.

Andrew steadied his gaze on me. "We are talking about the *St. Joan of Arc*? Painted by Walter William Ouless?"

I shook my head. "Horrible rumor that it's still out there somewhere."

Andrew visibly paled.

I rested my hand on his arm. "Are you all right?"

"Zara, your *Joan of Arc* is here. The painting arrived at Christie's last night."

My mouth felt so dry my tongue wedged to the roof of my mouth.

14

My head spun with the revelation. My reputation would be compromised, my fledging career dashed on the rocks of the art world before I'd even had the chance to make my mark in the only vocation I'd ever known.

My father was a good man. A kind man. A man of principle and ethics. So why was this happening to me? How could a painting that my father had told me had been destroyed, be here?

"We've yet to authenticate it." Andrew's voice sounded far off.

"I'm sorry?" My focus returned to his hand resting on the doorknob.

"*St. Joan* hasn't undergone any forensic tests yet. Just a visual by one of our analysts."

I swallowed past this lump in my throat. "Their conclusion?"

"Rudimentary."

His expression revealed they believed it was real.

He also looked regretful for even mentioning the painting

was here. Andrew hadn't accounted for dealing with a woman whose life was about to fall apart.

"Sure you want to do this?"

I gave a wary nod. It was too late to take a step back and think this through.

Andrew turned the handle—

St. Joan wasn't alone.

She hung at the far end of the room with a small tag hanging from her frame. I vaguely noticed the Renoir to the left of her. To the right, Jan Gossaert's *Portrait of a Merchant*, the subject's condemning eyes watching me...

I began the journey toward her.

As a child I'd never truly comprehended Walter William Ouless's work. I'd been too young, too naive to respect its true greatness. I'd always been more interested in my dad's other paintings, like that Raphael in his office, or the Renoir in our living room, or my beloved Vermeer that welcomed guests, though few, into the foyer.

Walter William Ouless's *St. Joan* had always intimidated with the revelation no one could live up to her.

Ironic how this painting now had my full attention.

"She shouldn't be in here," came a woman's whisper from behind me.

Drawn into the canvas, recognizing each stroke of the brush, each minute crack of wood, the strength in her left hand as she raised the hilt of her sword before her...

Real.

No scientific test would discount the profoundness of her authenticity. My heritage had been hidden behind a veil of lies. A sob escaped and I cupped my palm against my mouth to prevent another.

Ouless had immortalized this now martyr, bestowing her with a strong and beautiful face, lush brunette locks, and had clothed her in armor, that red sash over her left shoulder a flash of color to represent the blood she'd sacrificed for her cause—that sword held up proudly before her, proving her commitment to serve.

Joan had given her life for France, for God, a woman's martyrdom too profound to comprehend. Standing before her I knew she was no longer ours because we didn't deserve her. The truth of our unworthiness radiated from her.

Self-hate spilled out of me as I struggled to catch air in my lungs.

"Zara." The voice sounded familiar, a kindness in his tone.

Those butterflies returned to my chest, nudging out this dread.

"Turn around," he said.

Unsteady, this numbness enveloping, this terror holding me fixed and trembling.

A hand swept across my face and I closed my eyelids against the palm resting against them. This cruelest spell broken.

I spun around—

Tobias opened his arms, and I fell into them, warm and comforted against his chest, resting my cheek against him.

"I'm here now," he said.

Nuzzling in, a sense of refuge in his hold and his familiar scent soothing these spiraling thoughts.

My life had been a lie. Another sob escaped my lips.

"Listen to me," he whispered, "we're going to walk out and you're going to show no emotion. Do you understand?"

I peered up and blinked at him, vaguely aware he wasn't meant to be here. He looked dazzling in a three-piece suit.

"Zara." He tightened his grip. "Show no reaction."

"It's her," I stuttered out.

"We don't know that. There's been no forensic tests to

prove it." He rested a fingertip on my lips when I protested. "I need you to trust me."

I went to answer but the words failed to leave my lips.

He glanced over at Andrew, who was still standing respectfully at the back of the room. Tobias gave him a reassuring smile. "Looks like a fake."

I gripped Tobias tightly, hating this lie and feeling this betrayal of *St. Joan* twisting my heart. My fingers curled in his shirt as I silently pleaded with him to let me take her home.

But she wasn't mine anymore. Someone else had claimed her. Someone who must know the truth.

"Zara, we're leaving," he said. "We'll head out gracefully. Speak to no one."

Another nod as I crushed against his side, his arm wrapping around me as he led me toward the door.

We walked past Andrew and the woman beside him, a fortysomething curator with overly bleached blond hair and her concerned expression following us out.

Tobias snapped a command into his phone. "Bring the car round." He shoved it back into his pocket.

Out through the empty auction room, down the hallway, Tobias offering a polite smile to everyone we walked past.

The chill of the night met us when we stepped outside.

Puffing out cold air, proving autumn was barely holding on before winter.

That familiar silver Bentley pulled up to the curb and we hurried into the backseat. I recognized Cooper.

I sank low into the leather, shivering, my hand cupping my mouth to hold back the sobs.

Cooper gave a kind smile in the rearview. "Where to, boss?"

"Ms. Leighton's place." Tobias pulled me into a hug. "Fast as you can."

I managed to make it to my apartment before breaking down.

Vaguely, I was aware Tobias had followed me into my flat, but I was too busy crying into my pillow to give him much thought.

My dad had stood right beside me the night of the fire and together we'd watched our home go up in flames. We'd silently begged the firemen to move faster, save what they could. But afterward when the wreckage was examined, there came the awful realization the rest of the paintings were gone. Only the ones we'd managed to carry out had survived.

How had I not seen through his lie?

I'd stood right by his side outside the gate, both of us shaken from sleep, caught up in terror at what we saw. Our lives had gone up in flames.

Were there more paintings out there?

I'd trusted Dad more than anyone. He'd lovingly called me his "angel." Yet he'd betrayed me like I'd never meant anything to him. Left me with nothing but a legacy of shame. With him gone it would be me who would have to face the art world, the press and the inevitable fallout.

My life was over.

"Can I come in?" Tobias stood in the doorway.

My answer caught in my throat and to hide my embarrassment I buried my face into my tear-soaked pillow.

The bed dipped and I felt him sit close. "Made you some tea," he said softly.

"Don't deserve a cup of tea."

"Zara, the painting hasn't been authenticated—"

"I recognized it."

"Well, maybe your dad sold it before the fire? Perhaps he didn't tell you?"

I lifted my face and stared at him, swiping at tears. "He ran his fingers through the ashes of where *St. Joan* had once hung and sobbed his precious painting was gone."

"I'm sure there's a good explanation."

"It doesn't make any sense. Art was his life."

And at times it had felt like he'd loved art more than me.

"Apparently, I'm quite the tea maker," he said. "Here you go."

"I'll never breathe again." I buried my face deeper.

"Please, sit up and take this mug out of my hands before I get third-degree burns."

I turned and pushed myself up and rested back against the headboard. "You made me a cup of tea?" I took it from him.

"Why do you Brits call it a cup when it's a mug?"

"Don't know." I wiped my nose with my sleeve.

"Because most of you are bat-shit crazy, that's why." He reached for the box of tissues on the side table and handed it to me. "Anyone eating Marmite needs their head examined."

"I like Marmite."

"I rest my case."

I giggled but it morphed into a moan of despair. "He must have sold them and hung fakes in their place. Maybe he did it to defraud the insurance company? The art world? Surely he'd have considered they could have turned up?"

"Maybe he needed the money?"

"No, our estate was fine." I brought my knees up and rested my mug on them.

"What was his reaction? When he realized *St. Joan* was destroyed?"

"Devastation." My thoughts carried me back to that fire, the way he'd seemed so lost in thought, so dazed, shock stunning him into silence for the days and weeks that followed.

I'd also lost some part of my dad that night.

"It's not like he ever painted," I said. "He loved art but

didn't have a talent for it himself. Perhaps if he had I'd have given more thought to those accusations."

"Do you paint?" he asked.

"No, you?"

He shook his head. "Dabble in watercolors sometimes, but nothing worthy of anyone seeing them." He winked. "A fox or two."

"I'd like to see them."

"How old were you?"

"When the fire happened?"

He gave a nod.

"Ten. Can't believe this is happening now."

"Where was your mom?"

"She died when I was two."

"I'm sorry."

"This was her place."

He looked around the room and then gave me a comforting smile.

"Logan texted you?"

"I'm glad she did."

"That's why you were so close to Christie's?" I asked.

"Thought I'd surprise you at the auction house and take you out to dinner."

My tea was a golden brown and tasted how it looked, brewed to perfection and soothing. "You shouldn't be seen with me." I realized. "Not with this scandal. Your gallery in LA will suffer. Not to mention your reputation."

Perhaps...before this revelation there might have been a chance for us.

I scolded my rambling thoughts as I realized Tobias was just a friend who'd caught me midfall and had merely paused his day to be here.

"I can handle it." He frowned thoughtfully. "Let's wait and

see what they say before we condemn you to a life of cleaning chimneys."

"Cleaning chimneys?"

"Isn't that what happens to English people when they've fallen on hard times."

I burst out laughing.

He gave a shrug as he grinned his mischief. "Maybe I do admit to reading too much Charles Dickens as a boy."

"Why were you at The Otillie?" I said. "The night we met?"

"I was invited."

"By who?"

"Miles Tenant."

Of course, the director of the gallery.

"He's always been kind to me." I raked my fingers through my locks to tame them a little. "Not sure how he'll react to this. Probably give me back *Madame Rose*."

"I'll talk to him. Still, you've nothing to worry about as far as I can see."

Yet Tobias had trusted my ability to spot a fake when he'd taken me to the palace with him.

I pulled the blanket higher. "Miles was so generous to hold that reception. God, it was also meant to be a celebration of all my dad did for the art community."

"Let's not condemn him just yet."

No amount of regaling how my great-great-grandmother had been the toast of the royal Russian court would soften the strike of this current scandal.

It wasn't as though I'd seen behind the veil of Tobias's personal world, either; his mercurial, complex nature was as compelling as those beguiling hard edges that he never failed to show.

These unfolding moments where he revealed his true nature felt like a rare gift. This man was letting me in.

"You were very quiet that first evening we met at The Otillie?" he said.

"I was a little intimidated."

"By me?" He looked surprised and finished the rest of his tea and set his mug on the side table. "I'd borrowed the staff room to get changed. I'd have used Miles's office but he'd had it painted."

"The restoration program." I wrapped my hands around my mug. "Where had you come from that night?"

"Dinner with friends."

"Perhaps I should have asked you this before we shagged in my office, are you seeing anyone?"

"No."

"Me, neither."

"I know." He gave a crooked smile. "Art's your one true love. See, I remember."

My insides coiled with excitement that he seemed to get me.

"I love The Otillie," he broke the silence.

"I remember you saying that at the meeting with Adley."

"You blew us all away with that trick you pulled on the Pollock."

"Trust me. That came from years of study and my unhealthy obsession with art. Too many evenings spent alone at the National."

"There's worse things in life to be obsessed with." His gaze fixed on mine.

I never wanted him to leave. "What time is your flight?"

"Anytime I like." Tobias kicked off his shoes and joined me on the bed, sitting shoulder to shoulder next to me.

I looked at him. "You have a private jet, don't you?"

His face crinkled into a smile.

"Your pilot doesn't mind being on call?"

"I don't mind."

"You pilot your own plane?"

"Matter of convenience."

My jaw gaped. "That's impressive."

"You recognized a Pollack from across a room. *That's* impressive."

"When did you learn to fly?"

"Twenty-one. Family tradition." He broke my gaze.

I wondered if he was thinking of his parents and I inwardly cringed, hoping it hadn't been his dad flying the plane that went down.

"So do you normally sneak into homes and search out paintings?" I said.

He grinned. "Sometimes."

"You're not going to tell me how you knew that painting was there, are you?"

"I always protect my sources."

"So when you're not running around town hunting down pieces of art to buy up, you're running a tech business?"

"Yes."

"In LA?"

"I also have an office in Canary Wharf."

There was no surprise Tobias owned offices in one of the swankiest districts in East London, with some of Europe's tallest buildings.

My heart did a leap when I imagined visiting him there.

"We have a nice view of Cabot Square," he added.

"What kind of work do you do?"

"Design software, mostly."

"Are your inventions part of that?"

"Yes. We're currently developing virtual keyboards, phones, that kind of thing."

"How does that work?"

"Come visit me and I'll give you a tour."

"I'd love that." My toes curled with excitement.

He took my mug off me and rested it beside his. "You'll have to wear a hood over your face so people don't recognize you."

It was too late to hold back on my sulk.

"I'm joking, Leighton." He turned to face me.

He lifted my chin and leaned in to kiss me, his lips soft and gentle against mine, a contrast to the fierceness he'd kissed me with before.

"Maybe a quickie will help," I said.

"Who said anything about a quickie?"

Oh my God.

Tobias unbuttoned my blouse, making quick work of the rest of my clothes as he tugged me down to the bed. He remained fully clothed for now, and I felt vulnerable against his unmatchable strength, these tingles in my chest causing my breaths to quicken.

Shy of my nakedness, I held my arms against my breasts.

Tobias eased my hands away and his softness morphed into a raw desire. "God, at first I couldn't imagine how you'd fit into my life…it's so very complicated…but now, I can't imagine one without you. You take my breath away."

Would these words destroy me should I believe them?

A shiver of arousal alighted within. "I want to see your inventions."

"Do you, now?" He rolled onto his side. "I can show you one right now. If you like?"

"Really?

"I've yet to showcase it." He leaned in and licked around my nipple with the tip of his tongue and it beaded in response.

I sucked in a sharp breath.

His tongue swirling, lips sucking. "I'm rather proud of this brand-new invention."

"I can see why." I burst into a smile.

"Now this invention I'm about to show you is actually top secret." He rolled on top of me and began kissing my chest, moving leisurely down my abdomen and lower, trailing kisses as he went.

His head now between my legs, his short hair tickling my thighs.

"This one's going to need a lot of practice to refine." His tongue flicked over my sex and he strummed my clit with the tip.

"Oh my God." My head crashed onto the pillow. "I volunteer as a test subject!"

He chuckled in that deep husky way of his and set about suckling my clit, and I arched my back as my body went lax in his grip.

"Well, that's an interesting response from my subject. Something tells me this invention's going to be popular."

"Might want to trademark it!"

"You mean patent?"

"Yes, that's what I meant…patent." A shock of pleasure stole my breath when he circled his tongue slowly. "Oh, that's… amazing."

He owned my sex with his mouth, literally mastering with each stroke, his fingers peeling back my folds and lapping either side of my sensitized sex, proving he'd not only commanded in the boardroom but here too.

Wasn't I meant to be inconsolable? Hadn't my world just fallen apart? How did this virtual stranger have the power to soothe me beyond reason?

Don't think about that now. Enjoy it.

Enjoy him.

"Tobias, I'm going to come."

He growled against me as though his own arousal matched mine and I raised my head to watch this beautiful man focus between my thighs, my hand reaching out to grip his shoulder, digging my fingernails into his tattoo, taking in that intricate design, making out amongst those swirls and lines a small turtle in the center.

A rush of carnal want possessed me and I stared at the ceiling, mesmerized. Needing this so badly, more than breathing, I reached for his head and my fingers curled in his dark blond locks.

"Hands above your head," he commanded. "Wrists together."

I flung my arms up to complete my surrender, giving myself over, my sex now his to play with any way he wanted, trusting, giving up all control to *him*.

His mouth crushed back down onto me, filling me with these blinding sensations raking over my body, through me, and radiating out in waves of stunning pleasure, my body rigid when he reached up and caught my nipples in his fingers and began rolling and tweaking—

A moan escaped my lips and I was too stunned by bliss to move.

This climax sweeping me up and holding me in what felt like midair. Whimpering as I came, breaking through the silence.

Tobias took his time to bring me down, licking and kissing between my legs, and not letting up on his affection.

I cupped my hands over my face when he finally broke away. My cheeks on fire, my nakedness making me so vulnerable.

"Now that invention is still under wraps," he said. "I'd appreciate your discretion, Ms. Leighton."

"Little unknown fact about me," I said with a smile. "I'm an inventor too."

"Really?"

Shimmying down, I rolled onto my side and reached for him, unzipping his trousers and easing him out of his pants. I wrapped my fingers around his impressive girth and ran my hand up and down.

Tobias rested his head on the pillow and smiled down at me.

Swirling my tongue around the tip of his head, my eyelids fluttered at the thrill of his taste, so masculine, so virile, his skin silky smooth and taut, and I felt giddy with excitement when I sucked more of his pre-cum, greedy for more of him.

"This one is already patented I'm afraid," he said huskily. "But I'll let you use it."

"That's very generous of you."

His hand pressed me back onto him, his fingers curling in my hair and forcing the pace. "What you do to me, Leighton."

"Call me Zara, or I'll stop." A flick of my tongue teased around his head, running up and down the veins and worshipping every inch of him.

"Zara, Zara, Zara." He lifted his hips. "Oh, that's good, baby. Suck harder. That's it."

Taking him all the way back into my throat, I massaged him with my tongue and lips, from hilt to tip, his breathing now ragged, his stomach muscles tensing.

Knowing I was sending him into a frenzy like this, just how he'd done to me, made my pride soar.

"My sweet Zara," he whispered.

With my hand working him, my mouth lowered to suckle his balls, swirling my tongue around the delicate ridges, taking my own arousal to a fever pitch. My mouth now returned to the length of him, and took him all the way to the back of my throat, dragging my lips up to the tip and firmly down again, sucking in my cheeks as my hands cupped him gently.

"We need a condom," he said in a rush.

"I might have one."

"Might?" He sat up, half amused, half a man possessed as he gestured to me. "Hurry." He undressed quickly, removing his shirt and trousers in record time.

Scrambling, I dragged open the side table drawer and felt around for the packet. When he snatched it out of my hand with a devilish smirk, I squealed with laugher.

God, his cock looked beautifully erect as he rolled on the clear sheath, shiny now and rock hard, an unnerving extension of his powerful physique rearing majestically out of dark blond curls. A pure statement of power.

15

Rising and falling, my heart swelled as my body brushed against his.

Rising and falling, riding him swiftly, shuddering in ecstasy as I slammed down on him. His hips thrust to match my strikes with force, his face reading mine as though gauging my tolerance to the fiercest fucking.

Arching my back when he met my G-spot, my hair tumbling behind me, my fingers trailed over my breasts, only to be eased away by his hands. He took over pleasuring my sensitive nipples, blasting raw pleasure into them, bursting outward and downward and reaching all the way to my sex.

"Don't want it to end." I wanted to come again and again.

Just like I'd done half an hour ago when he'd pounced on me and pummeled me into a state of immovable bliss.

"We fit together perfectly, baby," he crooned. "Do you feel that?"

"Yes."

"Your skin feels like silk. I can't stop touching you." His hand reached between my thighs and his thumb circled, keeping his pounding inside me precise, revving me closer to the edge.

"Oh God," I said, "I love it when you play with my clit!"

"Jesus," he bit out.

Never had I felt so erotic, so feminine, and each time I caught wonderment as his gaze roamed over my curves.

"Titian would have killed to have painted you!" he whispered.

My gaze roamed over his sculptured torso and I knew I was making love to a sex god, a virile specimen of perfection, a sculptured art form who was breathtaking and talking and saying the kind of words I'd been starved of.

"I'm close, Zara." His jaw muscles tightened, his focus proven by that line of perspiration trickling down his brow. "I need you to come."

Unable to hold back anymore, my inner muscles milking him, my body crashing down hard to fill myself with him completely—

Snatched away into nothing but rapture.

"I like this plan," he said. "Come together." His body stilled beneath me, both of us coming hard, slick and wet from our mingled sweat, writhing in unison, losing ourselves, giving over to this moment and finally letting go.

Exhausted, I fell forward onto him and nuzzled onto his chest and rested my head there. Tobias slid me to the side with him still inside me, and he brought me into a tight hug and wrapped a leg possessively over mine.

We lay like that, not talking, the only sound was our contented sighs, the only sensation, his warm body against mine, our breathing in sync and his arms crushing me to him.

He'd brought peace to my storm.

Tobias only left me briefly to visit the bathroom and as he strolled away with that confident swagger, I ogled his sculpted back muscles and savored the way moonlight reflected off his impressive physique and my gaze drifted to his bum.

He turned quickly and grinned at me.

My hand slammed to my mouth to stop my squeal.

As he headed in I could no longer hold back my grin as this burst of happiness forced me back. My head met my pillow with a thump, my mind spiraling with thoughts of never wanting him to leave.

When he climbed back in, I felt safe again.

Easing back the blanket to expose him, I caught his amusement as I shimmied down and lowered my head to his groin.

"I want to know what this says." I ran my fingertip along the Latin inscription.

His cock was half-erect as it rested against his thigh; he could have been carved from marble he was so striking, those elegant veins, the ridged edges so exquisitely formed, and despite my closeness I strained to keep my focus on the Latin.

Tobias traced his fingers through my hair and found a strand to play with. "It's actually hidden down there for a reason."

My scalp tingled at his touch. "Now I am intrigued."

"This can be our little secret. I hide my ink so I'm not defined by it. Don't want to be seen coming."

"No pun intended." I traced my fingertip over the foreign writing. "Tell me about this one?"

"Promise to suck my dick again and I will."

"Deal."

"That was easy."

"Or, I could just memorize it and do a quick internet search on a translation site."

"Yes, but where's the fun in that?" He grinned and opened his arms. "Come here."

Beaming with joy, I moved upward and crashed against his chest and nuzzled in, melting as his strong arms wrapped around me. He reached for my faux fur blanket and pulled it up and over us.

His affection was keeping the world at bay. "Thank you."

He peered down at me. "What for?"

"Everything."

"Trust me, it's my pleasure."

"No one has ever touched me the way you do."

"I'm glad to hear it."

"I'm serious, Tobias. You have this way about you."

"You inspire me."

This ache in my heart morphed into a wave of dread as I realized this respite was merely borrowed time. Being in his arms was his way of comforting me. He couldn't prevent the inevitable. My body tensed at the thought of him leaving.

"Zara?" His gaze roamed over my face. "Yes?"

"It's time for you to come again." He reached down, his hand trailing over my abdomen.

I flinched at the erotic pulse when his fingertip found my clit.

My body trembled with the stunning rise of pleasure and my head crashed onto his chest as I squeezed my eyes shut, shifting my thighs slightly.

My fingers milking his forearms.

"See what I did there?" he whispered. "I've claimed you."

"Oh please."

"This beautiful pussy is now mine."

"Yes," I managed, my lips pressing against him, my tongue flicking and tasting his fresh sexy scent over his smooth, taut chest.

Wanting this to be true, needing to believe that after today he'd still want to know me, my heart aching with the suspicion that when my world inevitably fell apart, he'd be long gone.

"Rock your hips forward and backward," he whispered.

These erotic sensations caused my pelvis to shudder as I rocked against his hand.

"A little faster."

A throaty groan escaped my lips, this blinding bliss in my sex stealing my thoughts, my quickening pulse pounding, my breaths too ragged to control.

"Is that nice?" he said gruffly.

I managed a nod, this orgasm capturing me swiftly, unsure of where his finger stopped and my clit began, this delicate flicking morphing into a refined circling, proving he knew too well how to touch a woman.

His hand shifted and he slid two fingers inside me, the pad of his thumb now circling where his finger had been. I found my rhythm, riding his hand with steady thrusts, bleary-eyed, small sobs of need catching in my throat.

Tobias's lips pressed my temple. "God, you feel amazing, don't stop moving until you come, understand?"

A frantic nod.

"Look at me, Zara. Now give me permission to handle things from here for you."

Delirious, drowning in ecstasy, I tried to grasp his words. "Handle what?"

"Every detail."

"I don't understand."

"Open your eyes. That's it. Now look at me. Keep moving. Good."

"I'm going to come."

"Not until you say the words."

"You can handle everything." I was breathless.

He dipped his head to my ear. "Now you can come."

My mind and body splintered at the same time, thoughts reaching out to make sense of this, unsure why he'd want to take on the mess that was my life.

"Oh God," I cried out, trembling through this endless euphoria.

He flicked faster. "I'm going to watch over you. Do you want that?"

"Yes," my voice shaky. "Oh yes."

Shuddering through my orgasm, my core tight, thighs trembling, riding out these waves of pleasure, staring into his eyes, I fell deeper and deeper into the promise of him.

His fingers continued a steady beat, prolonging my climax on and on and on, and I laid my cheek against his chest and sucked in desperately to refill my lungs. My body stiffened and I moaned, coming harder still, caught in his grip and beholden to his brilliant fingers moving just so and extending this earth-shattering orgasm.

I collapsed on his side.

Tobias kissed my head. "It's going to be okay, Zara. I promise."

His words sent another thrill below as though his husky voice alone held power over me. This was the man I remembered from Oxford, the bossy, controlling man who'd persuaded me to strip down to my underwear and dress so provocatively.

It had felt like an awakening...

I couldn't work out which side of Tobias I liked more; there was so much more to him I needed to discover.

Lying safe in his arms, warm and snug by his side, with my leg thrown over him, it was easy to drift asleep.

Blinking into the darkness, remembering I had a gorgeous man in my bed, I reached for him, filled with disappointment when my hand ran over a cold sheet. I lifted my head off the pillow to check the time and caught a blur of movement at the end of the bed.

Tobias was sitting there. "Good morning."

He'd pulled on his shirt and underwear, his hair falling just so as though he'd merely dragged his fingers through it and it had fallen effortlessly into place.

I sat up and pulled the sheet around me. "What time is it?"

"Five."

Shaking off my sleepiness, I needed to brush my teeth. I needed my tea. "Good morning."

He rose to his feet and came over and sat on the side of the bed near me.

A rush of excitement raced through me as I roamed his beautiful face, his six-pack abs chiseled and kissed by the sun and conveniently visible through his unbuttoned shirt. His black boxer shorts taut around muscled thighs.

A grateful sigh escaped me. "Couldn't sleep?" I blamed my strange bed for his restlessness.

"Did some work. Shot off a few emails from my phone. Texts. That kind of thing." He looked back toward the living room. "Didn't want to disturb you."

"We missed dinner last night. Are you hungry?"

"Only for you." He gave a cheeky grin.

I broke his gaze. "Hope you felt comfortable enough to explore my fridge if you wanted something."

His eyes crinkled into a smile.

"Thank you for being here," I said.

"Of course."

I was still in denial about seeing *St. Joan* last night. I wanted to believe it was a bad dream, a mistake, but I'd seen the evidence with my own eyes and the truth was starkly real.

That gut-wrenching fear circled my chest. "What time do you have to be at work?"

"Eight, maybe."

"You make your own hours?"

"Pretty much."

And then I realized I'd have to face Adley this morning. Hopefully I'd get the chance to warn him about Christie's before anyone else did.

Tobias tilted my chin up. "You told me something last night…"

He really did have dreamy irises, and that dark blond hair crowned that handsome face; his five o'clock shadow enhanced his edginess.

God, what he'd done to me.

My sex tingled in memory.

He trailed a fingertip along my collarbone. "You mentioned you saved a few paintings from the fire?"

I rubbed my eyes, not remembering I'd told him that. "Yes, I carried three and dad carried the big one."

"Where are they?"

"Safe."

"Are they still at your old house?"

I pulled the sheet up and over my head and hid from him.

His soft gasp proved his realization.

Tobias dragged the sheet off me slowly until I had no choice but to look at him. His face lit up with intrigue. "Show me."

I slid off the bed and wrapped the sheet around me, fully aware his eyes drank me in as I scrambled to cover myself. My self-consciousness returning as though we'd not already seen each other naked and I'd not just had the most incredible sex of my entire life.

I padded out and down the hallway and into the spare bedroom. There wasn't much in here, just a bed with an antiqued white frame made to match the soft hue of the Laura Ashley wallpaper. There was that corner wicker chair that no one was ever going to sit in. The rose prints that hung on the far wall offered some red into the mix and balanced out the blue.

Tobias's gaze searched the room but his expression was unreadable. He leaned against the doorjamb with his arms crossed against his chest as he watched me—

Gripping the left side, I slid the walled antique mirror all the way to the left and revealed the cupboard-sized safe hidden behind it. After tapping in the ten-digit code, I waited for the mechanism to release. The door opened and I reached in and dragged out the large wooden pallet.

"Do you need a hand?" He stepped forward.

"I've got it, thank you." Carefully, I laid it flat on the carpet and slid off the lid.

He came over and knelt beside me. "What do we have here?"

I lifted out the first painting, which was separated from the others by brown paper. "Vermeer." I watched him swallow back his surprise.

Tobias's irises went from green to gold as his gaze swept over the portrait of the young woman staring back at us, her beauty mystical, the light shining off the canvas bringing a brilliant aura over her delicate face.

I rested that aside and went back to the wooden pallet and eased the next frame out.

Tobias's jaw gaped. "Da Vinci?" His eyes roamed over the sketch of a cannon gun, the image stained cream and brown, and faded only slightly by time.

"Did you know da Vinci was left-handed?" I said.

"Might have read that somewhere." His tone was soft.

I studied his face for a moment, seeing nothing but trust in his expression. The quietness lent itself to the reverence this moment deserved.

"I've never shown anyone this," I whispered.

"I already feel privileged, Zara."

"And this one." Sucking my bottom lip, still dazed from

last night, I peeled back the protective wrapper, revealing the final painting below.

Tobias's gaze swept over it in awe, his words just above a whisper. "Ho-ly shit."

16

A flawless rendition of Adam's elegant hand reaching out to the mighty hand of God, dramatically painted on a single panel in a breathtaking demonstration of how the artist practiced his vision of the *Creation of Adam*.

The final masterpiece was now set in the ceiling of the world's most prestigious palace, the Vatican's Sistine Chapel.

Sipping from our freshly brewed mugs of tea, Tobias and I sat on the floor of the spare bedroom sitting side by side, silently admiring its profoundness.

I'd propped up the Vermeer and da Vinci's sketch on either side of this tour de force, leaning their frames against the wall.

"You have a Michelangelo?" Tobias shook his head in disbelief.

It was impossible to comprehend the reality of us staring at a 1508 origin of one of the world's greatest treasures. The blue-white panel was cracked. But that took nothing away from the anatomically correct fingers nearly making contact and the profoundness that God had yet to touch Adam and yet, miraculously, his spiritual force had effortlessly breathed life into God's creation of man.

Tobias covered his face with his hands as though needing a moment to process what he was looking at.

"It's just that…" I strained to find the words.

His expression was full of understanding. "Letting these go would be you finally saying goodbye to your dad."

Tears stung my eyes but I pushed them back. "Yes."

Tobias understood. He truly got the ridiculousness of a girl living in a West London flat keeping priceless art hidden away.

"Oh, Zara." He reached out and hugged me into him.

"Isn't it beautiful?" I said.

"All of them are." He raised his hand to emphasize. "I'm lost for words."

"Dad had the Michelangelo privately authenticated in Italy. He would have made a fortune if he'd sold it. See, that's why I don't understand any of this. We never needed the money. Whatever his motivation wasn't about that."

"Your dad was a remarkable man."

I looked over at the paintings again and my heart ached for the ones we'd lost. "If someone stole *St. Joan* before the fire and replaced it with a fake do you think my dad would have noticed?"

He gave a slight shake of his head as if to say we'd never know.

"I have to phone Christie's," I said.

"Move forward cautiously."

"Yes, you're right."

"They can't stay here, Zara."

"Because of those thefts?"

"No one knows you have these here." He studied my face. "Right?"

"My friend Clara does."

"You trust her?"

"Of course."

He kissed the top of my head and I sensed that was his way of gentle encouragement. "Would you like them for The Wilder Museum?" I asked, my toes curling with the realization I was letting them go, *finally*.

He let out a long rush of air. "That would be something."

"I have the paperwork. The provenance goes all the way back. It's quite impressive. Dad had it in a box in his office safe."

"It survived the fire?"

"Thank God. The only photos of my mom were in there. I can help arrange to have these shipped to America if you like? Get the paperwork started."

"That's incredibly generous of you, but I think the best home for them is The Otillie. That way you can visit as much as you like. And know they're safe."

"Yes, you're right."

"Let's take them over tonight?"

I gazed at them lovingly. "Tomorrow. That way I get to enjoy them one final evening. When are you flying out?"

"I'm pushing my travel plans for now."

I cupped my face with my hands as a thrill of happiness washed over me.

He laughed brightly. "Miles Tenant is going to flip out when he sees what you have."

"Don't tell him where I've had them hidden."

"It'll be our secret."

"Hungry?"

"I should probably go." He took my hands and gave them a comforting squeeze. "I have an early meeting with a team of techies who flew in from Japan. Otherwise you couldn't drag me away."

"Were you planning on flying out afterward?"

"My schedule allows for versatility."

"Come on." I pushed myself to my feet and reached for his hand. "I'll make you some toast."

"How about a coffee?"

"I can do that."

Tobias waited in the living room as I poured freshly brewed beans into the filter and turned on the coffeemaker.

Staring out of the window, I tried to fathom this array of emotions sweeping over me. An overwhelming excitement that he felt the same way.

This gorgeous, incredible man wanted to be with me...*me*?

I searched my cupboards for that travel mug I rarely used. Within a few minutes I rejoined him.

He was standing by my hallway table—

Tobias was fully dressed now in that black bespoke well-fitting suit. I'd been too distracted to truly notice it yesterday, to see how gorgeous he looked during my crisis at Christie's. He moved with a masculine refinement as he turned to look at me.

"Hi." I smiled.

"Hi." He gave a coy smile and turned away, his gaze finding the Jaeger file. "Are you part of this investigation?"

"Yes, that's why I was at Christie's yesterday. To check on the provenance." Dread swept over me that in the hours ahead I'd have to face my work colleagues and go over everything and try to make sense of this mystery.

Tobias beamed my way when he saw the Sleeping Beauty travel cup I was holding.

It was impossible not to admire his stature. He had a commanding presence and I took advantage of drawing on his strength.

"Do you take sugar?" I asked.

"No, thank you, though." He took the mug from me. Tobias's focus returned to the file and his frown deepened.

"They had an Edvard Munch stolen," I said. "Isn't it terrible?"

"May I?"

I gestured he could.

Tobias opened the file. "Everything is here?"

I gave a nod. "The family is all set to submit their insurance claim."

"Any lead on the heist?"

"No evidence left. That's not been officially released yet. It was a professional job apparently."

"You found no discrepancy in their provenance?"

"No." I joined him by the table and stared down at the file. "Neither did Christie's. Why?"

Tobias frowned. "Jaeger's a German name?"

"Yes, but the Edvard Munch's provenance was tracked through Norway."

"Interesting." He peered down at the photo of Bill Jaeger's grandfather standing before a marble fireplace. The man stared directly at the camera. A few paintings hung on the walls behind him including that Edvard Munch.

Tobias turned the photo over and examined the paper. "Kodak?"

"Kodak was making this photo paper back in 1888."

"You've thought of everything, then?" He gave a thin smile.

"The police believe all those art thefts are connected in some way."

"Interesting." His grin widened as he checked the lid on the Sleepy Beauty mug. "This won't eviscerate my manhood at all."

"I make great coffee."

"Then it's worth it."

I stepped forward and wrapped my arms around him. "Thank you for everything." Resting my head against his chest, I swooned when I felt his right arm wrap around me, and he kissed the top of my head as he held me.

Reluctantly, I let go, not wanting to make him late.

He shrugged on his coat and then reached for his scarf, wrapping it around his neck and giving the knot a European flair.

"Last night..." I began.

"Yes?"

"Not sure I'd have made it out of Christie's alone."

Tobias was seemingly lost in his thoughts. "I'm glad I was there."

He had been kind to me but my guard was still up and no matter how incredible last night had been, I had to remain realistic. Tobias had comforted me through the first night of what would no doubt become a terrible ordeal, and my joining the dots all wrong was going to end in heartache if I wasn't careful.

And my father's legacy was about to lead me on into hell.

"I meant what I said, Zara." Tobias raised his chin. "The art world doesn't intimidate me like it does you. I make my own rules. You've nothing to be frightened of."

Yet facing the day could only be held back for so long.

After opening the front door for him I leaned against the doorjamb and wrapped my arms around myself. It was impossible to grasp that he still wanted to be with me.

He slid past me. "I'll call you, okay?"

Tobias kissed my cheek, and I closed my eyes to savor these final seconds with him.

When I locked the door behind him my body ached with the loss of his presence. Last night had been truly heart-stopping and I promised myself I'd hold on to these feelings to get through the day.

My gaze returned to the hallway and rested on the Jaeger file.

Navigating the many cubicles already filled with arriving employees, I maintained my forward gaze, not wanting to catch sight of any faces that might confirm rumors of *St. Joan*'s re-emergence had reached Huntly Pierre.

In a weak attempt to try and cheer myself up, I'd dressed in my favorite Ann Taylor little black dress, and these stilettos were now back on my stockinged feet, having come off when I'd made my usual ascent up the stairs. I'd thrown on this red silk scarf to add a touch of color and dabbed it with Elizabeth Arden's Green Tea perfume.

Making a beeline for my office, I hurried on in and shut the door behind me. I'd made it.

Though the worst still lay ahead, I was a step closer to getting this day behind me.

A small box rested on my desk and it was wrapped in a gorgeous golden bow. I threw my handbag onto the corner chair and almost pounced on the box.

Like Tobias had pounced on me last night.

Thoughts of him made my chest flutter...

I loved presents, especially having rarely gotten them and rarer still seeing the box covered in elegant paper with a pretty bow. After tearing it open, I set it on the desk and lifted the lid—

Upon a bed of black velvet rested a sleek silver screened phone.

Tobias.

He'd promised to get me a new one. I hugged it to my chest and drew strength from this rush of excitement that he was still in my life. With a flick of a button the screen lit up and I laughed when I saw the wallpaper set to a geisha girl.

A text appeared. Have a lovely day. Everything will be fine—Tobias.

I texted back, You shouldn't have, but I love it. Thank you!

Giddy with the idea of seeing him again, I grazed my lower lip with my teeth, anticipating if that meant another night of lovemaking with Tobias Wilder.

That Charles Dickens's quote from *A Tale of Two Cities* burned up my brain: "It was the best of times, it was the worst of times…"

Tobias: How are you doing?

I'm okay.

Tobias: Chat later?

I texted back: I would love that!

Tobias: Looking forward to it. Call me if you need anything!

Examining further, the phone was fully loaded with songs, but more thrilling still was seeing Tobias's phone number.

He was quite possibly one of the most thoughtful men I'd ever met. And he'd bought me a phone. A nice new shiny high-tech gadget that connected me right to him.

My gaze drifted over to Canary Wharf, and I wondered which one of those towering office buildings belonged to him.

That Blake on the wall drew my attention.

I let out a sigh of admiration for a piece of art that seemed to change before my eyes, those vivid greens morphing into brilliant blues depending on the way it caught the light. Liza's genius was an understated creation.

Settling into the morning, I grabbed a tea from the staff coffee room and returned to my office, needing one final read-through of the Jaeger file. Keeping my door closed for now may have been construed as a little standoffish but I needed to concentrate.

Working methodically from form to form, I couldn't find a flaw in the Jaeger case.

Taking one last look at the photo, I double-checked the date of the Kodak paper manufacturer just to be safe.

My heart went out to Bill and Patricia Jaeger and their ten-year-old twins. The photo of them had been taken by the press the day after the theft. Printed off and placed in their file to add a personal touch. They looked devastated, and I wondered what kind of an impression this would make on their children long-term.

Using my magnifier, I peered down at Bill Jaeger's grand-father. He was an elegant-looking man and you could see where Bill had inherited that strong nose, those kind German eyes and that dashing socialite demeanor that tangled with arrogance.

Looking closer at Hulbert Jaeger's clothes, there was nothing unusual about his suit, which was a clear reflection of the 1920s and inching downward his shoes checked out, nothing unusual there. Raising the lens, I studied his cuff links and then his wristwatch, slightly covered by a cuff.

Using the magnifier to again study the photo, I saw Hulbert Jaeger was wearing a Seiko Astron, the world's first quartz watch. A quick computer check showed that the company had first started selling watches in 1917. Visiting their website I admired Seiko's sleek designs and read up a little on them.

I sat back, stunned.

Needing a few more minutes to recheck the photo and gather my thoughts.

Quickly, I shot off an email to Abby, asking if we could all meet in the staff room. I wanted to share my new findings ASAP.

Her email replied briskly. Ten minutes?

I replied, Perfect.

A knock at the door startled me.

Instinctively, I flicked my screensaver up. "Come in."

Logan was already in the room. She shut the door behind her and rested her back against it.

I pushed myself to my feet.

"No need." She gestured.

But I was already on my feet and rounding my desk. "Can you thank Mr. Wilder for the phone?"

Logan's eyes widened as she looked at it and her frown deepened when she found the discarded box and its bow.

She was wearing a tight black Chanel suit and she looked stunning, wearing her usual sophisticated style with pure perfection, her makeup flawless, with not a hair out of place on her perfectly coiffed platinum chignon.

She came in farther. "Tobias filled me in on the incident at Christie's."

"Yes, we're waiting to see if it's authentic." I swallowed my fear but it wouldn't budge. I reached over for my leftover tea. "It's a little unsettling." It tasted cold. "Can I get you one?"

"Listen, Zara, we have a problem."

"Oh?"

"I understand that Mr. Wilder was seen with you at Christie's yesterday?"

"Yes, he was kind enough to—"

"Have you ever read or heard of any scandals or unpleasantries in Mr. Wilder's life?"

"No, I haven't."

She gave a knowing nod. "Thanks to me. He hired me to protect him in all legal matters. More specifically, to clean up his mess. Zara, you are an impending mess. You and I both know your family scandal is about to rear its ugly head and quite frankly, the shit's gonna hit the fan."

I reached up to my scarf and ran my fingers over the silk to loosen it, my heartbeat taking off at a rapid rate.

"You'll probably lose your job," continued Logan. "Huntly Pierre will attempt to save face before your reputation ruins theirs."

"What are you saying?" But I knew.

"Cut off all contact with my client. There will be no further interaction with Mr. Wilder, and should you reach out I'll slam you with a restraining order."

"I explained everything to Tobias."

"You can't use your wily ways on me, Ms. Leighton."

I blinked back the sting of tears. "I need to speak with him."

"Did you hear anything I just said?"

"You can't do this."

"I'm the one with integrity here, Zara. You were merely hired as our consultant. Your services are no longer required."

"Why are you doing this?"

"Seriously?"

I pushed her for an answer with a nod.

"Your father was embroiled in God knows what. Like most lies, it won't stay hidden for long. Perhaps you were privy to his criminal activity?"

"My dad was a good man."

"The evidence proving otherwise is at Christie's."

"How did you hear about it?"

"From Tobias, of course. We've both reassessed the situation and we're moving forward with closure with all contact with you."

"He just texted me and everything seemed fine."

"Don't make this any harder on yourself."

"We don't know if the painting is real yet."

"Seriously? You're not only an expert at spotting fakes, this one actually hung in your own home."

"What did Tobias tell you?"

She seemed to enjoy not responding to that. "Don't take advantage of his kindness."

It made me wonder if all those photos of Tobias escaping on his motorbike were of him trying to get away from her.

"I'm calling him right now—" I reached for my phone.

She got to it first and snatched it up. "I'm here on Mr. Wilder's behalf. I represent his wishes. Let's put this torrid situation to bed. Don't you want to be left with some dignity at least?"

"Please leave."

"I'm glad we've come to an understanding." She stepped back with my phone. "You won't need this."

"It was a gift!" I reached for it but the phone was already in her handbag.

"But of course you've fallen hard for the charismatic billionaire. You want to believe something more is possible. Woman to woman, stop embarrassing yourself."

"I object to that."

"If you care about Tobias, you'll do the right thing." She stormed out.

"Please tell your client we'll be in touch," I called after her.

"No need."

"Ruby?" I played my hunch. "Ruby Ryan?"

She paused in the doorway and twisted her head to the left, proving she knew that name. When she turned to face me, I saw the truth in her startled gaze and realized Tobias had used her elite membership to the private orgy to get us in.

Ruby was Logan's alias.

"You'll never see him again." She stormed off.

With weak legs I managed to make it to my chair.

I hated the idea Tobias might have attended one of those

parties with her. *No*, I reassured myself, he's already told you he doesn't share his women.

I'd merely glimpsed further into Logan's psyche; she was not only ambitious but also had a penchant for debauchery.

Mortified, I realized she'd seized my only way of contacting Tobias.

Logan's floral perfume lingered...

Sucking in a shaky breath I tried to center myself, draw on that courage I'd always managed to rally when life's edge went for my jugular.

I reached into my handbag and brought out my old iPhone. Its smashed screen was now an omen to all the crap I'd not seen coming. The thing still worked, thank goodness.

My gaze found those tall buildings rising out of Canary Wharf again. I was sure I'd find a number for Tobias's offices by a simple online search.

But what was the point?

My heart sank with the realization that if I was going down I had no right to take anyone with me, not Huntly Pierre, and certainly not Tobias.

Gathering my files I continued to prepare for that meeting I'd just asked for, determined to at least prove I had the talent for this job—

Even if it was my bloody last day.

All I had to do was keep it together and not embarrass myself by becoming a jabbering mess long enough to deliver what I'd discovered.

I was about to turn this case on its head.

Afterward, I'd offer Adley my resignation and hope he didn't accept it, and continue to do the right thing by putting my friendship with Tobias Wilder behind me.

Breathing through the pain, it was hard to work out which hurt more.

17

I was doing this.

Making my way around the cubicles and nodding to staff here and there, I tried to convey my usual chirpy nature. My smile might have been forced, but my enthusiasm to join the meeting was sincere. Maybe, just maybe, I could salvage my career at the wire.

Mostly everyone was gathered already, and it was a little daunting seeing Adley, Danny and Brandon all waiting on what I had to say.

Abby flew in and threw me an enthusiastic wave. "Got your email, Zara. You have something for us?"

A jolt of pride nudged me out of my melancholy. "I have something on the Jaeger case." I opened my file. "If I may?"

Adley gave a nod.

I slid out the photo of Hulbert Jaeger. "I studied the Jaeger file," I said. "There's a discrepancy." Their gazes locked on me.

I held up the photo of Hulbert for them. "This is staged."

"What makes you think that?" asked Abby.

I pointed to it. "This was meant to have been taken in 1920

of Hulbert Jaeger, their grandfather, and is meant to help prove the provenance."

"Looks authentic," said Shane. "Paper checked out."

I slid my fingertip and rested it on Hulbert's wrist. "Can someone please explain to me how Hulbert Jaeger is wearing a Seiko Astron?"

"It wasn't made yet?" asked Abby.

"This brand wasn't made until 1969," I clarified.

"Well done, Zara," she said.

"It's half-hidden by his cuff," I said.

"Look at this!" said Brandon as he tapped away on his keyboard. "You're not going to believe this."

A rush of excitement flushed my cheeks with the realization what I'd found really mattered.

"Got you, bitches." Brandon slapped his hand over his mouth. "Sorry, boss."

Adley gestured for him to continue.

Brandon slid his laptop around to show us the screen. "Just ran our Edvard Munch through the Nazi-era database."

My jaw dropped. "Our Edvard Munch is listed?"

"Hot as a jacket potato," said Shane.

"What's a jacket potato?" asked Danny.

"You call them baked potatoes," said Abby with a smile.

"Who cares," snapped Brandon. "Look, our Edvard Munch was once listed as being owned by a member of the Nazi SS."

"We never thought to check the Nazi database," said Shane. "The provenance looked solid."

"The painting came through Germany," I said. "Not Norway."

"And any painting coming through Germany in the 1940s has shaky provenance," agreed Adley. "We were thrown off by its history."

"Maybe the Jaegers know?" Danny suggested. "Maybe that's why they faked this?"

We moved onto our next agenda, Icon, and Adley pointed out it appeared the thief was becoming more brazen.

"A new clue has emerged," he said. "I received a call from the director of Interpol an hour ago."

We all leaned in, ready to hear.

"Interpol has kept this back until now," he continued. "It does seem relevant. There was a raven's feather left at the scene of the crime at the Jaeger home."

"Is he antagonizing us?" asked Danny.

"He's letting us know that no one will ever be hurt," I realized.

"'Cause he didn't hurt the raven at the Burells'?" asked Danny.

Adley seemed to give this some thought. "Icon's motivations are greed," he said. "If he is selling them on the black market to private estates, he's going to be caught. Sooner than later."

By then the damage would be irrevocable.

"The Met are holding a press conference later today," said Abby. "They'll be sharing with the public what they know so far about Icon."

There were so many questions to answer. With Abby leading the way, Shane, Brandon, Danny and I spent the rest of the day collating what we had and brainstorming how best to proceed.

We agreed to discuss our new concerns with the Jaeger family and hoped to garner a confession of sorts.

Chances were Interpol would find Icon first, but the high price tag on his reward had seen Adley giving us permission to at least try to beat them to the chase.

Adrenaline spiked my veins that I'd been accepted into

the team as one of them and I knew that Seiko watch was to thank. I prayed this wasn't short-lived.

After the meeting ended we agreed to reconvene on Monday, and were permitted to continue our individual projects at home as the best way to maintain our progress. That gave us three more days to study the file.

I'd left the conference room exhilarated right up until I remembered I still needed to speak with Adley about my own personal scandal.

I was merely holding my inevitable fall from grace at bay. I'd savored this brief interlude of popularity.

With this familiar lump in my throat, I made my way to his office. Adley wasn't there.

I stopped off at the reception desk to ask Elena where he was.

She finished up on a call. "Hey, Zara, heard there are exciting things coming out of the Icon meeting?"

"It's coming together," I said. "I'm looking for Mr. Adley?"

"He's visiting his mom. She lives in an assisted-living home in Kensington. He always goes there right from work on a Thursday. Is it urgent?"

"No." Though I wished I'd gotten this out of the way. "It can wait."

"Everything okay?"

"Kind of." I blew out a sigh of uneasiness. "Something came up yesterday, and I just wanted to keep Mr. Adley in the loop."

"Try his mobile?"

"Don't want to disturb him. Thank you, though."

"How would you like to join us for drinks? It's a Thursday tradition. It's me and Abby, Shane, Dan and Brandon."

"I think I'll go home." All this stress was starting to catch up with me, and I hadn't exactly gotten much sleep last night, merely a few hours in between my "Tobias time."

Vaguely, I wondered if he'd texted me.

After Logan had snatched my phone I'd probably never know.

"One drink?" said Elena. "You look like you need it."

"I do," I admitted. "I need a bloody big glass of wine."

Within the hour we'd locked up our offices and together with Elena, Abby, Shane, Danny and Brandon, made our way over to Covent Garden.

We settled at a corner table of the Coach and Horses pub. It didn't take long to realize this was a great decision.

The place had a modern, roomy feel, those black-and-white prints of old London covering the walls added a nice touch to the leather seating, private booths and dark wooden trim around the bar.

I stuck to just one glass of chardonnay, and began to relax a little.

The evening enabled me to get to know them all so much better. It was fun to hear Abby talk about how much she enjoyed journaling, Shane's love of Manchester United, and Brandon's obsession with Sherlock Holmes. Danny's enthusiasm for exploring London's historic sites was an inspiration and his passion invigorated mine.

The night out had been just what I'd needed to forget.

Huddled in my warm parka with my hood pulled up and warmed by the wine, I headed out of the pub and made my way toward Covent Garden tube station, dodging the other pedestrians.

Luckily, my old iPhone worked just fine and I popped in my earbuds and fired up my iTunes and people watched as the stations flew by.

I was still upset with Logan for stealing my new phone and

her ulterior motive was glaring. This wasn't about her protecting her boss—she was acting out of jealousy.

Still, in my own way I wanted to protect him, too.

18

After taking a leisurely hot shower, I wrapped a towel around my wet hair and pulled on my silk pajamas and threw myself into cleaning. This was the best way I knew to burn off nervous energy and hopefully get Tobias out of my system too.

I tackled the kitchen first and spaced out when I moved on to rearranging my spice rack. There was something comforting about normalcy and this also seemed to focus a part of my brain that problem solved.

I couldn't wait to visit The Courtauld Institute's library. The Witt's vaults held an impressive collection of well-worn books that could very well hold the clues we'd need, secrets that might connect all the stolen paintings. I felt like I was born for this kind of work.

The doorbell rang.

A quick glance in the bathroom mirror proved I was in no state to see anyone. I pulled off my towel and ran my fingers through my wayward damp locks. If it was Tobias, I'd probably put him off for good and get this heart-wrenching pain behind me.

The walk to my front door seemed endless and with each

step I regretted not dabbing my face with makeup. It didn't matter about my pj's, for goodness' sake, Tobias had already seen me naked.

Nervousness welled in my belly and my step quickened, all I could think of was having another chance to talk with him and get to explain what happened to his phone.

I flung open the door—

An ID was flashed in my face.

I stared beyond it at the pale, middle-aged woman, her salt-and-pepper hair highlighted by her face with etched hard lines around her mouth. Her formal trouser suit was covered by a long woolen coat. "Ms. Leighton?"

"Yes."

Her steely blue gaze moved past me into my flat. "I'm from Scotland Yard, ma'am. Inspector Ford. May I come in?"

My forearms prickled as I peered at her ID. She wasn't smiling in that photo, either. "What's this about?" I said.

But I knew, *St. Joan* had cracked open a can of worms. My life was about to nosedive.

My heartbeat took off at a rapid pace but I smiled through it, trying to look casually confident. A wave of guilt swept over me.

Yet I'd done nothing wrong.

"We're investigating an incident at Christie's. We're talking to everyone who visited the auction house yesterday."

"Oh, right, of course." I opened the door for her.

We made what felt like an endless journey to the kitchen.

"Sorry for this." I gestured to my hair. "Wasn't expecting anyone."

She waved it off with a smile and it was nice to see a flash of kindness. "Please." I pointed to the table. "Would you like some tea?"

"Love some." She dragged a chair and sat in it.

I busied with the kettle and put a tea bag inside a mug.

"You live alone?" She looked around.

"Yes."

She gave a slow steady nod. "Me too. Divorced. A kid in school."

"Sorry to hear that. About the divorce, I mean."

"We're much happier." She added a frown.

"How can I help?"

"You were at Christie's yesterday?"

"Yes, for work. I was checking on the provenance of a painting. I'm a forensic art specialist at Huntly Pierre. Provenance is—"

"I know what provenance is." She lowered her gaze. "Huntly Pierre's an exclusive place to work. Bet they pay well."

"Is this about that *St. Joan of Arc*?" I cursed myself for saying it.

She gave a slow steady nod.

A sharp knock startled me.

"That'll be my partner," she said. "He was trying to find parking."

"Oh, okay." I was so shaken I'd forgotten they traveled in twos.

"Ms. Leighton?"

I paused at the door. "Yes?"

"You don't seem too upset."

I blinked at her. "They haven't authenticated it yet." Somewhere in the far reaches of my addled mind I recalled Tobias telling me to say that.

"Wasn't that convenient," she muttered.

"Excuse me?"

Her pursed lips gave away her disapproval of something I'd done. That second knock startled me.

She gave a thin smile. "Can you let him in?"

Wasn't that convenient? Inspector Ford's words made no sense as I replayed them on my way back to the front door.

With the authentication process generally taking about twenty-four hours we were close to seeing scientific evidence to prove *St. Joan* was all too real. Though I didn't need a lab to tell me that no matter how much I wanted to believe it was fake.

I pulled open the door.

Tobias's grin widened. "It was the sexting, wasn't it?"

A rush of happiness swelled in my heart at seeing his friendly face and I beamed at him.

"Too much?" he added.

My grin faded as I glanced down the hallway for that second policeman.

God, Tobias looked gorgeous in his pinstripe suit, that black scarf wrapped around his neck just so, and his five o'clock stubble contradicting his otherwise snazzy appearance and making him ooze that bad boy aura.

He was holding up a lush bouquet of pink roses in one hand and in the other he was holding a Peppi's Kitchen Pizza box. The delicious scent of baked dough, tomatoes and mushrooms wafting; my stomach grumbled.

"The sexting?" he clarified. "I came on too strong?"

"Oh," I realized, anxious Logan might have read his texts. "No, I lost my phone."

"You only had it one day!"

"I'm sorry," I whispered.

"Maybe you lost it at work. Have you asked around?" He reached for his phone. "We can track it."

"Don't bother. Logan took it. She explained everything."

"Logan?" His frown deepened and I sensed his quiet resignation as it sunk in that I'd already gotten his message.

That kindness I'd seen in him was authentic at least.

"I thought you were away. I mean traveling?" Though he'd never actually told me where.

"Canceled it," he said brightly. "I needed to see you again."

Dread made my chest tight with confusion. "Tobias, you can't come in."

His gaze slid to my hallway and he blinked his concern.

I paused for a beat, realizing this was my chance to protect him and knowing full well this was the best way to do it.

His eyebrows raised in a question as he realized I wasn't alone.

"Yes," I managed.

His fingers tightened around the box.

I lowered my voice to a whisper. "You should go."

Dragging this goodbye out any longer was making things worse. All I wanted to do was fall into his arms and hug him.

"Thank you for everything," I said shakily.

Tobias lowered the flowers to his side and gave a nod of understanding. "Do you guys want the pizza?"

With a shake of my head I declined it. I'd never eat again from the way my stomach wrenched.

"What about taking your paintings to The Otillie?" he said softly.

"I'll take care of them."

He closed his eyes as though the embarrassment had caught up and then gave a reluctant nod.

With my chest tight and my throat hurting more than it should, I watched him stroll off.

Breathing through this doubt I questioned going after him.

With him out of sight the spell was broken.

I returned to the kitchen, telling myself I'd done the right thing, though doubting I had after replaying his expression.

After Tobias's compassion I'd betrayed him with the worst lie.

Trying to tame these trembling hands, I finished up making tea for the inspector.

"That wasn't him?" Her stare burned my back.

With a shake of my head I pretended to be focused on pouring hot water into her mug.

When the doorbell rang again I made my way back to the front door, concerned Tobias had ignored my attempt to send him away.

A rugged, tall man with a buzz cut raised his ID. "Sergeant Mitchel. Is Inspector Ford here?" His sharp gray eyes assessed me with the ease of habit and I tried to get a read on him too, taking in his trench coat that was seemingly a little too thin to hold off the cold.

I closed the door behind us and led him toward the kitchen.

The sergeant strolled beside me, carrying himself with the kind of confidence that came from a well-practiced routine. "Parking's a nightmare," he said. "Took me all this time to find a space."

"I'm sorry," I said, as though it was my fault.

Within a few minutes I made them both tea and sat opposite them, ready to face their questions.

The inspector talked me through my visit to Christie's and I explained how I'd intended to merely check on the provenance of an Edvard Munch and ended up discovering there was a painting there resembling the one that once belonged to my family.

"You were shown the *St. Joan of Arc*?" she clarified.

"Yes."

"Your thoughts?"

I shifted in my seat. "I'm waiting on Christie's evaluation."

"It looked like the one you once owned?" added Mitchel.

"My dad." I gave a nod. "I was ten when we had a house fire."

"It was meant to have been destroyed?" Ford flipped over her notepad. "Your dad filed an insurance claim? *St. Joan of Arc* by Walter William Ouless was included in that claim?"

Holding my hands in my lap I forced them to still. "I believe so."

Mitchel leaned forward. "Apparently, you have a knack for spotting fakes?"

My gaze stayed on his as I realized he'd spoken with Christie's staff who'd no doubt relayed to them about my time in their lab. I'd unwittingly proven my uncanny talent.

"It's a little confusing," I admitted.

"So it's the real deal, then?" said Mitchel.

My throat tightened as I fought with the answer. "I'm not sure…"

"Where were you last night?" asked Ford.

"Here. Why?"

"Alone?" Her tone cut through my resistance.

"No." I bit my lip. "I mean…"

My heart thundered as I ran through every way this could go and nothing looked good.

"Ms. Leighton?" Mitchel's fixed stare held mine.

"I was—"

"With me all night." Tobias stood in the kitchen doorway and threw me a comforting smile. "Pizza, anyone?"

Jaw gaping, my fear rose for Tobias's vulnerability as well as my confusion at having believed I'd locked my front door after letting Sergeant Mitchel in. Feeling dazed I watched Tobias casually wash his hands at the sink and then find four dinner plates. He sliced the pizza and placed them onto the plates and then handed them out to each of us. As well as one for himself.

"Where do we keep the vase?" he asked.

I pointed to the left cupboard and watched him retrieve it. Mitchel and Ford were also following his every move.

Tobias filled the vase with water and then dropped in the roses. "Looks like it's going to rain."

"This is Tobias." I forced a smile.

Ford and Mitchel introduced themselves. Their demeanors altered slightly, a visible shift in their level of respect, which was probably due to the way Tobias was dressed and his relaxed attitude.

"Tobias Wilder," he said with ease and leaned in to kiss my cheek. "See, I remembered, no anchovies. Do I get boyfriend points?"

My weak smile told him he did.

He also got my silent BAFTA nomination for the way he played the boyfriend role so convincingly. He even went into my fridge, pulled out a bottle of pinot grigio, uncorked it and poured two glasses of wine.

He handed me one.

"You guys are on duty," he said. "So I won't offer you one. Unless…"

"We're fine," said Mitchel. "Thank you."

Despite several gulps my mouth was still dry.

"You haven't asked why your girlfriend has two policemen sitting at her kitchen table?" Ford's tone was accusatory.

"I'm assuming you're here to apologize on behalf of Christie's?" He sat in the chair beside mine. "There's been a lot of confusion over a questionable piece."

I wanted to grab his arm and pull him out and privately ask what the hell he was thinking? And why was everyone talking cryptic?

"You're referring to the *St. Joan*?" asked Mitchel.

"Aren't you?" Tobias slid napkins toward them. "Here you go."

"We were asking Ms. Leighton about her whereabouts last night," said Mitchel. "Were you together all night?"

"Yes." Tobias bit into his pizza. "God, I'm starving."

I sipped my pinot and it tasted bitter.

"Excuse me for asking," added Ford, "did you both sleep in the same bed?"

Tobias shot me a look of affection. "Of course."

My blush burned my face.

"Do you take sleeping tablets?" asked Mitchel.

I shook my head. "No."

Mitchel turned to face Tobias. "You?"

Tobias shook his head. "Though I do admit to too much caffeine."

I bit into that slice Tobias was holding to my lips and a burst of tomato and basil melted on my tongue, these rich flavors and this crusty dough felt comforting. I'd not eaten since that packet of crisps in the pub and my stomach grumbled to remind me.

"Neither of you left this apartment?" said Ford.

A shake of my head as my cheeks burned up.

"What is this about?" I asked.

Tobias handed me a napkin. "I'm so happy to see you eat, Zara." He pointed to Ford's plate. "How is it?"

"Good," she answered in between chewing.

"Peppi's Kitchen." Tobias looked cheerful. "Just around the corner."

Mitchel pushed his plate aside. "Mr. Wilder—"

"Call me Tobias, please."

"Tobias, why would we need to apologize on behalf of Christie's?"

He shot them a look of surprise. "Seriously?"

The inspector narrowed her gaze.

Tobias glared at her and said, "Interesting technique to interrogate using the art of boredom."

Ford threw a wary glance at her partner.

Tobias reached for my hand and squeezed it. "Christie's had a break-in last night," he said. "You've not had the TV on? It's on the news."

"No, I've been cleaning." I used a napkin to wipe sauce off my lips. "Rearranging my spice rack."

Tobias looked amused. "Wish you'd waited for me."

I almost laughed. "Was anything damaged?"

"*St. Joan of Arc* was stolen," said Mitchel flatly.

Invisible icicles soaked into my bones as I replayed his words.

"Are you sure?" Blood drained from my face as I realized they were talking about my *St. Joan.*

Ford peered down at her notebook. "There's a lot resting on it getting authenticated. Isn't there?"

"Was anything else taken?" I managed to sound calm.

Ford's frown narrowed. "Just Walter Ouless's *St. Joan of Arc.* They did an inventory."

A chill ran up my spine at what this meant.

I'd lost St. Joan *all over again.*

Scattered thoughts came together in a collage of images as I marveled at Tobias's timing. He'd been one of the few people to even see *St. Joan* and, other than the staff, no one else knew about her.

And he was here, now, right when I needed him. He never did leave town when he'd told me he'd planned to. Instead, Tobias had turned up as my shining knight at Christie's.

Was the connection between us this profound or was something else going on?

My hand trembled as I reached for his, as though I'd be able to tap into his thoughts and see him more clearly, understand just what we were.

I needed to know what I meant to him.

"We're wondering on the motive?" said Mitchel.

"Isn't it always money driven?" said Tobias.

"Was there a power outage?" I whispered.

Ford's steely blue gaze held mine. "You've heard about Interpol's investigation?"

I swapped a glance with Tobias.

He looked remarkably serene, and I drew on his unwavering strength; my thoughts spiraling with just how well he handled this kind of drama. His ice-cool temperament impressive, the kind of nature that would be good for a thief like Icon.

Bloody ridiculous.

The stress was messing with my mind.

Tobias was an established businessman and a remarkable inventor who spent his free time as an ambassador for art.

I shook off this doubt and refocused on these questions I was going to have to get right.

"It came up in a meeting at work," I said. "The art thefts in London look like they're connected to the ones in Europe."

"There does appear to be a connection," admitted Ford.

"Only," I began, "all the others were from private homes."

"You're absolutely certain it's that *Joan of Arc* we saw yesterday?" Tobias asked. "They have a lot of paintings in there. It's a big place."

Ford's sympathetic gaze fell on me. "Afraid so."

"Tobias, you were there too, yesterday?" said Mitchel.

"I picked up Zara after work." Tobias reached for my hand and gave it a squeeze. "We were going to have dinner and then realized we just wanted a night in."

"If it's okay with you," said Mitchel, pushing himself to his feet. "We're just going to have a peek around?"

"Of course." Tobias held out his hand for the paperwork.

"We don't have a search warrant yet," admitted Ford.

"Ah," said Tobias. "Then it's a no."

Mitchel sat back down.

"It's okay," I said, "I've nothing to hide."

Tobias beamed. "Other than that priceless Michelangelo she has stashed away in her bedroom!" He roared with laughter.

I let out a feeble laugh.

Trying to fathom Tobias's motive for dutifully playing the boyfriend card, I reasoned he was the kind of friend who came through when you needed him.

Oh my God...

I'd locked my flat door and somehow he'd gotten in...

Yet, he was my greatest alibi in all of this.

"Michelangelo." Ford grinned at Tobias's joke. "Wouldn't that be something."

"Do you have the name of the owner?" Tobias asked flatly. "The person who dropped off the painting?"

I frowned, remembering Nigel mentioning it had turned up in Venice and wishing I'd paid more attention.

"That's confidential, for now," said Ford.

"The provenance would likely prove this painting belongs to your estate, Zara?" said Mitchel.

"The last time I saw it I was ten." There were more questions than answers.

Tobias smiled brightly. "It's a good thing it wasn't the real thing."

"What makes you say that?" said Mitchel.

"Didn't Zara tell you?" Tobias shook his head woefully. "The original was destroyed in a fire. Some idiot's gone and stolen a fake." He breathed in a sigh of relief and his gaze rested on the pizza. "Who wants the last slice?"

19

A chill of fear slithered up my spine.

Tobias was at the front door talking with the police. Their hushed tones possibly hinting at their realization of the distress they'd caused me. I heard the sound of the door closing and the latch being placed.

The kitchen door opened and Tobias strolled in. He eased my glass out of my hand and went ahead and poured more pinot into it and then refilled his own. He gave it back and then took his place against the counter, leaning casually and finally peeling off that scarf and throwing it aside. He picked up his wine and his focus zeroed in on me.

"None of this makes any sense," I said. "No one would risk being arrested for stealing a fake. How did they even know it was at Christie's? God knows how they knew it was real."

He blinked at me inquisitively.

The wine failed to quench my throat's dryness. "Tobias, what were you thinking?"

He didn't react, just continued to look calm and in control, his beautiful face staying as focused as when the police were here.

This silence raised the tension.

"What happens when they find out we've only known each other a few days? You acted like we've been together for years."

There was no way we'd managed to fast-forward to the kind of place where we looked like we'd been together any length of time.

"Have you quite finished?"

Pursing my lips, I forced back my response.

He looked thoughtful. "First, you accuse me of lying when you lied to me?"

"To protect you."

"I'm not the one who needs protecting. I was worried about you after not hearing from you all day—"

"Logan stole my phone—"

"I'll deal with her. You could have used a landline?"

"I don't have your number." I threw my hands up in frustration. "She threatened to put a restraining order on me if I reached out to you."

"When?"

"Today. I'll probably end up in prison anyway for bitch-slapping her."

He arched a curious brow. "I'll talk with her. She's out of line."

I pointed to the door. "I hated having to send you away."

"I was surprised after last night." His jaw clenched. "Logan went rogue. I'm sorry she upset you."

Logan had admitted she'd worked for Tobias for years and yet surely she'd well and truly overstepped her boundaries.

"Tobias," I relented. "What have you done? You lied to the police."

"Not necessarily. We are together. Aren't we?"

I set my glass on the table. "You want this?"

He came toward me and wrapped his arms around me. "God, yes."

I crushed against his firm chest with the kind of relief I'd not known I was holding in.

Breathing him in, nuzzling and refusing to deny myself him. "Why did you change your mind about leaving town?"

"I wanted to talk with you." He seemed conflicted. "About us."

I looked up at his gorgeous face, wanting to believe that, needing to, but was I willing to fall for someone so much like my father, a man just as mysterious?

"I had a suspicion there'd be residual details that might surface from *St. Joan*."

"Do you think it was Icon who stole her?"

He broke my gaze and stared off, seeming lost in thought. "Maybe."

"The police…do you think they believed us?"

"I gave you a solid alibi. Trust me, you don't want them digging around your office or your home, or more specifically your bedroom and finding priceless paintings stashed away in there. Even if they're locked away in a safe. Details like that tend to make the police antsy." He gulped his wine and looked revolted. "Where did you buy this?"

"Why?"

He blinked his disgust at the pinot and set his glass down. "I was keeping it especially for situations like Logan."

"Must I suffer too?" He gave a smile. "I need to explore your wine cellar."

"Funny. Look, I need to find out who dropped off *St. Joan* to Christie's. I have to ask them who they bought the painting from. Follow the provenance. I need to find out how anyone managed to bypass Christie's security. The police suspect me."

I ran my fingers through my hair. "Me, of all people? I have to find out if it's connected to those other heists—"

"You need to take a breath."

"This is my life we're talking about."

"I respect that. My team's on it."

"What does that mean?"

"This is a delicate situation that must be handled with precision."

"I've never experienced anything like this."

"I know." He shook his head wryly. "This is uncharted territory for you. I get that. My lawyers will talk with Christie's legal team—"

"How did you get in?"

His gaze narrowed on me.

"Your timing is uncanny. After I let Sergeant Mitchel in, I locked my door. You got creative, didn't you?"

He lowered his gaze.

"I'm not letting this go." I folded my arms across my chest.

"You've got me."

My breath stilted and my stomach flipped.

He raised his hands in surrender. "What gave me away? The report on how smart Icon is? How fit? Versatile? How brilliant and inventive he's proving to be? How dastardly he is to outwit the entire British police force along with Interpol who are tight on his heels?" He gave a smile. "Not to mention the reports on how handsome he is."

"This is serious. You know there's no mention of what he looks like."

"I confess. Somehow, in between running a billion-dollar company, landing my latest inventions and wooing you—"

"Toby!"

"—I'm just popping off to the Tate now, actually." He neared me. "Let me know if you need anything. Nice little

Rembrandt, maybe? How about a packet of Picasso-shaped gummy bears from the gallery store—"

I threw a tea towel at him, and he batted it away and laughed.

I crushed my body next to his and nuzzled in.

He wrapped his arms around me. "After nabbing those paintings, I hang them up in The Wilder and hope no one notices."

I tickled his ribs. "Thank you for being here. Are you sure you want to be associated with me right now? Maybe Logan's right?" I hated saying it.

"Of course I want to be here." He looked pained. "I thought I'd lost you."

"No." I rose onto my toes and pressed my lips to his. "I was trying to protect you."

"Zara." He nudged me against the wall and crashed his lips on mine, stealing my breath and stunning me into stillness as he trapped me there with his body, all firm muscle and uncompromising strength, his tongue lashing mine fiercely, his mouth forcing mine wider, his cock pressing against my lower abdomen.

Arousal blindsided me and my core tightened, my sex milking as though he was already inside me. His firm fingers ripped at my blouse, sending buttons flying.

His sharp tug at my bra yanked the cup down to free my nipple for his mouth. My head struck the wall when that shock of pleasure hit, making me needy as I responded to his firm suckling, his nibbling exquisite, the way he caught it between his thumb and forefinger to ease its pertness. It felt like a cord was attached from there right to my sex.

My thoughts swirled with confusion, the dread of having the police here, *St. Joan* now missing and my world spinning out of control.

He broke away. "I didn't lie to them. Look at us." His hand slipped beneath the waistband of my pj's and settled between my thighs. "I know you love it when I touch you like this. See how well I know your body. The way you respond."

The rhythm of his fingertip pressing my clit brought me close to the edge. He grazed his teeth along my neck, the warmth of his breath tickling, soothing.

"Tobias."

He pulled away and stepped back. "You're just so kissable."

"Help me understand all this."

"We both know that theft at Christie's looks suspicious. That's why you were first on their list of suspects. Look, Zara, the art world is full of wealthy collectors willing to do anything, and I mean *anything*, to get what they want. If they find a piece they want they'll go after it and nothing will stand in their way."

"Why are you helping me?"

"Because you're my girl. And you've already been through too much. You've risen out of a scandal that had nothing to do with you, and you're on the precipice of launching a stellar career. You're poised to make your mark. I admire that. You're ambitious because of your love for the profession and you see the true value of what art delivers. I won't see those wealthy collectors ruin you."

"You think they will?"

"You have something they want."

"What?"

"How can you be so sure rumors haven't surfaced about the other paintings you did manage to save that night?"

My legs weakened and my back pressed against the wall.

He stepped closer and took my hands in his. "I brought us food in because I figured it was best not to leave that Michelangelo unattended."

I stepped forward into his hug, resting my head against him, a pang of fear nestled into my chest when I realized that the thief might know where I live and worse still, might know about the paintings.

No one knows, I reassured myself, only Clara and Tobias, and I trusted them more than anything.

He hugged me tighter. "We take them to The Otillie. Tomorrow."

I held his gaze and conveyed how much his being here meant to me. Having a friend to navigate me through this storm meant everything. He was soothing this ache of uncertainty and supporting me in the best kind of way.

Tipping my chin up, I offered my lips to him and he kissed me leisurely, our tongues tangling. My body yearned for this, for him, for the way he mastered my body so thoroughly with his, the way he suckled at my neck, sending luscious tingles into my skin.

"I'm on the pill," I whispered.

His jaw tightened as he clenched his teeth, and my fingertips traced over his lips as I told him what I needed with that one gesture. Tobias's mouth brushed over my throat, his familiar fragrance of domination and sex rising, the heat radiating off him and sending shivers throughout me.

"You'll tell me everything," I said. "You share all you learn about where my painting came from."

"We'll never know if it was real."

I held his gaze; *I know.*

He gave a nod.

My forehead crashed onto his shoulder as I realized my dirty family secret had somehow been given a reprieve, and from the way he looked at me he knew it too.

My lips trembled. "I need answers."

He nibbled my earlobe. "We'll find them."

Yes, he had the resources and emotional stamina to do what I couldn't, but was I asking too much? Was he?

He caught me in that fierce glare of his. "Zara."

"You really want to deal with this?"

"Yes." His fingertips found my clit, making small circles…

Sending me into a writhing mess. "I need you inside me. Please, fuck me. Right now. Here."

His fingers left me and he made quick work of stripping me out of my pajamas.

Leaving me naked with my back pressed up against the wall, I drew from this alertness caused by the cold brick behind me; all senses hyperaware.

With a flick of his wrist he had his full length out, its rigidity nudging my entrance, and he lifted me up with ease and I flung my legs around his waist, allowing him to thrust deeper.

He slammed me against the wall and his cock slid farther in, bringing a luscious pang of taut pleasure, and my head lolled forward as I lost all will to fight back. All I needed in this moment was this, him taking me fiercely against the wall.

My vulnerability reached new heights with Tobias still dressed and me completely naked, my defenselessness glaring. The shock of this realization was short-lived as white-hot passion sent my hips into frenzied thrusts to greet his forced strikes slamming into me, alighting me, and I was stunned by the eroticism of being overpowered.

He sent my heart and mind reeling when he touched me, fucked me, controlled every aspect of my arousal to leave me breathless.

"I can't wait to fuck you properly, Zara."

"We are!"

"No, this is nothing compared to what I'm going to do to you."

Moaning as I neared orgasm, my teeth buried into his

shoulder tattoo just like I'd wanted to do from the first moment I'd set eyes on him, this man so vivid with dominance. A breathtaking vision of him furiously taking me.

His thrusts were frantic. "This feels amazing."

He crushed his lips to mine and his tongue fucked my mouth harder than it ever had, proving he meant it.

Frozen in a state of bliss, my sex gripping, milking, hungry for more of him, my clit a constant throb of need as his pelvis struck against it with an upward glide, sending deliberate shocks of bliss.

He pulled away. "I'm going to make it right."

With my legs still wrapped around him, he turned swiftly and moved toward the kitchen table. He swept off that wineglass with ease.

I barely heard the sound of it shattering on the floor. I was too gone to care.

He laid me back on the table, raising my legs and spreading them wide and resting the soles of my feet on each of his shoulders.

Tobias leaned forward and cupped the back of my head to rest it down. "Let me be everything you need."

His words rushed through my thoughts, sending ripples of desire into every cell, every sinew, and every inhalation of his cologne made me feel like he owned me.

My back arched. "Please."

He clenched his teeth. "Do you trust me?"

"Yes."

"There's nothing more wonderful than watching you come."

That was all I needed to free-fall into this blinding climax, my back arching further, my sex on fire with rippling ecstasy, my body rigid, my heart and mind yearning for everything he promised to show me.

My thighs slipped apart, unable to hold up anymore, and he caught them as they fell, holding them firmly and positioning my legs better for his access, to deepen his thrusts, his body taut and still with tension—

He was all hard muscle and ferocious control, his radiant jade irises morphing to emerald green. Then he closed his eyes, his face focused and his expression quietly powerful as he spilled his heat inside me, the rush of his cum tipping me over into oblivion...

Tobias's low grunts mingled with my own drawn-out groans, my body rigid and caught in this endless cycle of pleasure surging through my sex, my breathless sighs proving my need for this to never end.

Still coming, his hips steadily rocked in and out in this leisurely pace prolonging our pleasure, those shoves of power his only focus as his gaze roamed over where his cock glided in a continuous rhythm, and his fingers brushed over my slickness, stroking my cleft with affection.

Shuddering, I widened my thighs and tipped my hips upward, yearning for more flicking.

"You like this?" he asked.

I managed a nod as my cheeks flushed ever more brightly, my brow spotted with perspiration.

He used a single fingertip to circle my clit. "You're a goddamn masterpiece."

"You are." I breathed out in a rush.

Tobias carried me to the bedroom.

Weak in his arms, all I could do was close my eyes and surrender, my nerves raw from all that had happened.

I couldn't find the words to thank him for being here. Somehow, he'd convinced me everything was going to turn out fine. This man had superpowers when it came to making me forget.

Tobias stripped off the rest of his clothes.

That's right, I mused as my gaze drank in his sculptured body, remind me how lucky I am to have Tobias Wilder here in my flat, flexing those arm muscles as they reach for the blanket to pull it up over us.

I lifted my head off the pillow to admire my lover, who now lay beside me and looked just as sleepy. He sensed me looking at him and opened an eye and gave a devilish grin.

That gorgeous smile made my insides liquefy as he reached for me and pulled me over so my head rested on his chest. I let out a contented sigh of happiness.

How had I endured never knowing this man before? The way his fingers trailed up and down my arm comforting me, the way he tipped his head to kiss mine affectionately, were a reminder of what I'd been missing.

The rain striking the window stole my will to stay awake with its patter reminding us how toasty we were in here.

Sleep lured me into unconsciousness.

When I woke up it was to the sound of Tobias's low voice coming from the living room.

A glance at my bedside clock told me I'd slept straight through to 8:00 a.m. Thank goodness I was working from home today.

"No, you listen," he hissed. "It was a gift from me."

The edge in his voice startled me and I sat up and wrapped my arms around myself.

"I take it you read my messages to her?" he added.

His furiousness caused me to freeze.

"Never interfere with any decisions I make when it comes to Zara, understand? Do you understand?"

The severity of his tone reminded me of when I'd visited his home in Oxford, his uncompromising attitude forging ahead as he continued to master the conversation. I could only imagine what Logan must be feeling being on the other end. I felt sorry for her.

His voice softened. "I appreciate that, Logan. You know how I feel about you."

My breath stilted as I replayed his reassuring tone.

Quiet descended in my flat once more and I sensed he was taking the time to listen to her.

I slipped into my babydoll nightdress.

And tiptoed toward the living room.

The conversation with Logan sounded tamer now.

"It's looking good," came his husky voice. "I spoke with Magnus. He's in. He has the resources to deal with the level of attention this will bring. Well, I changed my mind. Made an executive decision." He listened a little more. "I will end this. It will be swift and sure. It will happen. And it will…kind."

He was talking about me.

A viselike grip tightened around my throat. Barefoot, I padded closer to him with my heart racing.

Tobias was dressed in that three-piece suit and waistcoat. He still had his back to me. His posture was stiff with tension and his left hand was clenched by his side.

"Give the phone to Coops." He turned and his jaw flexed tightly when he saw what I was wearing.

"Tea?" I mouthed.

"I made coffee," he mouthed back, and his gaze narrowed, those jade-green eyes hinting his appetite for me might be insatiable.

Still, doubt surged through me.

With a look of concentration, Tobias broke my stare and strolled over to the window, his focus centered on the street below. "Yes, Logan, I'm handling…it." He killed the call and remained transfixed by something on the street.

I stepped forward. "Everything okay?"

"You might want to put some clothes on."

"Why?"

"I've arranged for your paintings to be collected."

"What time?"

"Soon. I realized the ridiculousness of putting them in the back of my car. Or yours."

"They're in a pallet."

"They need to be handled by professionals, Zara. With expert supervision."

"I've taken good care of them."

He gave me a look that broke the truth out of its chains. I'd been negligent and had taken a risk keeping them here.

"If the police come back with that search warrant..." He let the sentence trail off and shrugged. "My team's discreet."

My brain told me not to go there and I ignored it. "Are you in a relationship with her?"

"Logan?"

I gave a wary nod.

When he didn't answer immediately it felt like a slap. All the clues had been there, the way she looked at him, her jealousy toward me. "Are you still..."

He stared down at his phone and tucked it away. "Not anymore."

"Why not?"

Considering Logan's model looks, an impressive career and bilingual skills that no doubt matched her other linguistic talents, she positively oozed sexy vixen.

"I found her a pleasant distraction. But later..."

"She wanted more?"

I sensed he'd sliced through her heart with a ruthless rejection.

He shook his head thoughtfully. "I need a lawyer who never loses."

Tobias answered my unspoken question on why she still worked for him. It was too late to pull back on my dismay. No wonder Logan went for my jugular each time she saw me.

"I know her alias is Ruby."

"She told me. I reassured her you'd guessed. She knows how smart you are."

"Have you ever gone to one of those parties with her?"

"No. She has unusual tastes. That's her private business."

"She was the one to tell you about the Goya?"

"Yes, she happened to catch the paintings one evening during a private tour of the palace."

"And she knows how much you love Goya."

"I'd do anything for you, Zara." His expression softened and rested his hand on his heart in a gesture of sincerity. "I'll always be here for you."

"I overheard you," I braved to say, "telling her she knows how you feel about her."

"Logan's worked for me for a long time. She's lent her loyalty. I owe her the same. That's not to say I tolerate inappropriate behavior."

Balling my fingers into fists, I hoped he wasn't skewing that remark toward me too for asking him about them.

"Have you any idea how beautiful, how gifted, how sweet you are?" His expression softened and I wanted to believe his outburst was authentic.

Perhaps Tobias was trying to placate me after I'd given away how close these two were.

"How about that coffee." He arched a brow.

I made my way into the kitchen and was met by the aroma of fresh beans brewing. I lifted the glass coffeepot and poured it into two mugs and added some milk to mine and left his black.

Tobias leaned on the door frame. "My work takes me abroad a lot."

My body tensed as I sensed where this was going.

Zach had stood there, right where Tobias stood now, giving those familiar excuses about life's commitments. Offering me a pretty bouquet of flowers, though nothing as lavish as Tobias's, but the purpose had been the same with those overly scented petals serving as a gentleman's apology.

Tobias's flowers were so very beautiful. They really were *kind*.

He strolled over to the counter and lifted his drink and took a sip. "I'm controlling. I can be demanding. As you just witnessed from the way I spoke with Logan." He blew a cool stream of air onto his drink.

I opened the fridge and put the milk away, hoping to hide my uneasiness.

He took another sip. "My private life is open to speculation from the press. I'm pursued like a deer during hunting season."

I reached for my mug and tried to read from him what I needed to hear.

"My life is complex." He put his drink down.

I held his gaze braving to say, "And you don't do love?"

Tobias's kind eyes crinkled into a smile as he said, "That was before…"

"Before?"

He went for his coffee again and wrapped his hands around it.

"Tobias?"

"You should take a shower."

Those few moments of his vulnerability slipped away.

And so did mine…

"Sometimes love, like art, cannot be defined," I said. "It

can't be contained. Controlled. Owned. It needs its freedom to become fully realized."

"Would that ever be enough for you?" he asked softly.

I raised my chin proudly and headed for the door. "Tobias, I was referring to me. I'll take that shower now."

Inside the bathroom I stripped off my babydoll nightdress. After turning on the faucet and adjusting the temperature I stepped in. That burst of heat felt incredible, the pressure pounding my head and flowing over my nakedness, cleansing my body as the water cascaded.

I'd allowed myself to go there and imagine what a relationship might be like with Tobias. It didn't take the wisdom of the ages to sense his reluctance to delve into a passionate affair with me. He'd realized our chemistry too. Something was holding him back, something more than just those seeds of doubt sewn by Logan. The self-respect I'd not known I had rose to the surface right when I needed it.

Our relationship also deserved to be on my terms as much as he wanted it to be on his. The challenge of learning more about Tobias had been a delicious pursuit.

Movement caught my eye and through the veil of steam I watched Tobias walk over to the corner chair and sit, crossing a leg over another. He stared at me with an expression void of any emotion.

Merely watching.

Lathering my body, I massaged soap over my heated skin, along my arms and legs, my abdomen and my sex, flitting a glance his way now and again and catching a glint of affection in his expression.

The way his tongue flickered and moistened his lower lip. His glare roamed over me, proving his desire, a stark passion reflected in his fierce green eyes.

I lathered shampoo into my hair.

This felt as sensuous as when we'd made love, a connection so profound I couldn't define it. His need to be close to me was more endearing than anything I'd experienced and I sensed he drew strength from me, just as I did from him.

Tobias rose from the chair and came over.

He pressed his palm to the glass and held it there. This, this was the reassurance I needed, that he felt the same way about me and no force or fear could keep us apart, and whatever the world might throw at us we'd handle together.

Mirroring, I raised my hand and placed my palm opposite his, my stare captured by his warm gaze, this moment of intimacy so honest.

Water continued to shower over me...

Silently I conveyed I had what it took to guide us where we needed to go and just as he'd asked me to do, I gave over my trust to him.

Tobias's hand slipped from the glass. And he left the room.

20

With my towel wrapped around me, I strolled into the bedroom feeling refreshed and with a sense of peace. These frantic hours worrying over *St. Joan* looked like they were over.

"Let's go out for breakfast," I called out to him. "You only had a slice of pizza. You must be starving."

My phone rang and Clara's bright face lit up the screen. I lifted it off the bedside table and yanked it out of its charger.

"Hey," I said, "how are you?"

"I left a message for you," she said. "What's going on over at Christie's? Didn't your dad once own that one?"

"St. Joan?"

"Are you okay? It was on the news. Was it stolen?"

"Right before they authenticated it."

"So you don't know if it was yours?"

"Not really." I hated lying to her.

"Has Nigel called you? Bet that got his nose twitching."

"Not yet." My stomach twisted at the thought of that sneaky journalist who'd no doubt want an exclusive.

A chill spiraled down my spine.

A trail of water trickled from my hair down my back. "Can I call you back? I just got out of the shower."

"Sure. I need you to fill me in."

I threw my phone on the bed and went in search of the most entertaining person I'd ever met.

"Tobias?" I called out. The kitchen was empty.

I made my way into the sitting room and when I didn't see him, a jolt of intuition told me to check if his coat was still in the hallway.

It wasn't.

A little fazed, I wondered if he was in the spare room preparing the paintings for their collection.

Dread seeped into my veins as I realized Tobias had left. I hurried over to the wall safe and peered in. The pallet was there. I pulled it out. "No!"

The paintings were gone.

Tears sprang to my eyes as I searched further for the envelope containing each proof of provenance. It wasn't there, either.

"No, please, no."

I sprang to my feet and in a daze ran into the sitting room and pressed my nose up against the window and stared out at the street. Cars driving by, a few pedestrians, a woman walking her boxer.

Back in my bedroom I dressed quickly, my hands too shaky on the zipper of my jeans, my chenille sweater feeling too tight around my neck. After a flurry of grabbing mismatched socks, finding shoes and scrambling for my handbag and phone, I flew out the door.

Drizzle fell on me.

It was too late to go back for my parka. A cab at the curb idled in front of me.

I grabbed the handle and leaped into the back. "The Otil-lie. Do you know where that is?"

The driver gave a nod and reached out to set the meter. He pulled away and I was shoved into the seat.

He's taken them to The Otillie, I reassured myself.

I was overreacting and sure to embarrass myself.

Fingers trembling, I pressed Logan's number and waited. It went to voice mail.

"Logan," I tried to steady my tone. "Please call me. It's urgent. It's concerning Tobias."

I killed the call and stared out at the passing scenery, old buildings mismatched with new, and pedestrians hurrying to work. This chill from the air-conditioning reached my damp hair and sent a stark coldness into my skull.

I forced my scattered thoughts into a stream of intelligent consciousness, running through what I knew about Tobias, the way he'd acted around me, the way he made me feel, and I cringed at how easily I'd fallen headfirst into this relationship.

Those final moments shared with him in the shower had been his way of saying goodbye.

Had I willingly given myself over to the crime of the century? The moment Tobias heard my name in The Otillie, when I'd introduced myself, his expression had proven he knew of me. And the very next day he'd turned up at my place of work…had that been the moment the seduction had begun?

Michelangelo had been his true love all along.

Rumors that not all my father's paintings had been destroyed in that fire had made it to America, apparently all the way to the Wilder estate.

Why had I ignored my gut feeling; why had I doubted myself?

Because you're about to prove yourself wrong, I chastised, *your paintings are fine and this is you overreacting and embarrassing yourself.*

In what felt like painful slow motion, I swiped my credit card through the meter and as soon as it cleared I flew out, my feet landing hard on the pavement.

Tripping forward and barely saving myself, I took two stairs at a time leading up to The Otillie's grand entrance. I went through the usual motions of the security screen and offered my handbag to be searched.

Miles's voice rose from the east wing and I headed in that direction, trying to maintain an aura of decorum and not sprint into his arms in a panic.

"Zara!" his clipped Cambridge accent echoed.

Even now Miles Tenant could intimidate with that booming tenor voice, his impressive dynamism evident by the way he ran this place and his generosity to always be willing to share his knowledge. Miles's African heritage gave him that elegant stature and that remarkable confidence that enhanced his charisma.

"Miles." I sucked in air.

"Come to see your girl?" He beamed at me. *"Madame Rose..."* His smile faded. "Zara? Are you okay?"

"Is Tobias Wilder here?" Terror caught me when I read his reaction.

"Are you meeting him here?"

"I thought so."

His eyes widened as his gaze swept over my disheveled appearance. "You got caught in the rain?"

"Do you have his number?"

"All calls go through Tobias's office."

"But you're friends?"

"He gets hundreds of calls a day. Busy man. They all get siphoned through his office."

I cringed at the obvious distance Tobias had placed between him and Miles. The same wall I'd faced when trying to reach him.

"Tobias didn't drop off any paintings?" Desperation dripped from my voice.

"No, was he meant to?" He smiled. "Now you have me intrigued. Let's go to my office."

"I can't stay."

I must keep moving.

"I'll tell Tobias you visited," he said.

"Call me as soon as he turns up, okay." I walked backward, heading for the exit.

"Of course." His squint of concern followed me out.

Turning on my heels and skirting through those damn rotating doors that freaked me out each time I used them, I burst into the freezing night air.

Pouring rain chased after me as I hurried back down the steps. I moaned with the thought of Tobias transporting my paintings in this weather.

From the curb, I looked left and right and gestured to an approaching taxi.

Hands shaking as they grasped my phone, I tapped away until I'd brought up the number for New Scotland Yard.

Think!

Go straight to the police and they'd demand a statement and no doubt have more questions regarding that incident at Christie's. That couldn't happen. I needed the time and freedom to hunt down Tobias.

How would I prove they were once mine?

And why had Tobias betrayed me like this? Stolen them from right under my nose? I'd been stupid enough to trust him. Believe in the chemistry that had been laid at my feet as a trap. I cursed my stupidity for falling so hard and fast for him.

"Ma'am, everything okay?"

I stirred from this trance and came to inside the back of the large black cab I'd climbed into.

"I'm fine," I told the driver. "Canary Wharf, please."

"Have an address?" his Cockney accent reassured me he'd know the backstreets.

My fingers flew across the screen as I did a Google search. "I'm working on it."

I found myself in front of a pristine black glass skyscraper that was crisscrossed with chrome. Wilder Tower was an imposing high-rise.

Crooking my neck, I guessed there was somewhere in the region of at least fifty floors to this building. I wiped rain from my eyes, vaguely aware I was drenched from head to toe.

The coldness soaked into my bones as I realized by the time I climbed those stairs, Tobias would have made his getaway.

If he was even here.

He could be boarding a plane right now and on his way to the States. With my paintings.

Stay focused.

Stepping inside, I clenched my teeth to endure the air-conditioning hitting my skin like broken shards of glass. These wet clothes clung with a cruel iciness.

Within this expansive foyer I could see the similarity with Tobias's Oxford home. Pristine chrome fixtures were offset by a stark fluorescence. A minimalist approach to a vast lonely space. That high ceiling the final stamp of grandeur.

How could a man so wealthy need to steal anything?

Because owning a Michelangelo was the last vestige of greed, I painfully mused, a priceless piece unlike any other that could be bought and privately owned.

These steps toward the receptionist's desk felt like the longest trek and as I looked around I knew the architect must have known Tobias well. This wide-open area reflected Tobias's need to throw off his opponents and control his enemies.

Across the way, two burly guards held me in their gazes with a look of suspicion, probably wondering why a bedraggled woman had any right to hurry through the Wilder foyer.

"Do you have an appointment?" asked the young pretty receptionist.

My fingers traced over the *GQ* magazine on the counter, flaunting Tobias's photo which was smack-dab on the cover and he looked so damn gorgeous, mocking me with his beauty in that usual arrogant, bespoke style.

The receptionist narrowed her gaze on me. "Miss?"

An unfamiliar burst of jealousy rose in my chest as I realized she'd see Tobias every day when he was in London, and perhaps, just perhaps she'd flirt a little.

"Yes." I bit back my embarrassment of looking so bad.

"Got caught in it, then?" She raised her chin to the door.

"Forgot my brolly." I gave a thin smile. "I'm Zara Leighton."

"Okay, great. Go ahead and sign in." She tapped away on her keyboard, her screen hidden from view behind that overly large marble reception desk.

"Do you have a pen, please?" I scanned the counter for one.

"First time here?"

"Yes. Is Mr. Wilder here?"

She hesitated for a beat and then narrowed her gaze. "He's expecting me."

Expecting to have his eyes gouged out, more likely.

Smiling I said, "Running a bit late for that meeting."

"Oh, are you from NG?"

NG?

"Yes." I blinked her way.

"I'll give you a key card for the lift."

My gaze followed hers and my throat tightened as I took in that large metal death trap, its gaping mouth threatening to devour and inevitably crush those stupid enough to enter.

"Which way are the stairs?"

"You can't use them unless there's an emergency. It's a security measure. You can't have access to all floors."

"What if people don't like lifts?"

"It's not an issue."

Not an issue for her, obviously, she merely sat here on the ground level protected by all this marble and chrome and didn't have to put her life on the line.

She pointed to the space between us and, on my look of confusion, added, "It's an air keyboard. If you could just sign in."

"I don't need a pen?"

"Use your finger."

"For what exactly?" Punch the air?

She punched the air and a transparent screen came down between us, her bored face reflecting clear on the other side.

"Did Tobias invent this?" I managed.

"Mr. Wilder? Yes. The whole building. There's a pool on the twelfth floor and a gym we can use during our lunch break."

I tried to hide the fact I was hyperventilating at the thought of having to use the stairs while being chased by those guards.

Punching my name into the keyboard with a pointed finger, I messed up and had to delete "Xars" and change it to "Zara."

She busied herself on her screen and I reached for that GQ, flipping through the pages, trying to calm my nerves.

There, a few pages in, were more photos of Wilder looking just as dashing along with an accompanying interview. Reading the highlighted points, I learned that Tobias had donated his holographic technology to medical schools in developing countries, so students could learn anatomy and physiology in the classroom before being let loose in laboratories. It was admirable but also turned my stomach a little when it previewed the detail of what was possible. The students could literally reach in and peel away three-dimensional body parts.

I scrunched up my nose. *Lovely.*

According to the article, Tobias was also a hero to gamers, after developing snazzy goggles for larger-than-life worlds that prevented the usual nausea associated with 3-D technology.

"I'm having trouble finding you in the system?" She piped up. "Let me try his private office. Maybe his secretary didn't sync."

"Thank you." Though with no appointment, I hoped she'd let me go ahead anyway; I was going to have to play it cool.

Skipping to the end, the article summarized Tobias was considered a high-tech equivalent of Albert Einstein when it came to gadgets.

Not everything he'd invented had come out a winner— two years ago he'd applied a neuron and synapse system to a computer that resulted in a neural awakening. Unfortunately, that experiment crashed the hard drive. The artificial intelligence had taken on a mind of its own and not in a good way.

I'd been flirting with a mad scientist.

Who was quite possibly Icon.

The receptionist set a key card on the counter but kept her fingertips on it. "Sure it's today?" She frowned at her screen.

I swallowed hard and kicked myself when she caught it. "You're not showing on his calendar, either," she said.

I grabbed the key card and bolted for the stairs, sprinting faster than I'd ever run. The clue that Tobias had a meeting with someone called NG kept spurring me on. I was damned if I was letting him get away with stealing my beloved possessions.

I was getting my paintings back. Today.

A guard sprang from out of nowhere and closed in on me. He cut me off from the entry to the stairwell.

I bolted right and in a blur of adrenaline and desperate heaves of panic, my legs carried me into the lift—even as my brain screamed against it.

I shoved the card into the strip on the wall panel…that guard looming closer and threatening to join me in here.

Frantically searching for buttons and not seeing any, one small gold knob to the right of the panel was my only choice.

I slammed my palm against it.

"Executive suite," came a virtual female voice. "Transparency mode activated."

"What?" I snapped.

No longer terrified by the guard whose hands reached out— the doors slid shut as he pulled his fingers free.

My scream echoed out on my final breath as I shot upward at a million miles an hour.

Terror gripped me as I watched the floor transforming from a steel base into see-through glass exposing the sheer drop below.

I dropped to my knees and froze. My ears popping.

Zooming upward like a rocket.

Finally, my walled prison came to a stop.

The doors slid open.

Twisting my head slightly, I made out the blurred image of a vast open floor plan. Stark white walls. A patterned couch and chairs were positioned to the left for guests who'd survived this face-off with death, and would need a place to sit and contemplate this miracle.

I crawled out on all fours.

Sucking in a gulp of air and hating this sense that the ground was unstable, I scrambled to my feet.

There he stood—

A few feet from the lift.

His expression predictably serene. The "too dashing for his own bloody good" Tobias *fucking* Wilder. That usual pose of his hands casually tucked inside his trouser pockets and his chin arrogantly raised.

Yes, buddy, I found you!

I pointed back to the lift and screamed at him, "Who was the mad, fuck-wit bastard who invented that piece of crap?"

Tobias's left brow arched inquisitively. "We can always rely on Miss Leighton to make a memorable entry."

21

Wriggling free from Tobias's ironclad grip was impossible.

We hurried past the stunned faces of his staff and continued along a hallway, speeding by a lengthy window to a conference room—

I sucked in a gasp when I saw my Michelangelo secure on an easel. Beside it rested my Vermeer and the da Vinci. The contents of several folders were strewn on the long dark wooden table.

Logan was in there talking with a balding man who had his back to me. I could only assume he was some private dealer ready to part with some serious cash. Logan gave me the stink-eye as we flew along the hall and I reciprocated with a scowl.

Tobias called off his guards and demanded one of his slew of pretty receptionists bring him a towel.

"You're a lying, cheating bastard," I said.

"Let's save the compliments until we're out of earshot, okay." We flew through a door.

I broke away from him and took a few steps back.

"Come here." He opened his arms for me to fall into. "I had no idea you were so scared of elevators? Or is it heights?"

I ignored him and snapped my head around at the posh-looking everything. The room so big it could only be his office. An enormous desk with a sleek computer facing that enormous TV hanging midair. A lounge with chairs and a leather sofa at the other end. The view of the city was spectacular with the River Thames winding off toward the horizon, and my legs wobbled as I remembered how high we were.

In the distance rose the fluorescent blue of the London Eye.

A young brunette came in and handed Tobias a towel. "Will there be anything else, sir?"

"No, thank you," he said. "No interruptions. Understand?"

"Yes, sir." She shrank out of the room and closed the door behind her.

"Unsurprisingly, you have quite the collection of tarts working for you," I said.

"I have an HR department." He threw the towel over my head and rubbed away.

Making me feel like a silly schoolgirl who'd stepped in from the rain.

"Where's your umbrella?" he said. "Didn't you wear a coat? We need to get you out of those clothes."

"Isn't that convenient!"

He went to speak and thought better of it.

I pointed at him. "Bet you're surprised how I found you."

"We're standing in one of the tallest buildings in London. Maybe the tower sticking up above all the others helped?"

"How could you?"

"What are you talking about, Zara?"

I glared at him from beneath the towel. "I went to The Otillie. Miles told me he hadn't seen you. And guess what I just copped a glance at?"

He arched a questioning brow.

"My paintings." I sucked in a sob. "You're selling them right under my nose."

He stepped back, leaned against his desk and folded his arms across his chest. "Although I can't deny this is thoroughly entertaining—"

"Fuck you."

He smiled his amusement. "God, you're gorgeous when you're angry. Delightfully fuckable. That snippety English demeanor pleasantly replaced by that fiery Welsh attitude finally rising to the surface to delight us all."

"You can't use your clever-speaking Americana to seduce me anymore. I've seen what you're capable of, and I'm immune to your charm."

"You gave me permission to deal with this."

"To take them to The Otillie."

"You didn't read my note, I take it?"

"What note?"

"The one I left on your hallway table."

"There was no note."

"For God sake, Zara, you missed it." He shook his head. "All you had to do was phone me."

"Yeah? How?"

"Give me your phone."

"Why?"

"Give it to me."

"No."

"Zara."

I rummaged through my handbag and held it up. "Why? What do you want it for?"

"I entered my number in it earlier. Before I left." He gestured. "Go on, take a look. I'm under *W*. Obviously."

Squinting at him, I searched through my contacts.

His name and number appeared right at the end. "Why didn't you tell me?"

"In retrospect it would have been a good idea. I hate seeing you like this."

"I've been freaking out."

"I'm so sorry, baby." Again he gestured for me to come to him.

"No, you don't get to call me that. Why are my paintings here and not at The Otillie?"

"We assessed the gallery's capabilities—"

"We?"

"My team."

"That's right, your elusive team."

"God help me I'll put you over my knee and spank you if you don't stop this."

"Why are they here?" I snapped.

"We, that is my legal team, decided the National Gallery is best suited for your Michelangelo. When the gallery announces there's a priceless painting of this magnitude, the attention will be unimaginable. We're talking millions of new visitors. The Otillie isn't set up to handle that kind of foot traffic."

"Why not take them straight to the National?" I raised my chin, proud of my reasoning.

"Getting a Michelangelo into a world-renowned gallery is relatively easy. Getting one out is virtually impossible. First, they must agree to our terms."

"Terms?"

"Yes, Zara, terms. A watertight contract that enables you as the exclusive owner, as stipulated in the paperwork, which you saw on the table, to remove the paintings from the gallery after five years. Should you so wish." He gave a shrug.

"You might want to have it tour the world. Perhaps stop off at The Wilder in LA."

"Oh."

"You're obviously not thinking straight. What girl keeps a Michelangelo in her bedroom? One who is clearly torn up with grief, that's who. If we've learned anything, it's you need me."

"Icon doesn't know I even exist," I whispered.

"I have a feeling he does."

"Why?" Fear slithered up my spine.

"You're investigating him."

"I've been in denial."

"That's not the safest place."

"But I'm part of a big team? I'm insignificant in the grand scheme of things."

"You may well be his biggest threat yet."

I blinked at him, trying to understand his reasoning.

"You're proving a great investigator," he added.

I wiped my hand across my nose. "Yeah, right, I just fell at your feet after melting down over some huge misunderstanding."

"I wish it wasn't me who had to shine a light on your naivety."

My feet wobbled as the madness of my last few decisions reared. I'd been scared, confused, and had totally mishandled those paintings.

I knew better.

Parting with them was my final goodbye to the art-filled life I cherished with my father.

All those memories clutched at me as they faded day by day.

I tried to remember Dad's face. His laugh. Those kind eyes that told me how much he loved me.

That bleak hospital room at Saint Bartholomew's Hospital.

The sympathetic expressions of the nurses as they relayed he didn't have long.

Take care of our paintings, Zara, he'd whispered as he'd clutched my hand. *Guard them with your life.*

Wilder took a step closer. "Do you want to talk about your elevator phobia?"

"No, not really."

"Something happened to you?" He looked at me with compassion. "Zara, I'm here for you," Tobias's voice sounded distant. "I can't believe you really thought I'd do that to you."

"I overheard you, Tobias, when you said, 'I will end this. It will be swift and sure. It will happen. And it will be…kind.'"

He blinked his confusion. "I was talking to Logan. That was my way of reining her in."

Staring down at my hands, I saw they were still shaking.

All that had gone before had thrown me off center. My past had ruined me in the worst kind of way, burned through my ability to trust or ever love again.

"You need to let the adrenaline wear off." He made his way over to his desk and pushed a button on his phone. "Hot tea for Ms. Leighton, please. Soon as you can."

"Right away, sir," came the reply.

"Now, let's get you—" he waved his hand at my hair "—tidied up so you can meet with Magnus Needham. He's the head curator at the National Gallery."

Oh God, I knew Magnus. Though he'd lost more hair since I'd last seen him. "NG?" I whispered.

"That's the one."

"Why didn't you say goodbye?"

"When?"

"You walked out of the bathroom and didn't wait to say goodbye?"

"When you were showering?"

"Yes."

"That was my goodbye. I took your words seriously."

"What words?"

"Minutes before, you made some big speech in the kitchen about freedom. About art, like love, not being defined. You mentioned something about hating the idea of it being 'controlled. Owned. One needs freedom to become fully realized.'"

My words came back to haunt me like a bad dream.

"I distinctly remember you saying you wanted your freedom." Tobias gave a nod to seal the memory. "The look of finality you gave me while you were in the shower proved it."

"What look?"

"This look." He mimicked an expression of stubbornness and of pure resignation, with a dash of indignation thrown in.

"I didn't give that look."

"You did."

"Well, you gave me a look of affection. Of you wanting to take us to the next level." I mimicked it to make sure he got my point. "Like this." My expression turned wistful.

"That was sadness. Because you didn't want to continue with us."

"That wasn't sadness." I pointed at him. "I can read faces."

"You put your hand on the glass."

"So did you."

"That was an obvious goodbye and good luck. That was clearly a 'It's been fun, Big Guy.'"

"The look I gave you was of me realizing you and I had something special." I arched my brows and widened my eyes just as I'd done back then. "This is me telling you I'm ready to see where our relationship might go."

"Seriously?"

"Yes."

"Damn, Zara, you're going to have to work on your expressions."

"You scared the hell out of me, Tobias."

"The only thing scary around here is your hair. Have a look in the mirror." He pointed across the room.

I eyed what suspiciously looked like a private bathroom.

"Do you have a brush?" He gestured to my bag.

I fumbled around in there for my comb.

"Come on, do something miraculous with your hair. I want to introduce you to Magnus and not scare him. He's old-school. You can read the paperwork and sign it."

"Might need some dry clothes."

"I'm sure my staff is working on it."

"How embarrassing."

"You've been under tremendous pressure. I understand."

A sob caught in my throat and I felt an ugly cry coming on. "It's going to be okay. Isn't it?"

Tobias stepped forward and wrapped his arms around me and he hugged me tight. "More than okay. We just admitted how we feel about each other. We averted a near disaster."

"Disaster?"

"You're my favorite, Zara."

I looked up at him. "How many Zaras do you know?"

"Actually, you're my first. And I'm ready to admit I've been secretly dating you."

"Secretly?"

"Well, it involves spending time with you, getting to kiss you, and the privilege of getting to taste you…"

My body weakened in his arms.

"Most off all," he whispered, "I get to be inside you. And nothing on this planet comes close to that."

22

Secretly dating me.

Sitting here on the edge of his desk, I was too busy swooning as I listened to Tobias explaining how a touch-air keyboard worked.

I'd complained about the stupid way I'd been asked to sign in and in usual stubborn Tobias fashion, he needed to convince me otherwise and provide a demo of his invention.

I'd been too full of fear upon my arrival to be impressed by any advanced technology I encountered. Now I tried to understand the need for a virtual keyboard as Tobias waved his hand, commanding it to appear out of thin air. He was rambling on about laser projection and nono-bytes of data which, while kind of hot coming from this hunk du jour, it was not as interesting as ogling him, and to be honest, he'd lost me with the involved details. I reasoned it was no surprise I'd feared Tobias was Icon, and even though I now knew my paintings were safe, I allowed my imagination to gather the clues. Like Tobias, our man would also have a great understanding of technology; he'd also have similar resources, and the same level of ingenuity.

Everything pointed to Icon having stolen *St. Joan*.

My gaze swept over Tobias's face and I slid off the desk to stand closer to him, reaching up to cup his cheek. He leaned into me, his gaze seemingly trying to convey something he wanted to tell me.

You're tired, I reassured myself, dazed from having believed I'd lost everything. Everyone becomes a suspect when your back is against the wall.

I daydreamed further that a better knowledge of Tobias's world would help me better understand the thief's universe, perhaps the way his mind worked.

His true motives.

My feet wobbled as the madness of my last few decisions reared. I'd been scared and confused and had totally mishandled those paintings.

I knew better.

Before the meeting with Magnus, I'd sat in Tobias's private office en suite bathroom, wearing a robe from the Tower's spa while his staff arranged for my clothes to be dry-cleaned. Apparently, the process could be expedited to less than twenty minutes, which gave me time to dry my hair with the blow-dryer borrowed from the gym. Turned out this was like a little village, with restaurants, that pool his receptionist had mentioned, and all sorts of other impressive amenities like a five-star restaurant and a cozy café—all I'd seen showcased on the promotional video he'd shown me.

Tobias kept opening his arms to me and I willingly fell into them, needing his hugs.

I imagined he had held back on sharing proof of his grand wealth so as not to intimidate me. Perhaps he'd also needed to explore my motives for being with him.

Maybe that was what he meant by "secretly dating" me.

My day had gone from one of the worst ever to blissfully happy now that I knew my paintings were in good hands.

The meeting with Magnus went well.

With Tobias's two-man legal team guiding us through the process of all that legalese, I'd gotten the reassurance I needed that our plan to secure the artwork in his prestigious gallery would go smoothly.

Dr. Needham had been giddy with excitement at the prospect of showcasing a Michelangelo. He'd also told us that having the painting by Vermeer and the sketch by da Vinci was "an astounding privilege." The works of art were now in the process of being transported to the National Gallery, where they'd be reframed and professionally cleaned.

Tobias was demonstrating now how fast he could type midair. "Am I boring you?" He gave a dashing smile.

"It's just a little over my head, that's all." I gave his arm a squeeze. "You're so clever."

He brushed his hand over my cheek. "Can I get you anything?"

"I'm fine."

"Coming to terms with your father's paintings finding a home? It's more than just a resolution to all you've been through."

"Not that I want to put any pressure on you," I said, "but you've been a nice distraction. Other than earlier, of course. When I was convinced you were that burglar Interpol's chasing."

"Icon?"

"Yes."

Tobias cupped my face with his hands and leaned in to kiss me, and I tipped my chin, my lips ready and needful for his lips.

He paused, his gaze narrowing. He stepped back from me. "Logan."

My head snapped round to catch her standing in the doorway.

She gave a nod my way. "Tobias, are you okay if I head home?"

"Yes, of course," he said. "Thank you for setting that meeting up for us."

I almost cringed when I saw the hurt in her eyes. "Would you like to join us for brunch, Logan?" It came out before I'd had the chance to think about it, but still, it felt like the right thing to do.

"No, thank you." She gave a nod, turned on her heels and headed back out, closing the door behind her.

"Why do I feel dreadful?" I muttered.

"You shouldn't. Everything's good between Logan and me."

"Clearly it's not."

"Look, you've had a difficult time."

"That's got nothing to do with me seeing her sadness."

"That's how she looks most of the time. She's intense. Driven. You don't know her like I do."

I bit the inside of my cheek to halt any more words from escaping. Tobias had only just admitted he wanted to date me and the last thing he needed was a jealous girlfriend.

I stared at the spot where Logan had stood. "You do know her better than me."

"Yeah, I see what you're doing there." He kissed my nose.

"What do you see?"

"Everything, Zara. You don't need to agree to placate me."

A tingle shot up my spine as I held his fierce gaze.

"Though I'm not an easy lover," he said. "I'm domineering and—"

"Bossy." My smile thinned. "I didn't mean…"

"Well, as I am the boss that makes perfect sense." His voice turned husky. "Wouldn't you agree?"

I blinked my amazement at the way even his voice affected me. My gaze slid to his mouth, and I yearned to be kissed by him.

"Zara, I want to possess you entirely."

Dragging my teeth over my bottom lip, I ran that through my brain as swirls of excitement rose from my core.

"Your mouth is dangerously delectable."

I doubted I'd ever be able to push him away as his kisses trailed over my throat and he eased my chenille sweater up. And it was impossible to protest at his mouth lowering to my bra, his firm hand easing the cup down to free my nipple and his lips encircling that sensitive skin until it knew only bliss. He set to work on the other breast, rolling his finger and thumb to maintain pleasure on the one he'd abandoned with his mouth.

I said breathlessly, "Possess me entirely?"

"Let me show you." He dragged his teeth over my nipple. "Now."

We strolled to the far corner of his office and paused before a blank white wall.

He faced it. "Jade, I've brought a guest. Allow." He gave me a heart-stopping grin of excitement.

The wall went from pure white to showing a doorway.

My free hand slapped to my mouth to prevent me from swearing. I'd never seen anything like this. An optical illusion so profound my brain strained to process it.

I felt the pull of his hand as we stepped inside a small, oval space. I waited for Tobias to push another button to take us through to the next room.

The space was too small, like a large cupboard, and I felt the hairs prickle on my forearms.

He leaned against the back wall. "Pick some music."

"Ellie Goulding."

"Jade, comply with guest."

The soft tones of Ellie Goulding oozed through hidden speakers, and I giggled at how quickly the computer reacted.

"What is this room?" I whispered.

With a wave of his hand the door slid closed. "My secret domain. Jade, dim the lighting a little. Little more." He laughed. "Not too much. I want to see my girlfriend. Good, bring the temperature up a degree. Activate invisible field."

"What's invisible field?"

He grinned.

"Why are we in here?" I whispered.

"I come in here to think with no distractions. I need complete silence when calculating unit conversions, hypothesizing engineering software and double-checking speculations. That's where Jade comes in. Right, Jade?"

I frowned at her silence. "She understands every word? Jade's not the computer that went haywire, is she?"

He brought his finger to his mouth. "Shush. Jade believes she's real." He frowned at me questioningly.

"I read GQ occasionally. You just so happened to be in the one I read."

"I'm flattered."

He didn't need to know I'd just read it.

Tobias looked amused that I'd researched him and leaned into my ear. "Don't believe everything you read."

"She didn't crash?"

"We discovered a cyber spy working for us. I sabotaged the AI. I've upgraded her since then."

"But the article?"

"A planted story. She works fine."

"You've turned her back on?"

"She was never off. And she's evolved." He gave a seductive smirk. "And she gets jealous."

"Seriously?"

"For example, she turns a little 'green' when I do this." He knelt at my feet, reached for my zipper and tugged my jeans down.

A soft green hue turned our space into a soothing hub.

His fingers touched my sex, his face inches away from the scorching heat rising between my thighs.

"This is your world?" I said wistfully.

"This—" Tobias eased apart my cleft and ran a thumb along it "—is my world."

I felt a tinge of pleasure at his caress.

"We're doing it in your secret room."

He grinned. "Yes."

"You're into kinky sex?"

"Into control." His tongue swept along my cleft and flickered there, his hands reaching up to pinch my nipples and tweak to the same rhythm. "And as you've learned I've mastered the ability to have you come at will."

The way Tobias suckled with precision felt and looked so erotic. I shattered into a thousand pieces, this stunning pleasure between my thighs forcing my eyes to shut and my jaw to clench in response.

Ellie Goulding was singing about chasing after love and finally finding it...

I grabbed locks of his hair and held him to me, my heart racing with excitement. These walls were closing in— "It's small in here." My uneasiness rose.

"You taste amazing."

A blast of pleasure radiated from my center and outward as my mind tranced out.

The tip of his tongue circled my clit slowly, and I tilted

my hips and thrust my sex forward nearing climax. My moan echoed and my short, sharp gasps proved I was about to fall into a climactic abyss.

He pulled away and rose to his feet. "I'm going to show you what it's like to be truly cherished."

"Tobias, I'm close." My breathing was ragged.

"You've never been nurtured the way you deserve."

I keeled forward, too weak to stand straight. "I'm grateful for all you've done."

He pinned me against the wall and crushed his lips on mine, his tongue rippled against mine, his mouth prying mine open farther to forge on through a deeper kiss. I tasted myself on him, causing my legs to weaken. His strength was the only thing keeping me upright.

His hands slid to his belt and he freed himself, lowering his body until the angle was perfect, his cock aligned, and with one quick shove he was inside me. A jolt of tightness and this tautness morphed into a shocking pleasure.

Hoisted up by him, I wrapped my legs around his waist and threw my arms around his neck.

He stepped back into the center. "Ride me. Hard and fast."

I gripped his forearms, and swirls of excitement distracted me from these looming walls.

His strong arms lifted me, guiding me through this thrilling pace, and gripping his hips with my thighs I set off rising and falling, my slickness enabling my glide, my head spinning with this rush.

"Let me know when you're close," he whispered.

With my pelvis thrust forward the pleasure was blinding, and I sucked in air to fuel my continued thrusts.

"Jade," Tobias whispered.

I dug my fingernails into his back to punish him for mentioning her.

He pulled me farther through my downward glide, sending a jolt of pleasure.

Trembling, coming hard, I buried my face into his neck, thighs shaking and my sex gripped him as I swept through each cycle.

"Tobias." I squeezed my thighs tighter as I ground against him.

"On my mark," he whispered. "One. Proceed."

My body detonated into brilliant prisms of pleasure, shuddering against him, a frenzied ride through this blinding orgasm; weightless as though free-falling, my stomach muscles and thighs had to work harder to fight this sensation of gravity.

He groaned as he came, his heat filling me and sending me over into a continuous state of bliss. We both froze, shuddering out the remnants of euphoria.

I leaned back a little and smiled at him, admiring his impressive strength, and reached up to swipe away a trickle of perspiration from his brow. "That was amazing."

"You're amazing." He lifted me off him. "And devilishly addictive."

This loss of him inside me caused a soft groan to escape.

Wearing the biggest grin, he tucked himself away, and then helped me to dress, pulling my jeans back on and straightening my clothes.

"I could do that all day," I muttered.

"Point taken."

I slammed my palm to my mouth in embarrassment.

"Glad to see the earth moved for you too." He waggled his eyebrows.

"Sure did."

"Close your eyes."

"Why?"

"Just do it. Don't open them until I say."

"Okay." I squeezed my eyes shut and felt the soft touch of his lips on my mouth. Tobias took my left hand and interlocked his fingers with mine.

Trying to obey, I wondered what other surprises he had in store. "What was all that 'on my mark' thing? Tobias, just so you know, women can't come at will like that."

"You seem to." He pulled me out and we reentered his office.

We walked for a little and I trusted him to watch out for the furniture so I didn't crash into anything.

There came the echo of our shoes, hushed voices… "Open your eyes," he said.

Adjusting to the wide-open space, my gaze tried to make sense of the expanse of the foyer, those tall pillars, that long marble desk with the perky receptionist, her face looking as stunned as mine, considering the last time I saw her I'd made a run for the—

Lift…

"You bastard," I hissed at him.

He waved off his security staff. "More compliments? It's my lucky day."

The receptionist ran toward us waving a Louis Vuitton umbrella. "Here you go, sir." She looked over at me, not quite sure how to react.

Tobias took the umbrella. "Thank you, Candice, all's well."

She gave a wary nod and hurried back behind her reception desk.

Glancing back, I tried to reason out that trip in Tobias's supersonic lift, and ran through my brain the trick he'd pulled. My heart raced as I realized the danger and was just a little mesmerized by his genius.

My legs weakened with the thought of the height from

which we'd descended. Tobias seemed to sense my unsteadiness and wrapped his arm around me.

"Not sure about you," he whispered, "but traveling at forty miles per hour always makes me hungry. Fancy some Belgian waffles?"

My feet wobbled and fond memories came flooding back of me tucked safely in my bed, a Kindle in one hand and a spoon in the other, a bowl of oatmeal balanced on my lap. Those comforting mornings where death-defying feats were only ever experienced on the telly. "Can we just go home?"

"Oh, Zara," Tobias said, "you're my woman now. This is where the fun starts."

We burst out of the building and he opened that large umbrella. We both huddled beneath it to hide from the rain, trailing down the steps toward the curb.

His Bentley idled there.

Cooper leaped out of the driver's side and opened the rear door for us. He took the umbrella from Tobias and shook it.

We climbed into the backseat and I snuggled against Tobias's warmth.

He reached for his Burberry woolen coat lying on the backseat and wrapped it around my shoulders. "We need to buy you a coat," he said. "You'll catch a cold."

"Oh no, look—" I pointed.

About fifty feet away, beneath a veil of rain, stood a young Buddhist monk with a shaven head who was clad in traditional orange robes. His expression was serene and he was seemingly unaffected by the downpour.

His eerie stance as he stared our way was trancelike.

"He's getting drenched," I said. "What's he doing all the way out here?"

Tobias leaned forward. "Coops, give him the umbrella and money for a cab."

"Yes, sir."

"That's a great idea," I said. "He must be freezing." Cooper opened his door.

"Oh, and Coops..." Tobias narrowed his gaze.

"Got it, boss," said Cooper, registering the message. He opened the umbrella and splashed his way over to him.

The monk's expression was painfully soulful. He acted thrown when Cooper offered the opened umbrella, but after some persuasion he accepted it.

I crooked my neck to see better. "He looks lost."

Tobias turned to face me and reached out. "Give me your hands." He rubbed them between his. "We need to warm you up."

Anguish coursed through me that I was being so spoiled as my gaze fell back on the monk. Cooper had hailed a cab for him and was leaning through the widow and speaking with the driver.

"Oh, look," I said, "Cooper's making sure he gets home. I wonder where he lives." I watched Coops open his wallet and pay for the taxi.

He returned his attention to the monk, who was now safely tucked away in the backseat.

Coops handed him cash.

Tobias gave a nod of approval.

I felt a pang of guilt at suspecting Tobias for stealing my paintings, I couldn't have been more wrong. This wonderful man came through every single time. I couldn't get over how wonderful he was and, right now, as I snuggled into his chest, I knew how lucky I was to have found him.

"Could you be any more wonderful," I said.

Tobias gave a smile. "We do what we can."

23

Standing in the middle of this luxury hotel suite, while wearing nothing but Coco de Mer bra and panties, I posed for Tobias.

Just as he'd told me to do.

The lavish decor was beyond exquisite with soft silver tones, which were the minimalist theme Tobias seemed to favor, and I wondered if that was why he liked this hotel, The Dorchester, on Park Lane. Everything was well thought out to provide lush surroundings that were also comfortable. That vase of lilies in the corner, that opulent seating area of high-back chairs and a long plush couch, that door leading to the bedroom and its four-poster bed where we'd made love all night long...

I'd been seduced into the very center of Wilder's world.

Half an hour ago he'd played Guns N' Roses and it had blared through the hidden speakers. This was my punishment for changing the music while he was shaving in the bathroom. Taylor Swift's "Wildest Dreams" blared in every room. Yes, I was being punished but my music continued to flow...

One tall chilled glass of champagne and I was up for this game; a siren glinting with happiness and almost naked before him. Tobias sat a few feet away in a large leather armchair. He looked so dashing in that tailored tuxedo with one long leg crossed over the other, his fierce green gaze reflecting a man admiring his prey.

We were heading out soon for a private party but there was still time to play. I'd grown fond of his frequent flashes of dominance that still made me feel safe.

I'd even relented when he'd requested The Dorchester's beautician to visit our room. She'd worked her magic on my wayward locks by hot-ironing them into voluminous, bouncy curls and had used a similar alchemy on my makeup. I'd searched the mirror, seeing nothing of the old me and everything of the kind of woman Tobias deserved to be with.

Never had I oozed such an erotic confidence before, and I hardly recognized these spiraling auburn locks that tumbled elegantly over my shoulders. My highlighted smoky eyes were dramatically larger and these long eyelashes were almost overshadowed by my overly rouged plumped lips forming an exotic pout.

"Part your legs a little," he said. "Very good. Place your hands behind your back. Wrists together."

I smirked at his request, feeling a little silly.

He suppressed a smile. "Do you find this funny?"

"No." I peered beneath long lashes. "I like it." And I did.

I loved the way he made me feel nurtured just as he'd promised. My gaze broke his and roamed the dramatic burgundy drapes that were closed now and swept across the two arched windows. I absorbed the lavishness surrounding us, giddy by this man whose command seemed effortless.

The weekend had been a whirlwind of expensive dining, a little shopping for new clothes for me at Harrods and Harvey Nichols, and then stopping off at The Otillie to see *Madame Rose*. It had been so wonderful seeing her and only now did

I truly understand that lovesick expression on Rose's beautiful face. It was as though I was seeing her wistful expression for the first time, a hint of her subdued passion. Only now I understood that timeless allure of love reflected in her gaze.

Tobias's affection was helping me see art through a different lens and by viewing through this prism of wonderment I opened my heart further.

We'd gone on from there to pay a much-needed visit to the National Gallery to see Magnus, and watch his restoration professionals work their magic on the Michelangelo. His talented team of renovation specialists had brought out the vibrant colors and were well into the process of restoring the paintings.

In awe, Tobias and I had admired all three of my portraits that deserved to be shared. Each majestic masterpiece would soon be given the opportunity to be adored by thousands of visitors to the gallery.

Sunday evening had brought with it more rain and lucky for us we were ensconced safely away in this luxury suite. I'd not seen the inside of my apartment all weekend. Instead, Tobias insisted we remain here and enjoy all the amenities close to hand. We'd been pampered beyond belief with endless sumptuous meals ordered up from room service, a private massage in our room, and a ceaseless supply of champagne and dark chocolates.

These two days had felt like nirvana and no matter how many times I cautioned myself to hold on and not fall, my heart rebelled and told me to risk it all.

"Turn around," he said. "Slowly."

I complied, more than aware my nipples were pert from the chill of the room, my lack of clothes making me vulnerable.

"Don't bite your lip," he chastised. "It draws attention to your mouth. We don't have the time."

I turned and grinned at him.

He grinned back. "Do you know how beautiful you are? How feminine? How kind you are? You take my breath away. I feel like I'm at the goddamn Tate, seeing modern art for the first time. Jesus, Zara, you're stunning."

It was impossible to pull back on my smile.

"I would do anything for you." That cute smile lit up his face. "Still, if you ever change my music again…"

The blaze of my cheeks forced my gaze away as I suppressed my smile at his brashness.

My sex thrummed with the need to have him touch me the way he always did. I'd fallen headfirst into the abyss of his universe. Climbing out from his heavenly lair seemed inconceivable.

The knock at the door startled me.

Tobias rose from the chair and made his way over toward the hall leading to the door. "Stay as you are."

I held my arms across my chest to cover myself, wary of this sense of defenselessness and watching the space where he'd just been standing while trying to listen to who he was talking with.

"Thanks, Coops. Half an hour." I heard the sound of the door closing. Tobias reappeared around the corner and he narrowed his gaze.

I snapped my arms down and glanced behind him to make sure he was alone.

He held a sleek phone, and it was the one he'd given me a few days ago.

He held up the phone. "Got it back."

"From Logan?"

"Coops ran a check on it. She read my texts but other than that no damage done."

"Damage?"

"My email and phone number haven't been erased." He

narrowed his gaze. "Arms behind you, please." He threw the phone onto the sofa.

It was reassuring he was just as suspicious of her emotional choices.

He made his way to stand in front of me and that dark gaze roamed over me. He drank in my body. I raised my chin proudly, assuming the posture of a lover trapped under his spell.

I wondered if he'd ever had Logan in this pose. Something told me after a passionate fling of this magnitude, there'd be no finding your way back to a humdrum life. It was obvious Logan couldn't bear to be away from him and couldn't move on, either. I felt sorry for her even after all she'd done to me.

How could I never have known what I'd been missing all these years and never suspect somewhere out there my prince was waiting?

"Take off your panties," he said.

I hesitated for a beat and then responded quickly, peeling off my thong.

"And bra."

Unclipping it, I wondered why we were moving backward—wasn't I meant to be getting dressed for a party?

"Excellent." He took my underwear from me and strolled over to the sofa and threw them on there.

"Hope this isn't one of your pervy parties?"

He looked severe. "First, you will remain dressed."

"No shenanigans?"

"Only with me." He gave a smile. "This is a unique encounter."

"What kind?"

"I want us to remain discreet. Experience this once-in-a-lifetime opportunity to view their art. We may even be privileged enough to view their most cherished artifact."

I perked up. "What kind?"

He waved it off. "We've been invited to a private viewing. Some of the wealthiest men in the world will be there."

And he was taking me...

Though I realized the soiree hinted at misogyny.

"Tonight, there will be some of the most priceless pieces of art ever showcased from East Asia. And despite all of that, you will be the highlight of the evening."

"Not sure I can live up to that."

He strolled over to me and wrapped his hands around my naked waist. "You have no idea how powerful you are. We need to change that, Zara."

I stared up at him.

Tobias walked away from me toward the couch and lifted the lid off the larger box. He reached in for the beautiful Escada gown he'd bought me just yesterday from Harrods.

"This is what you're wearing." He held up a delicate silk gold dress. "I'll be the envy of every man." He returned to my side with the gown and slid it over my head, pulling it over my curves.

It clung to me like spun gold, the material so fine it fell over my skin like water. Thin straps decorated with diamond-shaped beads caught the light. Turning slightly, I saw my reflection in the wall mirror and realized it was backless and the arch of the dress was just above my butt. "It's beautiful."

"As are you."

His mood seemed a little intense, as though he had something serious on his mind.

"Do you want to tell me?" I said softly.

He frowned my way.

"Something's bothering you?"

Tobias leaned into me and pressed his lips to mine, his tongue brushing my lower lip.

He broke away and trailed his fingers through a curl of my hair. "There, you've centered me."

I fiddled with the bra cups to make sure my breasts fit snuggly and resigned myself to the fact this design revealed an ample amount of my cleavage. A chill might have my nipples betraying me and perking to a deadly point—

Like they were doing now.

He quirked his lips into a smile. "I now know what true obsession is."

The same could be said about me. Tobias had never looked so dashing. Though I suspected it had little to do with that brand-new Brioni tuxedo he'd had tailored right here in the suite, and more to do with his hair ruffled playfully with that classic post-fucked flair.

Within minutes he'd helped me into the strappy heels and brushed falling locks off my shoulders, despite my attempt to use the length to cover my breasts.

"No bra?" I whispered.

"No, not tonight."

"I can wear panties, though, right?"

"No." He walked over to the chrome rack in the hallway and lifted off the satin coat he'd bought me. "Networking is essential in my line of work. You'll be my reward. Perhaps I'll take you during the evening to remind you you're mine."

A rush of excitement sent a flash of blood to my cheeks.

"It pleases me to know I'll be able to do this at will." He knelt before me and lifted the hem of my dress above my hips and his face closed in on my sex—

Sending a shudder spiraling between my thighs, my clit felt incredible as he kissed me, his tongue thrumming.

Leaning forward, swooning into the thrill of his flicking, I let out the softest mewl of pleasure.

He pushed himself to his feet. "You see the benefit of no panties?"

"Yes," I said in a rush, almost fainting at this lingering tingle between my thighs.

"Of course I don't want any other man to look at you." He pulled me into a hug. "But I must be reasonable and let you out sometimes." He peered down at me and winked.

Tobias tugged the belt of my satin coat tight around my waist.

Using the hallway mirror, he made a final adjustment to his bow tie.

I watched him, mesmerized, this devastation of beauty to behold, his suaveness a blending of broody dashing charisma enhanced by an edgy ruggedness.

And when he looked at me the way he was doing now with that undeniable authority, he made my core clench with want and my nipples bead and made me grateful to be hiding within this coat.

"Don't get too comfortable," he said. "The coat's coming off."

A thrill shot up my spine. I'd never gone out without underwear in my life. Luckily, no one would ever know.

We made our way down the corridor, and I felt Tobias's grip wrap firmly around my left arm. He was expecting me to take the lift *again*.

"Fear is merely an adversary," he said. "And adversaries only have power over us if we deliver it into their hands." He stepped inside and turned to face me.

I remained frozen before the open doors. That dreadful metal gape a cruel tease.

Now that happiness had found me this monster was going to end me.

I couldn't...not again.

I'd already braved this too many times this weekend.

"Zara." He held his hand out to me. "Overcome fear and you'll find freedom waiting for you on the other side."

I held my breath and stepped in and fell into his embrace, crashing against his firm chest.

"I'm here." He tipped my chin up as the doors closed shut behind me. "I've got you."

Staring into his eyes, I focused on him and his gorgeous face. If this was my last day on earth I'd be holding this beautiful image during these final seconds.

He grinned. "See, easy."

"For you." I shuddered as that first shake proved we were descending.

"Almost there."

"I want to know all about you," I stuttered out. "I want to know where you were born. If you have any siblings. Where did you go to school? What's your favorite food? Color?"

"Zara."

"Yes?"

"First floor."

Blinking at him, I pulled back a little to better read his face. That veil of mystery fell over him once more.

He grabbed my hand and interlocked his fingers with mine as he pulled me out. We hurried onward, bathed in the golden glow of the foyer, pure white marble beneath our feet, and above us swirls of light reflecting off the fine gold trimmings of a lavish decor.

The doorman pulled back on the handle and let us out with a respectful nod. We were met by the unique scent of freshly fallen rain, the weather holding off for a while to offer us a reprieve from the downpour, and the crispness of an autumn evening.

That familiar black Bentley waiting with Cooper loyally poised to open the passenger door.

A bright flash went off. "Get in," said Tobias.

Half-distracted by the photographer, I dipped my head and climbed into the back of the car.

Cooper waited by the driver's door and watched Tobias walk over to the photographer.

He started up a conversation with the man and I held my breath to see what he was going to do.

He gave his arm a friendly pat.

Tobias rejoined me in the Bentley, and Cooper climbed into the driver's seat.

"Who was that?" I asked.

"A photographer for *The London Times*." Tobias held Cooper's gaze in the rearview. "Usual protocol, please."

"Yes, sir." Cooper steered the Bentley away from the curb.

"What's the usual protocol?" I said.

"We prevent their publication. Either online or in print."

"How do you do that?"

"Whatever it takes." Tobias pulled out his phone and texted away. "Don't worry, no one gets hurt—" he arched a brow "—too much."

That didn't sound sinister at all.

I peered out. "Where are we going?"

"Kensington." Tobias raised his gaze to hold mine. "You'll be the most exquisite creature there."

I swooned at his words and sat back to admire this dark and dangerous enigma.

Tobias tucked his phone away and reached for my hand. "Usual protocol for us too, Zara."

"What's our protocol?"

"Don't let go of my hand."

24

The Tudor period had left all the eclectic touches of medieval England wrapped up in countryside charm. The dark wooden furnishings, colorful lattice windows and remarkable tapestries all evidence that the English aristocracy continued to thrive.

And should there be any doubt, one merely had to look around at the high-class guests at Hatwood House, one of the largest estates in Knightsbridge.

Those tailored tuxedos worn by suave-looking guests complemented the array of runway gowns draped over their pretty women. Discreet staff offered up endless trays of hors d'oeuvres and a constant offering of all sorts of booze.

I didn't belong here…

I loved every second of being with Tobias, but these last two days were overwhelming. I was regretting not getting to any of the work I'd lined up for Huntly Pierre. Instead of delving into my notes and preparing for the week ahead, I was fast heading into another late night.

With everything Tobias offered there was this sense of being swept along and continuously spoiled. It wasn't that I wasn't grateful but this was not my world and these were not my people.

Tobias turned to me. "You okay?" He'd sensed my reticence.

We'd spent too long getting ready for me to let him down and retreat. He leaned into me and whispered, "It'll be worth it. I promise."

It was no surprise that he attracted looks of admiration. Guests now and again stopped to introduce themselves, and the clipped accents and highbrow conversations proved my theory, these were moneyed visitors who could hold their own amongst London's elite.

We strolled from the foyer to the living room and onward into the luxury dining room.

There, lying on a central mahogany table was a scantily clad young woman. She looked no older than twenty. Upon her abdomen was a row of small plates lined from her chest to her groin, all containing small edible sweet delicacies.

Guests were helping themselves to her treats.

Tobias stared at her. "Are those DeLafée chocolate truffles?" He pointed to the plate between her breasts.

I scrunched up my nose in amusement.

"You know you want one." He led me toward the table.

Tobias leaned over her and picked up two chocolates. He threw her a smile of gratitude and she flushed brightly in response. She looked so vulnerable lying there, and with those tuxedo-wearing lions prowling around her it crossed my mind to sweep her up and get her out of there.

Tobias held a chocolate truffle to my lips. "Bite."

My mouth watered as the cocoa melted on my tongue.

He popped a chocolate into his mouth and let out an erotic groan. "Still not as delicious as you, Leighton."

I felt more daring than I ever had. "When will I get the privilege of tasting you? Tonight?"

"Careful, don't make me fall in love with you."

I let out a laugh. "Well, if that's all it takes…"

He broke into a smile. "Let's carve out some time later to explore that theory."

"Here?"

"I hear they have a pool grotto. We can skinny-dip. I'll show you my sea monster."

I burst out laughing. "You're on."

Through the swarm of guests came a striking vision—

The blonde's long stride and elegant form were equally as stunning as her beauty. She held herself with the glowing confidence of a supermodel, and I guessed her age at thirty-something. With her chiseled cheekbones and flawless complexion she owned perfection. Her red dress was as long and clingy as mine, though she easily stole the spotlight with that thick diamond necklace shimmering around her long neck, and more stones twinkled around her wrists.

If we were competing in the pert nipple awards, she'd be the front runner. Her low-cut dress and sheer gown revealed her thoroughbred genes in all their long-limbed glory.

She swept toward us with a catwalk stride. "Tobias!" Her accent as posh as a Sunday at Ascot. "You came."

"Violet." Tobias leaned in to kiss both her cheeks.

It wasn't so much a sense of jealousy as me soaking in the futility of competing with this goddess.

"This is Zara." He gestured to her. "Zara, this is our hostess, Violet Maxwell."

"I'm so glad you're here," she said.

"Thank you for inviting us," I replied.

Violet beamed. "Tobias, your bride is a real hottie."

"We're not married," I said.

"Not yet, but you two are a perfect match." She waved her hand. "Hugo will be so happy you're here. Hugo, come here."

A tall, handsomely weathered eighty-year-old stepped out of the crowd. "Well, look what the cat dragged in. Tobias."

"Hugo." He proffered his hand and shook his. "Always a pleasure, you both look wonderful. May I introduce Zara Leighton?"

From the way Hugo rested his hand on Violet's arse, this was not her father. That blinding ruby-and-gold band on her left ring finger proved they were married. This man was at least twice her age. And she looked so damn happy.

Tobias eloquently parlayed the conversation away from himself and managed to get Hugo talking about his morning golf, which of course Hugo had won. A few strategic questions later and Hugo was also sharing his plan to buy another hotel in Milan, an impressive addition to his apparent collection, Violet shared with us.

"We're off to Utah in January," said Violet.

"Perhaps we'll visit you?" said Tobias. "Stay at your Grand Royall. I hear you're taking five stars to the next level?"

Violet beamed at him. "We can attend Sundance together."

"Zara would love that," he said.

Hugo looked triumphant. "We have a rare conch shell trumpet on display!"

Tobias's face lit up with joy.

"We have all sorts of stuff here we know you'll like," said Violet. "Go take a look. We simply must do dinner."

"We'd love that." Tobias's gaze roamed toward where a crowd had turned the corner. "It's that way?"

"You don't have drinks?" Hugo sounded appalled.

"We want to enjoy the art first," said Tobias. "Give it our full attention."

"Wilder, you're ever an art connoisseur," said Hugo as he

turned to me. "Zara, the shell is a Nepalese antiquity. You can hold it if you like. Tell them to take it out of the case. The shell is one of five weapons of Vishnu, and can destroy your enemies if blown by an innocent who is worthy."

Tobias laughed. "I'm sure there's a joke in there somewhere."

They laughed and Violet leaned in to kiss both his cheeks again. "Don't leave it so long next time. We missed you."

He led me away from the Maxwells, and I sensed they were still staring at us as we walked away.

"They're nice," I said.

"They are."

"Looks like she did well."

"She did."

"She likes you."

"Violet married for love."

"She told you that?"

"Yes."

"How long have you known them?"

"A while."

I pulled on his arm. "Why are you always so elusive?"

He rested his hand on the lower curve of my back. "Look, there's the horn."

In the far glass cabinet rested an old shell wrapped in ornate silver and embedded with blue semiprecious stones. It was so pretty.

Two other guests were also milling around in here. Their attention had fallen on a collection of scary huge curved knives that looked like machetes.

"It's a kukri." Tobias pointed to the case. "The Nepalese use them to prepare their food. They also use them to kill. Hopefully not at the same time."

I waited until we were alone. "I'm serious."

"My favorite color is nude. Zara-nude to be specific."

I broke away from him and walked over to another glass case and stared at the conch shell trumpet.

"It's an instrument." Tobias neared me. "It's a means to enlightenment. Want me to get it out?"

"No. I might accidently bop you on your head with it."

He came closer. "You don't strike me as the violent type."

"I'm not talking to you. Not until you agree to open up." He stood by my side and his arm brushed mine.

I waited until we were alone. "Have you ever been married?"

He hesitated. "Let's not do this here."

Clenching my teeth, I stared at the horn. "We're alone."

"Still."

I turned to face him. "Yes, I love art. But what I also know is people are more important."

"I agree."

"Well, then."

"Zara, we've only been seriously dating for forty-eight hours."

The word *seriously* slipped through my defenses and I weakened. And then pulled myself back from his deflection.

"Why are you so evasive?" I raised my hand in protest. "When I ask you a question, you kiss me. Or…"

We were moving way beyond the boundaries of friends and yet, if he didn't let me in, how could there be an authentic *us*?

He arched a brow.

"What I do know about you is this—you're a talented inventor, which you've turned into a successful business. You have an incredible building with your name on it in the Wharf—"

"It's not a phallic representation. If that's where you're going with this."

"Tobias."

"Though it could be." He peered through the glass to take a closer look.

"There you go again." I peered in too. "Using humor to divert the truth."

"I am what you see."

"You're closed off. You refuse to let me in."

He stood straight and stared at me with those green eyes softening under the fluorescent light. "This might have been a mistake."

I swallowed hard.

He wasn't talking about the party.

"I'm sorry," he said. "I didn't mean that. You've come into my life like a breath of fresh air. Your happiness is more important than my own. It's just that I have certain commitments. It makes for a delicate balance."

Yet another encrypted meaning for me to wrap my head around. Tobias was like one of those icebergs, where you realize you're merely glimpsing the surface and yet beyond the depths there was so much more.

I broke his gaze.

"I've never been married. There, how was that?"

"I'm stronger than you think. You can lean on me."

He shoved his hands into his pockets.

Silence lingered and I let it, hoping it would feed back and unsettle him. "Anything else you want to tell me?" I said.

He let out a sigh. "I can be intense in the bedroom. Dominating. Some would say punishing."

"In what way?"

"I'm obsessive about how many orgasms I can give you over the course of a night."

I rolled my eyes.

"It's a fact."

My sex throbbed and I forced myself to pull back from this erotic brink.

"I've offended you?" he asked softly.

"What girl doesn't want to be taken hard by a hot guy?"

His eyebrows rose. "I make the *Kama Sutra* look vanilla."

I raised my chin proudly. "So, we're compatible in the bedroom, then."

"Well, it's a start."

"Wilder, I'm going to tie you down and torture you until you open up to me."

"Not into that."

I cupped his face in my hands and leaned in and kissed him, my tongue entering his mouth and swirling around his, demonstrating my power.

He pulled away and blinked at me. "You're going to have to do better than that if you want me to open up more."

"I'm not wearing any panties," I snapped. "Now how about some compromise?"

"Not quite seeing the connection."

Frustration welled in my belly. "I'm right here but you block me from getting close."

"I'm really rather boring. Nothing more to add really."

I walked away from him and quickly headed into the next room, relieved no one else was in here so I could calm my annoyance.

Upon the walls were paintings of the Himalayas. The artist seemingly the same for each one from what I could tell. Every season had been captured. That snow-covered tip of Mount Everest was worth revisiting when I cooled off and was calm enough to appreciate its Zen.

My feet jolted to a stop.

I saw him in the next room and even with his back to me I recognized that tweed-wearing threat. That unmistakable upper-crust English accent grating on my nerves. Nigel Turner, that wily *London Times* journalist was here.

I slid left and turned a doorknob and stepped into a hallway. Lifting my hem, I made my way down, unsure of the plan, just knowing I had to get as far away as possible.

I cursed him for using the same name as one of my favorite painters. Joseph Mallord William Turner was one of Britain's most talented romanticist landscape painters, and by all accounts he'd been the sweetest man and easily one of the most gifted masters of watercolor.

No, Nigel had no right to share his name.

I hurried round the corner and bumped right into Violet, our bodies clashing, and I almost fell backward. Steadying myself, I waved my apology and caught my breath as pain thrummed in my chest and my teeth chattered.

"Are you okay?" she said. "You look like you've seen a ghost?"

"Sorry," I said. "I was trying to get away from someone."

"Have you fallen out with Tobias?"

"No, it's not him. Just saw a journalist who's been hounding me."

"Why?"

"It's complicated. Has something to do with my father's estate." I didn't want to get into it.

She grabbed my hand and pulled me along the hallway. "Come on, I know where we can hide and no one will find us."

She burst out laughing with her playfulness, and it echoed behind us.

With my fingers interlocked with hers, we flew down the hallway in a cloud of her richly textured perfume that made me heady. Adrenaline pumped through my veins as I savored the thrill of escaping.

"What about Tobias?" I said.

"He'll be fine," she said. "Come on."

Having one up on Nigel with the host herself was hilarious, and I was grateful for Violet's generosity.

I knew Nigel would be cruel and ask all sorts of questions about *St. Joan* turning up at Christie's and his interrogation would no doubt turn nasty.

"In here."

We moved through a luxurious blue-themed bedroom.

Violet tapped a code into a walled keypad. "This is private."

The room was small. In the center stood a black marble pillared stand, and on top of it sat a glass case. Resting within the protective square was an ornate carved metal bowl and a gong beside it.

I approached respectfully. "It's beautiful."

"Tibetan singing bowl," Violet whispered as she closed the door behind us.

I looked around, realizing she'd brought me into a walk-in safe. "Why is it not on display with the others?"

"It's priceless. Goes all the way back to the first Dalai Lama."

"Seriously?"

Delicate symbols trailed around its lower base and around the rim were a swirl of lilies.

The handle of the gong looked bronze. A strange sense of peace emanated from its simple design.

It felt too sacred for this place.

"Hugo says it's like owning the equivalent of the Holy Grail." She waved it off and neared me. "Just a silly old pot if you ask me. I keep all my jewelry in here too. Sometimes I just drench myself in diamonds and run around naked."

She made me laugh as that visual flashed before me. "The stuff in here is worth millions."

"Then I feel honored." I took her hands and squeezed them. "Thank you for saving me."

"Better?"

"Much."

"It's my pleasure."

"Thank you, Violet. Sorry for taking you away from your guests."

"I'm so happy you came. Tobias never brings anyone to our parties usually." Her words made me feel selfishly happy. "He has lovely taste."

"The dress?" I ran my hand down the material over my belly. "It's more revealing than I'm used to."

"Curves are a gift. Use at will." She flirtatiously raised a shoulder. "I love Escada. Saw that one on the catwalk in New York."

I looked down at my shimmering dress and admired it.

She let out a sigh. "Tobias's such a mystery."

I went to tell her I was hoping to get him to reveal more about himself but thought better of it. "He's incredibly kind."

"Where did you meet?"

"At The Otillie." I pointed to the bowl. "I'm an art special-ist but this kind of thing is a little out of my league."

"Paintings?"

"Yes."

"Hugo has a few. He has a thing for Picasso."

"Does he own one?"

"Yes." She scrunched up her face. "It's silly. But he loves it. A dog. I could have drawn it and he could have paid me millions instead."

"It's a sausage dog." I shrugged. "Probably."

"Hugo says it's worth a fortune."

"How long have you been married?"

"Ten years. I was beginning my modeling career and he saved me."

"You didn't like it?"

"I love cheese more." She grinned. "I love cheddar. Brie." She caught her tongue between her teeth.

"Hugo seems lovely."

"He's adorable. Lets me do whatever I like. You know, within limits."

It was nice to see her happy.

"He lets me play." She pouted and stepped toward me. "Do you play?"

"Um…" Tennis came to mind but I'd never been any good at it.

Then I realized—

She came closer. "I can't get over how pretty you are."

"I thought that when I first saw you."

She captured me with her gaze, her dreamy aura proving she was the most beautiful woman I'd ever met. I imagined Hugo kept her on a tight leash.

A sigh escaped her lips…

She closed the gap between us. "Would you like some snow?"

I shook my head. "No, I don't do anything like that."

Her body pressed against mine. "Zara, such a pretty name." Her lips brushed mine. A flit of her tongue.

A wave of confliction as I feared offending her.

"I'm not—" I rested my hands above her chest and gave her a gentle nudge.

"There you are," said Tobias.

Violet stepped back and she looked back coyly at him. "Hello."

He strolled on in with his usual confidence. "Girl-on-girl action? And you started without me?"

I stood frozen, mortified.

He gave a cute smile. "I followed the exquisite scent of Obsession."

My perfume; the one gifted to me by him back at the hotel.

Perhaps this was his way of expressing how he felt about me, my beautiful, unfathomable Tobias.

He neared me and wrapped his arm around my waist and jerked me toward his firm chest, his hand sliding down my spine and continuing beneath my dress. He clutched a butt cheek and held me firmly against him.

I yelped as his hand squeezed my arse and he pressed his mouth to mine, kissing fiercely, controlling and giving me no choice but to surrender.

He pulled away and smiled. "Remember, we talked about this, baby. I. Don't. Share." He looked over at Violet. "But if you want to play with yourself while we watch, Violet, by all means."

"Tobias." I bit my lip.

Violet raised her chin proudly.

"You know I adore you, Violet." He stared at me as though I was the culprit. "But I'm the jealous kind."

"I'm not allowed to play with men." She arched a sexy brow. "You know that."

"Well, it's been fun, but Zara has to be up early." He let me go and strolled over to Violet and reached for her hand.

She raised it and smiled sweetly.

He kissed the back of it. "See you in Utah, Vi."

"Can't wait." She winked at me.

Tobias wrapped his arm around my waist and led me out. We headed back down the hallway toward the foyer.

I let out a deep sigh. "Still trying to work out what happened in there."

He nudged me against the wall and trapped me there. "Don't disappear like that again. Understand?"

A jolt of exhilaration made me shudder. "I was trying to avoid—"

His lips crushed mine, his body firm and unrelenting, his cock digging into my abdomen. "Zara, see what kind of trouble you get into when you leave my side." He broke into a wide grin.

My sudden coyness surprised me and I felt like a naughty schoolgirl. "I didn't encourage her. She just came to me. Offered me coke and, well, you saw the rest."

"My timing is impeccable, as always."

"You seem to know each other well?"

"I've never fucked her."

"Never asked."

"You thought it." He lifted my hands above my head and pinned them there. "And I certainly don't pursue married women. You and I, we're exclusive, right?"

"Yes, I want that more than anything."

"Good. You don't know how happy that makes me. Look, we have all the time in the world to get to know each other. Maybe the rest of our lives?"

"I need more of you." That came out wrong and I cringed.

He kissed the end of my nose. "Go on, then. Ask me anything."

There was no way we could avoid it any longer. Our pasts were so much of who we were and exposing ourselves completely and braving to be vulnerable in front of each other was how we'd sustain an *us*.

"Your parents?" I said softly.

"They're no longer alive. But you already know that from your research on me." He let go of my wrists and stepped back and said, "Sure you want to do this?"

"Yes."

His gaze swept over the ground.

"Your uncle took you in?"

"He's like a father."

"How old were you?"

"Nine."

"Thank God you weren't on that flight." He broke my gaze. I read his face. "You were?"

"Staying alive until help came proved more challenging. We crashed in the Outback."

"Australia? Were you alone?"

There came a pained hesitation. "Yes."

"What happened?"

His lips curved in a wry smile. "Well, I survived if that's what you're wondering."

"Oh, Tobias. I feel so…" *Stupid* came to mind and embarrassment bloomed for my tactlessness.

With his thumb he lifted my chin and leaned in, kissing me tenderly, a slow leisurely melding of tongues as our lips locked passionately. He'd taken this tense moment and morphed it into sweetness.

This man was letting me in.

His lips slid to my throat, planting kiss after kiss, running his lips along to my shoulder and then my ear. "I promise to tell you everything. But not here."

Hand in hand we moved fast and headed toward the sound of laughter from the other guests. Music became louder as we returned to the foyer.

"Let's go home," he said.

"Sorry you didn't get to see everything," I said. "Hope I didn't ruin the evening?"

"Never."

We hurried toward the front door.

"Zara Leighton?" came the screech of Nigel Turner.

I closed my eyes as though that alone would make the nightmare go away. Tobias gestured to the coat checker and she disappeared behind a wall.

He turned to face Nigel. "Good to see you again. Did you catch the swords? Great collection. Sorry we can't stay and chat."

"So it's true." Nigel looked triumphant. "You two are dating?"

"Your photographer caught us coming out of our hotel. I told him what I'll tell you now. Bury the photos."

Nigel smirked. "Or you'll bury us?"

"I'm not morally bankrupt, Nigel, but thank you for the vote of confidence." Tobias smiled as he took my coat from the coat checker. "Do you like being senior editor?"

Nigel turned to me. "Love to know where that *St. Joan* went. Any ideas?"

My gut wrenched and I turned to shrug into my coat that Tobias was holding for me.

"We were discussing your intrusion into our privacy," said Tobias. "I'm having lunch with your boss tomorrow. We'll discuss it then."

"With Bert Sanders?" Nigel smirked. "You'll be hard pushed to shut this down."

Tobias reached out and pulled me into a hug. "Actually, it's with Rufus."

Nigel paled and worked hard at swallowing a lump in this throat.

"Destroy the photos," said Tobias, and he led me away.

We headed out and down the steps.

Tobias gave me a sideways glance. "That's why you were hiding?"

I gave a nod. "Looks like you rattled him. Who are you meeting with?"

"Rufus Edwin Marshal." He waved his hand toward the Bentley.

I snapped my head to look at him. "Isn't he that mogul who owns the *Times*?"

"Let's take you home." Tobias gave Cooper a wave.

"So that's what you meant by 'usual protocol'?"

"We've had more than enough fun for one night. And by *we* I mean you."

"You missed it, then?"

Tobias stood up straight and turned to face me, his eyes inquisitive.

"In Violet's safe?" My elbow struck his ribs. "You were so busy ogling our tryst you missed the bowl."

"What bowl?"

"Exactly."

He opened the back door and ushered me in and I snuggled in the corner as a thrill of excitement curled up my spine. We were alone at last. *Kind of.*

"Coops," he called out. "Privacy, please."

"Of course, sir."

The Bentley pulled out of the driveway and the sleek black glass divider slid up and cordoned us off from our chauffeur.

"Violet told me the singing bowl is thousands of years old."

Tobias rolled his eyes.

The tip of my shoe tapped his calf. "Time to make it up to you. Us leaving so soon."

He gave a mischievous look. "Very inconvenient. Remember, I'm a demanding lover."

"Remember, I'm more than capable of appreciating rare treasures." I arched a brow. "I'm going to rock your world."

"Hands behind your back," he warned. "Use your teeth to unzip me."

"This isn't exactly what I'd call a punishment." I slid off the seat and positioned myself between his thighs, my mouth watering for him.

"What would you call it?"

"A reward." Through clenched teeth I lowered his zipper, my nose trailing down his groin, doing my best to calm my heart racing with how daring this felt.

It felt incredible to be this risqué. His cologne fired up my senses and mixed with his heady erotic scent, sending thrills of pleasure to my sex.

Tobias's impatience forced him to help and he eased his trousers over his hips. "I felt sorry for you there."

His erection burst free and I licked the tip.

"You're so thoughtful," I said with a Georgian lilt. "That's my Scarlett O'Hara." I caught him in my mouth and sucked the head.

He hissed through his teeth. "I have a clever retort but it's not worth the risk."

I peered up at him. "I've been fantasizing about doing this to you all evening." I ran my tongue along his full length.

His head crashed back against the headrest. "It's the least I can do."

I sucked in my cheeks and took him all the way to the back of my throat, using my tongue to swirl and caress, feeling his thighs tense either side of me. I brought my hands round and cupped his balls.

He rose off the seat a little. "Careful, I'm going to come if you don't stop."

My head bobbed as I continued to lavish him with affection, he was rock hard and felt powerful in my mouth, his sculpted marbled erection an extension of the dynamism he wielded.

Seeing his eyes closed, his jaw slack, and hearing his gasps that were short and sharp, I prided myself on the effect I was having on him.

Back at that grand Tudor house, Tobias had braved to open up to me a little. My chest heaved for the kind of grief he'd endured and now understood his reluctance to disclose more.

I soothed him with licks and kisses and then sucked him into my mouth even farther, all the way to the back of my throat.

Gently, I peeled back his shirt covering his Latin tattoo and wished I could read those italic words continuing down to his groin.

"Zara." He warned. "I'm close."

My tongue played around the edge of his head to torture him with pleasure and he let out ragged gasps, his fingers digging into leather until they made their way to my hair, his hands fisting in my locks and his strength owning my pace.

His breath stuttered. "You're the first person I've ever met who can make time stand still."

Never had we felt closer, so intensely connected, and my heart soared that we'd managed to find our way to this precious intimacy.

His final thrust came with a husky groan.

Swallowing him, drinking and gulping the finest nectar, it was as though I was tasting champagne for the first time again. I reveled in its potency that had my own sex clenching with need, the purest essence of him on my tongue, filling my mouth, my throat with *him*.

More than this, tonight I'd made a chink in his armor. He cupped his hand over his eyes. "How do you do that?"

I lapped at the rest, taking more, wanting more and demanding more with my tongue as my lips payed homage to his cock. "Do what?"

He sucked in the deepest breath. "You unhinge my soul."

And I looked up at him, at his beautiful face and the wonder of him.

25

We stopped off for a bottle of fine wine on the way home.

I'd snuggled with Tobias in the back of his Bentley, all the way to Notting Hill. He'd wanted to return to The Dorchester but I'd persuaded him to bring me back to my flat. I needed an early start tomorrow to go over my files.

"Zara," he whispered and pulled me in closer. "You're so right. You rock my world. God, you're an obsession like no other."

Nuzzling against his warm chest I let out a sigh of happiness.

I was relieved when he let Coops off for the rest of the night and held back my grin when I overheard him tell Cooper to pick him up from here in the morning.

My toes had curled with excitement.

In the kitchen, Tobias set about uncorking the cabernet sauvignon, a 2012 Laira from Australia, and I grabbed two glasses.

We settled in the living room.

"You seem to know a lot about wines," I said, taking a seat next to him on the couch.

He shrugged out of his tuxedo jacket and threw it over the back of the sofa. "French ancestry. It's in my blood."

It tasted amazing; delicious blackcurrants adding to the flavor.

"Clara loves wine too," I said. "She drags me along to wine tasting events." We'd also had some epic trips to France but I wasn't ready to share that right now.

"I can only imagine the mischief you both got up to."

I gave a crooked smile. "Why technology?"

"My uncle was into it. I suppose that's why you chose art, because of your dad?"

"Yes and no." I thought back to Dad sharing his love of art with me. "I was about five years old when I visited my first museum. I became mesmerized by one of the paintings and forgot where I was. I couldn't tell you the name of it now but there was a horse. I was worried because its rider was fighting a big dragon."

"St. George and the Dragon?"

"Probably. The rendition looked so real. Like a photograph. When I finally broke from my trance my dad had moved on to the next room."

"He should have been holding your hand."

"I don't remember being scared. Just ran off to look for him. He was in the adjoining showroom looking at another painting. Hadn't even realized I was missing. What I remember from that day was how that painting made me feel. Invisible, I suppose. It drew me in and made me feel safe. I didn't understand it then. Now I need to be around art or I get antsy."

He gave a nod of understanding. "Art set you free."

"Yes." The wine warmed me and I sighed with contentment. "Each time I step foot inside a gallery it's as though I'm drawing on the strength and the wisdom of the artists. Their profoundness. Art speaks to us. Connects without boundaries. There's no other explanation for why it feels so timeless." I placed my hand on my heart.

"Art teaches us how to be."

"It stirs love."

"Yes, it does."

"You help me see art differently, Tobias."

"How?"

Resting my palm on my chest, I let out a wistful sigh. "I feel like something's opened up inside me. These feelings go deeper now. They're more authentic."

I studied his face, trying to read his reaction.

He rose to his feet and strolled over to the window. He pulled back the curtain. "You have a nice neighborhood."

"I like it."

He seemed thoughtful as his gaze scanned the view.

I went to ask if he'd like me to put music on and thought better of it, sensing his comfort with the silence.

Pulling my legs under me I continued to nurse my wine and rested my head on my arm and watched him.

He peered out. "I like it here."

"Me too."

"I think you might have something to do with it."

He looked so beautiful standing there and seemed more relaxed than I'd ever seen him and I loved being part of the reason he'd allowed himself these precious hours to recharge.

The quiet between us felt welcome and I knew we both needed this time to decompress.

He turned and faced the room as he sipped his wine, his frown deepening. "My dad was flying a painting from France to Sydney," he began softly. "I'd accompanied him on the trip to Australia. Our plane went down in the middle of the night. The pilot and my dad died instantly. Mom…"

My hand went to my mouth and I held back from speaking, realizing how fragile this moment was.

"I don't remember much. Flashes here and there. The

mind's way of protecting me, I suppose. Tau, an Aborigine, found me just in time. I'd run out of water. I'd heard somewhere that you should stay with the plane. So I did. I'd never been so damn thirsty."

I wondered if Tau had seen the plane go down.

"He was on a tribal challenge. They're hunters and gatherers, as you know. He'd just turned seventeen and had been sent out there to prove he could survive in a rite of passage. They didn't expect him to bring back a souvenir in the way of a nine-year-old. The tribe took good care of me until help arrived."

My face flushed with the realization his tattoo on his right arm wasn't Polynesian, it was Aborigine. He'd immortalized his experience in ink.

"A team retrieved my parents' bodies and flew them to the States. The painting survived, if you can believe that. Two weeks later I made the journey that ensured it reached its destination. Reni was an old friend of my parents'." He breathed through a wave of pain. "These were my mother's final wishes spoken seconds before she passed away."

"Oh, Tobias."

"I'll never forget Reni's face when I turned up with her *Madonna Enthroned with Saint Matthew*."

"By Annibale Carracci?" I whispered it.

"It's at the Getty now."

And yet those people viewing the *Madonna* would never know the bravery behind it hanging there.

"My uncle Fabienne flew out and helped me get to Reni's place in Sydney. After my parents' funeral he took me back with him to France. He didn't want me to forget my dad's legacy, so when I turned fourteen we returned to Massachusetts and the town where I grew up. I enrolled in school there and later studied technology at Stanford. My uncle returned to France."

"He was good to you?"

"He's wonderful. Like a dad." He smiled. "Now I just hop on a plane and see him whenever I like."

It was so good to know he was still close to his uncle.

"Turned out I had a knack for business."

All that had happened to him was what drove him now, all that pain, all that fear, those suppressed memories his consciousness must have battled every day.

I swiped away a tear.

He gave a solemn nod. "Tau found me just in time. I'd woken up to see my leg gnawed off by a kangaroo."

I gasped and then realized his joke. "Tobias!"

He burst out laughing. "Don't feel sorry for me, Zara. Look at your life. Your house burned down as a kid. You never knew your mom. I got a good nine years with mine."

"Still." I blinked back tears as I thought of that small, scared boy.

He brushed his hand over where his tattoo lay beneath his shirt. "Once I turned eighteen I got this." He rested his palm on his arm. "Now I have the influence and money to repay their kindness. Much of the Aborigine land was taken. I'm part of a movement to restore it back to them. It's a delicate balance. We try not to disrupt their clans."

"What does the turtle mean?"

"The tribe told me it was my sign. When you're nine that tends to stick with you. It represents mother earth, strength and love."

"I love it."

"I've noticed."

My blush burned my cheeks.

"I'm not fucked up, Zara, but I am complicated in a way."

He shrugged. "I adore art and that's where my desire to open a gallery came from."

"You're following in your parents' footsteps."

He held my gaze for the longest time. "Do you have anything to eat? I'm starving."

"Oh yes." I leaped up. "I should have offered."

We made our way to the kitchen.

He peered into the fridge. "You don't have much."

I'd been so busy I'd not had time to shop. "I've got this." I held up the box of chocolate cake mix.

"Cake it is." He rolled up his sleeves.

I brought out the egg carton from the fridge.

"You're going to have to take it from here." I gestured to my beautiful gown.

"You could always take it off." He smirked as he read the back of the box.

"I'll let you do that afterward."

"You're on." Tobias looked adorable following the instructions. Adding the ingredients of vegetable oil, water, and then cracking that single egg open before adding it to the mixture in that large bowl. I handed him a wooden spoon to stir.

"You know it's cheating, right?" I pointed to the packet.

"I'm afraid I'm not much of a cook. But I love learning new skills. You're good for me."

I melted on the spot as I dropped his gaze, dipping my finger into the chocolaty mixture.

He grabbed my hand. "The egg's raw. You can't die on me. Not after waiting all my life to find you."

My hand froze midway and my eyes rose to meet his.

"What I meant was..." His smile broadened. "There's only one way to make this more perfect."

"How?" It slipped out wistfully.

"Add icing."

"Oh, I'll see if I have any." I opened a cupboard door.

"I wasn't talking about the cake," he said softly.

I turned to smile at him.

He leaned toward me and kissed my cheek. "But now we're on the subject let's bake it and have cake in bed."

I'd never known this kind of happiness before. I reached for that packet of icing. It was impossible not to smile.

"Zara."

I turned to face him.

"I think it's going to be amazing." He grinned. "More delicious than we ever imagined."

26

The week whirled by as I threw myself into work with passion. Those spontaneous dinner dates with Tobias had been exhilarating, and I couldn't wait to see him again tonight. Thoughts of him clouded my brain in the best kind of way, and thinking of Tobias was a welcome reprieve from the intensity of these hours spent huddled over a table at the Witt Library. I loved this place and had spent most of my student days here. It was named after art historian Sir Robert Witt and was a big part of The Courtauld Institute. This library had once been my home away from home.

Forcing my attention back on the file in front of me, I re-read the details of Interpol's case where a Titian had been stolen weeks ago, from the Burell family in Amboise in France.

For the last six hours I'd been entrenched in scrap pieces of paper, official records, old photos and tenuous provenance. With another twenty files to go through this was going to be a painstaking process.

Danny sat to my left at a desktop computer clicking away through the Witt's database.

He was chewing on a stick of licorice and now and again he huffed his frustration.

We'd not traveled far from The Tiriani Building, with Huntly Pierre's offices being a stone's throw from here.

Danny and I had been provided with one of their larger rooms to work in, enabling us to spread out our paperwork and focus in the quiet.

Danny leaned back in his chair. "What are we looking for again?"

"Anything that might link the artwork. Give us an idea of why these paintings were chosen by Icon."

"We know why. They're worth a fortune. And he's a greedy asshole."

"Come here." I stood and spread the paperwork out and pointed to the photo Danny had brought up on the screen during his earlier presentation.

We peered down at the image of a golden-lit rotunda, a grand feature at the Burells' family home. Also in the photo before us was an impressive collection of art, including many of the Old Masters, lining the circle of the room. That long wire hanging from the center of the roof was a stark reminder of what our thief had achieved.

"He stole the Titian," said Danny. "Rappelled in."

"He's fit. We know that. Probably works out."

"So what am I missing?"

"You told us he used a power tool to cut a hole in the ceiling's stained glass window? And the police report validates that."

"Yes."

"See anything interesting?" I pointed to the other paintings.

"They're all real? Right?"

"Yes. Our guy stole a Titian. Worth in the region of eight million pounds."

I slid my finger along. "That's a Paul Cezanne, right there. It's hanging five feet away from where the Titian hung. Take a guess at how much it's worth."

He shrugged. "Ten million?"

"This is one of a series of depictions Cezanne painted in the 1890s."

An oil on canvas of two men sitting opposite and leaning over a table and playing cards, a bottle of wine between them. An elegant prelude to Cezanne's final years.

"Only five *Card Players* exist," I added. "The last one was sold to the nation of Qatar for two hundred and fifty million dollars."

"What the fuck!"

"Exactly, so why did our thief go to all that trouble for a Titian?"

"Maybe he panicked when the bird flew in?"

"Yet the raven never set off the alarm. They found it happily perched on the van Gogh. He's cool enough to reevaluate the situation." I caressed my brow, something wasn't adding up.

"Maybe this time he cracked under pressure."

I grabbed that stick of licorice out of Danny's hand and took a bite. "What does all this tell us about his motive?"

"Icon's selective about what he steals?" Danny shrugged. "Maybe he's great at technology but an ignoramus when it comes to art."

"What do you do before you break into a house?"

"Case the joint." He smiled at that.

"Research." I looked at the photo. "He knew the Burells' rotunda floor was set to detect weight and movement. His scrap with the bird proves that."

"The loss of feathers."

"All the art is a private collection. Not publicized. So if he doesn't know what he's going for before he goes in, you'd think he'd learn a bit about art so his time and his risk are not wasted?"

"See something worth more—"

"Take that one, as well. Or at least instead of the other one."

He frowned at the photo. "Maybe he's working for a private collector?"

"The kind that's okay with him stealing a Titian—"

"But not a Cezanne." Danny frowned. "What's going on?"

"Exactly." I looked over at the computer. "Get back to work." I raised my invisible whip and struck him with it.

He feigned defending himself from my attack and laughed all the way back to his workstation.

He turned serious. "Zara? Can I ask you a personal question?"

"Sure."

"Do you think Ouless's *St. Joan of Arc* that was stolen from Christie's once belonged to your dad?"

"Does Adley know?" Everything tightened in my stomach.

He gave an apologetic nod.

"I'm sure we'll find out soon," I said. "Either way the investigation is added to these." I glanced over to the case files.

"I'm here for you if you need anything," he said.

"Thank you."

"Back to work then."

I gave a polite smile to hide my frustration and returned to the table.

Danny had fun cranking the library mechanism to open the shelves, and we slid between the thin corridor to retrieve the compendiums we needed to track the Titian's provenance. We carried the large books back to our private space.

Two hours later and we had our first breakthrough.

Danny stood beside me as I talked him through the painting's history.

I placed my scribbled Post-it notes in a line to represent the names of previous owners, and used them for reference before heaving open one of the larger compendiums that we'd pulled from the sixties section.

I pointed to the page. "Here's our Titian. Look, in July 1955 the painting turned up for auction in Amboise in France. The Ramirez family who lived in Bobigny reported it missing, stolen from their home. When they found out about the intended auction they argued against the sale and demanded their Titian back. It appears the Burells had the money to have their attorney deal with the mess. Says here, ownership landed with the Burells."

"Were the Ramirez family compensated?" Danny moved quickly back over to the computer and tapped away, searching out any news articles related to the contested ownership.

I scrolled through my phone, trying to come up with new and imaginative ways to coax Tobias to reply. I sent him a silly cat GIF and suppressed a smile.

"Found something." Danny centered the article. "This is from the local newspaper back then, *Le Rue Relais*."

I threw my phone back into my handbag and hurried over. We both stared at the headline enlarged on the screen.

Danny shot up straight. "No way."

"Make sure it's the same family."

"Same address."

"Same time frame?" My stomach churned with the revelation.

"It is." He stared at me. "Tell me that's not what I think it is?"

Our gazes returned to the screen—

Reading on, I cupped my hands over my mouth, aghast at the terrible truth.

27

Silence reigned in Huntly Pierre's conference room, emphasizing how traumatized we felt. Danny and I had returned to The Tiriani building just before 5:00 p.m.

The other staff were wrapping up their work for the day and preparing to head home.

I needed to document the details of what we'd found and Danny looked too shaken to be alone. He'd sat for the last twenty minutes with his head in his hands.

We were both grieving for the family. The injustice.

"Dan," I soothed.

"The Burells..." his voice cracked with emotion "...had them killed."

My weary gaze fell once more on *Le Rue Relais* newspaper article Danny had printed off from July 1955. It relayed the tragedy of a house fire at the Ramirez's home in Bobigny, and the loss of the family. Only their fifteen-year-old daughter, Sarah Louise, had survived. That large oak tree with its strong branches that reached her bedroom window had been her miraculous liberator.

Sarah Louise Ramirez would be in her seventies now, if

she was still alive. She'd no doubt remember that night and might even be able to shed more light on her family. Maybe even remember them owning the Titian.

Melancholy shattered me; I knew all about the suffering that followed surviving a house fire.

I wanted to say something to reassure Danny that we didn't know anything sinister had happened for sure but motive was key in a case like this. That legal battle of ownership over a Titian suggested foul play was a possibility. And the Burells' lawyers had dusted away the annoying rumors that followed.

Why did each revelation bring more questions?

My thoughts carried me back to *St. Joan* and her strange disappearance. I'd managed to keep my paranoia at bay but this sense of invasion prickled beneath my skin.

"What can we do about it?" said Danny.

"It's such a long time ago," I said.

"But surely there should be an investigation? Something done?"

"I know. Let's gather all the evidence on the other cases and maybe something can be done."

"When I first came into this job I knew there were some greedy cunts, but this is unspeakable."

I waved him back from the ledge. "The truth always rises, Danny. Maybe that's why you and I were chosen for this. Because we have the skills to know what we're looking at. And the determination to look deeper. We aren't willing to be silenced."

"Promise me you'll see this righted."

"I promise." That vow felt like an arrow to my heart.

I followed his gaze toward the conference door and saw a striking mirage—

Tobias was leaning casually on the doorjamb, his blue shirt and ripped jeans playing down the fact he ruled one of the most advanced tech empires. It was as though he'd purposefully dressed down to lessen his intimidation.

I always needed a few seconds to catch my breath with every new encounter. That kind face catching me off guard with its ethereal beauty, those refined masculine edges, the way his smile reached his eyes.

After this afternoon he felt like a goddamn miracle.

"Elena told me it was okay?" he said. "Hope I'm not disturbing you?"

"Of course not." I rounded the desk and made my way toward him.

Danny's inquisitive stare bounced to Tobias and back to me again.

"We were just finishing up." I reached for Tobias's hand and gave it a squeeze.

He came in farther and slipped his hand down to the small of my back and tipped me backward in one continuous movement to dip me, and I let out a gasp of surprise. I was powerless to resist as I hung completely off balance. All I could do was grin up at him.

He leaned in and kissed me, crushing those soft lips to mine, and the day slipped away... Tobias peered up at Danny. "This is how Zara greets all of Huntly Pierre's clients. Quite the service."

He lifted me up, and I sprang to steady my feet and tipped forward, leaning conveniently against his biceps. "You're incorrigible."

He peered across the room. "Where did the Pollock go?" He laughed and brought his arms up, shielding himself from a possible thump.

"I've been put through more than enough trials, mister."

He studied my face. "How was your day?"

"Challenging." I wrapped my arms around him and squeezed him tight and my entire body tingled.

Danny gathered his files and came over. "Good to see you again, Mr. Wilder." His eyes found mine and widened in a questioning way as he walked toward the door. "I'll let you continue with your consultation."

"Danny!" I chastised him playfully.

Tobias rolled his eyes and used his foot to kick the door closed behind him.

I knocked on the conference room window after Danny to get his attention and shouted through the glass, "Call me, okay? If you need to talk about today."

Danny offered me a thumbs-up.

I turned back to Tobias. "He'll tell everyone about us."

"You don't mind that?" He tipped my chin up. "Do you?"

"Of course not. I'm just not sure how Adley will take me moving in on his most prestigious client."

"Think of me as a perk." He waggled his eyebrows and pulled me into him.

"You don't know how wonderful it is to see you." I glanced back at my folder.

"Sounds like you both had a rough day."

"We found something at the Witt. The provenance of one of the paintings appears to have a sketchy history. We can't be certain but it looks like a possible homicide is connected to the theft, dating back to 1955."

"That would be difficult to prosecute now. Even with hard evidence."

"I know. And all to own a Titian."

His gaze drifted to the file. "Anything else turn up?"

There ran an insidious thread connecting Titian's painting, the Jaeger's Munch, and now my *St. Joan*. All of them sharing the one common denominator of a sketchy provenance.

I stilled as the pieces formed in my mind. "Looks like the work of Icon."

He gave a shrug. "Sounds like karma."

"Sounds like arrogance. Whoever this is, they're reckless. He's unpredictable. He's passing over pieces that far exceed what he's taking. For someone driven by money this doesn't add up."

"Maybe it's not what's driving him. There's more fuel than finance. Wealth isn't the only motivation."

"Well, I'm not letting up. That Titian is still out there and I'm not going to stop until I find it."

He leaned in to kiss my neck, and it was impossible to resist him. He crushed his lips to mine and kissed me greedily. When his hands cupped my butt and pulled me into him, I caved into his possessive hold and opened my mouth further, tangling with his tongue as this stir of arousal sent my thoughts scattering.

I smiled at him. "You're the best surprise a girl could wish for."

His expression became thoughtful. "You asked me to let you in."

I caressed his cheek and gave a smile of encouragement.

He leaned into my palm. "There's something I want to show you."

Our destination remained cloaked in secrecy.

With Tobias at the wheel of his sporty silver Jaguar, we drove along the backstreets of London and all the way to Copperfield Street.

Now and again, Tobias's eyes would lift from the road ahead and flit over to me, and each time I melted in my seat. When he reached over and held my hand I felt our closeness more than ever.

After thirty minutes of winding our way through traffic, Tobias parked his Jag alongside a large wall covered in lush greenery.

He reached over and kissed the back of my hand. "I've never shown anyone this. No one knows of my involvement. I'd very much like it to stay that way."

I peered up at that ancient wall strewn with wild, creeping ivy.

"I'm asking a lot." He leaned low and stared up at the wall. "But this is important."

"I promise."

We left the car and walked the rest of the way, and he pushed open a tall iron gate that squeaked on its hinges. We continued along a pathway covered with overgrown weeds and out-of-control plants. Either side of us were lines of half-sunken graves and most of them lost to the will of overgrown foliage.

Ahead of us rose tall Roman pillars on the side of a derelict church, appearing through the low hanging trees as if nature itself guarded this site. As we neared, I saw the powerful imagery of Christ crucified on the cross that was carved in stone and faded by time.

With my fingers interlocked with his we walked through the large double doorway and went on in, my gaze sweeping along the abandoned church. Above, the roof was so damaged it was partly open to the sky. Rotting remnants of what had once been pews were staged either side.

I jumped when a bird hopped on dry leaves to our left. More rustling here and there gave the wildlife away. The crisp night air surrounded us, and it felt naturally reverent as though an authentic spirituality had found its way in.

Tobias pulled me into him and gave me a reassuring hug. "This church was built in 1879." His face was full of wonder.

"This is what I love about British history. There's so much to learn from it." He pulled me along to the front of what had once been an aisle. "Look at the craftsmanship."

Overhead in a carved arch of stone was an intricate design that would have been worthy of the greatest of cathedrals with its complex layers of delicate flowers.

"Pagan?" I asked softly.

"Influenced by, yes." He pointed high toward the carved Roman faces set in the ceiling. "There's your first clue."

"Are you a member of a secret society?" I said. "We're going to dance around a central flame, praying to an ancient god."

"Preferably naked." He lowered his gaze to my lips. "I'll watch."

I gave his arm a tap. "You go first. I'll sit over there and enjoy the performance."

He laughed and shook his head, amused, but then his expression turned to sadness. "What you see here is about to be lost and all in the name of progress. This land is worth more than its heritage. It's going to be demolished. A new skyscraper is set to begin construction in less than a month."

A cold burst of air washed over me.

"Did you buy this land?" My voice broke with emotion.

"No. It was sold before I heard about it."

A dread welled and I realized this experience was going to haunt my dreams. "It's our last chance to see it?"

"This is why we're here." He took my hand again and led me farther down the aisle and I wondered if the path we took was through the old rectory. The walls were crumbling.

Descending into the murkiness we circled the stone steps lit up with modern lanterns that led the way. The chill prickled my forearms. Graffiti was scribbled on the walls in ink or sprayed with paint in a show of disrespectful plundering.

"The sacredness is still here," he whispered. "Do you feel it?"

"Yes, but there's a sadness too. I don't want it to be de-stroyed."

"There's always hope. We have that." He gestured the reason we were here was through that large wooden door ahead. "This is how we change the world. Through them."

He nudged the door open and I peered in at the sight ahead that was lit brightly with more lanterns—

Teenagers, twenty or so of them, and all of them dressed in work overalls and wearing hard hats. They sat here and there and they were working alongside ten adults. They were excavating.

"Who are they?" I whispered.

Tobias picked up a spare hard hat from a side table and placed it on my head. He took one for himself.

He tied my chin strap and whispered, "They're college students. The children of refugees. Don't worry, they only spend an hour down here one evening a week. But it's enough to stir their passion for conservation."

"Orphans?"

"Most of them. Many of their parents didn't make it. The system got overrun and we had to make special concessions to house all of them. If we send them back..." He gave a shrug.

"You own a charity?"

"Yes."

I was too speechless to answer.

He gave my arm a nudge. "Want a closer look at what we're working on?"

I shook my head as though coming out of a dream. "Yes."

When the teenagers recognized him, they dropped what they were doing, rose to their feet and ran to him. All of them reached out to wrap their arms around him. Their smiles hid the pain of what they'd gone through.

I stepped aside to give them more room and watched Tobias

interact with them with such kindness and patience that I had to squeeze back tears. He knew each of their names and turned around to include everyone. Their teachers came over to shake Tobias's hand and they chatted about their current progress.

He introduced me to everyone, and I knew I was witnessing a unique glimpse into his world. I understood why he kept it out of the headlines. That was his way of protecting these vulnerable children.

One of the male teenagers grabbed Tobias's hand and led him across the dirt floor to the back of the room. He wanted to show him what he'd accomplished and pointed to where he'd dusted away a Roman wall painting.

Standing back a little, I took it the magnificence of the ancient mural running along the entire wall. The painting depicting an ancient coliseum.

This was a peek into the profoundness that was London's history, a rich and never-ending insight into its past, stretching back all the way to 47 AD, when the Roman Empire owned the city and eventually turned it into the golden age of trade.

This priceless mural of Roman soldiers fighting in a coliseum, with its faded earth colors, was to be saved in a last-ditch effort to honor one of history's greatest times.

Tobias accepted the dry brush he was handed by the boy and set about joining him to dust away more debris. They chatted away about this and that and I overheard Tobias playfully arguing about football, and telling him that Liverpool was going to kick Manchester United's butt this weekend in Saturday's game.

Tobias glanced back at me and threw a wide grin.

This felt like the most precious of all the moments I'd ever spent with him. There were no flashy gadgets for him to hide behind, no alpha drama to protect him, this was the most authentic I'd ever seen him.

And he looked so happy.

Looking down at my arms there was already a fine layer of dust covering my skin and yet I didn't care.

"This is where I'd come from." Tobias peered up at me. "The night I met you at The Otillie."

It made sense now why he'd showered and changed in the staff room that evening and why he'd not wanted to tell me this before.

I now knew the privilege of him trusting me with this.

He patted the teen on his hard hat and rose to stand beside me again. "We're going to keep this wall intact and transport it to The Otillie. This is what the new wing is for. It will go on display in the early year."

"This is incredible."

And he'd just gone from mystery man to superhero status.

He leaned into me and whispered, "The sacrifice their parents made to get them to safety and ensure them a better life, it won't be wasted."

"I understand why you keep this so private."

He gestured to the others. "Their safety is my priority."

"That's why you keep out of the press too?"

"This, this is what's important." He raised his brush for me to take it. "Art is about chipping away until we get to the truth. When the truth protects others it should never be squandered."

"I'm wowed."

"Oh, I can do better." He broke into a smile and yelled, "Who wants fish and chips?" The roar of happiness echoed around us.

Tobias beamed at me. "Right there, that's my superpower."

28

I spent the following day working in my office at The Tiriani building while waiting for Abby, Shane and Adley to return. They'd had the uncomfortable task of visiting the Jaeger family to deliver the news their insurance claim was on hold until the provenance of their Munch could be further explored.

I had my own crises that needed airing with the team; that scandalous appearance of *St. Joan* wasn't going away.

By 6:00 p.m. I'd organized my office in preparation to head home, resigned to discussing my personal scandal tomorrow.

"We've got him!" Abby leaned on my office doorjamb and gave a victory wave.

"They arrested him?" I pushed myself to my feet. "Icon?"

"Ten minutes ago a security guard stakeout caught a glimpse of a man on the roof of the Tate Modern. They'd upped their security after the hit at Christie's. Private sector. He's drilling through the roof. The Met are closing in now."

"That's brilliant."

"I know, right?"

"Are they armed?" These words sent a slither of fear up my spine.

My intuition caused my mouth to go dry, and I reached for a bottle of sparkling water so I wouldn't have to look at her.

"Yes," she said. "I hope the fucker messes up and gets himself shot."

My throat tightened.

"I'll keep you updated." She turned on her heels and headed back to her office.

"I appreciate that," I called after her.

Trembling, I poured a few drops of water onto my bonsai tree and the delicate branches bounced as the water struck its leaves. Busying the creative part of my brain I ran through what I knew. Icon was supersmart, a man who understood technology and easily grasped the latest in security measures, so our man would no doubt love techie devices.

Was his reign as one of the world's most infamous thieves about to come to an end?

Don't.

Ignoring my dark musing, I recalled every interaction I'd ever had with Tobias, that first meeting at The Otillie. Where had he rushed off to later that night? Coincidentally the same evening that Munch was stolen. His financial status would provide him with the means to easily travel and his status could ensure his ability to jump on his private jet and fly to any destination on a whim.

Depending where the "job" was.

The suspect would know a lot about art and Tobias owned The Wilder, and was immersed in every aspect of this world.

The culprit wouldn't need to be greedy because he was already superrich. Perhaps the thrill of the heist was his main motive? His life would be complex and he'd no doubt have a busy schedule that would allow for an alibi when needed. He'd most certainly have contacts within high society so that when those elite invitations came along he'd have access into the private homes of the megarich.

Like an invitation to a secret society's orgy that would provide a reason to visit one of the grandest private collections of Goya on the planet.

Logan had never admitted she was Ruby. Maybe I'd read her wrong.

My hands tremored as I nudged the small plant's pot back a little. I was being absurd; I mean last night I'd spent a wonderful evening in that old church on Copperfield Street with Tobias. He was a good man. A kind man. Yet so many questions remained unanswered.

The evening Inspector Ford had visited my apartment I'd locked my door after I'd let Sergeant Mitchel in. Not only had Tobias accessed my flat, he'd turned up at the same time the police were there to question me.

I'd also been *his* alibi during the theft at Christie's.

My heart thundered as I remembered his unusual knowledge of Francisco Goya's *La Maja Desnuda* being hidden behind a fake painting in a state room at Blandford Palace.

Nausea welled in my stomach as I reached for my phone. What should I do? Warn him? No, that was ridiculous. Dangerous, even.

You've been burning the candle at both ends; your mind's rambling. But caressing my brow, I knew.

There was no use denying the truth anymore.

My hand reached for my phone and dialed his number—

"Hey," Tobias answered. "How's my girl?"

"Fine." Steadying my voice I stared at the bonsai tree. "I'm watering your gift."

"You're still at the office?"

"Yes. Where are you?"

He hesitated. "You're breaking up."

"Can I see you?"

"Can you hear me?"

I pressed my ear against the phone for ambient clues.

"Everything okay?" He came through faintly.

"Something came up that I need to talk to you about."

"Is it urgent?"

"Well—"

"Let me take you out to dinner later."

My heart pounded as I sensed him pulling away.

"You didn't say where you were?" I realized how that sounded. "I'm just interested."

He wasn't exactly going to tell me he was sawing through a roof. I was lucky he'd answered.

"Confession," he said softly.

"Oh?"

"I don't want to be here. I wish I was with you."

"Then be with me."

They're coming for you, Tobias, get out of there.

"I'm actually at the Coach and Horses."

"Covent Garden?"

"Yes. It's karaoke night. Office tradition. I always end up paying their bar bill. Sucker that I am."

My throat tightened at his lie but it was one that could easily be validated.

"It's a crappy line. I'll call you back."

He killed the call and left me staring at my phone in stunned silence.

Grabbing my phone and handbag, I flew out of there.

I reapplied fresh makeup in the cab on my way to the Coach and Horses, and let down my hair so the spiraling curls hid the fact I was staking him out if he really was there—

And not breaking into the Tate.

My heart was going to bloody well explode and I teetered

on the edge of having it smashed to smithereens. If anything happened to him I'd be to blame for not seeing this earlier. Not talking him out of it or warning the staff at Huntly Pierre.

This brazenness proved how far I'd fallen for him.

Still, there was uncertainty.

The pub was packed with wall-to-wall drinkers and the atmosphere crackled with the joy of friends hanging out.

I doubted I'd ever feel happiness again as I scanned the crowd.

A Beatles song blared from the karaoke stage, "Hey Jude," though the man's singing was terrible. The scent of booze wafted from the bar and the aroma of rich fried food came from the kitchen.

My phone vibrated in my hand and I stared down at the screen.

It was from Abby: We have him.

Heart pounding, I hurried into a corner and texted back, Do you have a name?

Abby: Not yet.

My fingers flew across the keys. Was he hurt? I backspaced, realizing how that sounded. Are they taking him to the Met?

Abby: Yes. More soon. Go celebrate. We're getting our art back!

I replied, Amazing Job. I managed that at least, wanting to roll into a ball and rock the rest of my life away.

Taking him right to the Metropolitan Police Station proved he wasn't injured at least. Hands shaking, I tucked my phone into my pocket, trying to see straight.

Should I go there?

My gaze locked on him across the bar and my brain exploded as I cringed against my insanity.

Thank God.

My gasp was muffled by the music.

Tobias sat in the middle of a crowded table at the far end of the bar. He was holding a bottle of Samuel Smith Imperial Stout, and was laughing at someone's joke. Logan sat beside him snuggled up close, her smile wide and her face flushed. She sipped from a tall glass of something fizzy.

This was what it felt to find my way to a well in a desert.

Tobias threw his friends a dashing smile as he shared a joke with them—

He looked extra gorgeous tonight, as though he'd gone out of his way to taunt me. That deep blue shirt, ripped blue jeans and black waistcoat emphasizing his knack for making casual look classy. His hair was extra messy as though he'd run his hand through it.

Lead ran through my veins as I realized I couldn't run up to him and wrap my arms around his neck and nuzzle in possessively.

Oh no, now I looked like the crazy stalker girlfriend.

Making my way to the bar all the way at the back, I eased through the mass of bodies, grateful for the camouflage.

I squeezed to the front and signaled to the barman. "Kamikaze, please."

And make it bloody quick, I mused darkly.

The young man with eighties' hair beamed at me and then got to work on my drink.

I needed to get the hell out of here and sleep away this horrible day.

The shot glass placed in front of me contained vodka, triple sec and lime and I threw it back with abandon, my mouth gaping at the burn.

Damn, I needed that.

Another one was placed it front of me and questioningly I stared at the barman.

"Happy hour," he shouted. "Two for one."

Damn it.

Why not, my nerves were raw from believing my boyfriend was Icon and I hated myself for doubting him.

I downed the glass.

Heading for the back door, I skirted the tables and headed to the restroom.

I worked on my hair and used the mirror, which swayed a bit too much, trying to smooth wayward strands into my curls.

Vaguely, I remembered Tobias mentioning my mom's Celtic heritage—though couldn't remember ever mentioning it to him. I staggered and caught myself on the sink and peered down to look for that offending loose tile. My attention rose to the mirror and my eyes reflected the confusion I was feeling.

Had my past decimated all chance of trust?

A knock startled me.

"Zara." It was Tobias. "You okay in there?"

"She's not in here." I crouched my shoulders, waiting for him to go away. "It's somebody else."

Music carried from the stage. The woman's singing sounded dreadful. I hoped I didn't sing as bad as that. With any luck it was Logan.

Silence.

Letting the minutes evaporate, I waited until it felt safe and reluctantly opened the door.

Peeking out, I saw the way was clear; I slid out and walked down to the end of the hall.

"Hello there," Tobias said.

I spun round and saw him with his arms folded across his chest.

"Oh hello," I said. "Fancy seeing you here."

He came closer and slid into a smile. "Fancy that."

"Well, that's super fun." I ran the words through my brain and stuck it in reverse. "Strange?"

"What is?"

"You being here and not on a roof." I peered at him through one eye.

"Roof?"

"Which I am so happy about. You don't even know."

"How much have you had?"

"Of heartbreak?"

"To drink? What did you have?"

"Some magical concoction that helps me see clearly."

"Are you upset I didn't invite you?"

"No, I'm busy at work."

"You're working now?"

Shit.

He gave a comforting smile and said, "We're moving at light speed. We have something special. I don't want to scare you off."

I gave a thin smile.

"Zara, please."

"It's been a difficult week." I waved my hand to let him know I didn't mean him.

"What happened?"

"I've always loved art. It's my first love. *Before you—*" I stared at him aghast. "Did I say that out loud?"

"Say what?" He grinned.

All that stuff about murder and stealing was breaking my heart. "The world is screwed up."

"You're worried about *St Joan*? I know it's been on your mind a lot."

"When that stuff comes out about my painting resurfacing—"

"*St. Joan*'s not coming back."

His friends were shouting over at him to come back.

"Come join us," he said.

"How do you know? About *St. Joan?*"

"A theory."

Theory...

All I could think about was that scared little girl climbing down a tree to get away from that house fire.

I couldn't let her name go unsaid, "Do you know the name Sarah Louise Ramirez?"

His frown deepened, proving I was embarrassing myself.

Closing my eyes, I cringed when I remembered the police had Icon in custody.

"I've had too much," I muttered.

"Want some water?"

"I should go."

"Wait for me, okay?"

I miss you.

But I daren't say it and from his stern expression I'd done enough damage.

He looked thoughtful. "That night I opened up about my parents..."

"I shouldn't have insisted you talk...about Australia and everything."

"It was good for me."

"You're not angry?"

"Why would I be?"

"We can still be friends?"

"Friends?" He swallowed hard and it kind of looked like sadness.

What had just happened there?

With all this booze swishing around my head it was hard to think.

"It's my turn." He pointed to the stage. "Have to win this."

I watched him walk away.

I'd just proven I was worthy of "clingy girlfriend of the

year." Or, I painfully mused, I'd unwittingly downgraded us to friends?

Tobias ran up the steps to the stage and within a few seconds he'd chosen his song.

He looked so damn handsome up there, so confident, the way he gripped the microphone, the way he rolled up his sleeves as he laughed back at his friends. The way his eyes searched me out in the crowd and gave me a sympathetic smile and then threw a big grin over to his table where he got a giddy wave back from Logan.

I sat down at an empty table and continued to watch him.

The music blared and Tobias's vocals were a husky baritone and annoyingly sexy. His table rose to their feet and cheered him on. He seemed to know the words well and turned away from the prompter.

The addictive bass thumped beneath my shoes. The crowd stomped their feet along with it and waved their arms. Some sang along with him using the audience teleprompter announcing he was singing "Witch Doctor" by De Staat.

I'd never seen Tobias so playful, so free from all that responsibility he carried.

Everyone was standing now, their arms raised above their heads as they screamed at his enigmatic performance. His deep voice boomed brilliantly, proving there was another thing I didn't know about him. He could sing.

He looked like a sex god, as hot as hell, masterfully riling up the crowd as electricity crackled through. They seemed mesmerized as he danced vibrantly in a circle, showing off that masculine power and his unstoppable exuberance.

Tobias was an enigma I couldn't get enough of.

He had the entire place whipped up in a fever of excitement.

The song ended and Tobias waved his arm triumphantly, apparently having won the sing off for his table.

He stepped down from the stage and weaved his way through the crowd, heading fast toward my table like a panther going in for its prey, nothing, not even celebratory pats on his back distracted him.

He zeroed in on me.

Tobias came closer and rose over me and I stared up at him, waiting for his goodbye...

He leaned in, cupped my face with his hands and crushed his lips to mine, snogging me so deliciously I almost fell off my chair. His tongue tangling with mine.

The crowd roared their approval.

Tobias pulled back. "Time to go home."

I blurted words; a slew of tipsy syllables that made him smile.

He beamed at me and held his hand out for me. "Let's get out of here."

29

I peeked from under the sumptuous duvet.

Blinking awake, my wristwatch pointed to 2:00 a.m. and I cringed that I'd got caught stalking Tobias at a bar after knocking back two shots. My head felt better than I deserved and then I remembered he'd given me two aspirin and made me drink a bottle of water before I'd fallen asleep.

The greatest revelation was they'd arrested Icon last night. Dragging my fingers through my hair nervously, I wondered if they'd find *St. Joan* in his stash of stolen property.

Tobias had brought me back to his suite at The Dorchester, though getting used to all this luxury was going to take some time. He seemed to effortlessly balance his philanthropic pursuits and his comfortable lifestyle.

He'd provided one of his T-shirts for me to wear and I sniffed the sleeve and swooned at the scent of his heady cologne.

Snuggled warmly, I waited for him.

Tobias strolled out of the en suite bathroom wearing only pajama bottoms, which gave me the advantage of being able to admire his six-pack as he made his way over to me.

I couldn't be apart from him any longer—

Reaching out for his hand, I pulled him onto the bed, and he fell willingly and brought his legs up. I climbed on top of him and wrapped my thighs astride his and grinned my joy of having captured the most beautiful, the most endearing, the most generous man on the planet.

"How are you feeling?" He gave a wry smile. "How's your head?"

"Fine. You?"

"Perfect."

"I can relax a little." I pushed myself up. "It's a secret right now."

He tipped my chin up. "Oh?"

"They've arrested Icon."

A flicker of interest flashed in his gaze. "Where?"

"He tried to break into the Tate."

Tobias rested his head on the pillow and stared at the ceiling. "Well, that's good."

I laid my head on his chest. "The work you do with those kids is incredible."

"It was of course an elaborate ruse. All of it. To get you to fall for me."

I tapped his chest playfully. "I'd already fallen for you. No ruse required."

He squeezed his eyes shut for a second. "I'm glad you could see the church before it's torn down."

"I want to work for your charity. I realized today how little I'm doing for other people." I shook my head ruefully.

"You're more than enough." He searched my face as though needing an answer; a flash of vulnerability crossing his face.

This low tremor of realization that he felt the same way about me caused my breath to catch. Reaching around to the back of his neck I brought his mouth up to mine.

"We're more," he whispered against my mouth. "Aren't we?"

"Yes, we're so much more."

He eased my T-shirt up and over my head and pulled it off me and chuckled.

"What's funny?"

"I was about to ask Jade to turn up the air-conditioning. Forgot where I was for a second."

"Jade's installed in your homes?"

"Homes, cars and offices."

"Don't you ever feel like she's stalking you?"

He laughed. "I created her. So, no."

I reached around and slipped my hand beneath the band of his pj's. "Bet she can't do this." I stroked the full length of him.

"Actually—" He arched a brow.

"That's so wrong!" I rested my head against his chest and heard his steady heartbeat.

"No one would ever replace you," he said. "You're one of a kind. You're a Salvador Dali amongst a sea of Rubenses."

"And you're a Pollock amongst a collection of Warhols."

He laughed. "I have no idea what we're talking about."

"You're complicated."

He stared up at me and seemed to swallow past his caution. "With you I come unraveled." He sat up and took my breast in his mouth, sucking my nipple and sending a shock of bliss. "You're more to me than anyone ever was."

My head fell back with the stun of pleasure.

He wiggled beneath me to pull down his pants and he grasped himself to direct his erection to slide along my cleft, that hard ridge caressing my sensitive clit. I let out a moan as he hardened further. With one firm thrust he slid inside me, sheathing himself completely. He arched his spine and closed his eyes as though he too was overcome with the pleasure.

With him still inside me he spun my body around and

rolled on top of me and I gripped his forearms and wrapped my thighs around his hips.

His body was all heat, all hard muscle, all furious pounding as he drove into me.

It was too late to hold back my heart from opening to him, this connection felt as though destiny had always intended this for us.

Both of us came together in a tirade of thrusts and moans, both of us blinded by this endless climax.

We fell asleep like that with him inside me and me never wanting to be let go.

I awoke to see Tobias out of bed and standing back at his tall computer desk typing away.

This guy was a workaholic.

A glance at the bedside clock told me it was six thirty.

He strolled over to the window and pulled back the heavy curtain and peered out.

He was on the phone and talking in French. I wondered if it was his uncle. I'd been crappy at French in school and had no idea what he was saying. The conversation sounded friendly enough. He looked so cute when he laughed away at what the other person was saying.

He caught me staring and smiled as he pointed to the food cart.

My superhero had ordered up room service. The tray conveniently positioned close.

Bleary eyed, I sipped the healthy-looking shake that tasted of pineapple and coconut, with some spinach thrown in to make it "healthier than thou."

I tucked into one of the pancakes, dipping it into a little syrup, and it tasted scrumptious.

Sipping the freshly brewed coffee, I settled in for my morning *Tobias* show.

Tobias at his computer. Tobias taking another call. Tobias coming over to kiss me. Tobias walking around the suite and munching on a slice of buttered toast and finishing off another coffee.

This I could wake up to every single day, I mused, as I sipped from a bottle of mineral water.

I slid out of bed and went to the loo.

When I came back he was sitting on the edge of the bed and he was dressed in gym clothes.

"That's impressive," I said.

"I thought so. Thought we'd do *it*."

I let out a nervous laugh.

"Get dressed and we'll get on with it." He gestured to the workout clothes laid out on the end of the bed. There was a Nike box beside it.

I lifted the lid and saw the running shoes. "Hope you're not suggesting...?"

"I am."

"When?"

"Now."

"You want me to go with you?"

"Get dressed, Zara. Or you'll be late for work."

"Why?"

"It'll clear your head."

Anything that involved breaking out in a sweat was not for me. "I think I'm just going to have a lie-in." I went to climb back in.

"A lion?" He grabbed my waist and pulled me back.

"No, a lie-in."

"Sometimes I have no idea what the hell you're saying." He held me still with his hands firmly around my waist.

"I don't think you should kiss me in front of Logan," I muttered.

"She knows how I feel about you."

"Oh?"

"She's knows I've fallen hard. She's happy for me." He grinned and continued to dress me in those expensive-looking gym clothes.

Feeling his hands sweep over my body felt divine. "When did you buy these?"

"Had them sent up from the hotel store."

"Remind me to thank them." I smirked.

Tobias waited for me to tie my shoelaces.

We headed out and took the elevator.

He hugged me into him the entire way down and I broke out in a sweat before we even made it to the gym on the fourth floor.

The place was as expected from a high-end hotel, chock-full of every kind of exercise equipment a human might like.

I blew off Tobias's offer to help me with my workout, instead going it alone on the treadmill. That wall mirror enabled me to ogle Tobias as he went through what looked like his usual routine.

He'd popped in his earbuds so he could listen to music, and seemed to space out as he went from lifting weights like a pro and generously flexing his muscles for me to enjoy, using the stair-climber, which conveniently revealed why he had such a lovely bum, and eventually moved on to sprinting fast on the other treadmill. He made my attempt at working out look feeble. Tobias insisted I try the rowing machine.

Pretending I was into this and there might be some chance I'd ever attempt rowing again in my lifetime, I made my way up this invisible river.

I climbed off the machine and sat on the floor mat. "Send help."

Tobias shoved a paper cup of water at me.

I drank it thirstily. "Did you get any sleep last night?"

"Not much."

"You're a workaholic."

"I have business stateside and they're on a different time."

"What kind?"

"We're rolling out our air keyboard at an LA tech expo. We're making the final touches to the design, securing a good position on the showroom floor, arranging my presentation time for the convention. That kind of thing."

"Can I help?"

"Yes."

I regretted asking. "How?"

"Get over there and lie down." He pointed to the corner.

"What if someone comes in?"

"We're not shagging, Zara. Down."

He followed me over and settled above me, lying along my body.

Tobias looked so damn gorgeous above me, all hard muscle and sexy perspiration glistening over his toned golden limbs. He began a grueling set of press-ups above me, each time he came down I raised my head and our lips met in a lingering kiss. A glance at his strong biceps revealed they were taut and bulging and carried him with ease. He paused above me on each descent, his body inches from mine and his smile reaching his eyes.

His breath minty fresh, his tongue swept over mine in one of the most cherished kisses he'd ever given me.

He resumed his press-ups, again proving the stamina worthy of this sex god.

"This isn't so bad," I said. "I could do this every morning." I snuck a peek at his tattooed biceps and ran my fingers over it.

"I'm trying to concentrate here." He kissed me again, effortlessly holding the tension in his arms.

"Sign me up for more sessions!" I laughed at my cheekiness.

He grinned down at me. "You're booked and good to go."

"With you, right?"

"Who else could endure your beauty?" He lowered his body and kissed the end of my nose. "Me, only me."

I let out the longest sigh of happiness.

It was behind us, all that dreadful Icon stress, all that awkwardness of getting to know each other and trusting in ourselves enough to fall, knowing he'd catch me. All those silent pauses between us were now morphing into moments of a deeper connection. This was the start of something greater than I'd ever dreamed possible for my life.

Falling in love felt so right.

30

Danny gave a wry smile.

I smirked back at him.

Funnily enough, he was the late one to arrive at our private research room at the Witt. "Get your mind out of the gutter," I said.

"I'm not saying anything."

"You don't need to."

"Personally, I think he's great. You're cute together."

"We are?"

"Shut up." He laughed.

"I have an idea. Let's get McDonald's for lunch." I winked at him.

"That's bound to keep my homesickness at bay."

We laughed and then realized how loud we were being.

Danny pulled back a chair and sat in it. "If they've arrested him, do we really need to be here?"

"We're going to help with providing discovery," I told him. "The more evidence we have to bring against him, the more paintings we'll retrieve. He may try to stash a few."

Danny gave an enthusiastic nod.

We worked diligently all day and were ecstatic to finally confirm the common thread between each of the paintings. The work had been exhausting, but worth it.

By 4:00 p.m. we were back at Huntly Pierre to present what we'd learned.

Within the conference room Abby, Shane and Brandon listened to Danny, and all of them were riveted with what we'd discovered.

Danny gestured for me to continue.

I flipped open my file and began, "We've collated images of each painting stolen in the Interpol case." I continued, methodically walking everyone through where and how each of the provenances had been broken.

Danny's voice cracked when he came to the Ramirez family, again sharing with the team the suspicious circumstances surrounding the loss of their Titian to the Burells.

"Were there any more deaths involved in our other cases?" asked Shane.

"We believe the Ramirez family were the only ones who suffered like this," I said. "Still, one family dying in a fire is one too many."

"Icon's not hurt anyone, right?" asked Shane. "No reports of any violence from him?"

"None so far," said Abby.

Danny pointed to our file. "Every single painting we researched has a break in its provenance."

"Each one of them once stolen," I added. "And stolen again. That's our pattern."

"Well, we have a lot more to work with," said Abby. "Let's share our findings with the Met and Interpol."

Brandon sat forward. "Talking of provenance, Zara, what are your thoughts on the theft at Christie's?"

The blood drained from my face. *"St. Joan?"*

Had they found my painting on *him*?

"We're your friends," said Abby. "We're here for you. Like we are for each one of us."

"I was mortified," I admitted. "And everything else that goes along with discovering there may be a painting out there you were told shouldn't exist." I took a sip of water and added, "When I was ten my home almost burned down. My dad was an art collector. We lost most of our paintings. We managed to save a few. *St. Joan* was one of the 'destroyed' paintings."

"Sounds like your dad sold it." Danny gave a comforting smile. "You were a kid. How could you keep track of something like that?"

"I remember my dad grieving for that particular painting," I said.

"You were probably in shock," Abby reassured me. "Memories have a funny way of being skewed after a traumatic event."

That dreadful memory of my father sifting through the remains of *St. Joan*'s ashes through his fingers was too dreadful to bear.

"I bet Ouless painted two," said Shane. "There's your answer. Walter Ouless painted more than one. Maybe he practiced on the first and didn't like it?"

Guilt dripped off me with the unfairness of innocence. "Christie's never got a chance to authenticate it. It was stolen the night after it arrived."

"Who dropped it off at Christie's?" asked Danny. "Bet they have answers."

"They want to remain anonymous," I told them. "Right now, Christie's won't reveal their client's name."

"We'll find out more," said Abby. "I'm sorry it's gotten caught up in the Icon case."

The memory of seeing *St. Joan* made me feel vulnerable and I inhaled a steadying breath.

Shane glanced at his ringing iPhone. "It's New Scotland Yard." He rose and headed out of the conference room to take the call.

Brandon held up a flash drive. "I got this for you."

I tried to swallow past this dryness. "What is it?"

"Security footage from Christie's. The night your *St. Joan* went missing. I went over there this morning and they gave me a copy. Told them I worked for Adley."

Mixed feelings rose over whether tampering with this potential hornet's nest was wise and, after all, Tobias had told me to let it go.

"Have you looked at it?" I asked.

"Not yet." Brandon glanced at the others. "We were going to see what you thought first."

"Have the police seen it?" I said.

"Yes," said Abby. "The footage is a little confusing apparently."

I sat forward. "In what way?"

"Let's look at it," she said. "Try to understand their confusion."

"At least I'm not on there." I leaned back and breathed a sigh of relief. "An inspector from New Scotland Yard paid me a visit at home. I told her I didn't know anything. Sorry I didn't tell you. It was never the right time."

I was hoping it would go away.

Shane hurried back into the room. "We have a problem on the Icon case."

Danny and I swapped a wary glance.

"How do you mean?" he asked.

"The man caught—" Shane gestured for us to remain calm. "He's a thief. Just not ours."

Air rushed from my lungs. "A copycat?"

Shane gave a nod. "He tasered a guard before they got to

him. He was released from Brixton prison a week ago after serving a three-year term."

"And Icon never harms anyone," I muttered, remembering that feather serving as a symbol of that promise.

"Onward then." Abby looked devastated as she gestured to my file. "May I look?"

"Of course." I slid it over to her.

"I'm going to grab a sandwich." Danny rose to his feet sharply and stormed out.

"Want to watch this with me?" Brandon waved the flash drive in the air. "I'll get it set up. How about ten minutes?"

"Sure. Did Christie's staff say they saw who took the painting?" I pointed to the flash drive.

He frowned. "There's one suspicious individual but he has an alibi."

"I'll grab a sandwich and join you." I pushed to my feet and said, "Thank you. I appreciate this."

"Zara," Elena called to me, gesturing from the door.

"Yes?"

"Adley wants to see you."

I cringed inwardly as I assumed this was about *St. Joan*. I'd be hard pushed to explain why it had taken me so long to report this to him.

I made my way to his office. The door was ajar.

Adley rose to greet me. "Zara, heard things are going great on your investigation? Though it's a shame about our copycat?"

I stepped in farther. "Thank you, sir, yes. I'll email my report. Let me know if you have any questions."

"Quite the revelation."

"I'm sorry it's taken me this long to tell you about—" My gaze froze on the square-jawed, redheaded man sitting in Adley's armchair.

Pulling back on my surprise, I faked I'd never seen him before. Nor had the displeasure of attending an orgy he'd been at. It wasn't just the man's build, it was his cold gray eyes that I remembered, an icy stare peering through the mask he'd worn that night.

"Hi," I managed.

He rose out of his chair. "I've been hearing good things about you, Zara."

My gaze shot to Adley, and I wondered if he knew now that I'd visited the palace. He didn't seem annoyed, shocked or any other manner of facial expressions I'd expect from discovering his employee had attended a bangfest.

Adley gestured to him. "This is—"

"Francis." He frowned my way. "Have we met?"

"Don't believe so." I shook his firm hand and recalled all too starkly standing in front of the fireplace at the back of that ballroom. "I have one of those faces."

Francis had ogled me from that small distance between us. That masked woman by his side. The one I'd asked for the direction to the loo.

You were wearing a mask, I reassured myself.

He tilted his head. "I'm glad I caught you."

"I'm sorry?"

"This was all last-minute," he added. "I was visiting the Reform Club and thought I'd pop in and see Adley."

I looked apologetic. "If you'll excuse me. Have to make a quick call. I'll be right back. Ten seconds?" I glanced at Adley for permission.

With a nod he gave it.

I strolled out of there and then I rushed round the corner and pulled my phone out. And dialed Tobias.

"Wilder." His voice sounded husky. "Zara? You caught me between meetings. Lucky me. Stay in Oxford with me tonight. I'll send a car."

"Thank you," I said. "I'll drive. It'll help me decompress."

"What happened?"

"Tobias," I whispered. "You know that palace we went to? The one in Oxfordshire?"

"How's your day going?"

"Not too good. Look, there's a man here from the party. You know the orgy thing."

"Where?"

"Adley's office. I can't tell if he recognizes me."

The silence lingered on the other end. "Are you sure?"

I swallowed hard. "He has red hair. Same eyes. I'm sure of it. His name's Francis."

"Lord Francis Blandford?"

I swallowed hard. "It was his party?"

"It's fine, Zara. We did nothing wrong. Take a deep breath and get on with your day."

"But he wants to talk with me."

"About?"

Adley appeared and gestured for me. "I have to go," I said. "I'll call you."

"Zara," Tobias's voice sounded stern. "Don't go back in."

I hung up and walked toward Adley.

My phone buzzed in my pocket but I ignored it.

"Use my office," Adley said. "Take as long as you like."

"You're not staying?"

"Francis wants to talk with you privately."

31

Don't go back in.

Tobias's words hung like a noose around my neck waiting to tighten.

Francis sat on the edge of Adley's desk with his arms folded across his chest. He gave a thin smile.

"It's a pleasure to meet you," I said. "I've read wonderful things about your art collection."

He lowered his gaze. "Which you've seen."

"Excuse me?"

"I'd never forget your eyes, Zara."

My gaze flittered toward the door.

"It's refreshing to meet others who share our taste in the finer delights of life."

I studied his face, trying to gauge if he knew I'd also seen his secret Goya. The thought of Adley finding out what had happened that night made me sick to my stomach.

"I looked for you later," he said. "That Neanderthal you were with hid you away."

I breathed a sigh of relief. "How can I help you?"

He scratched his nose thoughtfully. "You'd be surprised how many people enjoy our lifestyle."

"You have a painting to be appraised?"

"We're concerned with all these thefts. We need our home reevaluated. An expert to secure our paintings. This man's very good. This Icon. Our system may be outdated."

"We'll have our team visit."

"I want you there."

"I'm an appraiser, Lord Blandford. Security—"

"Francis, please."

"We have a fine team here who specialize in security consulting." My fingernails trailed over the nape of my neck. "We'll keep your paintings safe, sir."

He stepped forward. "Sir? I like that."

"I didn't stay. You know, for the... Wasn't my thing. To be honest."

"Zara." He stepped closer. "You prefer one-on-one?" His fingers trailed along my throat. I pulled away.

He scowled. "Shall I inform Mr. Huntly about your attendance at my party?"

"And expose your own?"

His left eye twitched. "See you Friday. With your team. Be prepared for some private time."

"I don't respond to threats, Francis."

"Excuse me?"

I stepped back, putting more distance between us and trying to hide the fact my heart was racing. "Glad we cleared that up. Huntly Pierre will be delighted to provide a security consultation. I'll have Shane Hannah, one of our lead investigators, contact you with the details."

A knock at the door.

Abby leaned round the door. "Sorry to interrupt, but Brandon's found something interesting on that case you're both working on." She gave me a knowing look.

"Thank you." I turned back to Francis. "You'll see our team on Friday, Lord Blandford. Have a safe trip back to Oxfordshire."

He gave a thin smile. "Friday it is."

I hurried out of Adley's office. "Thank you, Abby. How did you know I needed saving?"

"I didn't." She glanced behind her. "Are you okay? What happened?"

"He's a creepy bastard."

"No more meetings with him alone."

"That's my intention."

"Well, are you going to fill me in on the deets?"

My head snapped to look at her. "What?"

"Tobias Wilder?" She grinned. "Are you guys just shagging or is there more going on there?"

I gave her an incredulous look. "Mind your own bloody business."

She burst out laughing. "Oh my God, you're shagging Tobias Wilder!"

"Does everyone know?"

"He kissed you in front of Danny. Then you headed off into the sunset together."

"How embarrassing."

"Are you kidding me, he's a bloody catch."

"Yes, he's pretty special."

"Imagine how cute your babies are going to look."

"Shut up."

We walked into Brandon's office and he gestured for me to take a seat. I was too wound up after my run-in with Francis to take it and talking about Tobias had muddled my brain.

I paced a little to refocus.

He used a napkin to wipe crumbs off his hands and pushed his half-eaten sandwich aside.

"What have you found?" I pulled my phone out and saw five missed calls from Tobias. He probably needed reassuring my meeting with Lord Blandford went smoothly.

I texted him, Will call soon. All okay.

Tobias: Call me. Now.

"This is what we managed to get from Christie's." Brandon pointed to his Apple's flat screen. "Watch this. This is what has the police baffled."

I placed my phone on the desk and concentrated on the film. I recognized the room at Christie's, the same one I'd visited and recognized the three paintings on display in the private showroom. My *St. Joan* was flanked by the Renoir to the left and to the right, Jan Gossaert's *Portrait of a Merchant*.

The wall camera swept left and then right painfully slowly and taking in the full view of the showroom. The time clock stamped on the lower right screen was 03.01.

A chubby security guard strolled in, looked around and strolled out again. "Watch this—" Brandon froze the frame.

St. Joan vanished.

"But the guard's right there!" I said. "He's in the room."

"And no one else is in there," said Brandon. "You just saw what we saw. The room is empty. Officer Fields strolls in. He strolls out. Touches nothing. Then, bam! Painting behind him is gone."

An uneasiness rose in my chest.

"This is Icon's MO." Abby threw me a wary glance.

Elena appeared at the door. "Zara, you have a call."

I forced a friendly smile her way. "Tell Tobias I'll call him in a minute."

She grinned. "How did you know it was him?"

"Wild guess," I said.

"You might want to answer that." Abby stared at my cell phone.

I relented and picked it up and strolled over to the corner near the window. If I crooked my neck I'd see the Wharf.

"Are you alone?" Tobias said.

"No."

"Are you okay?"

"I'm fine."

"What did Francis want?"

"Help with securing his paintings. You know, with all these recent thefts it's got him rattled. He needs a security review of the palace."

"Did he recognize you?"

"This is a bad time."

"Please answer the question." His voice sounded eerily calm.

I turned to see Abby staring at me. Her frown was proof she disapproved of me sharing confidential information of a client's business.

"I'm looking at some footage," I said. "Can I call you back?"

"What footage?"

"Christie's. The night *St. Joan* went missing." I moved closer to the screen. "We may have something."

"Zara." He let out a long sigh.

"Hold on." I clutched my phone to my chest and rewatched the film Brandon had on replay.

"And you're sure about that guard's time card?" Abby pointed to him.

"Yes." Brandon looked up at her. "Officer Fields told the police he was on his break from two forty-five to three thirty. And that's what's on his time card that he used with an electronic thumbprint stamp. He clocked in and out and is seen doing just that."

"But he's right there," she said. "In the same room as the *Joan of Arc*."

And I hated the idea of watching someone manhandle her.

"How do you explain it?" Brandon pressed his finger to the screen.

"Where did he go for his break?" I asked.

"Staff coffee room." Brandon clicked through the other files.

Five more clicks and he had the coffee room footage up for that same night. Brandon sped up the time frame to match the same time *St. Joan* was stolen.

Officer Fields was sitting at a table and enjoying his soup and sandwich and watching a football game on a walled TV. The time unraveled on the right lower clock, proving he didn't move from that spot.

"Fuck me." Brandon pressed a fingertip to the screen's time stamp. "How is Fields in two places at the same time?"

We stared at the image, all of us aghast.

"Does he have a twin working there?" asked Abby.

"First thing I asked," said Brandon. "And no, he doesn't."

"Play the footage again," I said. "No, the one of Fields in the gallery with *St. Joan*."

Brandon got right on it.

We watched Officer Fields walk in, look around and then head for the door again. A split-second later, with Fields almost out the door, *St. Joan* vanished midframe.

That same feeling arose in my gut as my gaze lingered on the face of Officer Fields. A well of uneasiness rising as I watched his image flicker and waver before he stepped out of view.

My chest tightened with this flash of panic as I recognized what I was seeing…and feeling…

The uncanny valley.

I stared at my phone and with a trembling hand I hung up on Tobias.

Half an hour ago, I'd flown past the sign welcoming me to Oxford. Heavy traffic along the M40 had slowed me down. It had taken two hours to get here.

My thoughts raced as I ran through each interaction I'd had with Tobias, recalling that night when we'd first slept together, the same one *St. Joan* had been stolen. I'd woken up to find him half-dressed and perched on the end of my bed.

Had that given him enough time to sneak out and steal *St. Joan*? *Bloody ridiculous.*

Or was it?

What Brandon had shown me today in that Christie's security footage looked uncannily like a holographic projection of a security guard. What other explanation could be given of seeing him in two places at the same time. And there had been no evidence of the footage being tampered with.

The theft of those paintings Huntly Pierre had been tasked with reviewing spanned all continents. All professional jobs, and all connected by the fact each portrait had a provenance that had been broken at some point.

And stolen again.

Why would our thief go for a Titian and not a Cezanne? Why would someone steal a painting already stolen? That clear pattern of it being a home targeted was broken when Christie's had succumbed to the robbery of *St. Joan*.

Again, the thief had stolen only one painting when so many others were there.

Christie's footage proved he'd been feet from a Renoir and a Gossaert and yet had only taken *St. Joan*.

For me, personally, there was so much riding on that painting turning up. I hated my heart for telling me Tobias had anything to do with this.

After navigating his driveway, I parked my Rover near his front door and raised my gaze to see his helicopter perched on his roof. An impressive collection of Jags parked outside.

His home was lit up brightly. I made my way in—

Recognizing the music blaring from hidden speakers— "Weak" by Wet was playing, and I followed the sound of the singer's dreamy lyrics.

This was how Tobias made me feel, weak, brought to my knees, and he'd told me he felt just as changed by me and that I'd even "unhinged his soul."

The shattering of my own had begun.

If I'd learned anything it was we both kept our secrets close. Tobias and I were alike in so many ways. Caressing this ache in my chest, I tried to focus and act with nonchalance.

The aroma of cooking wafted through the house and smelled divine. I nudged open a door.

Tobias stood before a stove and he was stirring a spoon dipped in a large stainless steel pot.

His kitchen was homey with an Italian flair offsetting all the chrome and steel appliances.

He wore black trousers and a loose white T-shirt, and his hair was ruffled; his innocence radiating off him with the persuasion of beauty.

"I was worried when you didn't answer." He turned to look at me. "You hung up on me?"

"Call dropped." I stepped in. "How did you know I was here?"

"Jade." He rested the spoon by the side. "I wanted to surprise you with dinner."

"I thought you can't cook?"

He gestured to the open recipe. "It's kind of fun. You inspire me."

I came in farther. "Smells incredible."

"I would have sent a car for you."

"Needed time to think."

"Come here."

I walked quickly toward him and fell into his arms, my eyes closed and needing to be with him again, needing to feel what we had wasn't lost.

That I was wrong.

There were too many facts addling my brain and the dots were too disjointed to join, too confusing and misguiding the truth from where it deserved to lie.

I peered up into his eyes, wishing the truth would just reveal itself.

"I've been working on this hug all day." He pulled me tighter. "Worked up the schematics. Ran a software trial." He squeezed me.

So safe, so nurturing, his cologne so damn sexy it muddled my brain.

"Refused to stop until I knew this hug was scientifically accurate," he added. "And would garner satisfying results. The kind that would make you happy."

Tears stung my eyes.

He looked concerned. "You okay?"

"A little tired."

He kissed my forehead and pulled back. "Here." He used the spoon to scoop out a loose clam that was free of its shell. "Taste."

I leaned forward and let him tip the small mollusk into my mouth; it tasted of garlic and butter and melted deliciously on my tongue. "Amazing." I managed a smile. "I wanted to thank you."

A tilt of his head. A narrowing gaze. An expression of acknowledgment.

"For all you've done. You've helped me in so many ways. Dealing with my dad's paintings and securing them at the National. Being with me when the police wanted to know more about *St. Joan*—" I studied his face.

"I'd do anything for you, Zara, you know that."

"You've done so much."

"Let's eat."

He dished up the clams into china bowls and removed piping hot garlic bread from the oven. He uncorked a bottle of pinot grigio and poured white wine into two glasses. He handed one to me.

We sat on bar stools at the central island and dipped our bread into the sauce. I made noises of pleasure at how delicious it all tasted. He was so good at so many things, a man who quite possibly was capable of anything.

Was I breaking bread with Icon?

I feigned that all was well as I dipped my torn-off piece of bread into my sauce and chewed, grateful for this incredible meal.

Was this our last together?

Nursing my wine, I listened to Tobias tell me about his day and I told him about mine.

"You can't go back to the palace," he said.

"Don't worry. I have no plans of ever seeing Francis Blandford ever again."

"Tell me if he contacts you."

"Okay. Any news on when Francis is going to sell his Goya, *La Maja Desnuda*, the painting we went to see?"

"No." He lowered his gaze. "It would be wise never to mention it to anyone."

"Of course."

"So, how did Christie's security footage look?" He broke off some bread. "See anything interesting? You hung up on me so I assumed you'd caught a break?"

"The guard's in two places at the same time." I held his gaze.

"Technical issue?"

"Well, you know more about all that than me." My fingertip circled the rim of my glass.

"You seem distracted. Everything okay?"

"I'm fine."

"Is what you found at the Witt still upsetting you?"

"Apparently, every single painting stolen in the Interpol case has a prior broken provenance."

"In what way?"

"Each and every one was stolen. Before it was stolen again." I couldn't say by Icon. Couldn't let him know I knew.

He took a sip. "That's quite a revelation."

"It's doesn't appear coincidental. Too many paintings for that."

"What's your theory?"

"Perhaps there's a collector out there who covets what other men covet."

"Perhaps."

"What do you think, Tobias? Why would he steal them?"

He lowered his gaze.

My forearms prickled as the fine hairs reacted to the way he looked at me. I raised my glass and chinked it next to his. "To us."

He raised his. "Us."

I stared upward. "How do you get Jade to respond to your voice?"

"Calibration."

"How do you do that?"

"Jade, command imminent."

My gaze roamed the ceiling as though his invisible friend could see us.

"Permit house commands to Zara Leighton." He reached out and rested his hand on mine. "Say something."

"Jade—" I clenched my tongue between my teeth. "This is Zara, I'd love to be able to lower the lights."

"Are you using my technology to seduce me?"

"Did it work?"

The lights dimmed several degrees.

"She likes you." He lifted his glass and took a long sip.

A trickle of moisture spiraled down his glass and dripped onto the counter. He wiped it away all while holding my gaze.

"What else does Jade do?" I asked.

"She performs a mean pole dance."

I hit his arm and laughed.

"What do you want, Zara?"

"Let me be all you need. All you want. Fulfill you in every way."

"That would make me very happy."

I held my hands together in a prayer, waiting, hoping he was ready to tell me the truth. Confess.

He leaned forward. "The only way I can prove how I feel about you is to show you," he said.

I slid off my bar stool and circled the counter.

Leaning into him and resting my head against his chest. The room fell quiet.

"Jade, lock all the doors," he said. "Secure the house." He clasped my hand and interlocked his fingers through mine and led me out.

Down the sprawling hallway.

I recognized this way from that first time I'd visited.

That felt like a million years ago now.

Upon the walls were prints of modern art dotted here and there, a mismatch that somehow made sense.

"Clara knows I'm here," I stuttered.

He led me farther along. "We should have her over for dinner."

"Where are we going?"

"It's my turn to show you what nirvana feels like." He shoved open the door to his bedroom.

We entered together.

The room was minimalist, like the others, white linen on a steel four-poster bed with wisps of lush netting swept above. No other furniture, not even a chair, as though that bed was the center point, and something told me this wasn't his bedroom.

Yet I went willingly, wanting this more than breathing itself, and if this was wrong I refused to blame myself for wanting it, wanting *him*.

He had me stand in the center of the room.

Tobias undressed me slowly, like a dark ritual of sorts, then moved around me with the swagger of a man who held all the power.

"Zara." His voice was low. "Trust me. That's all I'll ever ask."

I wanted to believe him.

"I won't hurt you, baby. Never would I do that to you." He stepped back and stripped his clothes off. "I want to spoil you."

Stripped naked and standing in the center, I patiently waited, my heart patting away like scared sparrows unable to fly.

Perhaps, just perhaps, this would purge all need for him and I'd begin a pathway to setting myself free from this addiction that was Wilder.

He stood behind me and his lips trailed kisses along the

nape of my neck making my insides liquefy and my breathing quicken. He eased back locks from my shoulder and kissed me tenderly, taking his time to woo me into an erotic trance.

He circled to face me again. "I care deeply for you. This is how I'm going to prove it." His fingers lowered to my abdomen and lower still until he'd reached between my thighs and gently parted my labia. "Hold this apart."

Looking down, I held myself just how he showed me. My clit peeked out, that little nub erect with excitement.

He lowered himself to his knees and leaned in, his tongue sweeping along my cleft, and he lapped at me passionately. "Don't let go of your pussy. It proves you're giving it to me when you hold it like this." He took my hands and directed them either side of my labia.

That sudden rush of bliss as his kiss intensified there, my thighs trembling, this overwhelming urge to moan.

"I want something too," I burst out.

"Ask."

"You promised to tell me what it says? Your tattoo?"

"Soon."

Under his direction he'd turned me round and walked me forward a few steps, and I leaned forward and placed my palms on the wall to support my bent-over body, my bum out and offered to him. He knelt behind me again and I shuddered as he resumed suckling my sex, his tongue savagely taking me.

I moaned through an orgasm and yet he was unrelenting, his lapping insistent on destroying my will to resist and I rode his mouth, hips rocking, rubbing my clit along his tongue.

He paused and pulled back, rising to his feet. We stared into each other's eyes.

I lowered myself to kneel before him. "You promised." I ran my fingers along his cock and trailed them over the inked Latin.

"I know."

Suckling his balls, lapping and lovingly worshipping them, my hand working his cock that was rigid, and his deep sigh proved he was succumbing. Running my tongue along the full length of him, taking him in and then setting him free from my lips to tap the ridge of his cock with my tongue.

"Jesus, Zara."

"Tell me," I said.

"Ubi non est poena. Victurus de Saluto." He ran a finger along the writing. "Retribution where there is none. He who is about to win, salutes you."

I broke away and stared up at him.

My thoughts swirled with what he might have done.

Tobias swept me up into his arms and carried me over to the bed and flung me into the center. I bounced on the mattress and over soft pillows, my breath gone and my equilibrium off.

In a haze, I watched him bring over four red silk ties.

"You mentioned you wanted to be tied up." He smiled devilishly. "Remember?"

Vaguely, I did, at the Maxwells' party, though now was the worst time for us to explore this fantasy.

I went to pull my wrist away but he was too fast, making quick work of my other arm, securing it upward and outward either side and tying me to the posts.

He did the same with my ankles.

Too dizzy from the wine, my thoughts scattered as I struggled to get free, my movement frantic as the tautness of these binds proved inescapable.

I'd made a terrible mistake.

He rose over me and I stilled as his steely gaze met mine. His green eyes capturing me—

My chest rose and fell with each pant, my breasts trembling, nipples pert and sensitized beads of need betraying my uneasiness.

Had I given myself away?

Yet his expression was so loving, the way he stroked his hand up and down my belly, the way he held my gaze with affection.

My entire being craved this, craved him, desired Tobias above all things, and my body burst alight with tremors sending an eruption of arousal through my body. His hand swept over my breasts and tweaked my nipples, bringing this arousal to a fever pitch.

Exhilaration surged though my veins at this overwhelming domination.

I've lost my mind.

Obsession had stolen all logic.

He came closer and brought his cock to my mouth and I let out a sigh of gratitude, my head lifting off the pillow as I took him in, lapping his pre-cum and wanting more and sucking hard for it.

My own need so vital I never wanted this to end. Bound and yet free.

My body on fire with passion as he trailed his fingers along my cleft and then raised it to show me how wet he'd made me.

His hands clenched my breasts, kneading them, ignoring my plea that this was too much. My back arched, captured in an erotic suspension right on the edge of falling—

With a swift movement he twisted his body onto all fours and buried his face between my thighs into a perfect sixty-nine and he lavished affection with his mouth, using his fingers to ease back the folds so he could own my clit, sucking and letting go, sucking and letting go…

Until all I could do was lap weakly at the tip of his cock, too gone to think straight or respond, reeling into another orgasm.

At last he untied me.

Bringing me up to sit on his lap facing him and stilled long enough for me to adjust to his girth as his cock slid all the way in.

"Circle your hips," he ordered.

Looking into his beautiful green eyes, circling my pelvis round and around, making a wider circumference, thighs shaking through another rising orgasm, my scream silenced by his mouth as his lips crushed mine and he kissed passionately, endlessly.

Time fell away...

Proving not only Tobias's ability to refrain from coming, but his mastery at every position. He fucked me from behind, taking me from the side, hanging off the bed, moving my limbs into inconvincible poses—

We settled with his back against the headboard and me sitting on his lap again, only facing the front, my back to his chest with my thighs strewn over his.

I rose and fell, rose and fell, taking him all the way into me and keening forward when his fingertips danced on my clit, flicking and circling, slowly at first and then fast until I exploded into a million pieces of blinding light.

Mesmerized...

Joy at the feeling of him coming within me, his final burst of aggression and I loved every second of his show of force.

We stilled, our bodies drenched in perspiration and the remnants of sex, our bodies a perfect lock as his fingers trailed over me, my breasts, my throat and back to my sex where he possessively cupped me with his hand.

He held me like this for a long time.

Not moving. Not letting go. Proving his ownership. Until I collapsed in a heap, too exhausted to go on.

"See how good we are together?" His thumb brushed my clit. "We're perfect for each other."

My heart ached so bad, needing this to be true. All I had to do was believe in us. In *him*.

I gave a weak nod. He let me sleep.

At last.

And semi-consciousness took me down with it.

My eyes popped open and I raised my head off the pillow, my vision adjusting through the dark to look over at Tobias. He was fast asleep, his limbs stretched out on the bed with a leg over mine.

I slid away from him and maneuvered out of bed, feeling sore and achy.

I bent to retrieve my panties and pulled them on. I left the rest not wanting to waste time.

Pausing by the door, I glanced back to confirm he was still sleeping. Tobias looked so calm, so peaceful, and guilt found me in the dark as I felt my way along the wall.

I entered the living room and after a brisk search found nothing. I hurried on and soon discovered the door to his den. There was nothing suspicious in there, either, and I went back the way I'd come, toward the east side, through the kitchen where the scent of our delicious dinner lingered.

I found his office. The desk large and the room tidy. A blank wall calendar. An antique typewriter on a shelf. And near it were books on archeology and others on art. A photo of a young couple who could have been his parents, their similarity familiar. A photo of an older man. His uncle, Fabienne, perhaps?

There was another door at the back.

Retribution where there is none.

Recalling his words, the meaning sent a shiver through me.

I opened the door and walked right into another hallway. There, at the end, lay a chrome door. And it looked heavy on its hinges.

I hurried toward it.

My fingers brushed over the control panel and I tried to guess the combination. A sense of futility caught in my throat along with guilt for violating his privacy, and after all he'd done for me.

All the wonderful work he was doing for others.

But I'd come too far…

"Jade," I whispered. "Open the door." I glanced behind me.

A trickle of sweat ran down my spine.

Raising my voice a little, I said, "Jade, I need you to open this door." I rested my forehead against it, questioning what the hell I was doing.

A noise startled me and I listened out for another. "Jade, open the fucking door." The lock clicked.

I shoved it open.

The deep-boned chill of air-conditioning hit me and it re-minded me of the same coldness of a gallery.

He who is about to win, salutes you.

My hand cupped to my mouth—

Walter William Ouless's *St. Joan of Arc* rested upon a stand to the left of the room.

Moving closer, my chest heaved as I took in Joan's beautiful expression of faith, and the bright red sash across her. Closer still I recognized that minute spiderweb of cracked paint in the left hand corner of her canvas, right above Ouless's signature.

Turning, my gaze roamed… A Rembrandt.

Monet. Vermeer.

All of them originals.

All of them on the list of paintings stolen. I snapped my head around, frantically looking for the Titian, but couldn't see it.

I gasped—

There, in the center upon a marble stand sat the Maxwells' Tibetan singing bowl and around its rim ran a swirl of lilies and lying beside it was that familiar gong.

The silence shattered with my sob.

He'd stolen it from them. Used me to access the room and then pretended he had no interest in it.

The air was suffocating. I had to get out.

I rushed across the room and slid out the door, quickly closing it behind me. Heading back down the hallway, through his office and on through the house.

My palm clamped over my mouth—Tobias was in the kitchen.

He'd opened the fridge door and was peering in and was basked in a fluorescent white.

Expressionless, he turned to look at me.

"I was looking for the loo."

"Our bedroom has a bathroom en suite."

"It was dark."

"Find one?"

"Yes."

"Thirsty?" He reached in and removed a bottle of water. And offered it to me.

My gaze jumped between him and the bottle. He twisted the lid and offered it again.

I mentally counted the steps from here to the front door, reconciling with the fact I was only wearing my panties and would just have to go for it.

Tobias's stare held mine and he took a sip himself and then smiled after taking several gulps. "Was it too much?"

I bit my lip, using pain to hold back panic. "What?"

"Next time I'll be gentler." He tilted his head. "Told you

I make the kama sutra look vanilla. God, Zara, what you do to me."

"I liked it."

"Let's go back to bed." He held the bottle out to me again.

I stepped forward and took the water from him and sipped and then gulped a little more, my thirst refusing to quench.

Hand in hand we walked back to the bedroom. We got back into bed.

Tobias rolled me onto my side and spooned behind me, pulling me into a hug, and I prayed he couldn't feel my heart racing so fast it pounded my rib cage.

I ran through what I'd seen and the stark danger I'd placed myself in came at me like a tsunami.

"You're cold." He hugged me tighter.

My breathing stuttered and I realized I'd made the worst mistake of my life.

"I want to cherish this," he whispered.

It didn't make any sense... I'd watched him drink from the same water... I fought the urge to let go.

Limbs weakening...

"What did you give me?" My fingers clutched the sheet. "Tobias..."

"Shush," he soothed. "I've got you. Sleep."

32

With heavy eyes, I blinked awake.

I was in my own bed.

Home.

My hands covered my face as memories swarmed in—all the pieces came together, bringing a tidal wave of panic and forcing me to suck in calming breaths. When I'd mentioned the name Sarah Louise Ramirez to him, his expression hadn't been frustration, it had been recognition.

God, I needed to pee.

Peeking beneath the duvet I realized he'd dressed me in my babydoll nightdress. He'd brought me home and put me to bed.

I shot a glance at the bedside clock: 8:00 a.m.

My feet were unsteady as I padded out to my bathroom, my hand trailing along the wall to support me as I tried to shake off this postdrugged daze. After using the loo I brushed my teeth to try and rid myself of this taste of betrayal.

Feeling a little better, I checked each room to make sure he wasn't here. I reached the kitchen—

The Tibetan singing bowl was on my kitchen table. "No!"

I was already a suspect for that theft at Christie's, and it wouldn't take much more of a stretch to have them believe I had anything to do with this.

Oh my God.

I'd spent time in that private safe with Violet as my witness.

I burst into action and ran into my bedroom, quickly finding a box and that Harrods paper bag that Tobias had given me when he'd gifted those strappy new shoes. I'd had no idea then I'd be using it to transport a priceless artifact.

I dressed in a hurry, pulling on jeans and a jumper, and tugging on my boots and grabbing my parka.

In a blind panic I flew out the door.

There was no other way to prove my innocence but take full responsibility for being caught in this web.

I hailed a taxi and within minutes the black cab pulled away from the curb.

Clutching the Harrods bag to my chest, I cycled through why Tobias had set me up by staging evidence. My heart felt like fragile glass on the brink of shattering; I begged God to numb this agony.

I could have loved him…

Some part of me felt as though I had.

Oh no…

I'd accompanied Tobias to Blandford Palace and helped him stake out the painting by Goya. The one suspiciously hidden behind a fake. And I'd been forbidden from filing a report and relented to his demands for secrecy.

I'd been so naive.

The journey to Scotland Yard was an endless drive into the mouth of hell. I knew I was about to succumb to the worst kind of questioning. A cruel treatment worthy of the police's finest detectives. An interrogation so fierce they'd have me believing I'd played a part in this dreadful crime.

If I thought my life was bad before, it was circling the drain now.

I reached into my handbag and pulled out my phone and dialed Tobias's number. It went to voice mail. He'd not canceled his line yet. There was hope I might speak with him one more time. Get answers to why.

My voice sounded shaky. "Tobias, please call me. I'm begging you. We have to talk." I killed the call and dialed Abby's number.

Her voice mail answered.

I canceled the call, unsure of leaving words on record that might later hang me.

With the taxi paid for I climbed out and hesitated on the curb. That tall police station of New Scotland Yard threatened to keep me in there.

There was no other way...

I began the trek up the steps.

Hands trembling, I resigned myself to my fate and continued up.

A flash of inspiration hit me, and I plopped down and rested on the stone step. With a sweep across my phone and a tap, I had the number for the operator. Within seconds I was being put through to a Sarah Louise Ramirez, the only one listed in Canterbury. At some point she'd moved from France to here.

Tobias had met with Sarah the same night he'd had Cooper drive me home from the palace. He'd flown to Canterbury to give her back her family heirloom.

A woman answered. "Hello?" She sounded elderly, just as Tobias had described her.

"Ms. Ramirez?" I said. "Are you enjoying your Titian?"

She gasped and hung up.

Squeezing my eyes shut, I cursed myself for needing more proof.

Tobias had stolen *St. Joan* to protect me.

It was over.

My gaze rose and froze on the image across the street—

Standing there, clad in orange robes, was a young monk, serene and completely still. He was staring right at me.

He was the same monk who'd been outside the Wilder building.

He walked away.

Taking two at a time, I hurried down the steps.

I dodged the other pedestrians and rushed after him, terrified I'd lose this fine thread that might lead me to Tobias.

The monk headed into the entrance of Charing Cross tube station, and I quickly got in line for a ticket.

At the bottom of the escalator he was gone. "Please." I begged the universe.

My shoulders slumped with frustration as I looked left and right into the crowd. A tube pulled up.

A flash of orange. He was sitting on a seat on the tube. I ran toward the compartment right in front of me and pried open the doors. I slid through and grabbed the center pole to steady my feet as the train took off, not taking my eyes off the monk.

He got off at Bermondsey.

Making his way out of the tube station and along. His steady pace was easy to follow.

After fifteen minutes he opened the towering iron gates of a large brick manor set back on the street. He continued up the steps and through a turquoise-colored door.

He went inside.

I pulled open the gate and it squealed on its hinges. And made my way inside—

The scent of incense hung heavy and the quiet seemed to be trying to calm my thundering heart. Stepping in farther, I soaked in the oriental decor of carved wooden furniture and took in the deep red walls that offered a womb-like peace.

The monk stood at the end of a long, dimly lit hall, and he was looking back at me. Standing beside him was an older priest who was also clad in robes.

The older priest stepped forward. "You have it?"

I clutched the bag to my chest.

"Please." He gestured the way. "He's waiting for you."

Hands trembling, I took a wary step forward. "It was stolen from you?"

"Yes."

"When?"

The old monk hesitated. "A year ago."

"You asked Icon to get it back?" I said.

He gave a kind smile. "We prayed for its safe return."

"Did you know who had it?"

"We were spared such details. We were told it's better that way." The young monk earned himself a nudge of disapproval.

Tobias was returning it through me.

Was he returning them all?

"You must take off your shoes first," said the younger monk.

"I have questions," I said.

"'True love is born from understanding,'" said the older monk and gestured. "This is the way."

Light-headed, my feet teetered.

A sense of reverence with this small action of removing my boots. I rested the paper bag on a long side table and lifted out the box. Carefully, I removed the singing bowl with the gong inside it and clasped it tightly.

I held it out to them. "Here."

Their gazes fell upon it and they bowed their heads. The older monk gestured left.

Carved wooden doors lay ahead, foreign whispers... The doors opening—

A low chanting emanated from fifty or so monks who kneeled before a large wooden bed and under those covers slept an elderly priest, his head propped up by pillows.

The monks turned to look at me, and as their gazes fell onto the bowl I saw recognition in their faces.

It was hope.

Step by step, as though outside of myself, I walked toward the left side of the bed. "You cannot touch him," said a monk to my left.

I gave a nod of understanding and moved closer until I stood next to the elderly monk. He looked so peaceful and my gaze fell to his clasped hands.

The spiraling fine wisps of incense rose here and there, the soft lighting calming. Whispers rose around me.

The old man stirred awake and he turned his head to look at me. His kind chestnut gaze found mine and lowered to see the bowl, and he gave a nod of acknowledgment, a glimmer of relief.

Kneeling, I bowed my head in respect and raised the bowl for him.

It was taken from me and handed to him by the same young monk who'd guided me here.

The elderly monk raised himself higher in the bed, freeing his hands from the blankets and waving off help from the others. He wrapped his hands around the singing bowl, his eyes closing once again as though in prayer.

The younger monk sat on the edge of the other side of the bed and took the bowl. He rested it close to the old man and leaned in farther to continuously stir the gong around the inner edge...

The room was filled with the ethereal sound of shards of

white light shattering into a million crystals and this was music unlike anything I'd ever heard, as though prisms of color had transmuted into notes...

Squeezing my eyes shut, I thought of Tobias, realizing this was what he'd wanted me to know.

Being here was the only way I'd have understood.

I knew this with all my heart and a sigh of understanding escaped my lips.

The elderly monk's right hand rested on the top of my head and his words flowed, sending peace coursing through me. Time evaporated...

Outside, I blinked against the light of the sun, unsure how long I'd been lost in this meditation.

Soothed by prayer, the truth glared as brightly as this morning light: Tobias used his mastery of technology to right the wrongs of this world. Art and science had a common denominator and it was spirituality.

Icon was fighting back.

33

Madame Rose Récamier emanated the kind of calmness I'd come to appreciate over the last seven days since Tobias Wilder had left my life.

Rose emanated empowerment too. Her Grecian dress not just a fashionable choice of the early 1800s, it also emphasized her self-respect as she reclined on that long sofa, her posture of facing away with her arm relaxed along her body and her hand open revealed she made decisions on her terms.

Perhaps that was why my dad had bought her for me and hung her in my bedroom at such a young age, so I'd wake every day to see this strong woman who embraced her femininity.

Rose wasn't the only painting to have altered the pathway of my life.

St. Joan's momentary appearance at Christie's had sparked controversy for a while. This portrait felt like the tip of the iceberg in an intriguing mystery that was now my life. Perhaps somewhere within those leftover boxes of heirlooms stored in the basement of my dad's old house were clues.

For now, the storm had settled, and I let out a sigh of gratitude that calm had returned to my life again. It was so easy to become absorbed in a painting and forget the world around me.

After all that had happened I still believed *Rose* would be safe here.

I wondered how many visitors would ever realize what they were looking at when they viewed her. Perhaps they'd assume she was nothing but a pretty girl in a simple white dress who had been lucky enough to be immortalized on canvas.

If only they knew her like I did.

Rose's bravery in entertaining free-thinking artists and painters at her private salon apparently caused Napoleon, France's most famous military and political leader, to banish her from Paris. She'd hosted one too many of his opponents, apparently, and Napoleon had a reputation for exiling those who'd threatened him.

Madame Rose had been no wallflower.

And neither was I.

I'd cracked open a conspiracy within the art world, and I refused to disappear into the fabric of a life that had no meaning. Only when the veil is lifted do we see the world as it really is, a sometimes heartbreaking creation that we can only comprehend through art.

And art was in my blood.

Though it was Tobias Wilder who had found his way into my heart.

I was no longer angry with myself for letting him in. He, like me, had been exposed to the lengths men would go to possess, and centuries had seen too many of them get away with it. Until Wilder had swept in and demanded retribution.

As he'd reassured me, *no one gets hurt*. He was merely reuniting the paintings with their rightful owners.

Though it was still highly illegal and morally questionable.

I gave a nod of respect to Rose and made my way back to the other end of the gallery. Punching the button to call the lift.

I'd not heard from Tobias since I'd drifted to sleep at his home in Oxford. Afterward, I'd been dropped off at my London home and my adventure had ended abruptly.

Or had it begun?

Stepping into the lift, my thoughts stayed with him.

The moment you see through the veil of truth there is no unseeing it.

I mused it was still interesting how thoughts of Tobias lifted my spirits, his gorgeous smile, the way he laughed at my silly jokes, and how he'd risked so much to hide *St. Joan* away and suppress the evidence of my father's undiscovered secrets.

My descent took me to the ground level.

I'd taken this brief detour on my way to Huntly Pierre and felt centered again and inspired by these remarkable artists.

The lift doors opened and I headed toward the foyer.

Ahead of me lay an 11:00 a.m. appointment where I'd get to appraise a Raphael. Later, I'd attend a routine staff meeting and somewhere during the day I'd water my bonsai tree.

I paused to admire a corner marble sculpture of Aphrodite. It was new to The Otillie, and I quietly thanked those who'd donated her. She was beautiful, her sweeping dress carved masterfully and her oval face exquisite. I knew what it meant to hand over a cherished piece of art to share with the world and also knew that peace came with such a decision.

My phone buzzed in my pocket and I pulled it out. I turned the corner and huddled against the wall.

A quick glance around reassured me I was alone.

I accepted the incoming video and saw Tobias's smiling face looking back. His enduring dashing looks concealed the mystery behind the man.

"Have you forgiven me?" He gave a kind smile.

"Yes and no."

"I'm sorry I… You look so beautiful when you sleep."

"If you ever drug me again…so help me God."

"I'm strangely aroused." He chuckled. "I'm glad you're open to sleeping with me again."

"I wish you'd trusted me. You like to live dangerously. I got all the way to New Scotland Yard. You cut it close."

"I had faith in you. Thank you for returning the artifact. The priests are eternally grateful."

"Your way of implicating me?"

"Secrecy is our code."

My heart ached as I asked this nagging question. "Did you use me to get closer to the case?"

"Never… I care deeply for you. I let you in. That's all the proof you need."

I closed my eyes and tried to fathom those words and how I'd ever get over him.

"I hear you received a blessing from a high priest Lama?" he said.

"Yes."

"That's life changing."

"You're life changing."

"As are you." He let out a long sigh. "Whenever you want you can have *St. Joan* back. She is yours, after all."

"You know that for sure?"

"I do, yes."

I sucked in a sharp breath. "Are you still in England?"

"No."

"How can you be sure I'm not recording this?"

"It's my phone."

My eyes closed for a beat as I realized he'd probably been

tracking my every move. "Does anyone else know you're Icon? Coops? Logan?"

His silence lingered too long.

"Throw yourself into your inventions, Tobias. You're gifted and capable of so much good."

"Necessity is the mother of invention and my inventions serve a need."

"You've got to stop this. This will end badly. I know you believe this is your purpose and this is who you are but you can't save everyone. You can't turn back the past."

My heart ached that he'd risked everything to let me in and I was now his greatest threat.

"I tried not to get close to you." His voice cracked with emotion. "My need for you is my greatest weakness. You've utterly destroyed me."

The more we resisted each other the greater the pull of gravity between us.

"Please, do this for me," I said. "Walk away from this life. Isn't there another way to help these people?"

"I wish there was. I started out trying every avenue to right these wrongs. Every means to work within the law. If there was any other way don't you think I'd choose that?"

"But why you?"

"I'm the only one who can. I have the knowledge, the resources and the will. No one else can do what I'm doing."

"All of it just for art?"

"Zara." His voice softened. "You were the one who told me it's more than a painting."

"It's still wrong."

"I've made peace with that. But you know what's right? It's people reconnecting with these works that go beyond life saving. They're life affirming. Everything has more meaning if you look beyond the evidence. If I'm the one to carry this burden, then so be it."

This ache in my chest would never lift.

"I will always love you."

I nudged up closer to the wall. "Then don't leave."

"It must be this way for now."

I clutched my stomach to lessen this dreadful pang of loss.

"You know what surprises me the most, my sweet Zara?"

"What?"

"You of all people never once questioned your own provenance."

My chest heaved with the revelation…

Would I ever be brave enough to explore his implication? I wasn't sure I was.

Silence lingered… "Zara."

"Yes?"

"*Madame extraordinaire.* You'd create such a sensation in Paris." He'd just told me how to find him.

My thumb slid across the screen. "I'm coming to get you… Icon."

Before he could respond, I ended the call.

I slipped the phone into my handbag, steeled my nerves and left The Otillie, passing a multitude of lavish masterpieces, their ageless faces gazing upon me with an aura of regard.

We both knew we'd meet again. It was only a matter of when.

★ ★ ★ ★ ★

In THE GAME, the second novel of the ICON trilogy, bestselling romance author Vanessa Fewings widens the canvas of an intoxicating and thrilling world as Zara must make the ultimate choice at a moment when all is not what it seems.